MICHAEL WEBB

Shadow of Destiny

Cover design by jeffbrowngraphics.com.

First edition

ISBN: 978-1-7375788-3-3

This book was professionally typeset on Reedsy.
Find out more at reedsy.com

Books by Michael Webb

Shadow Knights: Origine - Novella

The Shadow Knights Trilogy:
The Last Shadow Knight
Rise of the Shadow
Shadow of Destiny

Contents

III   Destiny

Land of Terrenor
North Sea
Bryveld
Nortris
Noravorre River
Daratill
Norshewa
Korob Mountains
Rydland
Gap of Thardor
Kyrd Forest
Molyaigh
Karad
Karondir
Westfale Ocean
Feldor
Nasco
Bromhill
Tienn
Benevorre River
Kandis
Felting
Rynor
Felavorre River
Straith Mountains
Lorranis
Transvorre River
Tarving
Palenting
Isle of Paratill
Tarphan
Portris
Searis
Marris
Gulf of Tartis
Parathan Ocean
Parthe Mountains
N

I

Hope

1

A New Regime

The table's smooth grain radiated a warm glow from the candles dotting the chamber. A handful of stuffed chairs spread around the area, and the large windows revealed a dark courtyard outside. The late King Wesley once used the intimate space as a private meeting room. Paintings of animals and children covered the walls. King Edmund Bale scoffed as he looked around. Wesley's taste in decorations betrayed his misplaced sense of compassion.

A smaller display table rested against the wall, displaying decorative vases and trinkets. He waited, rubbing his hand across the table's wooden surface, when something caught his eye. A plaque with a symbol displayed on a stand. The letters S and K intertwined with a sword running down the middle.

He touched the symbol, feeling the grooves of the letters. Sweat dotted his forehead as his pulse increased. The Shadow Knights marked his past and haunted his future, and the last knight—Veron Stormbridge—eluded him. Conquering Tarphan and Rynor should be simple now, but Bale refused to rejoice. Hand clenched, he pounded once on top of the seal. The letters stared back, unmoved.

A door opened. Desmond entered and nodded. "It's time," the man confirmed. Bale inhaled then followed his advisor of many years into the adjacent room.

After walking through the door, he squinted at the brightness of the Hall of the King. Columns flanked either side of the space, and windows adorned the eastern wall. An army of lanterns filled the hall, erasing the darkness outside, while the ceiling towered above. The carved wooden throne of the previous king rested on a raised dais.

A dull thrum of voices rumbled through the room but hushed as Bale entered and proceeded to the front of the platform. His metal armor chinked while he moved, its slight metallic scraping the only sound to be heard.

Desmond joined his trusted officers, Ryker and Cyrus, standing on one side of the throne. Opposite them, the Feldorians who betrayed their previous king adjusted their feet, flitting their eyes around the room. Bale laughed to himself. *They're worried about what I'll do now. They don't even realize what I'm capable of.*

Raynor Fiero, the newly appointed Regent of Feldor, held his chin up, projecting confidence, but Bale saw through the false front. Next to him, Gareth Billings used his cane to steady himself, sword hanging on his hip. Captain Gannon scanned the room, and Brixton Fiero stood straight at the end of the line, eyes darting around the hall. All four of the native Feldorians wore red-and-black Norshewan badges pinned to their shoulders.

Bale turned to look down the hall. In front of him, the remaining captains of Felting's army and the city's high lords rested on their knees, cowering before him. Bale's loyal soldiers guarded them on all sides.

Behind them, men and women filled the room, lining the sides and the entire back half, but most looked ready to flee at a moment's notice. Women clutched men's hands, and even a few children grabbed onto their mother's dresses. Bale smirked. Their eyes revealed the reason they were there—curiosity.

"A new age began yesterday," Bale said, his booming voice echoing off the far wall. "For hundreds of years, Feldor stumbled blindly. Kings came and went, blundering through selfish decrees and inept decisions. Your kingdom fell into ruin. Corrupt officials took what they wanted, and despots like King Wesley lived in opulence while the common person suffered."

A few cries of assent echoed in the hall before Bale continued. "The people of Feldor deserve hope! You deserve a place to live where your children have an opportunity for a better life! This is my pledge to you. As we unite all of Terrenor, I promise to bring greatness again to your land." Mumbles of approval rolled through the audience, accented by a handful of cheers.

Bale stepped forward, approaching the Felting soldiers. "Stand!" he commanded, prompting the six captains to rise. Norshewan troops in red-and-black uniforms lined behind them. "Are you men willing to pledge your loyalty to Norshewa?"

The officers looked between each other, faces long and shoulders slumped. They nodded.

"Say it!" he shouted.

"Aye," the men confirmed in a scattered response.

A grin grew on Bale's face. "I will look past what came before, and I accept your offers of fealty."

"We will support your rule," one captain blurted, "but we will not take the lives of other Feldorian citizens." He looked toward the ground as he replied.

Bale stiffened as he inhaled. He strolled along the line of men, staring into their faces. "All of you feel this way?"

After a beat, the other captains nodded almost imperceptibly.

Bale's head bobbed when he spoke. "I understand. It's what I expected to hear."

Shoulders relaxed and sighs dotted the line, the tension melting.

Bale paused for a long moment while the hall silently hung on his words. He gestured slightly to one of the soldiers in red and black before turning and walking toward the throne. The shriek of a mass of people drowned out the metallic ring of unsheathing swords and the chaos of scrambling men, trying unsuccessfully to live a moment longer.

Bale sat in the carved wooden chair. In the hall before him, six captains lay motionless on the floor with pools of blood growing around them. Whimpers continued from the crowd.

Bale jerked his chin, and the soldiers prodded the high lords to their feet. The men shifted their weight and danced their eyes around the room. One overweight lord with a large beard pressed his hands against his shaking legs.

"What about you all?" Bale asked.

Silence filtered into the hall behind his question's fading resonance. The men averted their eyes.

Bale tapped the arm of the throne while he waited for a response. "Are you men willing to do what your king requires?"

They continued to avoid his gaze. Bale gripped the wood as his blood boiled. In a smooth motion, he jumped up from the chair and pulled his sword out. The men tried to shrink away, but the sword tips of the soldiers at their back kept them in place.

"You! What's your name?" Bale asked, pointing his weapon at the end of the line.

Heads snapped to the man, whose head seemed to retreat into his shoulders. Bruises and cuts, mottled in black and blue, covered his face. "Me? I—I'm Darcius Marlow, High Lord of Commerce for Feldor."

Bale smirked as he stepped forward. "High Lord of Commerce . . . Ah yes. Thank you for delivering us to the king, by the way. I demand unwavering loyalty, High Lord Marlow. You must support my decrees and see they are followed—even if that means turning on someone you've known and loved. So, I repeat my question. Are you willing to do what I require?" He pressed the tip of his sword against the man's chest.

Sweat dotted the high lord's brow, his chest rising and falling rapidly. His eyes settled on Bale as they hardened. Marlow extended his chin and opened his mouth.

"Your Majesty!" a voice called behind him. Bale spun, and Brixton Fiero stepped forward, legs shaking. "I spoke with High Lord Marlow, and all the high lords, earlier. We need them to assist with a smooth transition of power. Marlow assured me he was willing to do whatever you ask. Isn't that right, Darcius?"

Bale turned back to the line of men. With a pained expression, Marlow exhaled then nodded. Bale softened the press of his blade then dropped it to his side. After a hard stare at the lords, he sheathed his weapon and returned to the throne.

Remaining standing, he raised his voice and addressed the entire hall. "Anyone who can bring me the head of Veron Stormbridge will receive twenty gold sol in return!" Muttering resumed as the crowd looked at each other. Bale turned to the men on the dais. "Join me."

He strode toward the smaller meeting room. The men followed, pressing in to fill the intimate space.

"What news?" Bale asked Lord Billings.

"Nothing, Your Majesty," Gareth replied. "My men scoured the city for the last day. No one has seen or heard of Veron."

Raynor Fiero spoke up. "Brixton, think again. Did you hear or see anything?"

Brixton shook his head. "Nothing. I only saw him briefly on

the balcony—" he nodded to Bale "—when he was with you, Your Majesty."

"What about the house where he lived? That was Marlow, right?" Bale asked.

Captain Gannon cleared his throat. "I handled that, Your Majesty. We beat him . . . mercilessly, but he revealed nothing. He admitted Stormbridge showed up, but Veron knocked him out and ran off with a stolen horse, some food, and his daughter. We even offered the twenty sol, but he didn't waver. He doesn't know anything."

"I find that believable," Brixton added. "The high lord had no love for Veron after he corrupted his daughter. He wouldn't withhold information."

Bale gripped the back of a chair, pushing into the fabric as he stewed. "I want him found! The signs weren't enough. Triple them! Put them on every street in every town in Feldor. Have trackers search the woods. This *boy* must be killed! In the meantime, I want no less than fifty men guarding me day and night."

"It will be done, Your Majesty," Raynor said.

"I will personally choose the men," Ryker added.

Bale exhaled a long breath. "Good. Now, to the affairs of the city. Raynor, as Regent of Feldor, you will govern as the late King Wesley once did."

The corner of Raynor's mouth turned up. "Thank you, Your Majesty. I look forward to it."

"You may do what you like with it, but I have two requirements," Bale said, causing the half-grin on Fiero's face to falter. "First, let's discuss taxes. They are collected from sales, property, and licenses, correct?"

"That's correct."

"I require one argen per head per season to be paid to me in my home capital of Daratill."

Raynor's eyes bulged. He glanced at Gareth Billings before sputtering, "B—b—but there are hundreds of thousands of people in Feldor!" Bale cocked his head but didn't reply. "That . . . that would be impossible to collect! Many live in farmhouses or small villages buried in the woods. How are we supposed to—"

Bale's fierce glare cut him off. "Are you saying you're not up to the task, Regent Fiero? Do you wish I would find someone else for the job?"

Fiero swallowed hard as he stared back. With a tight shake of his head, he answered, "No, Your Majesty. But half of the kingdom is not yet under our control. What do—" He swallowed again before choosing different words. "I'm not sure how we'll approach taxes from Tienn and Karondir until they are aligned."

"Leave that part to me," Bale said.

"What was the other requirement?" Fiero asked after a tense moment of silence.

"I need men."

"Men? You mean . . . soldiers?" Billings asked.

"No, workers," Bale confirmed, "to join me in Daratill."

Fiero stiffened. "Workers? To do what, exactly?"

Bale's jaw tightened, and his chest rumbled. "Does it matter?" he growled.

Raynor shifted his weight before looking to the ground. "Of course not, Your Majesty."

"Good. I want ten thousand able-bodied men or women ready to march to Daratill in ten weeks."

"Ten thousand men! From Felting?"

Bale scratched his chin. "Some from Felting. Some from Karad. I hear there are several villages hidden in the woods. And we can pick up some in Tienn and Karondir on the way to Norshewa."

He looked between the men of the room, but none dared speak

back. He smirked. *These fools finally realize what they've signed up for.* "That will be all," he said to the group.

"Brixton," Bale said as the crowd moved to leave. Both Fieros turned. "Stay a moment. Please."

Through noticeable effort, Brixton's eyes remained calm. Strands of loose, blond hair touched his furrowed forehead. He remained standing, holding onto the back of a chair while they waited for the others to leave.

"Sit, please," Bale said, pointing to a chair while he walked to a table with several tall, narrow flagons. Lifting one carafe for closer inspection, he pulled the cork and swirled it, holding the opening to his nose as he inhaled. A smile crept over his face. He set out two cups and poured from the vessel. A thin, red liquid streamed into the cup with a hiss as smoke rolled over the lip. After setting the flagon down, Bale carried the drinks to Brixton. He extended a cup.

"Is this . . . firetonic?" Brixton asked with a slight shake in his voice as he tentatively accepted.

"It is. Have you ever had it before?"

The young man shook his head.

"I would expect not. The lower three kingdoms banned production of the drink eighty years ago."

"So, how is it here? How did Wesley have it?"

"According to the bottle, it was a gift from Rynor to Feldor. I'm guessing it was never opened until today.

"But . . . isn't firetonic supposed to kill people?" Brixton asked as he held the cup close to his face.

"Ha!" Bale chortled. "Swords kill people. Drowning kills people. That doesn't mean you'll never splash in the river on a hot day, does it?" Bale winked as he raised his glass then downed the drink in one gulp, setting the empty cup down with alacrity.

Brixton blanched, turning back to his drink. He lifted it gingerly to his lips, pausing to sniff. His body tensed as he tipped it, allowing a small amount to flow into his mouth. For a moment, he seemed to freeze, but as he tried to swallow, his face twisted, and red liquid spewed into the air.

Bale exploded, doubling with laughter while Brixton bent over in a coughing fit. The young man covered his mouth with one hand and held his throat with another.

"You've surprised and impressed me, young Fiero," Bale said, leaning into his chair's high backing.

After several more coughs and wiping the sides of his face and blood-shot eyes, Brixton looked to Bale. "Me?"

"I wasn't sure about your ability to complete the job, but you proved yourself brilliantly."

"Thank you," Brixton said, clearing his throat.

"Many people come to me, flattering and trying to impress. They say whatever they think I want to hear, but I know they only crave power and money."

His coughing finally under control, Brixton nodded his head and listened.

"Of course, I know you desire these things, too. I'm no fool," Bale added, prompting Brixton's shoulders to relax. "But you've shown an impressive dedication in your support. Veron used to be your friend. It must have been difficult to turn him in, and I respect that. Also, you've lived in Feldor under King Wesley all your life. Turning on him couldn't have been a decision made lightly."

"It's true, Your Majesty. It wasn't easy, but . . . I wanted to show you and my father how resolute I was."

Bale held back a smirk. *He's ready to follow me anywhere.* His forehead wrinkled. *Me or his father.* "Your father . . . He's a hard man, isn't he?"

Brixton froze. His eyes glanced around the room.

"It's okay. It's just us."

Brixton sighed and nodded slowly. "Yes, he is."

"Nothing you do is good enough for him, is it?"

A light twinkled in Brixton's eye. "No, it's not."

Bale nodded and continued to listen.

"He never recognizes the things I do well . . . only points out my mistakes."

"Brixton," Bale said, leaning forward and looking him in the eyes. "I see what you're capable of. You are intelligent and brave, and I'm thankful to have you with me. We couldn't have accomplished what we did without you."

Brixton's face lightened, and he sat up straighter. "Thank you."

"To get where we need to go, I'm going to call on you even more. Are you prepared for that?" Bale asked. Brixton nodded. "As Commercial Envoy, I need you to organize what commerce between a united Norshewa looks like. Also, it'll be difficult convincing Feldor to provide the taxes and workers I need. You must work with your father and the high lords of Feldor to make it happen. Can you do this?"

"I can," Brixton said without hesitation.

"I knew you could," Bale said with a wry grin. He stood, Brixton following. Bale placed his arm over the young man's shoulder as they walked to the door. "Now . . . let's see what we can do about making your life here a little nicer."

2

Introductions

"Father?" Veron said as his sword clattered on the wooden floor. He took a step forward. His heart pounded, and his breath came irregularly. His gaze locked with the strangely familiar man.

Behind the man's long brown hair and unkempt beard, the hazel eyes staring back softened, and the fists held in attack position dropped. "Son? It's me, William." The words cracked with emotion, and a tear rolled down his face. He hurried to close the distance.

Before their bodies met, Veron held up his hand, stopping the man short.

"What—" William started, but Veron shook his head as he stepped backward.

His lungs refused to work. He reached behind until he arrived at the door. Veron fumbled with the knob. Turning it, he yanked it open and flew outside, leaving behind five shocked expressions.

Veron gasped for air as he ran through the village of Nasco. He pulled from the origine, fueling his muscles as he pushed them to their limits. He passed houses and dirt streets. A woman sitting on a porch turned her head as he sped by. The cool night brought relief from the stuffy, suffocating wooden house.

After a brief sprint, Veron slowed his effort. His legs stumbled into a rectangular, grassy area surrounded by benches and stores. The space was empty. A lone lantern hung from a post, but the full moon's bright glow rendered it unnecessary. He paced next to the grass, his mind racing. When he felt ready to burst, he sat on a bench and lowered his head into his hands.

His breath shuddered. Of all the things he was prepared for, meeting his father was nowhere on the list. His body ached, battling between physical exhaustion and emotional shock. *Why did I run? I have so much to talk about!* He wanted to return to the house, but his legs felt bound in chains as tears dripped down his hands. He pressed his palms into his eyes, but the emotions were overwhelming.

"Veron?"

His head snapped up. Chelci approached, panting and walking tentatively toward his bench. Her long brown hair swayed behind her. He wiped his face and looked away.

"Can I sit?" she asked.

Veron nodded.

She sat but didn't speak.

"I haven't seen him since I was five," he said after a long moment. "He was supposed to be dead." Chelci rested her hand on his shoulder, giving him a speck of comfort. "If he wasn't dead, then why didn't he ever come to me? Why did he leave me to fend for myself?" Veron's fist clenched.

"I imagine that's something you can ask him," Chelci said in a gentle voice.

"I don't even know why I ran!"

"It's okay. You don't have to know. It's a lot to take in."

Veron wiped his eyes again, and the two sat in silence. Chelci took his hand in hers and squeezed.

"You want to head back?" Veron asked.

Chelci nodded. "I'm ready if you are." She kept hold of his hand as they stood and returned the way they came.

"So you know him?" Veron asked.

"Bensen? Er—William, I guess. Yeah, I know him. He's a good man."

A tinge of jealousy crept in. Veron had only made up stories about who his father was and his adventures. The chance to learn something real made him want more.

Chelci continued, "He was an instructor with the village guard. That's where I got to know him. He was strict but had a soft place in his heart for us all."

"What should I feel?" Veron asked. "What would you think if you were me?"

"I don't know, Veron. I don't think there's anything you're *supposed* to feel. What matters is how you *do* feel. You've been given a gift though. People who lose their parents when they're young never get a chance like you have."

Chelci slowed her gait as they approached the house, and Veron tensed. His footsteps brought him to the base of the porch, where he stopped.

"Go ahead, Veron."

As he placed his foot on the bottom step, the door in front of him opened. William walked through it, backlit by the light inside and leaning on a staff. The two stared at each other for a long moment. Veron's legs trembled, so he reached out to steady himself on the railing.

"Veron, I—uh . . ." William rubbed the back of his neck and looked down at the porch floor.

The wind picked up, blowing a cool breeze across Veron's face and tossing his hair. *I've wondered so much my whole life,* Veron thought.

Now is my chance. He opened his mouth to speak, but his words caught. A scent wafted across his nose, turning his head down the street. The smell of decay was faint but poignant. His stomach turned. *What would give off an odor like that?*

Piercing the night, the crisp, deep ring of a bell echoed over the village. Chelci snapped to attention next to him. William and the man named Russell rushed outside and looked to the source of the sound. Shouting erupted at the far end of the village.

"It's back," William said.

At once, William, Russell, and Chelci took off toward the noise. Veron looked at Morgan, who poked his head through the doorway and shrugged. Unsure of what happened, Veron pursued the runners, quickly catching up.

"Has it returned before this?" Chelci asked mid-stride.

"This would be the fourth," William replied.

"Four times!" she yelled. "Have we lost anyone?"

"Yeah, three guardsmen and two children."

Chelci groaned. "I wish I would have finished it off."

The crew slowed as they approached a young man wearing a loose, black uniform with a sword and shield emblem on the front. A metal helmet tucked under his arm, resting against his body. In a moment, several other men in similar uniforms arrived.

"Where is it, Finley?" William asked in a commanding voice.

"It was just in the woods, right there." The young man held a shaking arm out and pointed down the hill toward the trees. "I was—" He stopped, and his eyes opened wide as a smile grew on his face. "Elise! I mean, Chelci! What are you—"

"Finley!" Russell shouted. "Focus!"

"I'm sorry. I—It's good to see you, Chelci."

"Is anyone taken or hurt?" William asked.

Finley looked back to the woods. "No, I . . . It, uh . . ."

"What happened, Finley!" Russell yelled.

The young man took a deep breath and collected himself. "I heard a noise in the woods, so I went down to check it out. I got just to the edge but didn't want to enter. That's when I heard it—the growl. The wind also changed directions, and the smell hit me at the same time I saw it. It was *huge!*" He turned to Chelci. "It had the scar . . . on its snout where you—"

"Where'd it go? Did it run away?" William asked.

"I . . . uh . . . drew my sword and backed up. It followed me at first, but when it stepped into the clearing, it flinched."

"What do you mean?" Chelci asked.

"When its front half emerged into the moonlight, it recoiled. It stared up toward the moon and growled but then slunk back into the woods."

"The moon! Could that be it?" William breathed.

"I shouted to Royce, who ran for the bell."

"This could change everything," Russell said, turning to William.

"All attacks have been at night under the cover of trees," William added.

What's afraid of the moon? Veron partially lifted a hand. "What is it? A bear?" All heads looked at him.

"Who are you?" Finley asked.

"It's not a bear," William said in a low voice. "It's a valcor."

Chills ran through Veron. He wanted to laugh, but the seriousness of everyone there told him it was no joke. He replayed Finley's story over in his head with a whole new meaning as he thought back to all the stories he'd heard of the legendary creature.

"No one can defeat a valcor," he said. "How are you supposed to—" He stopped when Chelci covered a giggle with her hand. "What?" He glanced between Chelci and the others.

William chuckled. "There's at least one person who can."

Veron stared, trying to figure out his meaning. Another giggle from Chelci drew his attention back to her. "What . . . You?"

"Men on watch," Russell said to the crowd. "Be extra alert tonight, but let's use this new knowledge from Finley. Don't go into the woods."

The men in uniforms all nodded then dispersed.

"Chelci, I'll talk with you tomorrow, okay?" Finley said, prompting Chelci to nod. "I'll tell Aleks, too. He'll be so happy to see you!"

Russell and William talked together as they walked back toward the house. Veron fell in line with Chelci. A crooked grin pulled at the corners of her mouth as Veron stared.

"You really fought a valcor?" he asked.

"What? You don't think I'm good enough?"

"No, I just . . . um . . . That's amazing!"

Chelci laughed. "Yeah, it was no big deal. I followed it up a tree. After fighting back and forth for a while, I stabbed it through its mouth and knocked it to the ground."

Veron's mouth hung open.

"You should ask your father about it, actually."

Veron looked ahead where the older men continued to talk. *I have so much to ask about.* "Why were you called Elise?"

Chelci laughed softly. "Just like you used to be called Ash, I used to be called Elise."

After a brief walk, they arrived back at the house. Russell and William climbed the porch to talk with Nevi, and Morgan came down to join Veron and Chelci.

"Everything okay?" Morgan asked with eyebrows raised. "Nevi said something about a valcor?"

Chelci nodded. "It didn't hurt anyone tonight—ran off in the woods."

Morgan's head shook. "I never thought they were real! Do you think we'll be able to stay here?"

"I'm sure. The villagers are good people."

"I wonder if Bale will search out this far?" Veron asked. "I wish I knew his plans."

Nevi cleared her throat, drawing their attention. "We're so glad you all came, and we're happy for you to stay. Chelci, if you like, you can have your old bed back. And, Morgan, we have space to make a pallet on the floor in the living room for you."

"And I can sleep one at my house," William said, looking at Veron.

Veron swallowed hard, but his heart leaped at the same time. A smile fought to grow on his face, but something in him resisted.

"It's getting late now. Shall we . . . ?" William held his arm out, pointing down the path.

Chelci grasped Veron's hand in hers and squeezed. Her eyes sparkled, and her brows lifted. Her long brown hair jostled while she offered a tight nod. The hope she tried to instill in him took root, and a grin tugged at his mouth.

"I'll see you two tomorrow," Veron said, squeezing her hand a final time before turning to join William.

Butterflies danced in Veron's stomach as he looked forward, head angled down. He walked along the dirt path next to his father, racking his brain for something to say. They turned down a path that led along the village center and crossed to the other side. Veron chanced a glance at William, who opened his mouth but said nothing. Veron laughed to himself. *He doesn't know what to say either.*

William led the way to a modest wood-frame house with a low porch and door centered between two windows. A large tree grew against one side, and a raked roof hung over the edge of the house.

Veron followed his father inside, the smell of wood and earth greeting him while William lit a candle. A countertop and stove filled one side of the tight living space. Shelves on the wall above contained a few basic dishes and some food. Opposite it, two cushioned chairs angled toward each other in the corner with an oval rug on the floor. A small table with a pair of stools pushed against the third wall with a window above it. A doorway in the last wall showed a low pallet of straw in the adjacent room.

Veron removed his back scabbard and set it with the sword against the wall. "What happened to your leg?"

William glanced down as he rested the lit candle on the table. "That would be courtesy of our village friend you almost had the privilege to meet a bit ago."

Veron's eyes widened. "The valcor!"

William nodded.

"Chelci said I should ask you about it. What happened?"

William laughed. "Of course she would want to bring that up." He took the coiled rope off from where it looped across his body and laid it on the floor. Then he rested his staff against the wall and hobbled across the room to a chair. "Chelci was training for the village guard when we ran into it the first time. I fought it until it knocked me out and dragged me into the woods."

Veron raised an eyebrow. "But . . . you're a shadow knight . . . right? How did it get you?"

"A shadow knight is still a person. We can bleed and die just like anyone else." Veron joined him in the other chair while William continued, staring at the candle, lost in the memory. "I used only a small amount of origine while I stabbed it. I didn't expect my sword to be useless on its hide. Its claws were as fast as lightning, and it shredded my leg. I wasn't ready. After that, I was useless."

Veron leaned forward, elbows on his knees. "What happened with Chelci?"

A smile formed on William's face as he shook his head and chuckled. "She saw the animal take me down. Then . . . armed with nothing but a child's blunted sword and a uniform too large for her, with no one to back her up, she ran deep into the woods, following my trail of blood."

Veron's jaw hung loose again.

"She ran the valcor off, almost killing it. Then she dragged my body back as she nearly bled out herself. When I was still conscious, I used origine to heal my wounds as best I could, but it wasn't enough. I'd be dead if it weren't for her. I was fortunate I only lost a leg."

The two men settled into silence and watched the candle flicker. *Is he going to ask something, or should I?* Veron swallowed and turned toward his father. "I have so many questions I don't know where to start. I wasn't expecting this."

William nodded. "I know. Neither was I." After another pause, his father continued. "Maybe we should get some sleep and try in the morning?"

Veron's shoulders relaxed. "Yeah, that sounds good."

William pressed down on the arms of the chair and stood. After picking up the candle, he led Veron to the other room. A musty odor filled the room from the large, straw pallet that took up most of the floor.

William took a pile of blankets from the shelf and handed them to Veron. "Should be plenty of room for us both," he said, motioning to the far end of the pallet.

"Yeah, this is fine." Veron removed his Shadow Knights cloak and laid it on the wooden boards next to the pallet. A warm feeling rolled through him as he lay down and pulled the blankets over. His father settled down next to him. Veron stared at the thatched roof's underside. The foreign feeling of being with his father left him on edge and alert. Soft, rhythmic breathing soon sounded next to him, and Veron relaxed. In no time, he fell fast asleep.

3

The Elders of Nasco

A chirping bird roused Veron from a deep sleep. For a moment, the unfamiliar location left him disoriented. When he opened his eyes, the straw pallet and the open window displaying a limb full of leaves reminded him where he was. Sunlight drifted past the leaves, filling the room with a morning glow.

Veron sat up and rubbed his eyes. The space next to him was empty. *How long did I sleep?* He threw his blankets off and rose to his feet. "William?"

"Out here!"

Veron dusted off pieces of straw stuck to his arms and legs as he left the room. The sizzling of a frying pan greeted him, the spicy aroma making his mouth water.

"Sausage? Bread?" William asked.

Veron nodded as his stomach growled. He sat at the tiny table where two table settings waited. "Sorry I slept so late."

"It's fine. You had a long trip." William divided sausage onto two plates and added slices of bread. He brought the plates over and sat with Veron.

Veron skewered a sausage link with a fork and took a bite. His eyes opened wide. "Wow! This is good," he said with his mouth full.

William chuckled. "You sound surprised."

"I just assumed . . . well . . . Artimus wasn't the best cook."

William stopped mid-bite and breathed in sharply. "Artimus," he said, looking out the window. "Is he still . . ."

Veron's face fell as he shook his head.

William's mouth formed a tight line.

"I lived with him in Karad for four years," Veron said.

William continued to stare out the window. "I figured it was him. He was the only one missing when I came to."

"After Bale's attack?"

William nodded.

"You healed yourself?" Veron asked.

William flashed a feeble smile.

"What'd you do then?"

William looked down at his plate and pushed his sausages around. "Bale would never stop hunting me if he knew I lived, so I hid. I left Felting and . . . everything, and I ended up here." A trickle of a tear traversed his cheek before he wiped it away.

"Everything. You mean, me?" Veron said with an edge in his voice.

William looked up. "I'm so sorry. I wanted to get you. I really did. But . . . I was scared . . . for *you*. Bale wanted to kill me, and I didn't want to put you in the middle of that."

Veron leaned back and crossed his arms. "So you thought it better to leave me to fend for myself—living on the streets, begging, stealing?"

Tears fell again. William's fork clattered to his plate as he grabbed Veron's arm. "I didn't know what to do. I wish I could undo it."

Veron gazed out the window.

"I did return for you," William added.

Veron's head snapped back. "When?"

"I was too late. I wrestled with my choice for too long. After three years, I made the trip back to Felting to find you."

Veron counted in his head.

"You had just left."

"I left with Fend—an older boy. He took care of me." Veron's chair scraped as he stood. "I'm sorry. I need some air."

William didn't protest as Veron walked to the door. Over Veron's shoulder, a quiet voice said, "I wish Julia could have seen you."

The words hit him hard and paralyzed him. His hand shook, holding onto the door frame, and his feet paused mid-step. *Mother.* He half-turned around but stopped. The desire to learn about his mother warred against the rage toward his father for abandoning him. With heavy feet, he continued off the porch, leaving his father alone.

Veron wandered the village for close to an hour. He passed the main square with the grass and benches he had found the night before. Villagers chatted in front of stores, throwing curious glances in his direction. His path took him past a large garden filled with leafy greens and recently harvested stalks. A memory of Artimus kneeling in the dirt in Karad came to his mind, bringing a wistful smile to his face.

The village's homes sprawled along winding dirt paths, eventually ending at the surrounding woods. He skirted the woods, traveling on the dirt path. He warily watched the trees, half-expecting a valcor to jump out.

Am I being too hard on him? Should I forgive him and accept him as my father? Does he deserve forgiveness? His questions generated no answers, and eventually, he made his way to Chelci and Morgan.

"Veron!" Morgan waved from the porch.

Veron mounted the porch steps and took a free chair. "Where's Chelci?"

"She's walking with Nevi. So . . . how was it?" Morgan's eyes sparkled as he spoke.

Veron extended his chin. "How was what?"

"Talking with your father! Was it amazing?"

"Oh. Yeah, I guess it was good."

Morgan raised an eyebrow. "Ohhhkay . . . We need to discuss this."

"What?"

"What happened?" Morgan asked, folding his arms across his chest.

Veron exhaled a frustrated sigh as he shook his head. "He just . . . He left me. I was five, and he knew where I was, but he—" Veron covered his mouth then blinked several times in succession. He stood to lean against the railing, staring out at the woods. "He *says* it was a hard decision—that he was afraid about Bale. He says he came back to get me, but I was gone."

"Mmm," Morgan mumbled.

Veron spun. "What?"

Wrinkles lined Morgan's forehead as his brows pinched together. "It's just that . . ." He adjusted himself to sit on the edge of his chair and gestured with his hands as he spoke. "Imagine you were in his shoes."

"What do you mean?"

"If you expected someone to track you down and kill you, would you bring your five-year-old with you and put him in harm's way, too? He probably did the best he knew how to do."

Veron sighed but refused to give in to the logic. He wasn't ready to let go of his anger yet. He turned back to the woods to keep Morgan from reading his face.

"If William wants to connect with you now, it may be a good idea to give him a chance."

Walking along the dirt path, Russell joined them, wearing one of the black uniforms they saw the night before. "The elders are gathering to discuss the valcor and Bale. Veron, they've asked you to come."

Veron glanced at Morgan.

"Have fun," Morgan said before breaking into a broad grin. "And say hello to your father for me."

At the edge of the village center, Veron followed Russell through a wooden doorway to a well-lit meeting room. Chelci jumped up to greet him. Seeing her smile filled him with the warmth he craved after the emotional last day. When she reached him, Chelci held his hand and gave him a quick kiss on the cheek. Veron blushed.

"I heard your talk started out rocky?" she said.

"What? How did you—" Veron followed her gaze to where William sat on a bench, watching them. "I can't just act like everything is fine."

"You don't have to act. Just be yourself," she said, squeezing his hand and leaning against him.

A circle of benches with a handful of people filled the room. Veron already knew William and Russell. Three older men, who Veron assumed to be the elders, sat together, and two other men wearing matching black uniforms made seven total. Veron pulled Chelci's hand, leading her toward seats in the back row.

"Thanks for joining us," William said, leaning in his direction.

Veron didn't reply.

"Elise, it's good to have you back," one of the elders said, throwing a smile in Chelci's direction. His aged voice wavered, reminding Veron of Artimus. "I think we can begin. We have two topics to discuss. First, what happened with the valcor last night?"

"No one was hurt, thankfully," Russell said. "Finley found it, but he was unharmed."

"How is that possible?" the elder asked.

William jumped in. "We believe it may fear the moon. It appeared to shrink back from the moonlight and wouldn't leave the safety of the trees."

"Why have we never known this before?"

William shrugged. "We've only seen it a handful of times, and those have all been in the woods."

"So if we stay out of the woods at night, we'll be safe?"

"We don't know for sure, Peter, but we think that may be the case," Russell said.

The elder addressed as Peter glanced between Russell and William. "Should we attempt hunting it again?"

"We tried for a week with no success," William said. "It may be worth simply staying out of the woods around the village at night for a while. Maybe we can get lucky with some traps."

"I agree," Russell chimed in. "I ordered a team to begin clearing a wider ring around the village. If we're wrong about the moonlight, we can always change the plan, but for now, that should be enough."

Peter frowned. "I want to make sure our people are safe."

Russell leaned forward. "As do we, and we think this is the best plan to do that."

The elders looked between themselves and nodded. "Very well," Peter said. "Now, let's discuss this issue of Bale.'

Russell turned. "Veron and Chelci?"

Veron sat up straight as all heads turned to them. Chelci answered, "Edmund Bale aligned with Karad and has taken over Felting. They killed King Wesley and plan to take over the rest of Terrenor."

"We saw the soldiers when they marched through . . . around a week ago," William added.

"We expect widespread ruin and oppression. His influence will grow with time," Veron said.

"We've lived in our quiet village for years without being bothered," another of the elders said. "It's been twenty years since we've seen an official visitor from the kingdom. It shouldn't be any different now."

"I agree," the last elder chimed in. "I know little about Bale, but I can't imagine how this affects things here."

Veron adjusted in his seat.

Peter's brows narrowed. "You came here to get away from them?"

Veron glanced at Chelci before looking at his hands. He cleared his throat and swallowed. "Bale's been hunting me because . . ." All eyes bored down on him as his pulse's thump grew in his ears. "I'm a shadow knight."

The three elders muttered between themselves.

"And so am I," William added as he stood. "Veron and I are the last ones, and it's prophesied that one of us will kill Bale. As a result, the Norshewan ruler wants us dead. That's why I came here to begin with, and it's why Veron's here now."

The muttering increased in volume.

William remained standing, eyes locked on Veron. "Plus . . . Veron is my son. I hadn't seen him in fourteen years until yesterday."

The room grew silent, and all heads turned to either William or Veron.

William looked at his hands as he continued. "I made some mistakes as a father, ones I can never take back. All his life, I've loved him and wanted to be with him—" William's eyes glistened. "—but he never knew it. He grew up abandoned." He looked up to meet Veron's eyes. "I can't correct the past . . . but I can do better, now."

Veron clenched his jaw to keep from spilling tears. Chelci squeezed his hand as his father sat back on his bench. The three elders conferred for a moment between themselves. William stared at

Veron from across the circle. His father's eyes were soft. Veron turned away from the weak smile, the ache in his heart pounding against the hard exterior he'd built.

"Is there a chance Bale knows you're here?" Peter asked.

Veron looked at Chelci then shook his head. "I don't think so. No one knows where we are."

Peter nodded. "In that case, our course is clear. We stay where we are and leave the business of Terrenor to Terrenor." The other elders nodded in agreement. "That will be it for today."

Veron's heart twitched, thankful to remain in hiding yet regretful at the same time. As the gathering dismissed, he hurried outside.

"Are you okay?" Chelci asked, catching up in a hurry. Veron continued walking forward, even as she slipped her hand into his. "How are you feeling?"

"About what?" Veron asked.

"About what your father said."

He shrugged. "I'm fine."

"Veron." Chelci pulled on him, turning his body to look at her. They stood at the edge of the village center's grassy courtyard. One eyebrow arched as she stared at him. "He sounded genuine. You should give him a shot."

Veron's gaze drifted past her shoulder to where his father walked by. William passed with a doleful smile, filling Veron with a tinge of regret.

"Yeah," he said with a nod. "I think you're right. I asked him about the valcor, by the way."

"Oh, yeah?" Chelci smiled as she swung his arm. "Did he tell you about how I was the bravest in the class?"

"He didn't mention that, no. You must have been trying to impress one of the boys or something, huh?"

Chelci's mouth dropped as she snatched her hand free. She hit him on the shoulder, sending a spasm of pain through his arm.

"Ow!"

"I wasn't trying to impress a boy!" Wrinkles lined her forehead as her face furrowed into a frown.

"Finley? Was that his name?"

"No!"

"Or was it Aleks?"

"Ha!" Chelci scoffed.

A crooked smile grew on Veron's face. "You liked him, didn't you?"

"What? No!"

"I think you had a thing for this *Aleks* guy."

Chelci's pursed lips and narrowed eyes didn't conceal her desire to laugh. "He's a good guy. They both are, but they're like brothers to me."

Veron's shoulders relaxed as the insecurity faded. "Okay. We'll see." He took her hand back, and she didn't fight him. They turned and walked down the street toward Chelci's house.

"What do you think about staying here?" Chelci asked.

Veron exhaled. "Honestly, I'm not sure. Part of me feels like I should go back to confront Bale. What if he finds me here?" Veron motioned to the houses. "What might happen to this village?"

Ahead, William stopped to help an old woman who struggled to carry a load of vegetables in a wooden box. Veron was too far away to hear what was said, but his father smiled and laughed with the woman. He walked alongside her, talking as he limped along with his staff, carrying her burden against his hip.

"But . . . part of me wants to stay for a while."

Chelci turned her head and held his hand with both of hers. "Well, I know what *I* want."

Veron nodded. "Yeah, I think I do, too."

4

An Uncomfortable Job

Brixton smoothed his hair as he ascended the steps to the Department of Commerce. The stately building intimidated him, even though his current position was of much higher esteem.

When he opened the door, a woman sitting behind a desk greeted him with a smile. "Good morning! How can I help you?" she said. Her eyes moved to the red-and-black badge on his shoulder, and the smile turned into a frown.

"I'm . . . uh . . . here to see High Lord Marlow," Brixton replied.

"Is he expecting you?"

"Yes, I'm Brixton Fiero, Commercial Envoy of Terrenor."

Her mouth formed a hard line. "Of course. Have a seat, please. I'll let him know you're here." She motioned to an empty chair.

Brixton sat as the woman walked down the hall, disappearing into another room. He pressed his new cloak taut against his chest. Bale compensated him well for his position, and he didn't waste any time putting his wealth to work. Brixton leaned forward to stare after her. *Where is she?* He huffed as he waited.

Finally, the woman returned. "The High Lord will be with you shortly."

Brixton's temper flared. *How dare he keep me waiting? Does he not realize I outrank him?* He sat for a moment, bouncing his foot on the ground. "This is insulting," he muttered before standing.

"Please, sir, you can't just—"

Brixton ignored her protest. He passed her desk and marched down the hall to the room she had gone into. He opened the door and entered unannounced.

High Lord Marlow and an old woman sitting opposite his desk turned to look. She dabbed at her red, puffy eyes.

"Brixton?" Marlow said. "We are *almost* finished here."

"It's okay," the woman said as she stood. "I need to leave. Darcius, thank you for your help and kind words. You don't know how much it means."

Marlow stood and nodded before glaring at Brixton.

Brixton averted his eyes and shifted his weight as the woman passed him, leaving the room. "I . . . uh . . . thought you were making me wait. I didn't realize . . ."

"Why would I make you wait?"

Brixton left the question alone. "What was going on with her?" he asked louder than necessary as he walked to the chair.

"Mrs. Sturgess? Her husband passed away last week. She's taking over his herb shop and needed some advice."

"So, you just . . . helped her?"

Darcius quizzically tilted his head. "Of course. Does King Bale have a problem with that?"

Brixton scoffed and stared back at the high lord, refusing to answer the smart remark. The older man looked haggard. Nasty-looking purple bruises covered the side of his face and part of his neck, and a dark scar ran down the opposite cheek. Brixton winced, imagining the pain he must have gone through at Captain Gannon's hand.

"What brings you here today, Brixton?" Darcius asked.

He stiffened at the informal address. "You should refer to me as Commercial Envoy Fiero." An abrupt laugh escaped Darcius' mouth, prompting Brixton's face to redden. "What?"

"I'm sorry," Darcius said. "It's a new title to me."

Brixton's jaw clenched. He chose to move past the insult. "We need to work out how to collect Bale's tax. One argen per head is steep."

"*I* don't need to work out how to collect it. It seems to me that's *your* problem."

"This affects us all, Darcius. If Bale doesn't get what he wants, none of us want to be around to see the consequences."

Marlow stared back for a long moment, forcing Brixton to shuffle in his seat. "Why are you doing this?"

"Doing what?"

"All of it. Aligning with Bale, betraying your kingdom."

Brixton leaned back and tried to sit as upright as possible. "It does no good to support the losing side of a war. It's foolish."

"I say it's brave."

Brixton clenched his jaw as he held it out, unsure how to respond.

"You think not wanting to be on the losing side justifies killing the king?" Darcius asked.

"He was going to die one way or another." A smug grin formed on Brixton's face. "I took action that ensured I'd be successful in the aftermath."

"In that case, congratulations, Commercial Envoy Fiero. You've shown us all what wisdom truly looks like."

Brixton swallowed hard and gritted his teeth against the thinly veiled sarcasm. "Look, I'm no fan of Bale's. I worry about what he's going to do to our kingdom, but there's no fighting this. He's here, and he's in charge. The best thing to do is to be part of his trusted group. At least this way we have some control over how things play out."

Marlow stared back without responding, forcing Brixton to revisit his question. "So, about taxes . . . I'm meeting with High Lord Plummer later to get his ideas. My first thought was to keep it simple—have a seasonal census where each person pays one argen."

"Ha!" Marlow exclaimed. "Good luck with that!"

A flush crept up Brixton's neck. "Why do you say that? It's fair. Everyone pays their tax."

Marlow shook his head as he responded. "Have you ever walked through the Red Quarter, Brixton?"

Brixton gritted his teeth.

"I don't think you have. I'd like to see you tell one of those people living on the street they need to pay an argen to Edmund Bale and not for a basket of food."

Brixton squirmed at the thought.

"You'll have an uprising on your hands."

"Then we throw them in prison!" Brixton shouted. "Bale isn't bluffing about this. He won't be satisfied with less than the full amount."

"How much space do you have in the prisons?" Marlow raised an eyebrow before breaking into a laugh.

A light burning feeling covered Brixton's entire face. "Okay, then. We don't take one argen. We only ask for five tid." Marlow didn't object to the lowered amount, and Brixton regained some confidence. He nodded at his own suggestion. "I'll bring it up to Ernest when we meet. That will get us halfway there."

"What about the rest?" Marlow asked.

"We'll have to raise it through commercial taxes."

Marlow's jaw set as he stared daggers. "Feldor already taxes commercial trade at the maximum level. Increasing it would create hardships on the people."

"It would allow those with no money to not pay."

"And those with money to pay double," Marlow noted. "They'll love that."

"Well, what do you propose?" Brixton's blood heated up. They needed a solution, and Marlow wasn't being as helpful as he had hoped.

"I propose we *don't* kill King Wesley and allow him to continue to rule in the manner he has for years."

"Wesley's dead!" Brixton stood and slammed his fist on the desk, causing Marlow to jump. "Bale is here, and we can't change that!"

Brixton breathed heavily, his hand in a ball. He edged back from the desk and returned to his chair. Marlow smoothed out the front of his tunic as he leaned forward.

"How high would we need to tax commerce?" Marlow asked. "Have you worked it out?"

Brixton squirmed. His eyes darted around the room, wishing he could avoid the truth. "If we're only getting half from a census tax, commercial goods is the best way."

"How high?"

Brixton tapped his finger on the arm of his chair. "Thirteen percent."

"What?" Marlow threw his hands up. "How are our vendors supposed to raise rates thirteen percent? People can't pay that!"

"They'll have to."

"Or what?" The question hung in the air for a long moment. "People are going to fight it. There will be resistance. Vendors won't raise rates or pay the tax. What will you do then?"

"You figure it out. You're the High Lord of Commerce!" Brixton blustered.

"Who reports to the Commercial Envoy of Terrenor, apparently."

"I don't know! Throw them in prison!"

"Sounds like a party in the prison with all those bodies."

"Gah!" Brixton exclaimed. "Close their businesses! Take their property! We need this money, and people need to know we mean business. We only need to make example of a few, and the rest will fall in line."

Marlow shook his head. "This leads down a dangerous path filled with ruin and heartache."

"Not for me!" Brixton's chest heaved from the heavy breaths. "What else is there to do?"

"I already told you what I would have done."

Brixton sighed. There was no way to turn back. "We need all business owners to sign updated license agreements, agreeing to the new tax rates. Make it happen."

"And when they refuse?"

Brixton took a deep breath. "Let me know. I'll make an example of them."

After a long moment, Marlow nodded with a look of resignation.

"Where's Chelci?" Brixton asked.

The change of subject seemed to catch the high lord by surprise. "I—I don't know."

"They didn't indicate where they went?"

"I told that captain everything," Marlow said as his hand absently touched the bruise on the side of his head. "She ran off with that *servant.*"

Brixton smirked as he stood. "Have those new licenses signed within a week, Darcius." Without waiting for a response, he walked to the door.

"Brixton . . ."

Brixton stopped and turned.

Marlow's eyes softened. "Thank you for speaking up the other night with Bale. I appreciate it—all the high lords do."

Brixton nodded, locking eyes, then left.

Outside, Brixton ducked through the crowd to continue toward the Department of Treasury. As he walked, a friendly voice called his name, halting him in his tracks and prompting him to turn around. He scanned the road but couldn't find the greeting's source. Finally, a young man waved a hand as he approached, drawing Brixton's focus.

"Brixton! It's good to see you again!"

Where do I know him from? Brixton smiled as he racked his brain. The young man's disheveled hair stuck up in tufts, and a flour-dusted apron covered his front. *The baker! Chelci's friend!* "It's good to see you again, too!" he said before narrowing his eyes. "Remind me of your name again . . ."

The light dimmed in the baker's eyes. "Matthew."

"Yes! Of course! I'm sorry. And you're married to . . ." Both young men leaned their heads forward until Brixton chanced a guess. "Emma?"

Matthew's smile returned as he nodded. "That's right. I, uh . . . heard things didn't work out for you and Chelci. Sorry about that."

"Yeah, well . . . it's okay. It's worked out well in other areas." He glanced toward the treasury office before turning back.

"I heard about the . . . Emissary of Commerce thing, too."

"Commercial Envoy," Brixton corrected.

"Yeah, that. Congratulations, I guess."

Brixton nodded, unsure what to say. "Well, I really should . . ." He gestured down the street in the direction he'd been heading.

"Of course!" Matthew said, reaching out his hand. "I won't keep you. It's good to run into you though."

Brixton cringed as he pulled away from the parting handshake, flour and dirt depositing on his palm. He didn't want to wipe it on his clothes, so he held out his hands and rubbed them against each other.

"Sorry about that," Matthew said. "I guess I don't even think about it."

Brixton grunted in response.

"Say, I know you're new to Felting. If you ever need to hang out with someone around your age, let me know! Come by the shop anytime."

Matthew's smile dredged up guilt as Brixton turned to leave. *I can't spend time with bakers now that I have such an esteemed position,* he thought as he walked down the street. *Still . . . it does feel nice to talk with someone who isn't scheming and jostling for position.*

Brixton's meeting with High Lord Plummer went as expected. The man wasn't excited about the idea of the census tax, but he didn't fight Brixton on it. Feeling victorious, Brixton returned to his new house with a grin of satisfaction.

His choreman opened the door as he approached. "Welcome back, sir."

Brixton took off his cloak and handed it to him without a word. He couldn't remember the man's name, so he avoided a response.

Bale had arranged for the living quarters while Brixton was in Felting. Near the castle and one street over from the Marlows' home, he found it quite adequate. It wasn't as large as his family's old place in Karad, but the decorations and fixtures were of the finest quality, and expensive art filled most rooms. He didn't know what happened to the family who used to live there. It was easier not to ask. The choreman, housekeeper, and cook came with the house. Timid—almost scared—they took care of everything he needed.

Brixton called for a glass of wine and went to the sitting room to relax while he waited for dinner. The ticking of the clock echoed through the empty chamber. He sat with his drink for only a moment, the silence grating on his nerves. Hoping the patio would be more to his liking, he exited the back doors.

Cooler air greeted him, lifting his spirits. The sun fell low in the sky, painting a red and purple scene. Conversation percolated from a gathering at a nearby house. On the opposite side of the unseen property, a woman called children's names, resulting in a distant fit of giggling.

A frown tugged at Brixton's face. A longing for something he couldn't place his finger on pulled at him. *I'm one of the most important leaders in the kingdom. Why do I feel like something is missing?* He fixed his jaw then took a long drink, draining the glass. *I know what I need to do.*

Heading inside, he again forgot the choreman's name. Brixton walked the rooms, unsure how to call out for the man. He cleared his throat, but no one responded. He found the cook hard at work in the kitchen. "Um . . . have you seen the choreman?" he asked.

The cook stopped stirring a pot with a wooden ladle as he tilted his head. "Nigel? He should be around." He leaned toward the doorway. "Nigel!"

"Remind me of your name again," Brixton said.

"Quinn . . . sir." The cook gave a slight bow.

"And the housekeeper is . . . ?"

"Corina."

"That's right," Brixton said, acting as if it had just been on the tip of his tongue.

"Yes?" Nigel said, entering the kitchen before he noticed Brixton. "Oh! Master Fiero. What can I do for you?"

"I want to host a party," Brixton said, standing tall with his shoulders back. "Next Weekterm. I want to invite all the important people of Felting, and it must be . . . impressive."

Nigel glanced at Quinn. "We would need to hire additional help, and . . ."

"I have plenty of money," Brixton said. "Make it happen."

Nigel bowed. "Very well. I'll see to it."

After refilling his glass, Brixton left the kitchen and wandered into the sitting room. He grinned as he pictured his house filled with guests—people from all over the city who came to be around him.

5

A Chance to Impress

Brixton straightened his collar as he gazed in the mirror. A strand of blond hair fell down, and he licked his fingers before tucking it behind his ear. He looked sharp in his new outfit. The crisp black suit folded in sharp lines, and the brilliant white tunic underneath peeked out with silver buttons reflecting the light. A shop in Turba Square made the suit for him. It cost a hefty tid but was a necessary expense to impress.

His stomach fluttered as he thought of the crowd gathering below. Laughter rumbled up through the floor, and glasses clinked together. Still, Brixton waited—not quite time for his appearance. He took a stiff drink, draining the glass of brandy—his third of the night. A foggy sensation already danced through his mind.

A soft knock rapped on the door. "Come in," Brixton said.

Nigel opened the door. "Sir, I believe most of the guests have arrived."

"Is my father here yet?"

"I've not seen Regent Fiero."

"What about Bale? Has he shown?"

Nigel shook his head. "Not yet."

"Hmph," Brixton mumbled. He took another look in the mirror and pulled at his collar. "Very well."

Nigel held the door open while Brixton exited the room. Warm air from a house filled with bodies hit him as he walked to the top of the stairs. The raucous conversations and light music from below brought a grin to his face. Brixton stepped lively as he descended until his vision spun, forcing him to hold the railing and slow down.

The staircase emptied into the foyer, where two rooms spilled from both sides, packed with guests. Tables covered with food lined the far wall, and people loaded small plates with bite-sized treats of the finest fare Felting had to offer. He inhaled, savoring the moment.

Turning to the tea room first, Brixton meandered between the guests, scanning their faces. Several people appeared to have already had a handful of drinks—confirmed by the volume of speech and the lack of coordination. No one returned his gaze, and he didn't recognize anyone. *I guess most wouldn't know me yet. Should I introduce myself?* He made his way to the sitting room, where he found a similarly unfamiliar scene. *Who are all these people?*

"Can I have a fresh brandy?" A greasy man with dark hair barked, shoving an empty glass at Brixton and nearly tripping over his own feet.

Brixton reflexively took the glass but screwed his face up as he stared back. "What? No, I'm not a server. I'm the host!"

"I'm sorry, I thought you looked like . . ." The man's words faded as he swayed on his feet. "Well, can I have a brandy?"

"Um . . . sure." Brixton glanced around and waved down a server they'd hired for the party. He paled. The server's outfit appeared similar to the suit he wore. "Get this man a drink," he said with as much authority as he could muster. "And one for me, too!" The server snapped to attention and made off straight away.

Brixton turned back to the guest. "What's your name, sir?"

"Kurtis," he replied, extending his hand to shake. "I own the Tensington Law House."

"I'm Brixton Fiero, Commercial Envoy of Terrenor." Kurtis twitched, covering his mouth. Brixton wasn't sure if it was a laugh or a hiccup. "I've been working with King Bale and my father, Regent Fiero, to ensure—"

"Yes! Thank you!" Kurtis said, interrupting him as the server approached. Ignoring Brixton, he grabbed his filled glass and turned away, disappearing into the crowd of bodies.

"Wha—" Brixton's mouth hung open. He closed it with a snap and seized his glass with a force that sloshed some of the liquid onto the floor. He took a long drink then frowned. A fog washed through his head as he scanned the room again. The familiar face of Byron Hampton, his sister's father-in-law, perked him up. Brixton jostled between guests to approach the High Lord of Trade.

"High Lord Hampton!" Brixton said cheerfully. The man paused his conversation with another guest Brixton didn't recognize. "I'm glad you could make it to my party."

"Yes, well . . ." Byron glanced around the room as he spoke. "There wasn't anything else going on tonight."

"How's Magnus doing? Still working hard at that accountant job, is he?" Brixton took a drink as he gloated on the inside. At one point, his jealousy of the high lord's son consumed him, but now, he had far surpassed his brother-in-law's station.

"Your sister struggles to give him a child."

Brixton jolted into a coughing fit as the liquor went down the wrong pipe. He took a moment to collect himself as his eyes filled with water. "Sorry about that," he said between coughs, pressing his fist against his chest.

Byron made a face toward the man with him. Brixton continued to clear his throat, attempting to compose himself.

"You haven't seen my father tonight, have you?" Brixton asked.

"The regent?" Byron said condescendingly. "No, I haven't."

Brixton nodded. "I figured as much. Look . . . I appreciate you being here tonight, Byron. Some people have held it against me with what all has gone on recently. But . . . family is important, and I thank you for the support."

Hampton tossed back the last of his drink then glared at him. "I couldn't care less about supporting you and Bale's insatiable thirst for power. I'm here because there are free drinks. Now, if you'll excuse me, I could use a refill." The high lord and the other man walked away, leaving Brixton alone again.

Anger simmered just under the surface. *Is that why no one I know is here? Do they all think ill of me?* He stood alone, surrounded by a crowd engrossed in their own conversations. A small group of musicians played stringed instruments in the corner. The music was light and festive, contrasting the growing sourness of Brixton's mood.

He pushed his way to a server, polishing off his glass and trading it for a full one. Feeling bolder with a fresh drink in his hand, he stood on a chair and faced the crowded room, raising his hands in the air.

"Attention, everyone! Can I have a moment?" The music stopped. The crowd noise dimmed to a murmur. People pressed in from the adjacent rooms as all eyes rested on him. A smile formed on his face. "Thank you all for being here at my party. For those I haven't met, I am Brixton Fiero, Commercial Envoy of Terrenor." A snicker echoed from the back of the room, but he forced himself to ignore it. "Being new to Felting, I'm excited to get to know you all. I hope we can all use our influence and resources to help each other be successful in our endeavors. So . . . enjoy the food and drink, and have a good time tonight!"

He lifted his glass as he finished. A few people joined him in drinking, but the response was not enthusiastic. After a moment, the music picked back up and conversations resumed. Hopping down from his chair, Brixton grinned as he waited for a guest to approach him. *Surely, someone will want to speak with me now that they know who I am.* As the seconds ticked by and he stood alone, his smile faltered. Soon, his mouth fixed in a tight line, and he breathed heavily through his nose.

"Master Fiero," Nigel said to the side.

"What!" Brixton shouted, louder than he intended.

The choreman shrank back. "I'm sorry, sir, but there's someone here for the party. They're not on the list, but they say they know you and you'd be okay with them coming in."

Brixton's eyebrows furrowed. *Who could that be?* He invited all high lords, government officials, and prominent businessmen of the city. *Who did I miss?*

He followed to the front room where Nigel pulled a curtain aside at the window. Brixton's stomach turned. The baker, Matthew, and his wife, Emma, stood on the stoop. Matthew wore a suit with a messy head of hair. Made up nicely, Emma's dress was passable for a party. They both smiled and chattered between each other. Emma held a basket under an arm where loaves of bread poked out from beneath a cloth.

I can't have them here! They're bakers! Brixton glanced around him. The people would shun them. His hands felt clammy as he looked back at the window and stepped closer to the pane.

"Sir?" Nigel asked. "Should I . . . allow them in?"

Brixton swallowed hard. He stared at Matthew, jealous of his genuine smile. *How can he look content when he works so hard and barely makes a living?* Matthew's gaze turned to the window and Brixton jumped, pulling the curtain closed. "No," Brixton said. "Don't let them in." He left without a second glance.

Keeping his back to the front door, Brixton clumsily lapped through the rooms of the party. With no one talking to him, he drank to give his mouth something to do. A warm, muddling haze seeped into his mind as the brandy took effect. He welcomed the dulling of his senses and drank more, hoping it would come quicker.

What do all these people want? he wondered. *Food and drink? Is that the only reason they're here? Why hasn't Father come? He should be here to support me!*

Wandering the rooms, Brixton's thoughts turned to his past. *What if I'd been earnest with Chelci? Would things have worked out between us?* She seemed genuine but was driven away when Brixton pulled down his facade. The notion of a regular life with her refreshed him, but it was far too late for that.

As the surrounding crowd avoided making eye contact, he thought of Veron and their time together. They would sit around and talk. *Veron didn't use me for my position. He wasn't a friend because of my money.* His jaw clenched tighter. *When he became successful, it got to his head. He refused to share anything with me, then he took everything I had!*

"Excuse me, did you say your name was Brixton?"

The light voice snapped him back to the present. He sat on a lone couch in the corner of the sitting room, and in front of him, a young woman stood, leaning forward with a drink in her hands. Brixton blinked several times to clear his blurred vision, but it wasn't successful. From what he could tell, she wore a long, light blue dress with white gloves. Her brown hair formed a bun, while loose tendrils fell to her shoulders. Her dark eyes had a smoky look, and a grin tugged at her face. He stared back, mouth agape.

"Um . . . Yes! I'm Brixton," he replied in a voice that was probably too loud. "Who are you?"

"Alina. Nice speech a bit ago. Can I sit?"

Brixton's eyes widened. "Of course!" He sat up straighter, adjusting his position to give her room while angling his body to hers. A wave of dizziness washed over him at the sudden motion. He took a drink to calm himself as she settled confidently onto the couch. "So . . . Who are . . . What do you, um . . ." His foggy brain struggled. *What am I trying to ask?*

Alina held herself with intimidating poise. She looked younger than him yet more mature. "I will graduate from King's Academy next year," she said. "I'm not sure what I want to do after. For now, I'm keeping my options open."

"I went there, too!" Brixton said, placing his free arm along the back of the couch. "You must'a started during my last year." His words contained a slight slur.

"Yes, I remember you," Alina said with a smirk. "I was young then, but the champion swordsman from the graduating class left an impression on me." She raised an eyebrow and scooted her body closer. Brixton swallowed hard as she rested her hand on his leg.

"So . . . uh . . . are you here by yourself? I don't 'member sendin' invites to the Academy," Brixton said, experiencing a creeping warmth. He took another drink to settle his nerves.

Alina glanced around the room and motioned with her hand holding the glass. "My father's here somewhere. He's master of the textile guild."

"I'd love to meet him."

"I'm sure I can arrange that. So, tell me about yourself, Brixton. How did you get to be Commercial Envoy?"

His smile grew. *This is what I've been looking for! This is what all of this is about!* "Well, I's the right man for the job. I've had constant promotions since I graduated from King's. Bale noticed me and thought I's the best choice after he took control."

"I guess the position pays well, huh?" Alina asked. "To get a house like this and throw this sort of party." She grazed the top of his leg with her fingers as she spoke.

Brixton fought between feelings of excitement and discomfort at her forward behavior. Against his better judgment, he edged his body closer to hers, allowing his arm to rest against the back of her neck. The move brought another wave of dizziness, forcing him to blink to see her clearly. Her warm breath teased his skin as she continued tracing her fingers along the top of his leg. He swallowed another gulp of brandy. "I'm looking forward to the 'citement of travelin'. I'll be in charge of all of Terrenor, so I'll visit Tarphan, Rynor, and Norshewa. I'll probably be stayin' in the nicest places and have loads of money." His voice sounded distant and muffled. He had to yell, using large hand gestures to emphasize his words.

Brixton's gaze drifted to a spinning ceiling. His head floated to the side, and he pulled with his neck muscles to straighten it, but the effort didn't seem to help. Looking back to Alina, her mouth worked, but he couldn't understand the words. Her lips held him transfixed. Their perfect shapes moved in slow motion as if beckoning him.

Across the room, a familiar body approached. His blurry eyes widened as his father came into focus. Brixton sprung to his feet and reached out to steady himself on the wall as he lurched in his direction. "Honored guests, I love t'rinduce you my father—Regent Fiero!" Brixton shouted as he raised both hands in excitement, but he could barely hear himself. He wasn't even sure he'd made a coherent introduction. Brandy sloshed onto his face from his raised glass, forcing him to wipe his eyes with his free hand. He tossed the now empty glass to the ground, the resulting crash sounding distant.

His father's head tilted with a raised eyebrow. Is he the one tilting, or is it me? "And now, I want everyone ta meet Alina." He gestured dramatically toward the couch where she sat. "I don't know her last name yet, but I pretty sure we're gonna get married."

He ignored the crowd's muffled murmur as he stumbled the few steps to where she shrank in her seat. Brixton smiled as he leaned over, both arms resting against the back of the couch. He stared at her wide eyes for a long moment. Her lips called to him. He couldn't feel his legs or arms except for a general tingle that filled his body.

As he leaned in to meet her lips, a sinking feeling turned in his stomach. His insides rebelled, desperately trying to get his attention. The sensation felt dull. He ignored it until he couldn't. His body retched violently. Leaning over Alina, in her light blue dress and made-up hair, his stomach suddenly, violently expelled its liquid contents.

The cacophony erupting around the room seemed vague to Brixton. He fell to his knees, succumbing to multiple bouts of tumultuous heaving. Finally, he collapsed to the floor, gasping for breath. Lying on his back, he stared up with a cloudy sense of feeling. Footsteps and shouts sounded around him, but he only saw a blur. Soon, the blurry sight turned into a hazy darkness.

6

Repercussions

His head pounded even before he could see. Brixton pressed his palm against his forehead, but it didn't ease the throbbing pain. His mouth felt sticky, and he wished away the awful taste. When he opened his eyes, he glanced around, unsure how he got into his bedroom. *What happened to me?*

He sat up, dressed in his undergarments. A sickly odor reached his nose. He glanced around to locate the source and stopped when he found his stained suit draped over the end of the bed. A cold sweat rushed over him as the night's hazy events returned. He painfully threw his legs over the side and stood then fumbled through his wardrobe to find clean clothes.

After stumbling downstairs, Brixton held his head and squinted as he entered the kitchen. Quinn worked over the stove. Nigel sat at the table on the far side of the room with Corina, but the housekeeper stood and left, glaring at Brixton.

"Does anyone know of anything to help head pain?" Brixton asked.

Nigel raised an eyebrow. "The best way, sir, is to, um . . . avoid alcohol."

Brixton's anger bubbled to the surface. "Well, it's too late for that, isn't it?" he shouted, causing Nigel to sit straight with a jerk.

Quinn grabbed some containers off of a shelf. "I know of things that can help," he said. "Give me a moment, and I'll brew you up a tea and prepare some food."

Brixton mumbled thanks before plodding across the room and sitting at the table.

"Is there anything I can do for you, sir?" Nigel asked.

"Can you remind me what happened last night?"

Nigel looked askance at Quinn. "Er . . ."

"Out with it! Come on!" Brixton insisted.

"You drank a heavy amount in a short time," Nigel said.

Brixton pinched the bridge of his nose. "Yes, I gathered that."

"Do you remember the girl, sir?"

Brixton tilted his head and tapped the table. "Alina?"

"I believe that was her name."

"Did I . . . ?" Brixton mimed things coming out of his mouth. Even the motion made him feel nauseous again.

Nigel nodded. "I'm afraid so, sir."

"And my father? He was there for that?" The nodding continued. Brixton sighed as he sat back in his chair. "Those are the only hazy memories I have. What happened after that?"

"The girl was in shock, and her father escorted her out. The rest of the partygoers departed soon after you passed out."

"And how did I get to my bed?"

Nigel looked at Quinn again. "We carried you upstairs, sir."

Brixton nodded. "Thank you for that."

"Of course."

Nigel left as Quinn brought over a cup of tea mixed with ground-up herbs and bark. It smelled like dirt and tasted worse, but he drank it all despite the roiling in his stomach.

"Within the hour, you should feel much better," Quinn said.

At Quinn's insistence, Brixton forced himself to take a few bites of eggs and bread, but they didn't sit well in his stomach. He washed them down with some juice. Noticing the morning sun high in the sky, Brixton cursed to himself. It was Marketday—time to report to the castle, and he was already late.

Bale's shouting carried down the hall as Brixton hurried along. His aching head had settled into a dull throb, but the nauseous feeling had not left. Rushing up flights of stairs to reach Bale's council room didn't help. Dozens of soldiers in full uniform with swords and shields clustered around the opening. They nodded at his Norshewan badge and parted to allow him through. Watching with wary eyes and breathing heavily, he walked through their midst and entered the chamber.

Inside the hall, a large oval table stretched across the space. His father, Lord Billings, and Captain Gannon sat on one side while Bale's men—Desmond, Cyrus, and Ryker—sat opposite. Bale paced back and forth between the sides. His face was red, and his chest rose and fell quickly. Along the balcony's arched openings, dozens more soldiers stood on alert. *Wow, he wasn't kidding about having fifty men around!*

"Brixton!" Bale said. "Thank you for joining us, even if it is late."

Brixton held the back of a chair at the end of the table while standing. "I'm so sorry, Your Majesty. I—"

"I hear you had quite the event last night."

Brixton glanced at his father, who raised an eyebrow and stared back. "Yes. I, uh . . . It was . . ."

"A man unable to control his actions cannot be trusted," Bale said.

The air escaped Brixton's lungs. He swallowed as he hung his head.

"I trust that is the final time we'll see such foolishness from you?"

Brixton nodded. "Yes, Your Majesty. I promise. It won't happen again."

"Good." Bale paused for a long moment before changing subjects. "Your father seems to think we're going to have trouble gathering workers for Norshewa. He thinks they will revolt if we push them too hard."

Brixton looked at his father, who squirmed in his seat.

"Do you have any suggestions?"

Brixton's head snapped toward the ruler. "Me?"

"Yes. How do you suggest we gather our ten thousand workers?"

All eyes turned to Brixton. His neck grew warm. He kept the chair back between him and the rest of the men, but the barrier didn't shield him from responding. "I assume we won't have volunteers." Bale inclined his head forward as if waiting on Brixton to complete his thought. "We'll have to take them by force, I guess."

"And if they resist?" Bale asked. "If they rise against us?"

Brixton gulped to clear his throat's dryness. "Then we beat them down . . . hard. If they're afraid enough, they won't resist."

A grin formed on Bale's face, but Brixton's mouth turned down in contrast.

"That's what I've been saying!" Cyrus shouted. "They need to know we mean business!" Opposite him, Captain Gannon nodded.

"Thank you, Brixton," Bale said. "I hear you've had some good ideas on the tax front as well."

Brixton brightened. "I like to think they're good ideas."

"High Lord Plummer prepares to conduct a census, and High Lord Marlow told me of the new tax plan. However, Marlow also mentioned many of Felting's businesses have refused to sign the new licenses." Brixton's eyes grew wider while Bale continued. "They had a week to agree to the terms, but it seems we have a small uprising with our businesses."

"They can't afford the new terms," Brixton's father said. "It's going to put some of them out of business. If we push too hard, even more will resist."

"Hold on," Bale said, holding up his hand to the regent. "I want to hear from Brixton."

Brixton glanced around the table while all eyes watched for his reaction. His gaze finally settled on his father, staring back with a hard expression. "We could . . . uh . . . give them another week? Maybe they just need a bit of time." Bale's raised eyebrow caused Brixton to scramble. "But—of course—if they refused to sign in the first week, they're unlikely to change their mind with more time. So . . . we need to show them we're not to be messed with. If they're afraid enough, they'll comply."

"I agree," Gannon muttered.

Bale smirked as he walked around the table toward Brixton. "What would you do?"

"I would seize a business—one in a prominent, visible loca-tion—and close it down, putting a large sign on the front indicating they refused to endorse the new tax law."

"What else?"

"I would take all of their clothing, medicines, food—whatever they have—and pile it in the street to be burned." Cries of affirmation around the table encouraged him to continue. "Finally, I would flog them and place them in the stocks for all to see. After a while, they should go to prison to rot."

"Yes!" Gannon shouted.

Standing an arm's length away, Bale nodded with a solemn expression. He placed a hand on Brixton's shoulder. "These are local Feldor businesses, Brixton. Are you okay with this? Do you have what it takes to make this happen? Or will your history in this kingdom make you soft?"

His father's grave expression caught Brixton's attention, but he shrugged it off and turned to Bale. "My allegiance is to you, Your Majesty."

"Good," Bale said, clapping his shoulder. "Do it."

"I can't wait to see the look on their faces," Gannon said as he and Brixton navigated the street.

He's a little quick to make people suffer, Brixton thought, feeling less enthusiastic than the captain about what needed to be done. Six soldiers followed as they headed toward the Department of Commerce.

"We should choose a lawyer or an accountant. Think of the great fire we could make in the street with all of that paper!" Gannon said. Brixton sniffed in response. "Who do you think we should pick?"

"I don't know," Brixton said, cringing as he imagined dragging a lawyer into the street and having him flogged. His stomach turned. *This wasn't what I had in mind when I joined up with Bale.* At least, if it had to be done, he would rather not have to see it happen, but Bale tasked him to carry it out. He glanced over his shoulder at the men following him. *There's no way out of this.*

He opened the Department of Commerce's door to find the lady from before sitting at the desk. She shrank away from Gannon as he stomped into the room, knocking the end of his sword against the walls. The other soldiers waited outside.

"I need to see High Lord Marlow," Brixton said.

"I'm sorry, sir. He's not in today."

"It's Marketday! How is he not here?" Gannon interjected.

"I don't question his comings and goings."

Brixton sighed as he turned to Gannon, relieved. "Well, I guess we'll have to do this another time."

"Where's his office? I'm sure we can find what we need," the captain said.

Brixton blanched. He wasn't about to ransack Darcius Marlow's office.

"What do you need? Perhaps I can get it for you?" the lady offered.

Gannon sniffed, holding up his nose in her direction.

"Yes, perhaps," Brixton said. "There should be a list of businesses who have not signed the new licenses. We need to—"

"Oh yes, I know where that is," the lady said. "I helped his high lordship put it together."

Brixton's shoulders fell. "Retrieve it for us."

The lady's face screwed up. "Why do you need it?"

"Because we said so!" Gannon shouted, stomping his foot on the wooden floor.

She straightened her dress, collected herself, and scurried down the hall to the office.

While waiting, Brixton turned to the front window and glanced outside. Six soldiers stood by, ready to act on whatever orders they gave. *Such incredible power,* he thought. *To give a command and have men follow it.* His role as Commercial Envoy was similar. All Terrenor commerce bowed to his commands, from the high lords to lowly shopkeepers. A smirk crossed his face. *Even market owners, like who Veron used to be.*

The lady's steps returned. She handed a sheet of paper to Gannon, who grabbed it with a flourish and left through the door.

"Thank you," Brixton said, nodding to her before he followed the captain.

"Who do you want?" Gannon asked, scanning the list, standing by the group of soldiers. "It's in alphabetical order. Just go with the first one?"

Aitken's Apparel popped into Brixton's mind. The tailor shop across from his house had already made several of his fine outfits. He had no idea if they would be on the list but didn't want to risk it. "No, that doesn't seem fair to whoever's at the top. Just choose someone."

"To the back of the list, then." Gannon flipped the paper over then looked up and down the street. "This way," he said, moving with purpose.

Brixton followed with less enthusiasm. His steps felt heavy as they marched through the street. The captain kept a fast pace, and Brixton struggled to keep up. The fast walk brought his nausea back and drew attention to his lingering headache. He avoided making eye contact with anyone, imagining the hatred all might feel toward him.

"You ready for this, Brixton?" Gannon asked, looking over his shoulder and slowing for Brixton to catch up.

"For . . . ?"

"Showing your power! Letting the people of this city know what happens when they defy you!"

Brixton cocked his head. "I hadn't thought about it that way. They are defying me, aren't they?"

"Yes! This tax plan was your idea, right? Anyone holding out is spitting in *your face!*"

Brixton strode with more purpose. If there was one thing he wanted more than power, it was respect. "Give me that sheet. I want to see who you chose."

Gannon handed him the paper. "No need. We've arrived."

Brixton looked up from the paper as they slowed to a halt. He blanched as he read the words on the window display. *No, not them!* Westcott Bakery stood before him—Matthew and Emma's shop.

"You ready to show this city the strength of your authority?" Gannon asked with a twisted grin. His hand rested on his sword's hilt. He motioned for the soldiers to follow as he led the way to the door.

"Wait! No!" Brixton shouted after a moment of statuesque stillness.

Gannon turned. "What is it?"

The other men stared at him, but Brixton wasn't sure what to say. "We can't—Um . . ."

"What's wrong?" Gannon said, stamping his feet.

"Um . . . Let me go in first."

Gannon took his hand off the sword and shrugged. "Sure, go ahead."

Brixton stepped toward the door, pondering what to do. After resting his hand on the knob, he sighed before pushing it open and entering.

The bell announced his presence, and both Matthew and Emma glanced his way from behind the counter. "Brixton! Welcome!" Matthew said with a grin. Emma handed a loaf of bread to a customer at the counter while two more patrons waited in line.

"Matthew, Emma . . . we need to talk," Brixton said, trying to keep his voice casual.

"Sure, give us just a moment," Matthew said as he worked to pull something out of the oven.

Brixton glanced over the array of baked goods as the customers chatted back and forth with Emma and Matthew. Their words sounded jumbled in his ears, and their laughter caused him to wince. *I can't do this to them. Maybe if they run . . . ?* After the last customer left, Brixton approached the counter. An entire sheet of warm buttery pastries rested next to him. The sight turned his stomach as sweat dotted his brow.

"You two are in trouble. You need to get out of here, now!" Brixton said.

Matthew's forehead wrinkled. "I don't understand. What's wrong?"

"Run to the Department of Commerce and sign the new business tax agreement. Tell them you were sick and couldn't get to it last week or something! Do you have a back door you can sneak out?" Matthew shook his head. Brixton cursed under his breath then glanced around the shop. The pounding in his head grew.

"If this is about the new tax agreement, we can't sign it. It will put us out of business!" Matthew said.

"What's going on?" Emma asked, her brows knit together.

Through the windows, the soldiers fingered the clubs on their hips out in the street. Brixton spied a saucepan on the counter and pointed to it. "Hit me over the head with that!"

"What? No, we're not going to—"

"Come on! Knock me out, then sprint out the door and don't come back. You don't realize—"

The bell over the door rang, silencing Brixton mid-sentence. He clenched his jaw as multiple pairs of shoes clunked across the floor.

"Getting tense in here, I gather," Gannon said with a laugh. "Thought I'd come in and back you up, Commercial Envoy Fiero."

Brixton's eyes held Matthew's. He attempted to tell him to run by a slight nod of his head, but the baker didn't seem to understand. "Yes, these people insist they've already signed the forms. I wonder if there's been a misunderstanding," Brixton said, hoping to buy them some time.

Gannon approached the counter, staring at Matthew and Emma with a twisted smirk. "They insist, huh? Come on, Brixton. Surely, you don't believe these *liars!*" He punctuated the last word by flipping the sheet of pastries over, sending them flying and the pan clanging to the ground.

Emma shrieked. Matthew stepped near and put an arm around her as the soldiers pulled out their clubs and stepped closer. Moving in front of his wife, Matthew stood tall, staring down the captain. "You're right. We didn't sign them. And we never will." Brixton groaned inside at his defiance.

The captain turned to Brixton, raising an eyebrow. "There you go. The obstinate rebel confessed. Are we good to proceed, Brixton?"

The entire room looked to Brixton with bated breath. His throat felt dry, and his head pounded once more. The roiling in his stomach redoubled. Tears rolled down Emma's face, her eyes pleading with him. Matthew pulled his wife closer, standing tall and staring back with his jaw set. Gannon waited next to him, but Brixton couldn't tear his eyes from the young baker. "You ca—" He cleared his throat and swallowed. Finally, he nodded. "Proceed," he whispered.

Matthew's eyes widened as the soldiers sprung. Brixton turned away, unwilling to watch the havoc he unleashed. Glass shattered. Pans crashed. Emma screamed, and Matthew shouted. Two soldiers dragged the bakers outside, flinging them to the stones. The others loaded their arms with crates of bread, sacks of flour, and any pans or ingredients they could carry, dumping it all into the street. Loaves of bread and delicate pastries fell into the dirt. They upended sacks of flour, leaving a mess in the road and a cloud of white in the air.

"You can't do this! Brixton, help us, please!" Matthew shouted.

A soldier poured a container of oil on the mess. Standing in the doorway to the shop, Brixton choked on the caustic fumes. As the soldiers backed away, another threw a lit candle at the pile, which burst into flames. The searing heat forced him to cover his face with his hands.

Emma fell to her knees, wailing as she stared at the fire. Blood dripped down the front of her legs where she'd scraped them on the street.

I couldn't do anything about this, Brixton told himself. *This was Bale's doing. It's his requirement for the tax. If it wasn't me instituting it, it would be someone else.*

"This is good," Gannon said, drawing near. "We needed a firm response, and this should get the others to fall in line." He clapped

Brixton on the back. "Nice work."

Brixton fought to keep his inner horror from showing. He wasn't able to respond, but stared at the bakers, hollow inside.

"Take them to the stocks, men!" Gannon shouted.

Wicked laughter echoed in the street as the soldiers circled around the bakers, holding out their clubs. Brixton turned away as the first bludgeon fell. His stomach churned, screaming against his excess from the night before and the horror he wreaked on the friendly couple. Unable to stop himself, he vomited again, spewing his body's vile contents onto the building's wall.

Spitting away the bile, he closed his eyes, but the yells of pain behind him assaulted his ears as he screamed along with them on the inside.

* * *

Raynor Fiero ascended the spiral staircase, stepping lightly to keep his boots from making noise. His torch flickered, chasing away the shadows of the dark passage. His heart sped and thoughts raced as he ascended. At the top, he pulled a handle to an old wooden door. A draft came out of the space, making his light dance.

His feet scraped on the dusty floor as he entered the room. "Hello?" he whispered into the darkness.

A shadowy form stepped from the corner, giving Raynor a start. "Billings! You scared me."

Gareth Billings leaned on his cane with a grave look on his face. "I trust you have a good reason to ask me here at this hour?"

Raynor nodded. "I want to hear your honest opinion about . . ." His eyes danced around the room. ". . . how things are going."

Gareth raised an eyebrow. "You mean with Bale?" Raynor didn't reply. "I think . . . things aren't as smooth as they *could* be." He enunciated his words carefully while keeping his voice down.

"I agree," Raynor said. "I fear his taxes and worker quotas will leave a marked impression on Feldor. When we aligned with Bale, this isn't what I had in mind."

Gareth nodded his head slowly. "Nor I. What do you propose we do about it?"

A grim smile formed on Raynor's face. "I have some ideas."

7

Life in Nasco

The dirt squished as Chelci sank her knees into the ground. The smell of earth filled her soul and brought a smile to her face. She brushed a bug off the leaves in front of her before she pruned several to toss in a crate.

"This'll be some of the last we get this season," Nevi said. "I'm gonna miss these wild greens." The older woman pulled a few rooted vegetables out of the community garden and shook the dirt loose. "In a few more weeks, we'll plant the suether crops."

Chelci leaned back, sitting against her feet, and sighed. "I've missed this place."

"It's missed you, too," Nevi replied, tossing her handful into the crate. "How was your family after you returned?"

"My father's been good." A smile tugged at one side of Chelci's mouth as she stared at the dirt. "He was so glad to have me back. Sometimes I think he's not sure what to do with me . . . but he loves me."

"Does he know you fled?"

Chelci nodded. "Yeah. He helped us escape. I didn't actually get to see my brother. He's an army captain, stationed at Karondir, but we wrote to each other."

"What about your mother?"

The question still rattled her, even though she knew it was coming. She breathed in and slowly let the air out. "She died almost two weeks ago."

Nevi gasped. "Oh, no! I'm so sorry!"

Chelci shook her head. "It's okay. She . . . She hadn't changed much. I was sad, not because I lost her but because I lost the chance for things to be made right." A drop formed at the corner of her eye. She wiped it away.

Nevi's eyes were soft as she listened. "How did she die—if you don't mind my asking?"

"Bale sent some men. They were after Veron, and she got in the way."

Nevi rested a gentle hand on her leg. Chelci sighed, reminded of why she loved Nasco.

"I'm glad I went home when I did, but . . . I'm happy to be back here with you, now." Chelci stood and dusted the dirt off her lower legs. "Enough of all that."

Nevi joined her and picked up the crate. "So, what I *really* want to hear about is this Veron character," Nevi said with a smirk and a raised eyebrow as she started walking to their house.

Chelci laughed, following beside her. "Oh, what to say . . . he's incredible!"

"Look at you . . . falling for the—" she leaned in closer and whispered, "dashing shadow knight."

"Hey," Chelci said, pointing at her. "He was only a servant when I met him."

"Really? So, what do you like about him?"

A musing smile covered her face as her steps crackled in the dry, dirt path. "He's as smart as anyone I know, but he'd never admit it.

He's not above working any job, even cleaning floors and fireplaces. Of course, he's strong and handsome, but I think what I like most is that he's interested in me—what I like, who I am. It's refreshing."

Nevi smiled then bounced her head back and forth. "And . . . that he's a shadow knight?"

"Okay, fine." Chelci hit her on the arm. "That doesn't hurt." They turned a corner, revealing Nevi's house down the path.

"Do you think you two will . . . get married?" Nevi asked.

"So many questions!" Chelci cried out then attempted to cover her grin with her hand. "I don't know. I've only known him for half a season. We'll see."

"We'll see, what?" a boisterous voice called from behind.

Chelci spun to find Aleks and Finley bounding along the path toward her. Both wore their village guard uniforms with swords dangling from their hips.

"We'll talk more later," Nevi said, waving her away with a smile.

"Aleks! Finley!" Chelci shouted before throwing her arms around them both and pulling them in a three-way hug. "I've been here a day and a half, and you're just now finding me?"

"It's been busy!" Finley said. "Russell works us like dogs."

"Yeah, we were on duty all day yesterday," Aleks added. "This valcor has everyone on edge."

"I thought they're afraid of the moon . . . and the daylight?" Chelci asked.

"Well, that's a theory, but I don't think anyone wants to pin all their hopes on it," Finley said.

"So, you couldn't stand to be away from us for even one season and had to hurry back, right?" Aleks playfully asked.

"Well, that's not exactly it."

He laughed. "Yeah, I know. We heard about Bale's attack. I'm glad you're okay."

Barks came from behind. Soon, a white curly-haired dog jumped against the boys, nuzzling their hands to force them to pet it.

"Hey there, Charlie," Aleks said, crouching to scratch the animal.

"So . . . we saw your boyfriend this morning," Finley said with a grin as he clapped his hands and rubbed them together. A flush washed over Chelci's face. "What's his name? Vermin? Vixen?"

She rolled her eyes. "Veron."

"That's right," Finley said. "He was with Bensen."

"Did you talk with him?" Chelci asked. Finley shook his head.

"I thought he was supposed to be a great warrior or something?" Aleks said while continuing to pet the dog. "He didn't look that impressive to me. Maybe we should have a little duel? You know—for fun. See who's the better swordsman?"

"Ha!" Chelci blurted before covering her mouth.

Aleks' eyebrows pressed together.

"I'm sorry," she said with a grin. "I would love to see that."

"Maybe you two could come by the Academy?"

Chelci's eyes lit up. "There's a new class?"

"A *big* one. Either the valcor's got everyone motivated or your story inspired them. Either way, we're filled to the brim. Russell and I are the main instructors. Bensen—er, William, I guess now—is helping some, but he's more limited than he used to be."

"Sure, we'll come by. Maybe we could have a rematch on the course to see who's the fastest now?"

Aleks pursed his lips and turned to Finley. "Or maybe a race around the village trail with weighted bags instead?"

Chelci punched him in the arm.

"Ow!"

"You want that because you know you'll win!"

"Just like you know you'll win a race on the course!"

Chelci and Aleks stared at each other until they both broke down in laughing fits.

"I hate to be the one to break up this competition, but Aleks and I have to go," Finley said.

Aleks nodded. "Yeah, we do. See you soon, Chelci?"

"See you soon," she said with a smile as her friends walked away.

Chelci knocked on the door to William's house, but the lack of response indicated neither he nor Veron were home. She followed the sound of chopping wood to the edge of the woods, where she found them tucked behind some trees. Both held axes. Veron faced a large, flat stump that held two smaller logs, balancing one on top of the other. William stood a few paces back, coaching him.

Past memories of chopping wood rushed back. She winced and pulled on her shoulder as she remembered aching arms hurting for days. An enormous pile of split logs—far greater than she'd ever created—lay in a jumble on the ground. As she approached, Veron turned to face the log. With pushed-up sleeves, he held the axe at the ready then lifted it over his head, rising to his toes. His forearms rippled as he brought it down, cleaving through both logs in one fluid motion.

"Wow!" Chelci shouted, causing them both to turn. When she had to chop wood, it took her several swings to get through even one. "Sorry! I didn't mean to distract, but—How'd you do that?"

"We're working on focus and control," William said.

Veron grinned as she approached. "That was cool, wasn't it?" His bushy-brown hair pressed against the side of his face in sweaty clumps.

William stepped up to the stump. "You're using too much, though. See how far you buried the axe?" Over half of it was planted deep in the stump.

"Whoa," Veron said as he extended an arm to balance. His face looked pale as he leaned against the stump.

"Breathe and relax every muscle," William instructed. "The fatigue will fade as long as you give it a chance."

Veron took several breaths, looking to the ground. After a moment, he looked up at William and nodded. He moved his hand up the handle of the axe and tugged. Nothing happened. He brought his other arm in and braced a foot against the stump as he pulled harder. The tendons in his neck strained. A groan emanated from his throat, but the tool remained stuck.

"Use origine, but only just enough," William said.

Veron stood up straight and took a deep breath before leaning back in. With one arm, he pulled on the axe. It popped free, seemingly without effort.

William nodded as he stepped back. "Good. Now, do it again. Remember control."

Veron stacked two new logs. After a quick breath, he swung again. The axe cut through them but stopped with barely a nick in the wood below.

"Nice!" Chelci shouted.

"Well done," William added.

Chelci stepped in closer. "So, how are you doing that? Does the origine help you aim better or stop the axe just right?"

Veron rested the axe on the ground and turned to her. "Yeah, when I pull the blade down, I use the origine to think quicker. If I'm off the mark, my muscles quicky respond to get it right."

"Controlling the power is most difficult," William said. "To cut through the logs, you must exert more force, but if you use too much, the axe ends up buried. The goal is to use the right amount, then pull back at the end to keep from overextending."

"So, in a battle, you'd want to give more power from a sword strike or a punch or kick, but also be able to pull it back if you needed, right?" Chelci said.

"Exactly. Veron's learning well," William said, turning to his son. "So, Artimus' training was only physical? He didn't teach you anything about the origine?"

"I only found out about it the day before he died. He wanted to keep me from becoming a shadow knight because of the prophecy."

"Ah, yes . . . the prophecy," William said. "I think about it a lot."

"Do you think it's true?" Veron tossed a furtive glance toward Chelci while they waited for William to consider his answer.

"I like to think my future is what I make of it rather than something fixed in stone," he said. "But, I believe Dreams to be reliable . . . for the most part. So . . . I'm not sure."

Chelci stood silently as father and son stared at each other. The unspoken question of who was the one from the Dream rested in the air between them. Her stomach turned at the thought Veron may be the one to perish.

"Why didn't you go after Bale?" Veron asked.

Chelci breathed in quickly through her nose. The older man sighed as he looked at the grass.

"I thought about it," he said. He lowered his chin and paused for a moment. "I tried to be brave and selfless as a knight, but after the others died, I guess I turned inward. Plus, Artimus was alive somewhere, so I didn't know if it might be me or him. I decided not to invite trouble until it was the right time . . . *if* there was to be a time." He looked up at Veron. "And now there are two of us again. I can't believe you've developed the ability this far on your own."

A grin formed on Veron's face.

"I ran into Aleks and Finley a bit ago," Chelci said, interrupting the moment of silence. "Aleks said we should come by the Academy sometime and see how it's going."

William nodded. "I think that would be great."

"I think he wanted me to teach them how to run the course."

"Ha! More likely, he wants to set up a sword-fighting demonstration, so he can show the young ones how their instructor can beat the 'valcor slayer.'"

Chelci's face soured.

"Why don't you both come Marketday?" William suggested. "We could include you as guest trainers."

Chelci looked to Veron, who shrugged. "Sure. That sounds fun," she said. "Veron, whenever you're done here, can you come by the Martins' house, where I'm staying?"

"Of course," Veron said.

"Nevi and I are about to work on dinner, and I thought it would be fun if you joined us. I'd love for her to get to know you better."

He twinkled his fingers in her direction. "See you soon."

His eyes' softness and face's eagerness filled Chelci's soul. She turned to walk back into the village, excited at the prospect of going to the Academy with Veron.

Before rounding a corner, she glanced back at the men. Veron had stacked two new logs on the stump, and William mouthed instructions. The older man gestured as Veron nodded along. A smile grew. *This is just what Veron needed.*

8

Academy Demonstrations

"You sure you're ready for this?" Chelci asked. Veron's hand felt gentle in hers as they walked up the hill toward the Academy's training building.

"Of course," Veron replied. "I'm looking forward to it. You'll know all these people?"

Chelci shrugged. "Probably, but I haven't seen the applicants for this class yet."

Her heart pumped with excitement as the building approached. She remembered her apprehension two years earlier when she entered for the first time, but that changed with time and experience. Her sword dangled at her hip, and she wore her favorite active clothing, good for any sort of training.

Veron looked less confident. His lean arms and legs were ready for anything, but he seemed wary. His shaggy brown hair fell along the side of his face, and his sword slung over his shoulder. Chelci squeezed his hand and flashed him a smile.

Aleks and Finley stood outside the building as they approached. Aleks held his sword out and appeared to be explaining something as he traced his hand along the flat of the blade. His eyes lifted, and a grin formed as he sheathed his weapon. "You made it!"

"Hey, guys," Chelci said, glancing around. "Where are all the trainees?"

Finley pointed toward the woods. "Running a loop with Russell."

"Yeah, I guess William won't do that anymore, huh?" Chelci said.

"He gets around well for only having one leg," Aleks said.

"Surprisingly so," Finley interrupted.

Chelci glanced at Veron from the corner of her eye. He strained to keep a straight face.

"But running like that would be a stretch," Aleks continued. "He's inside getting the swords ready. Russell and I take turns on the runs, now."

"Are you an instructor, too?" Chelci asked Finley.

He shook his head. "Nah, I have a day off from guard duty today. I just came to hang out."

"So, this is the warrior, huh?" Aleks said, extending his hand to Veron. "I'm Aleks. Veron, right?"

Veron nodded. "Yeah, I've heard about you." The two boys shook for an extended time, hands clenched and forearms strained. Veron finally let go. "And you're Finley, right? Nice to officially meet you. I've never run into a valcor before, so I have to say I'm impressed with you from the other night. I'm sure I would have been too terrified to do anything."

Finley blinked several times while a grin grew on his face. He straightened his shoulders as they shook hands. "Thank you! Yeah, it was frightening, but . . . that's what we train for. I had a job to do—you know?"

Chelci rolled her eyes.

"So I hear you're with Chelci. What makes you worthy of being with her?" Aleks asked.

"Aleks!" Chelci protested.

"What?" he replied, holding his hands open. "I just want to make sure he's treating you right."

His instinct to protect—like an older brother—comforted her, but she didn't want Veron put off by her friends' blunt questions.

"I can't claim to be worthy of her," Veron replied with a disarming smile. "I couldn't even tell you what she sees in me."

"He did rescue me on three separate occasions," Chelci said, taking his hand in hers and leaning into his side.

"Wow," Finley said. "Usually, she's the one saving others around here."

"A hero, huh?" Aleks said.

Veron glanced at Chelci. "I don't know about hero. It was usually my fault she was in danger to begin with."

Eager to change the subject, Chelci looked toward the woods where Russell headed their way, leading a group of runners. "So, how are these applicants? Anyone good?"

Aleks shrugged. "Eh . . . We'll see. They have their work cut out for them."

"No one's killed any monsters yet," Finley added with a laugh.

Russell arrived first, breathing heavily and sweating with a weighted bag over his shoulder. He lowered it and flashed a quick smile before glancing at his pocket watch. More sweat-laden boys trickled in after him.

"Reece! Hey!" she yelled, waving to get the boy's attention. While still shorter than her, he had grown several inches since they'd both started the Academy together two years before.

"Hey!" he panted. He flashed a smile and dropped his bag to the ground in front of her.

"You're trying again, huh?"

"Yeah, you motivated me. I wanted to give it another shot. My time on the course is down to 8:29."

"Wow, nice!"

The sight of a girl with long hair pulled back in a ponytail drew her attention to the arriving runners. She knew Emily—a year older than her.

"Hey, you have another girl!" she said to Aleks.

He chuckled. "Four of them, actually."

"What?" She looked back at the runners. Three more girls arrived, mixed in between some boys.

"I think you inspired them, Chelci," Finley said.

A warm feeling grew inside, along with a smile on her face.

"Nice job, Reece," a short girl said as she dropped her bag and panted next to him. "I tried to catch up with you, but I wore myself out on the hill."

"Yeah, I heard you yelling at me. It helped me run faster, I think." Reece gave a weak laugh as he continued to even out his breathing.

"Grace, I can't believe you're in the Academy. That's great!" Chelci said. Grace was younger than Chelci by a year and shorter by a foot. They were at the village school together several years before. Her arms and legs had toned up since Chelci last saw her, and her light brown hair was shorter.

"Yeah, I want to be like you, Chelci." Grace's eyes were bright, and sweat glistened on her face. Her labored breathing continued. "You made it. I figure if I work hard enough, perhaps I can, too! Plus, after I told Reece I was thinking about it, he decided to give it another shot. Now we can hang out!"

Chelci looked at Reece, eyebrow raised. "Oh, really? I thought it was my inspiration that led you to join back up, Reece? Was it something else?"

The shorter boy blushed, avoiding her eye contact.

"Good!" Russell said as the last boy arrived. "You're all within one minute now. Drop your bags inside, then we'll resume sword work."

"There are more than I expected," Veron said, prompting her to count the crowd that bunched to file inside the building.

"Yeah, eighteen. That's huge!"

Inside the building, William passed out wooden swords to all the candidates, nodding as Veron entered. Aleks and Russell made their way to the far end.

"Before Aleks and I demonstrate today's lesson, I want to introduce our guests," Russell said, gesturing to the back of the room.

All heads pivoted to Chelci and Veron. Two years before, the looks toward her contained judgment and superiority, but now they were filled with awe and wonder—a welcome change.

"You all know Chelci—who used to go by Elise—I'm sure," Russell said. "And this is Veron, who comes to us from Felting."

Veron offered a wave and a sheepish smile.

"I heard you fought against Bale," a boy around Chelci's age asked, looking at Veron. "Is that true?"

Veron glanced at Chelci as he scratched his head. "Uh, yeah . . . I did."

Gasps sounded around the room.

"Wow, we should have *him* show us how to fight," a voice mumbled.

"Did you kill anyone?" another voice asked in an excited tone.

Veron shuffled his feet without responding until Aleks cleared his throat. "Okay, everyone. Eyes up here!" he called.

"Aleks, can you fight Veron? Who would win?" a boy asked, supported by several cries of approval.

Aleks glanced at Russell, looked back toward Veron, then lifted an eyebrow in invitation.

"Do they know about me being a shadow knight?" Veron whispered to Chelci.

She replied in a hushed voice. "No, I don't think anyone else knows. They're probably just hoping to see their instructor put in his place."

Turning back to Aleks, Veron shook his hand in a gesture of friendly refusal. "I don't want to interfere with your training. You two please continue."

Chelci smirked. *Too bad. That could have been fun to see.*

"Aleks is the best in the village guard," an applicant said. "We'd love to see what someone from Felting could do!"

"It wouldn't interfere at all," Aleks said to Veron. "Just a friendly display. Please . . ." He beckoned Veron with his outstretched hand.

William caught Chelci's eye as he leaned against the wall across the room, chuckling.

Veron looked at Chelci and raised his shoulders. "I could try to let him win?" he whispered. The people in the room stared wide-eyed.

"How about me?" Chelci said, taking a step.

The eager look on Aleks' face faded.

"Unless you're afraid of fighting a girl?"

Aleks shook his head and chuckled with a resigned smile. "Come on," he said, waving her up.

Russell cleared out of the way as Chelci approached, pulling the sword Aleks gave her as a present earlier that season. The candidates pushed back to give them plenty of space, and Aleks grabbed his own weapon that lay on the floor by the wall.

"You better not take it easy on me," Chelci said.

"Against the 'valcor slayer?' I wouldn't consider it!"

The room hushed as Chelci and Aleks held their weapons in salute before lowering into a slight crouch. It had been a long time since Chelci had sparred with Aleks. His skill with the blade was far superior to hers, but she was fast and had practiced a lot with Veron.

Chelci moved first. She swung to connect with his sword and push it to the side. He parried and returned with a matching strike of his own. She pulled away as they rotated in a circle. He lunged to tap her on her side, but she maneuvered her blade to knock it away. While he reset, Chelci extended her leg and kicked him.

"Oof," he cried, taking a step back and shaking his head as he rubbed his side. "So, that's how it's gonna be, huh?"

"That's right. I would have thought the number one selection for the village guard would be prepared for that," she taunted.

Aleks lunged toward her. His sword whistled as it sliced through the air, but Chelci's blade twirled and sang in response. The two lunged and struck. Steel crashed as they grunted from the exertion. Chelci spun, moving to fend off the older boy's attack. The crowd of onlookers gasped in awe. They shouted and cheered at the two recent Academy graduates, locked in a display of skill and power. Sweat flung from their arms as their swords danced in response to each other.

"You've been practicing," Aleks said through a labored breath.

Chelci smirked, chancing a glance to Veron, who smiled from the back of the room. When Aleks swung his sword, Chelci used a move she'd learned from Veron. Instead of parrying, she stepped in and attacked back, striking his sword just above the hilt. Aleks' eyes flared as his weapon moved out of position, leaving his body wide open. Chelci elbowed him in the stomach, causing him to double over, and she kicked his sword arm farther away. Victory was in her grasp. Stepping to the side, she moved her sword to his neck, ready to declare victory, but as she opened her mouth, her legs fell out from under her, swept by a jerk of his foot.

Chelci's stomach jumped as she crashed to the floor. The sharp impact of her hand hitting the wooden slats knocked her weapon away. Chelci scrambled to find it again but froze as she saw Aleks' long sword blade extended, hovering over her chest.

"Argh!" she yelled. "I was so close!"

Aleks grinned, trading the sword for his hand to help her stand to her feet. "Are you okay?"

"Of course!" she blurted, not wanting to admit the amount of pain in her tailbone.

"That was great, Chelci. You almost had me." Aleks turned back to the audience. "Give a hand for Chelci, everyone!"

Chelci scowled as the applicants cheered for her. The eager looks on the girl's faces softened the feeling of disappointment. She sheathed her sword and returned to Veron. Russell rejoined Aleks, and the two launched into a discussion about parrying techniques.

"Nice fight," Veron said when she made it to the back of the room.

"He won," Chelci replied, crossing her arms with a sulk on her face.

"That doesn't matter. You were great. You almost had him."

"Yeah, but I didn't." Her gaze drifted toward the window to avoid eye contact.

"Chelci," Veron said, resting his hand on her arm. "Look at him."

She looked at Aleks at the front of the room. Taller than her by six inches, his broad shoulders and arms put him in a different class despite the hard work she'd put into strengthening her body. Years before, she had a crush on the boy until she realized he was more like a brother. *He still is an impressive fighter.*

"You said he's the son of a blacksmith, right? That he's been fighting all his life and is the best in Nasco? You're the daughter of a high lord and only started using a sword a couple of years ago. The fact that you nearly took him down proves how amazing your skill is."

The sulk on her face faded, and she sighed after his encouraging words. "Yeah, I guess so."

"Be proud of yourself," Veron said. "I'm impressed with you, and I guarantee Aleks is, too."

"Okay, I'll be proud," she replied, her mouth curling into a smirk. "But next time . . . I want *you* to fight him. And I want you to teach him what it means to lose."

9

The Test

Veron watched from below as Chelci swung her leg over the tree limb and pulled her body up. "Here. Take my hand," she said, reaching out.

With her help, Veron made it on the molopyr tree's branch, where he sat next to her, dangling his feet in the air.

"This was my resting spot—when we had breaks," Chelci said. She rubbed her hand along the smooth bark, appearing to be lost in a memory.

Veron glanced up the hill at the Academy training building, where the applicants continued to work. "I like it here in Nasco."

"Yeah, me too. What do you like about it?"

"I appreciate that no one is trying to kill me," Veron said, drawing a laugh from her. "Actually, I enjoy the people. Russell and Nevi seem kind. Finley and Aleks are welcoming. Well . . . Aleks seems as if he doesn't like me."

"I think he feels like you're competition. He's used to being the best, but he's a nice guy."

"I'm sure he is. And . . . I'm glad William's here."

"No more hard feelings between you two?"

Veron furrowed his brow. *Are there?* His feelings toward his father were softer than they had been. "I guess I'm feeling more accepting."

"Speaking of whom . . ." Chelci said, nodding toward the training building where William walked down the hill. He held a staff but barely seemed to need it.

"How do you walk so well?" Veron asked as his father grew close. "I imagine walking with one leg would be more difficult than you make it seem."

William glanced at his artificial limb as he stopped before the branch where they sat. "You know how you used the origine to guide the axe as you chopped the wood?"

Veron tilted his head. "Yeah, I can use a small amount at the right time to aim it. Is walking the same way?"

"Pretty much. The wooden leg is well made and secure. I use the origine to make sure I'm balanced on it. When walking slowly, I barely need any energy. If I need to run, I can go a while without support, but that tires me out quickly."

"That's incredible," Chelci said. "So, why do you even have the staff?"

William glanced at the long wooden rod and stamped it into the ground. "Well . . . I don't use the origine if I don't need to. Plus, other than the elders, you two, and the Martins, no one knows about our abilities.

"So, I'm curious about these abilities. Why do you two have them, but no one else?" Chelci asked.

Veron and William exchanged a glance, but Veron wasn't sure how to answer it.

"Can anyone learn?"

"There's a test," Veron said. "I'm not even sure what it was, but it determines if someone can learn the origine. Passing is rare though. Artimus said only one in three thousand people qualify."

A chuckle from William drew Veron's attention down to the ground. "What?" His father covered his mouth with a hand as his laughter grew. Veron jumped down from the limb, landing softly in the dirt next to him. "What's so funny?"

"Artimus. He told us all the same when we first started," William said, but a sparkle in his eye told Veron there was more to the story. "It's not true."

Veron's breath stopped. He based everything he knew about the Shadow Knights on what Artimus taught him. "What's not true? Was the test a lie?"

"Oh, no. There is a test, but it's a lie that only one in three thousand can learn how to use the origine."

"What do you mean?"

After glancing around, William leaned in closer and spoke in a low voice. "Anyone can learn."

Veron's eyes widened as the world seemed to shift. "Wha—What do you mean? That—That doesn't make sense."

"What doesn't make sense about it?"

Veron's mouth dropped open for a long moment while he thought. "Why don't you train a ton of people?"

"Yeah," Chelci chimed in from the tree limb. "You could create an army of shadow knights!"

William shook his head. "It's too dangerous—too much power."

"What do you mean?" Veron asked.

"Imagine if—who was the captain you told me about from Karad? Mortinson? What if *he* learned how to use it? What if someone like that taught a bunch of like-minded people?"

Veron squirmed as he remembered Mortinson lusting after the power and begging to be taught. "Well, we just wouldn't teach people like him. We'd make sure they were good people before they learned."

"And how would you determine that?"

Veron glanced up at Chelci and shrugged his shoulders. "Maybe we could—um . . ." He snapped his fingers and turned back to William. "A test! We could test them to see what type of—" Veron stopped as it dawned on him, and a grin grew on William's face as he chuckled again. "That's what the test is about?"

"The test is to determine two things," William said. "While it's *possible* for anyone to learn, it is only easy for a few. Someone needs to have the right amount of focus, drive, and internal strength for the training to work, which is what most of the test looks for. For someone who lacks these traits, the one in three thousand number is pretty close to accurate for their chances of learning the origine."

"What's the second thing?" Chelci asked.

"Character. We check to see what type of person they are—what motivates the decisions they make. Greed? Selfishness? If given power, will they use it to advance themselves or help others?"

"How do you test for that?" Veron asked.

"It's not as easy. We ask questions—'What would you do if . . .' scenarios. Mostly, we tried to look at a person's actions and see how they lived."

"But I was a thief, living on the street when Artimus took me in. There's no way he saw me and decided I had good enough character to learn."

"He knew me," William said. "Maybe he assumed you'd inherit some of my traits. Plus, didn't you say he waited four years before teaching you the origine?" Veron nodded as William continued. "Artimus' line about few people being able to learn was to keep power seekers from getting greedy. And that's the reason we have rule number eight of the code—never allow your abilities to be known. The fewer people who know what the Shadow Knights are capable of the better."

Veron grimaced toward Chelci as a knot twisted in his stomach.

"Yeah . . . so I wasn't always great about that one."

"That's okay," William replied. "You did what you needed to do."

Veron's mind whirled as he took in the new information.

After a moment of silence, Chelci landed on the dirt next to him. She stood tall and faced William with her chin held out. "Teach me."

Veron and William locked eyes. Veron wasn't sure if it was a good idea or an awful one, so he was thankful when William shook his head.

"Why not?"

"It will put you in danger," William replied.

"Because of Bale? He wouldn't know! We don't have to tell anyone in Nasco." William looked to his feet, avoiding her eyes. "You of all people know I have drive and strength, and I like to think I've proven my character! Come on! You'll need more knights to keep the tradition alive, right?"

Veron lifted his hand, drawing the other two's attention. "I . . . don't mind trying to teach you." A smile grew on Chelci's face. "But I barely understand it myself, so I'm not sure how effective I'll be."

William sighed. "Fine. I'll *test* you, but that's all I'll agree to." Chelci squealed, grabbing William around the neck in a hug. "Okay. Okay," William said as he extricated himself. "But don't get your hopes up."

Veron looked through the open window in William's house. The sun had fallen behind the trees, and the sky glowed with a warm sunset.

"It's beautiful," Chelci said from over his shoulder, causing him to turn to her.

"Not as beautiful as what's in this room," he said in a suggestive tone.

Chelci rolled her eyes.

William chuckled as he entered from the bedroom. He carried a small basket and walked to a chair.

"I don't care if you think it's cheesy," Veron said toward his father. "I stand by it."

"Oh, I'm not laughing at you," William said. "I used to say things like that to Julia all the time. You reminded me of me." He turned to Chelci. "Now, you come and sit here."

Chelci crossed the room to take the other cushioned chair, leaning forward at the edge. William pulled a ball just smaller than a fist out of the basket.

"Hold out one hand palm down," he instructed. Chelci complied, and William set the ball on the back of her hand. He removed his hand, allowing the ball to rest motionless. "Now, I want you to move your hand quickly and grasp the ball while still keeping your palm down. The goal is for the object to move as little as possible."

Veron sat on a stool while he watched. He held his sword in front of him, the tip against the wooden floor and the hilt spinning slowly in his palm.

A nervous laugh issued from Chelci, and the ball trembled. In a sudden movement, Chelci pulled her hand back and grabbed for the ball. It fell to the floor with a thunk.

"It's okay," William said. "It can take a few attempts." He returned it to her hand.

Chelci's eyes focused. The ball shook before her arm jerked. That time, she caught it. "Aha!" She grinned at Veron.

William reset the ball. "Good. Do it again." Chelci flicked her hand to catch it another time. William nodded. "Nice. Keep repeating that. Remember to see how little you can move it."

She repeated it around a dozen times, only dropping it a couple times. Veron wasn't sure how little it was supposed to move, but he thought she did great.

"Trade with me," William said, taking the ball and handing Chelci a rough, lumpy stone.

"What's this?" she asked. "An amulet that gives me special powers?"

William tilted his head. "It's a rock. I pulled it from the dirt next to the woods."

A laugh snuck out before Veron could stop it. "Maybe it's a magic rock?" he suggested, earning a scowl from Chelci.

"It's heavy," Chelci said, turning it in her hand.

"Yes, it is. Hold it out straight." William said, demonstrating by holding his own arm extended. While she followed his example, William glanced at a pocket watch. "I want you to hold that as long as you can."

"Gah!" Chelci said, adjusting her posture to sit up straight. "Couldn't you have picked a smaller rock?"

Veron watched the ruby turn in his sword as he spun it. "So . . . should you keep the sword now?" he asked after a moment of sitting in the silence.

William turned to him and looked at the sword. "Farrathan?"

"You're the only real shadow knight. It feels kind of wrong for me to have it."

William chuckled. "You're as real as I am. Plus, Artimus gave it to you."

A smile pulled at Veron's mouth. He touched the leather of the grip, thinking of the weapon's history. After a moment, he looked up. The room was silent, and Chelci sat motionless. Her arm was still, and her eyes locked on her hand. William monitored the time.

"What was she like?" Veron asked after a moment, drawing a look from his father. "My mother. What kind of person was she?"

A grin grew on William's face. "Julia," he said as if seeing her in front of him. "Her smile lit up a room. Whenever I had a bad day, all it took was one glance from her to make me forget my woes. Her eyes had a sparkle to them, as if joy filled every moment. When she sang, the world stopped to listen. Her voice enchanted me."

Chelci's arm shook and perspiration dotted her forehead.

"What else?" Veron asked.

"We had little money, but you'd never know it to watch her."

"She was quick to spend it all?"

"No, she gave it all away! It annoyed me at first, but the more I got to see the looks on the people's faces she helped, the more I understood."

"Understood what?"

"We were fine. We had each other. We had food. Our needs were met. But there were so many people who needed more, and that's what drew her."

"Argh!" Chelci yelled as her hand fell into her lap.

William glanced at his pocket watch. "Impressive," he said. "Three minutes twenty-two seconds."

"I remember doing that," Veron said. "With Artimus."

"Yeah?" Chelci asked as she shook her arm out. "What was your time?"

"Well . . ." Veron started.

"Well, what?"

Veron sighed. "I was holding a sword that weighed, probably . . . *fifty* pounds."

Chelci raised an eyebrow. "Fifty pounds? For a sword?"

"That's right," Veron insisted. "It was a fifty-pound sword."

"So . . . you're saying your time wasn't longer than mine. Right?"

Veron groaned, and Chelci laughed.

"Okay, hold out your other arm now," William instructed.

"Not the rock again!"

"No, no rock this time." William held a stick out just above her hand. "Make an open fist with a circle on the top. That's it. I'm going to drop this, and I want you to catch it as soon as you can."

"This sounds much better," she said, staring at the stick. Veron sat quietly so as not to distract. Suddenly, the stick dropped, and Chelci's hand snapped shut. She barely caught it. "Ha ha!" she cried in victory.

During the next fifteen minutes, they moved from test to test. William had her balance on one leg while catching a ball with her opposite hand. She had to remember a series of phrases and repeat it back while William distracted her with other words. He blindfolded her and had her describe in detail the room they were in. Veron sat patiently while the tests continued, cheering her on every time she did something right.

"Good," William said, taking the blindfold back. "One more test to go. How's your right arm? Rested?"

Chelci shook it again then rolled it around her shoulder joint. "It's good."

"Okay, hold it out," William said, pulling a dull gray bracelet from his basket. He slid it over her hand. "Now, you can take the rock back."

"Ugh, no!" Chelci groaned.

"It's the final time, I promise. Again, hold it out as long as you can."

"My arm's going to be weak from last time!"

"It's okay. The second attempt is always shorter." William glanced at his watch as she extended her arm again.

I remember doing the same thing, Veron thought as he watched her concentrate. He jerked, sitting up straight. William turned. "Like a metal ring circulates the transfer of energy!' You're testing the metal blocking abilities thing!"

William smirked. "Artimus taught you about it?"

Veron scoffed. "No! I wish he had, though. I spent most of wiether thinking I'd lost the origine for good. King Wesley taught me only a couple of weeks ago. How does it work?"

William shook his head. "I'm not the best to explain it, but it deals with the connection between mind and body. That's how the origine functions. Your mind convinces your body to do more than it normally is capable of, but metal interferes with that connection."

"How?"

"Have you ever put on a wool tunic and your hair stood up?"

"Yeah, that's crazy."

"That's the same type of energy the mind uses to connect with the body. When your body is circled with metal, for whatever reason, that energy connection is gone.

Chelci's arm began to shake. Her jaw locked tight, and her eyes narrowed as they focused on her hand.

"So, the part in the book about 'a pure connection' giving the body nearly unlimited capacity? Does that mean, if you get it just right, you can do anything?"

William issued a short laugh. "Sure . . . anything you want . . . until you collapse from using all your energy."

"But, what if the connection to the origine was perfectly pure? Could you possibly—"

"Nothing is perfect, Veron. Your body is flawed. Your mind gets distracted. Your body gives out. The metal ring amplifies those flaws."

"In Felting, I healed myself while wearing an anklet, but it took a ton of effort and wiped me out after only a bit. Is that because—"

"What do you mean?" William asked, interrupting him with his brows knit together. Veron stared back, unsure of the question. "You healed yourself using the origine *while* wearing a metal anklet?"

"Yeah, a few times. It was like normal, but it took more effort, and I tired quickly." William stared back with narrowed eyes. "Is that . . . typical?" Veron asked.

"As I said, a metal band disrupts the connection between the mind and body to use the origine."

"Yeah, I could feel the difference," Veron said.

"That's not what I mean," William said, quizzically staring. "It should *prevent* the ability completely."

Veron breathed in. "It didn't. I could still—"

A low growl grew from Chelci, drawing both of their attention. Her arm flexed as she gritted her teeth. After a long roar, her hand dropped to her lap with a sigh. William looked at his watch, his eyes betraying the shock behind them.

"What? How long?" Veron asked.

"Did I make it?" Chelci asked. "Did I get close to three twenty-two?"

William swallowed hard as he looked up. "Four minutes flat."

Veron inhaled sharply. "What does that mean?"

William didn't answer but only blinked his eyes, staring straight.

Chelci waved in front of his face. "How did I do? Did I pass?"

After a moment of silence, William looked at her. His voice was flat as he spoke. "I always had a feeling about you. How quickly you learned the sword. The bravery you showed. How you fought off a valcor on your own. Part of me wanted to test you for a long while."

"What's the normal rock test result?" Veron asked.

"The metal is supposed to prevent any shadow knight hopeful from being able to draw on extra energy. Most future knights don't even make it halfway through the previous time, and I've never tested someone who went longer on their second attempt."

Chelci's eyes grew wide. "You're saying I have *that* much more ability?

William shook his head. "Your reflexes are weak. Your balance is average. Your focus suffers in the lightest of distractions." Chelci screwed up her face as he continued. "I had almost given up hope during the test, but I knew how much you wanted to pass . . . so I kept going."

"And the rock test proved she was great?" Veron asked, leaning forward.

"The rock test—the proof that she wasn't impeded in the slightest by the metal—proved what the other tests indicated. She has zero connection to the origine." William turned to Chelci and slightly shrugged. "You could never learn to be a knight."

10

Felting Common Hall

Brixton dragged his feet as he shuffled down castle's hall. He received an invitation from the Regent of Felting—who sent an official coach to pick him up. Having dinner with his father was the last thing on his wishlist, but he couldn't decline.

He wanted to wear his new suit, but Corina hadn't yet removed all the stains. Instead, he wore an old brown outfit. He tugged at the waist while he walked. *I need to get some more clothes soon. I don't remember these pants feeling so tight.*

The servant in front of him opened an ornately carved door and motioned for Brixton to proceed. The room was the informal dining room of the castle—used whenever there weren't guests or larger events requiring a grander space. Even so, the table could seat a dozen people.

His mother stood as he entered, but the prior light in her eyes was nowhere to be found. He acknowledged her with a kiss on the cheek and a hollow greeting. His father—sitting in front of a half-drunk glass of wine—glanced up from his seat but didn't stand.

"How's Mila?" Brixton asked as he took a chair. Servers immediately came in and piled the table with bread, cheese, and sliced meats.

"She's well," Elenor replied. "Her and Magnus have moved into the old house in Karad."

"Magnus!" Brixton groaned in frustration.

"They're married, Brixton."

"I hear she hasn't been able to get pregnant." His mother's look soured. "I bet it's Magnus' fault," he added.

A server came with a pitcher and filled Brixton's empty glass with water. He picked up the glass and scoffed. "Water?"

His mother averted her gaze at her plate, but Raynor stared back. "That's right. Some people cannot be trusted with harder drinks."

Brixton's stomach dropped as he thought of the fuzzy image of his father at the party. "It was one night! I was—" He stopped in a huff. Brixton lifted his glass and took a long drink of water without breaking his father's eye contact. "Ahh," he said, smacking his lips in mock satisfaction. "Excellent water. Thank you."

"How do you feel about your new job, Brixton?" Elenor asked as he reached for some meat and cheese to add to his plate.

"It's great," he said, his stomach turning at the lie. After a moment, he sighed. "Actually, it's been more difficult than I expected."

"How so?"

"These taxes Bale requires are troublesome." Brixton glanced at his father, surprised to see a hint of sympathy on his face. "We got much of the city to comply, but many of the businesses are holding out. They talk and the unrest builds."

"I heard what you did with the bakers," his father said, face devoid of emotion. "Any results?"

Brixton wobbled his head. "Some have fallen in line, but unrest from the others is even worse now. There's been vandalism on the commerce and treasury buildings. You need to get your people in line, Father."

Raynor pounded his fist on the table, causing Brixton to flinch. "I am Regent of Feldor! And I'm still your father . . . no matter what *title* Bale gives you. Besides, you're the one who came up with the taxing plan."

"What about you and all the *workers* you're collecting?" Brixton asked. "That's the real reason everyone is so upset."

Raynor's jaw fixed in a line as he stared back. His voice lowered to a nervous tone Brixton rarely heard. "It's not me . . . and it's not you."

Brixton's caught his breath, his mind curious of his father's intent.

Raynor glanced around as if to make sure they were alone. He mumbled almost too quietly to hear. "It's Bale."

"Raynor, watch it," Elenor snapped.

"It's true," Raynor said, leaning forward and whispering. "The taxes—the workers—it's all Bale's doing. That's why the city is filled with unrest. We've been under him for only a couple of weeks, and the city already falls apart."

"How many have you gathered so far?" Brixton asked, unwilling to engage in the treasonous conversation.

His father sighed. "We need ten thousand. We have around four so far, including the two that arrived from Karad this morning."

"Have they left for Norshewa yet?"

Raynor shook his head. "Bale wants to clear the route past Karondir first. He sent some battalions ahead. I imagine he'll want to move before long."

"Did you get people to volunteer?"

"We tried that, but it didn't work. We had to find more direct methods."

Brixton and his mother exchanged a furtive look. "More direct?" Elenor said. "So, you forced people."

Raynor leaned toward his wife and pointed at her. "You don't know what I've had to deal with! Stay out of it!"

"If you hadn't turned your back on this country—"

Smack! The back of Raynor's hand struck her across the face, drawing a sharp cry. Brixton clenched his jaw as his mother held her cheek and shrank back. A thick silence filled the room after the moment of violence. Brixton looked at his mother, but she wouldn't meet his eyes.

The door to the dining room opened, causing Elenor to jump. A Norshewan soldier entered and spoke in a commanding voice. "Raynor Fiero. King Bale requires your presence."

Raynor raised an eyebrow but didn't move. "Now? What is it?"

"People have gathered at the Felting Common Hall to protest. He wants you to speak with them."

Raynor grumbled as he stood, grabbing a roll and a hunk of cheese.

"I'm coming, too," Brixton said, rising to join him. His father didn't object.

They followed the soldier outside the castle and entered a waiting carriage. With the snap of a whip, the vehicle lurched into movement.

"Look, Brixton . . ." Raynor glanced out both windows before leaning forward and speaking in a low voice. "The people of Felting aren't standing for this."

"For what?"

"For Bale. For any of it. It was one thing to take over a country, but the taxes and the slaves . . ." Raynor faded out and swallowed hard. "It's too much. He's going to run us into the ground. Do you agree?"

Brixton's eyes grew as his father spoke. Slowly he nodded. "What do you suggest?"

Raynor leaned in further, whispering, "We're going to overthrow Bale."

"What?" Brixton yelled before covering his own mouth. "Sorry," he whispered.

"This isn't what Billings or I had in mind when all of this started," Raynor said. "Once Bale is gone and his men have run back north, it will be just us. No more extra taxes, and no more shipping our men away. We'll control it all, and the people will thank us for saving them."

"Uh . . . how are you planning to do it? He has fifty men around at all times. Veron couldn't get to him. How would you do it?"

"Bale's men are to protect him from shadow knights. He's not looking to defend against Felting soldiers or his trusted partners."

The vision was easy to get behind. *I won't have to throw people into prison for trying to earn a living.*

"We might need your help," Raynor said. Brixton inhaled quickly. "Not to kill him, but when the time comes, you may need to help us get him alone."

Brixton's heart sped. "I—I can't."

"What? Of course, you can."

He shook his head. "I did it with King Wesley and with Veron, but—"

"And you can do it again," Raynor snapped.

"Father, please!"

Raynor waved a finger in Brixton's face. His words were quiet but sharp. "You asked for this position. You wanted power and money, and now you have it. But keeping it requires doing what must be done. Don't beg and plead with me to show you leniency. You wanted to be here . . . now you need to do your part if you want to remain."

Brixton leaned against the back of his seat, and a moment later, the carriage slowed to a halt. His father glared at him until the driver opened the door for them to exit.

A dull roar greeted Brixton as he stared up at Felting Common Hall. The wooden beams and stone walls rose high above the street to create a marvel of a structure. Angry voices from inside bounced through the open door, confirming a discontented crowd. Groups of soldiers stood at alert, and a dangerous energy filled the street.

Brixton followed his father and a soldier to the side door of the hall. Glancing through the open doorway confirmed his assessment. The space was packed. Men made up most of the crowd, but a smattering of women and children yelled along with them. Every face contained a scowl. Bale stood next to the side door with his arms crossed over his chest and a slight crook in his mouth. *He's not upset or scared. What is that? Does he find this humorous?*

"What's going on?" Raynor asked, barely audible over the shouts spilling through the doorway.

"Brixton," Bale said with a warm grin. "I'm glad you could join us, too." He turned to Raynor, and his smile faded. "Your city finds it amusing to protest against what we're trying to do for them."

Raynor glanced through the door and tugged at his collar. "What do they want?"

"Talk to them, *Regent*," Bale said with a harsh emphasis. "If you're going to run this region, you need to be able to control one city. Calm them down. Help them see what we're doing and accept it. Unrest like this is a disease that will spread if not stamped out."

Raynor nodded a long time before he crossed through the doorway and pushed through the phalanx of soldiers between the rabble and the stage.

Bale and Brixton followed behind, standing to the side as Raynor lifted his hands from the stage and shouted. "Quiet!" The crowd settled. "What are your complaints?"

For a moment, the crowd seemed to wait for a spokesman from their ranks, but when no one took charge, voices cried out. "We can't pay the taxes!" "My business is failing!" "You took my husband!" "We're losing our customers!"

"Whoa, whoa!" Raynor raised a hand again. "Let's start with the taxes. You signed the new business agreements, correct?" Several faces looked toward the floor, and an indistinct murmur filled the room. "If you agreed to the taxes, why are you complaining?"

"I agreed because I had to! I couldn't go to prison!" a voice shouted.

Brixton shrank back a step as his father glanced at him. "We don't have enough money to pay the tax!" another man cried out. A round of agreements echoed through the hall.

"You need to include the tax in the price of your products. That's how taxes work," Raynor said, his irritation showing in his voice. He pointed to the man who'd spoken up. "What do you sell?"

"Shoes. I'm a cobbler," he answered. "I tried including the tax in my shoes, but my customers have stopped coming! If I don't include it, I'm left with no money, but if I do, no one can afford to buy anything, and I'm left with no money!"

A roar of discontent filled the hall. Raynor raised his hands, but the shouting continued.

"Get control of them, Regent," Bale growled, leaning toward Raynor.

Sweat dotted Brixton's brow as he scanned the angry crowd. *I'm glad these guards are in front of the stage.*

"Quiet!" his father yelled, finally getting the room to hush. "The taxes are here. Get used to it. It takes money to run a kingdom, and there is no way around it. Unless you want to find yourselves in prison, make it work."

The crowd did not shout back. Brixton wiped his sweat-laden forehead.

"What about my husband being taken?" A woman yelled after a moment of silence. "He was an apothecary, and I don't know how to take over for him! Plus, I have three young children, so I couldn't even if I knew how!"

Brixton's father shifted his feet. "We—Um . . . Building a kingdom requires a lot. It takes money, and it takes workers. Don't worry, your men will be back!"

Bale's mouth flinched at the promise of the men's return.

"When?" a voice shouted. "When will they be back?"

"Soon!" Raynor replied.

"But how am I supposed to live now?" the apothecary's wife asked.

"What are they even doing?" another asked.

"The workers are . . . to build infrastructure," Raynor replied after a brief pause. Brixton's forehead creased. "Roads . . . bridges . . . They're making our kingdom better."

"We want our men back!" another voice shouted.

Raynor blinked as his head swiveled around the room. He glanced back to Bale, who stood like a statue with his arms crossed. "I don't know . . ." Raynor mouthed, holding his palms up.

A hole grew in the pit of Brixton's stomach. *I've never seen Father unsure what to do.* Shouts of "taxes" and "out of business" came from all directions along with pleas to return those taken.

The noise crescendoed until Bale stepped forward, raising his hands. "Silence!" The crowd instantly quieted. "We appreciate all of your thoughts," he said with a false smile on his face. "You've given us a lot to think about. Please give us a moment to speak. Wait here, and we'll be back momentarily with a solution for how we can make this right for you all."

Bale motioned for Raynor and Brixton to follow as he led out the side door, joined by his fifty soldiers. When they arrived in the alley, Bale turned to Raynor with a snarl on his face. "That was pathetic, Fiero! You can't kowtow to these ignorants whenever they don't like something."

Raynor stepped back while his eyebrows lifted. "But they bring up good points," he replied. "How are they supposed to—"

"Your weakness enables them! You need to be firm! They're not making it work because they don't want to make it work. They *can* pay the taxes. Their customers will adapt. They sense a weakness in your leadership, and they're pulling on it to break you."

Captain Cyrus approached amidst the reprimand. "Shall we proceed, Your Majesty?" the captain asked.

Bale nodded then waved a finger in Fiero's face. "Get your stuff together, Raynor. If you can't be firm enough to do what needs to be done, I'll find someone else who can."

Brixton's eyes followed soldiers shuffling around the building. *What are they doing?*

"Come on. Let's go," Bale said, ushering them out the end of the alley.

When they arrived at the main entrance, soldiers jammed thick braces in front of the doors. Others did the same down the alley.

"What's going on?" Raynor asked. "What are you doing?"

"What needs to be done," Bale said. "Hopefully, it's the last time I have to intervene for your shortcomings, Regent."

Brixton turned to the hall. He gasped as men with torches came around the corner. *No!* He screamed inside, but his jaw remained locked. He swallowed and glanced at his father, whose eyes showed the same. Raynor Fiero was selfish and cruel, but he was no killer. The soldiers touched the torches to the structure, igniting the wooden beams. Flames crept up the building. Smoke billowed into the air as screams emanated from within.

Brixton blinked away a tear before glancing at Bale. A smirk tugged on the dark-haired man's face. *Is Father right? Will Bale ruin us?* As he watched the Felting Common Hall turn into a blazing inferno with hundreds of innocent people trapped inside, Brixton's confidence in his next steps crumbled.

11

Purpose Explained

Brixton pounded for a third time on Darcius Marlow's door. No one responded, and his frustration grew. Finally, the door clicked open, revealing their choreman.

"Jensen, it's about time. What took you so—"

"I'm sorry, sir, but the high lord isn't receiving guests."

Brixton scoffed. "I'm not a—" He blinked several times before he pushed past Jensen to enter. "Where is he?"

Jensen scurried after him. "Excuse me, but I told you—"

"I'm not a *guest*, Jensen. I'm the Commercial Envoy of Terrenor. Darcius reports to me, and as such, I demand to see him." Jensen recoiled from the harsh words and left him alone.

Brixton stepped lively, searching through the house. Servants bustled around cleaning and straightening.

"Brixton?" a familiar-looking young man said. He stopped scrubbing the floors and looked up. "I'm Nathaniel. We met several weeks back when you were, uh . . ."

"Yes, I remember."

"Chelci's not here anymore," Nathaniel said.

"I'm not here for her. Where's High Lord Marlow?"

The servant raised an eyebrow. "Last I saw, he was walking the garden paths."

Brixton walked to the nearest window and spotted the man outside. Without a word, he crossed to the back door and exited.

The midday sun beat down, but the shaded paths still held a chill in late wiether. Brixton pulled his cloak together as he jogged to catch up with the high lord. "Darcius!" Brixton called as he approached.

The older man froze without blinking. "Brixton, I wasn't expecting you at my home."

"We need to talk. I couldn't wait."

Marlow motioned Brixton to walk with him. "I presume this concerns the business crisis in the city?"

Brixton took a deep breath and exhaled. "I need help. I think you were right about Bale, and honestly, I don't know what to do about it. Forty shops are closed because of the taxes. Some couldn't stay in business, and many fled to avoid being taken as one of Bale's workers. The fallout from the common hall burning is affecting everyone. Did you know all the city's cobblers were gathered at that meeting?"

"Yes, I heard," Marlow said. "There's not a shoe to be bought in all of Felting."

"Meat is the same way. Several butcher shops already closed because of pricing sensitivity. People stopped buying it when it became too expensive. Most of the rest died in the fire. Now there are only a few stores left, but they can't supply enough for the city."

Marlow nodded. "Prices of everything are skyrocketing. Brixton, I've worked in commerce all my life, and I've never seen anything like this."

"How do we fix it?" Brixton asked, coming to a halt at the end of the path and turning to Marlow. "We can't keep going on!"

"You're right, Brixton. We can't. These taxes must end. The killing and forced slavery must stop. We need stability so the people of

Felting can heal from their shock."

"I agree. We need stability." Brixton's heart pounded. *Would Darcius be on board with Father's plan?*

"Bale should have more sense than this," Marlow said. "He wants more taxes, but he murders off his tax base. How has he been in power in Norshewa for so long with such decision-making?"

Brixton nodded, his brain feeling clearer. "You know, that's a good question. I wonder . . ." he paused for a moment. "I need to talk with him. If he understands what's going on, maybe we don't have to—" He cut himself off before revealing too much. "I've gotta go. I'll come by and see you on Marketday."

"Brixton," Marlow called, turning him around as he walked away. "You don't need to be like him. Don't let him push you into doing something that's not right."

Brixton nodded then pulled his cloak together as he left.

"Brixton!" Bale shouted as Brixton entered. The king hunched over a desk signing papers while his advisor, Desmond, stood to the side. "To what do I owe the honor?"

"I—uh . . . hoped to speak with you."

Bale stopped writing and raised his head. He looked Brixton in the eyes. "I'm glad you came by then. I can't wait to hear what you have to discuss." He turned back to the documents. "Give me *just* a moment." Brixton glanced at Desmond, who returned a weak smile. "There!" Bale said with a flourish. He collected a pile of papers and handed them to his advisor. "What time is it?"

"Nearly three," Desmond answered.

As Bale nodded, a soldier poked his head into the office. "Your Majesty. They've arrived."

"Great!" Bale said. "Brixton, talk with me while we walk."

Brixton fell in stride while they left the room into the midst of the army of guards stationed just outside. A few went before them, but most trailed behind.

"What's on your mind, Brixton?"

Brixton's heart pounded. His father's plan to overthrow Bale itched at the back of his mind. "We're running into more trouble in the city," he said.

"After the protest at the Common Hall?"

Brixton nodded. *"Because* of what happened there, I believe."

"How so?"

"Your Majesty, I know the intent behind your actions—the hard response to force people to comply—but I worry that it's not panning out the way you'd hoped."

Bale rested a hand on his shoulder, and both halted at the top of a staircase. He raised an eyebrow, inviting Brixton to explain further.

"The—um . . ." Brixton's throat suddenly felt dry. "The people who've said they can't afford the taxes . . . They're not exaggerating about their situation. I've spoken with several of them and even looked at their books. They can't afford them. And for those that raise their rates, customers stop coming. The goal is to make more money in taxes, but we're making *less* right now because stores are closing."

Brixton couldn't read Bale's expressionless, stony visage no matter how hard he tried. He cleared his throat before continuing. "And after killing the protesters, we're seeing even more trouble. Many products have supply problems, and nearly all deal with skyrocketing prices. All of this results in citizens hoarding what little money they have, which further grows the problems with businesses and the taxes we hoped to collect."

"So, what are you saying?" Bale asked, causing Brixton's insides to feel like water.

Brixton swallowed hard. "I'm saying . . . I know what you want from the people, and I understand why you've done what you've done. But I don't believe it's having the desired result, and I think it may be necessary to change the approach."

Bale breathed deeply as he leaned his head back. Brixton's pulse pounded in his ears as he waited for a response. The king's mouth formed into a smile, and Bale erupted into a hearty laugh while he hit Brixton on the shoulder. "Oh, Brixton! Ha! You have even more guts than I gave you credit for." As his laughter settled, he looked Brixton in the eyes. "And more wisdom, too." He nodded toward the stairs as they descended.

"There are two types of rulers, Brixton," Bale said. "The first type controls by fear, where disobedience is met with harsh consequences. People remain in line, not because they want to, but because they're afraid of what will happen if they don't. The ruler can't give in to demands, or they weaken their ability to control. Any compromise is poison to their power. The second type of leader governs with kindness. They want everyone to be their friend so they'll do the right thing of their own free will." Bale scoffed. "*Wesley* was such a fool. Thank you for helping us rid this kingdom of his ineptitude."

"So, you want to be the first type?"

"I want something different. I prefer the people to do what I require of their own choosing, but at the same time, be afraid of *not* doing it."

Brixton furrowed his brow. "I don't understand. How can you do that?"

"You're right in your assessment of the city. Things are falling apart, and the current state is not beneficial to me, you, or anyone. Now that the kingdom is primed, it's time to demand what I want, which is only five tid per head per season. The announcement is already being posted this afternoon."

Brixton's mouth turned up and his brows lifted. "Only five tid! That's great! That will be so much easier to get! I'm sure people will have no trouble getting by with—" Brixton stopped walking and turned to Bale. The dark-haired ruler stared back with a wicked grin on his face. "Oh, that is brilliant," Brixton said. "They'll be happy to pay after experiencing something worse."

Bale nodded.

"Ha!" Brixton shook his head as they continued down the hall. "But people are still afraid of you, so not only will they pay the tax, but they wouldn't dare protest anymore." Brixton's face darkened. "But all those deaths. Surely there was another way?"

Bale's mouth formed into a tight line. "That was regrettable but necessary. Sometimes a city needs to be purged of those who aren't productive. Anyone whose business struggled and anyone who rankled against authority was at that meeting. In one fell swoop, we eliminated them. Now, the city can regrow with new, healthier citizens taking their place."

"What about the workers you're taking to Norshewa? People are upset, and reducing their taxes won't change that."

"That's true. They'll be on board when they see what we build. People want to have something they can be proud of. It will take hard work to get there, but they'll come around."

Brixton pursed his lips together. *I'm not sure building something on the other side of Terrenor will excite the people of Felting.*

Bale continued. "Getting them to comply is where the *fear* aspect comes in. For now, we need them to obey."

After descending another flight of stairs, they arrived at the ground floor and proceeded through the entrance hall. *I wonder who's arriving?* Brixton thought.

"I'm impressed with your insight and bravery, Brixton. These past few weeks have been a difficult but necessary period. Things will turn around, and I see you having a bright future in what's coming."

Brixton beamed as they exited the castle. The dark cloud that blanketed him lifted as his fears for the city and what would come dissipated.

A chorus of trumpets blared, and he jerked to attention. Bale halted at the top of the steps, where a line of soldiers extended down. They stood in formation, alternately holding swords and Norshewan flags. In the stone circle below, a caravan of people approached. Brixton gaped at the sight before him as a chilly gust of wind rustled the end of his cloak.

Soldiers wearing blue and white uniforms flanked dozens of silver-trimmed carriages. They marched in formation with swords at their sides and large feathers sticking from their caps. The vehicles were all pulled by rydanor—the enormous beasts Brixton had only seen in books from the Academy. Their muscular legs and massive bodies seemed to pull the vehicles without effort.

"What is this?" Brixton asked, gaping.

Men emerged from the carriages as they came to a halt. Their outfits were exquisite. Sharp lines, bold colors, and decorative hats distinguished the visitors. After stretching their legs and gathering together, they approached. An older man with stripes of gold on his cloak ascended the steps with authority and purpose.

"That would be King Jabari of Tarphan," Bale said, glancing at Brixton. "I invited him."

Brixton's eyes widened. Until a few weeks before, he had never met a single king. Unsure if he should be there or not, he remained next to Bale as the contingent of men came to meet them.

"Welcome, King Jabari!" Bale said in a booming voice.

A cautious smile formed on the approaching man's face. He glanced at the man on his right before bending his knee and flourishing his arm in a bow. "Thank you, King Edmund," he said, his words stilted. "Please excuse my speech. My Common Norshic is mostly weak."

Bale smiled. "Your speech is excellent. I hope your travel was easy."

"Yes, much easy." Jabari nodded.

"And the weather is not too cool for you?" Bale asked, his light cloak hanging loosely and blowing in the breeze.

"Oh, no," Jabari said, clutching the front of his cloak with white knuckles. "The weather in Searis is warm, so the chill here is . . . what's the word . . . refreshing."

He motioned to a man standing behind him and uttered a command in his native Tarphic language. The man approached, carrying a small box. He knelt and extended it toward Bale, his arms straining. King Jabari lifted a clasp and opened the lid. A padded surface lined the inside with a matted gray object in the middle. "As a token of our . . . grouping, I present you this rydanor figurine—the symbol of Tarphan. It means the strength and working of our country. I offer it to you as promise of our friend line."

It's so small. Brixton's eyes widened. "Is that . . . baltham?" Brixton asked, his voice trembling.

Jabari's wistful smile confirmed he was correct. "Donated by the . . . happy families of Tarphan."

"Impressive," Bale said, nodding as he reached out to grasp the gift. He grinned and picked up the small object.

That much baltham could feed one hundred families for an entire season.

"Does this mean you accept my terms?" Bale asked, turning the figurine over in his hands.

"If so, you no attack? Yes?"

"You have my word."

Jabari swallowed and looked back at the man at his side. "We, uh . . ." He turned back to Bale and stood straight, extending his neck. "Yes, we accept. We agree to the tax want. We will pay at each season."

Bale raised an eyebrow while his mouth formed a tight line. "And the other piece?"

Jabari adjusted his weight. "Yes. We provide the, uh . . . *workers* you say."

"Good!" Bale set the figure back into the box.

"Will you be sending men to, um . . . occupy Searis?" Jabari asked.

Bale cocked his head and stared. "Do I *need* to send men to occupy Searis?"

"Oh, no!" the older man blurted. "I just wondered . . . so we could be prepared."

Bale sniffed and held his gaze for a long moment. "I will send a small battalion. I trust you will make sure they are housed and fed well?"

"Of course, Your Majesty!"

"And they will have full access to any information they require?"

"They will."

"And your title?"

Jabari seemed to falter a second, but he recovered his composure. "I will name have Jabari Grint, Regent of Tarphan." He lowered himself to both knees and bowed his head. "And I submit to you, King Edmund Bale, ruler of Terrenor."

12

Betrayal

B rixton walked down the long hall where Feldor's empty throne sat on its raised dais. His boots clunked on the stone and echoed through the barren room. Despite the chill inside the castle, he wiped sweat from his brow. His hands were clammy, and his heart thumped. Regent Grint had only stayed a week before scurrying back south with his people. With the visitors gone, it was time for a change. When he arrived at the opposite end, his arm shook as he reached to turn the handle.

His father jumped as he entered the room. "Brixton!" He held a carafe and glanced toward the door. "I thought you were him." Smoke inched over the edge of the vessel where red liquid swirled inside. After pushing a cork into the top of it, he set it on the table before him along with several other flagons. Lord Billings sat in one of the high-backed chairs with a leg propped on the opposite knee.

"Is it done?" Brixton asked.

His father glanced back at the carafe and picked up a vial resting on the table. He clenched his jaw and nodded while placing the empty container in his pocket. "It's ready."

"Bale will be here in a moment," Brixton said. Neither man replied.

His father paced about the chamber. Two lit torches rested on the wall at either end of the meeting room. A clock ticked off seconds as the anticipation built.

"Remember, we can't be the ones to suggest it," Raynor said, breaking the silence. "The poison should act quickly, so make sure you don't drink any."

"We know, Raynor," Billings said.

"And your captains are ready to respond?"

Billings nodded. "Gannon is with them now, ready for my signal."

"Are you sure you want to do this, Father?" Brixton said. "This new rate reduction is much more reasonable. Perhaps we should—"

"I'm sure," Raynor snapped, leaving the words hanging in the air.

Brixton clenched his jaw. "I believe you're missing the fact that—"

"Enough! You don't know about these things as I do." Raynor took a deep breath as Brixton hushed. Although his father sounded confident, worried lines marked his forehead. "If he doesn't go for it . . . we may need to—"

The door opened suddenly, and all three heads turned. Edmund Bale led the way. His sword swung at his hip, and he walked with a purposeful gait. Bale, Ryker, and Cyrus followed with four more Norshewan soldiers bringing up the rear. The soldiers stopped just inside the door and stood at alert. Brixton glanced at his father. A sharp intake of breath lifted his chest as Raynor looked at Billings.

"I'm told you have news," Bale said.

Raynor's face morphed into a broad grin as he crossed the room. "We do, Your Majesty. I'm excited to say that we have six thousand workers waiting for your word to travel to Daratill. I'm sure we can pick up four more from cities along the route."

Bale tilted his head as his eyebrows narrowed. "I thought you only had four thousand ready."

"We did," Raynor said. "But we've been hard at work these last few days."

"That's good," Bale said, nodding in the silence that followed. He rested a hand on the back of a chair, but his body angled as if he wanted to leave. "Is there anything else?"

Raynor shuffled his feet closer as he glanced at the table of bottled spirits. "We thought that was something worth celebrating, Your Majesty." He allowed a brief pause before barreling on. "But we have even more good news. After your decisive display at the Felting Common Hall, the city's business leaders are finally submitting to the new rules."

"Are they?"

"Yes," Raynor gestured to Brixton. "My son confirmed nearly all the business agreements have now been signed."

Bale turned. "Is that so, Brixton?"

Brixton swallowed and nodded slowly as his insides churned. "It's true. It seems the message got through." His voice cracked as he spoke.

Bale tilted his head back. "I thought the commercial state of Felting was in chaos?"

"It was, Your Majesty." Brixton cleared his throat and flicked his eyes to his father. "But I think your rate reduction convinced them to comply."

"I imagine we'll see things turning around soon," Raynor added.

"Well, I'm glad to hear it." Bale pointed to Brixton, Billings, then Raynor. "You leaders have been pivotal in helping us work through this transition time, and I thank you." Bale turned, and his party made to leave.

Brixton's father stepped closer again and wrung his hands, looking to Billings. "Your Majesty!" he said, stopping the men. "I would like to thank you! The last few weeks have been a whirlwind of activity, and I feel we should recognize the leadership and bravery you've shown." He gestured between himself, Billings, and Brixton. "We wouldn't be here today without you."

"Thank you, Regent Fiero," Bale said.

Raynor rested a hand on the table of drinks as sweat beaded on his forehead. "We should toast!" he said, raising a hand suddenly and looking around the room. "It's a Feldorian tradition to drink to the success of a new partnership." He turned to the table. "Do you think we should, um . . ."

"We aren't here to continue Feldorian traditions," Bale said in a hard voice that left no room for debate. Brixton cringed at his father's awkward display. After a moment, Bale's face softened, and a smile grew upon his mouth. "However, it is custom in Norshewa to drink after a successful battle, which we neglected. Are you willing to support our Norshewan traditions, Raynor?"

His father's shoulders relaxed as he returned the smile. "Of course, Your Majesty."

Bale stood and walked to join Raynor at the table. He glanced over at the various carafes. "What drink do you suggest?"

Raynor looked at the drinks. "Me? Oh, I'm not sure. These were all Wesley's." He leaned in to inspect the labels. "We have a dark wine from Tienn, a brandy from Tarving, a gin from Lorranis, a—" He jerked back. "Firetonic! I didn't know Wesley kept some of this. I've never actually had it before."

Bale looked hard at him. "Are you proposing we toast with firetonic, Regent Fiero?"

Raynor froze. He glanced at Billings and then Brixton. Thick tension filled the room as Brixton held his breath. "I am," Raynor said with a slight catch.

Bale stared back as the ticking clock seemed to increase in volume. "Very well," he said after a pause.

Brixton released his breath, but his palms sweat. Bale crossed to join his father at the table and picked up the flagon of firetonic. He lifted the glass container toward the flickering torch. A red glow projected onto his face as the light filtered through it. "Your son and I shared a drink of this a few weeks ago," he said as he removed the cork. "You should have seen his reaction. He spewed most of it across the room."

Raynor laughed. "It probably put some hair on his chest."

Bale laughed before turning to him with an upturned eyebrow. "You're up for trying it again today, aren't you, Brixton?"

Brixton stood straighter as he gave a tight nod. Bale laid out six glasses. Smoke poured onto the table as the thin red liquid filled each glass in turn. When finished, Bale passed the hissing drinks out, first to Ryker and Cyrus, then to Brixton and Billings, and finally one to his father while keeping the last for himself. "So, what should we toast to, Regent Fiero?"

Raynor's eyes locked onto the drink in his hand. Brixton thought he saw his arm tremble until his father brought the other to steady it. Finally, he lifted his drink into the air. "To a new, greater Terrenor, united under King Bale—may he live forever." His voice's falter disappeared as the rest of the men raised their glasses and repeated the last words.

For a long moment, the drinks remained raised in the air as the men waited. His father lowered his as if he were going to drink it but paused. No one drank. Raynor inclined his head and offered a half-smile. A nervous laugh escaped his lips. "Is no one going to drink?"

Bale lifted his chin as he extended his glass. "You agreed to follow Norshewan customs, Raynor." His words were hard and even, his hand solid like a rock.

Raynor's eyes shifted around the room. "Wh—what do you mean?"

Bale took a step closer. "In Norshewa, it is customary for whoever offers a toast to be the first to drink." His icy gaze filled the room with a chill.

Raynor's face looked green. An abrupt laugh betrayed his nervousness. He lifted his glass, the red liquid jostling as his hand shook. He touched the rim to his lips and tipped it to where the liquid barely touched them. When he lowered it, his throat demonstrated an exaggerated swallow. "Mmm, excellent," he said.

"Do you *intend* to insult me?" Bale asked, leaning in with a hand on his chest. Raynor's eyes grew as the king continued. "Our custom states that when you offer a toast, the amount you drink shows if your words are genuine or not. Surely you weren't aware of this or you would have drunk fully."

Brixton's father took a step backward. "Your Highness, I . . . I'm sorry. I didn't mean to insult you. It's just that I've heard rumors about firetonic and how dangerous it can be."

"Yet you just said it was good for your son?"

Raynor looked between the people in the room. "I—uh . . . I'm not—"

"Drink it," Bale said in a menacing voice as he stepped closer. The four soldiers by the door unsheathed their swords and aggressively crossed the room.

Raynor's eyes held a crazed look. "Please, I—I just . . ." He looked across the room. "Gareth, maybe we should—" His father stopped speaking as Billings averted his gaze.

"Are you afraid of a little poison, Fiero?" Bale asked with a sneer.

Silence filled the room as Raynor's face twisted in confusion. "Gareth? You told him?"

A deep laugh bellowed from Bale's chest. "Oh, Fiero, it wasn't Gareth who sold you out."

Raynor turned to Brixton. His eyes looked crazed as his chest rose and fell. "Son?" Brixton lowered his eyes. "No! How could you?"

Brixton's breath grew ragged. His pulse thumped, and he steadied himself against the wall.

Bale drew his sword. "Now, after all these years and how you've treated him, you expect him to stand beside you?" Raynor bumped into the table as he attempted to step backward. There was nowhere to go.

"But we had a plan," Raynor whimpered. His jaw quivered.

"I was never on board with your plan," Brixton spat. He looked at the floor, averting his gaze from his once powerful, dominant father reduced to a quivering heap.

Bale turned to his soldiers. "See to it that Regent Fiero finishes his drink."

"No! Please!" Raynor yelled.

The soldiers surrounded him as Bale motioned for Brixton and the others to follow him out of the room. Brixton didn't hesitate. His father's protests chilled his bones, but it wasn't until he heard the horrendous gurgling sound that his stomach turned. He held onto the door frame for balance as he fled. When the door closed and the sounds faded, Brixton bent over, holding his hands on his knees while his father died in the room next to him. His stomach roiled as beads of sweat dotted his forehead.

To the side, Bale mumbled something to the others before he came to Brixton and sat on the dais next to him. He patted a hand on the hard surface. "Thank you for warning me. That was brave of you."

Brixton inhaled deeply as he sat. "I couldn't take him looking at me."

"I know how difficult that decision was," Bale said. "I made the same one many years ago with my own father." Brixton raised an eyebrow as Bale continued. "Part of me felt guilty. He was my family, so I felt like I had to stand up for him, but I realized that was misplaced. He gave up his right to demand my loyalty long before. Your father put you in the same position."

Brixton nodded. "He never cared about me. He abused and mistreated Mother and me all of our lives. All he wanted was money and power."

"And now he's gone," Bale said as he clasped him on the shoulder. "It's normal to feel conflicted, but don't take that as a sign of you making a mistake. You have a freer life ahead of you filled with promise."

Bale stood, and Brixton followed. His legs wobbled, but after a moment, his strength returned.

"Gareth, I trust we will have no more issues with you as regent?"

"Of course not, Your Majesty," Billings said with a bow. "By the way, Fiero lied about the workers."

"I figured as much."

"We are close but not quite there."

Bale turned to Brixton. "You've proven trustworthy in many things, Brixton. Can I trust you to help with something new?"

Brixton swallowed as he faced the king. "You know you can."

"Take a few days to see your mother is cared for, then I have a task for you."

* * *

Brixton avoided his mother for the next two days. His insides tore at him for what he did to his father. He told himself it was for his mother's own benefit, but that wasn't why he betrayed him. He had much more to gain aligning with Bale than his father.

Unable to stay away any longer, his feet felt heavy as he approached the main entrance to the castle where two carriages parked out front. Servants laden with enormous trunks bustled down the steps and loaded them on top of the vehicles.

"That's the last of them, my lady," a servant said as Brixton rounded the end of a carriage.

"Mother?" he said, freezing in his tracks.

Elenor Fiero stood next to the front carriage, dressed in black. She turned her head and stiffened. "It's time to go, Loren," she said to the man adjusting the reins on the horses.

Brixton approached her. "Mother, what's going on? Where are you heading?"

Her jaw was tight as she looked back. "I'm returning home—to Karad where I will stay with your sister."

"You weren't even going to tell me goodbye?"

She raised an eyebrow and stared him down. Brixton withered under her sharp glare. She took a step closer and spoke under her breath. "Raynor told me of your plan. I knew what you, Billings, and he were supposed to do. But somehow, he's the one who ended up poisoned."

Brixton opened his mouth but couldn't think of words.

"How dare you turn on him," she whispered.

Brixton reeled. "But . . . But he hit you, and he yelled at us, and . . ."

"He was your father!" The nearby servants' heads turned.

Brixton clenched his jaw as he took a deep breath.

"He wasn't a perfect husband or father by any means, but he was the only one you have. Bale can never fill that role." After staring him down for a long moment, Elenor grasped the rail of the carriage and stepped inside.

"Shouldn't we bury him first?" Brixton asked.

Her eyes were cold as she looked back at him. "I already did."

Brixton's chest ached as the carriages rolled away. *I thought this would help her feel free.* While he stared after the cloud of dust kicked up by the castle gate, footsteps approached down the steps behind him. He turned to find Edmund Bale with his mass of guards lingering nearby.

"She's grieving," the king said. "Give her some time."

Brixton glanced back to the settling dust. "I thought it might relieve her, but I guess I was wrong."

"A lifetime of loyalty can't change overnight. Don't worry, you'll always have a place in her heart." Bale extended his arm to usher him into the castle. "Come now, Brixton. We have work to do."

Brixton looked up the steps and nodded as he followed.

13

Premweek of Suether

Veron dusted off his hands as he rolled his neck and stood up straight. A long line of tilled soil extended before him with freshly covered mounds and watered dirt. Around him, dozens of villagers finished their own work in the large community garden.

In the row next to Veron, Chelci bent over as she completed planting her row. Her brown hair fell around her face. She continually tried to brush it away, but it kept falling back. Her shirt clung to her from sweat, and brown pants hugged her legs. Despite the physical effort, a casual joy covered her face. Smile lines at her eyes accented the smooth skin of her face. He smiled, noticing her ever-present beauty.

"You need any help?" Veron asked.

Chelci looked back at him while remaining bent over. Her red, upside-down face had wild strands of hair stuck to it. "No, I'm almost done—but thanks. Hey, you're not back there checking me out, are you?"

Veron jerked his head. "What? No! I was just offering to help."

With a laugh, Chelci turned her attention back to the dirt to finish up her row while Veron's gaze drifted toward her backside. A quick shake of the head averted his eyes.

"You all done, Veron?" Nevi asked as she approached.

He spun toward her. "I wasn't—" He stopped after seeing the innocent look on her face. "Oh . . . the garden. Yes, I just finished." He pressed his cheeks, wishing the flush would go away. He nodded to another plot of dirt. "What about that section?"

"The wiether cabbage needs another week before we harvest it. Then, we'll plant there as well. You sure seem to know what you're doing here."

Veron chuckled. "I've spent my share of time around a garden. So, I'm curious . . . since everyone seems to work together in the garden, who decides who gets what when you harvest?"

"No one, really, or we all do—depending on how you look at it. Everyone takes what they need, knowing that we have to share."

"What if the crop is poor or someone takes too much?"

Nevi shrugged. "We work it out. The village elders settle concerns when needed. But it's rarely needed."

"You're all quite different from the rest of Feldor," Veron said.

"We prefer it that way. We try to stay clear from the issues of the kingdom, and they leave us alone."

"Whew! Now I'm done," Chelci said as she straightened and dusted her hands on her legs. The rest of the workers all finished as well. "You ready to go?"

The three of them picked up their sacks and tools, and Nevi led the way toward the Martin house. Chelci leaned close to Veron. "I saw you looking," she said in a mock-accusatory voice, prompting a sheepish grin to cover Veron's face.

"So, are you two ready to party tonight?" Nevi asked, looking over her shoulder.

"Oh, Veron, you're gonna love it!" Chelci said. "The premweek of suether celebration is my favorite of the entire year!"

"What do you enjoy about it most?" Veron asked.

She sighed. "The food, the music, the dancing."

A wave of nerves washed over Veron at the prospect of dancing.

"It's so much fun!"

"Don't forget the guard performance," Nevi added.

"That's right," Chelci said. "It was always my favorite part when I was younger. They show off their sword skills. It's amazing to see."

"When does it start?" Veron asked, eager despite his nerves.

"In a few hours."

Nevi glanced over her shoulder again. "Until then, we all have some baking to do."

Veron carried a large wooden platter, balancing two bowls as they walked along the dusty path to the village center. The spicy aroma of garront stew caused his mouth to water, but he most looked forward to the bortleberry pie with steam coming through the slit in the crust.

Nevi and Chelci led the way, walking arm-in-arm, and Veron and Morgan followed. Although Veron had to be careful carrying the food, he had trouble taking his eyes off Chelci. She wore a light-blue, long-sleeved dress that fell just past her knees. Her brown hair was curled and pinned up on top of her head, making her appear several inches taller than normal. Veron admired her long, elegant neck and straight shoulders.

"I'm happy for you, Veron," Morgan said.

Veron looked at his friend. "Oh yeah? What for?"

"You've been through a lot in the last few years. You're a good person, and it's about time you had something go right."

"Thanks. Yeah, it feels like I've had a cloud over my head for years. I loved our market in Karad, but this feels . . . somehow even better." His insides trembled as he steeled himself to get out the next words.

He lowered his voice close to a whisper. "You know, I'm considering asking Chelci to marry me."

Morgan jerked his head toward Veron. "Really?" With his eyebrows lifted, a smile crept on his face.

Veron winced, "Yeah . . . Good idea or bad? Is it too soon?"

Morgan's grin widened as he continued walking. Creases grew around his eyes. Finally, he chuckled to himself. "I asked Catherine to marry me a week after I met her. My only regret is I didn't do it sooner." He turned back to Veron. "If someone is the right person, what's the point of waiting?"

"What if she doesn't feel the same? What if she thinks I'm some starry-eyed street kid turned slave? Maybe the thought of marrying me revolts her?"

"Ha!" Morgan's sharp laugh turned the heads of the ladies ahead of them. He lowered his voice again. "Have you seen the way she looks at you? I've only known her for a few weeks, but if you think she sees you as a street kid, then you don't know her well."

Veron nodded while a smile grew.

Morgan rested his hand on Veron's shoulder, and the two stopped. "I know what happened with Chloe in Karad when you opened up to her, and I'm sure that makes you hesitant to do it again. But you're a blasted shadow knight! You were an advisor to the king and one of the most successful businessmen in Karad. If you can fight street thugs and face Edmund Bale, I think you can summon enough courage to talk to Chelci."

A broad smile covered Veron's face. "Yeah, you're right. I can do it, but it still scares me." They resumed walking.

"Speaking of Bale . . . what will you do about him?" Morgan asked.

"What do you mean?"

"Do you plan to keep hiding? Or are you going to seek him out?"

"I'm not hiding," Veron said, his thoughts about Chelci fading as defensiveness crept in. "I just need to lie low for a week or so to give things time to settle down."

Morgan nodded. "You realize we've been here for three weeks already, right?"

Veron stopped walking and turned to Morgan. He pursed his lips and took in a deep breath. "I know. I just love it here, and I find myself less interested in making a decision that has a one in two chance of leaving me dead."

Morgan stepped closer as his face softened. "You are an amazing person, Veron. You have gifts that far surpass what I could ever hope for, and I'm not just referring to your shadow knight abilities. I want you to live a long and happy life—but that's not something for me to decide. You *do* have a decision to make, and I know it's not an easy one."

Veron swallowed hard, the metal of the Shadow Knights medallion pressing against his chest. "Do you think I have to make it now?"

"What I want is for you to be purposeful about making it. Don't stumble into your future. If you have a decision to make about Bale, don't ignore the question—that's all I'm saying. I won't judge what you choose."

Veron nodded then sighed. "I guess I've avoided thinking about it, hoping the problem might disappear. Thanks for bringing it up."

"Come on, you two!" Chelci called from ahead down the street. "We're already late!"

Veron turned to her. "Sorry, we're coming!"

When they rounded the corner, Veron gawked at the festive display of the village green. Colorful paper animals and flowers hung from lines strung between the buildings. Multiple long tables piled high with assorted foods—boar, chicken, still-smoking shredded beef, plenty of greens and vegetables, and an entire table filled with sumptuous desserts. Kids played tag on the grass, and adults talked and laughed while a band's bouncing melody filled the air.

"Wow, Chelci, you weren't kidding," Morgan said. "This is amazing!"

Chelci stood waiting as they walked up. "Did you think I was exaggerating?"

"Over here, dear," Nevi said, motioning for Veron to place the dishes down at an open space on a table. After he set them down, she shooed the three of them away. "I'll take care of the food. You all have fun."

"Thanks, Nevi," Chelci said before pulling on Veron's sleeve. "Come on!"

Veron and Morgan followed as Chelci led them around the perimeter of the village green. His stomach growled at the sight of all the food, but no one else was eating. Chelci stopped and talked with villagers as they meandered through the crowd. Some people were excited to meet Veron. Several even wrapped him in hugs.

Morgan had made a great deal of friends in his few weeks in Nasco. The food vendors knew him by name, and he seemed as at home walking through the crowd as Chelci did.

"Veron!" Finley called as the young man approached their group. "Chelci! Morgan! I worried you all weren't coming."

"Are you kidding?" Chelci replied. "We wouldn't miss this. The pie took longer than we expected."

"You almost missed the Academy demonstration," Finley added, pointing up the hill where the training facility looked down on the village center. "They're getting ready now." Young men and women moved into position in the outdoor courtyard. The music faded, and the crowd hushed. Russell, Aleks, and William walked down the rows of candidates, inspecting them.

"What do they do?" Veron whispered to Chelci.

"The candidates show off their sword skills. I'm so glad we didn't miss it," Chelci said. "I took part in it the last two years."

When the instructors seemed content, they moved to the side, giving the rows of young men and women direct sight to the crowd below. For a moment, the village was quiet. A few candidates glanced between each other, but most stared straight ahead. The young man in front raised his sword and loosed a guttural yell. The two lines of Academy hopefuls snapped to attention, raising their swords in sync.

Veron gasped, unprepared for the sudden movement. After a beat, the young warriors flowed into a striking display of power and control. They chanted in unison as they slashed their blades through the air. Synchronized kicks and spins blended with shouts to emphasize when they struck an invisible opponent. Their mouths fixed in fierce lines. The muscles in the candidates' arms rippled as they moved through form after form.

That's horn stance! Veron realized with a jolt. *And that's dragon . . . and snake.* The forms were all familiar. William caught his eye, observing the candidates from the side as they performed. *I guess that makes sense with William teaching them.*

Chelci cheered under her breath as they moved. Veron glanced to see a broad grin covering her face. *I can picture her doing something like this.* A shout of approval from the crowd turned his attention back to the presentation.

The lines broke and two people took turns facing off in brief but intense displays of swordsmanship. Two young men clanged their weapons multiple times in a quick exchange, then spun to trade sides. A sharp advance from the shorter fighter left the other with a sword against his neck. The crowd clapped as the fighters bowed, and two more immediately took their place. The next pairing had a similar display, but this group had a young man versus a young woman.

"Get him, Emily," Chelci muttered.

Emily and the young man exchanged furious blows. The staged fight was clearly choreographed, but Veron cheered for the girl, too. After knocking her sword away, the young man aimed an exaggerated swing at her feet. The crowd roared as Emily leaped backward, flipping upside down to spring off her hands and land on her feet a safe distance away. She scooped up her discarded blade, and the two fighters froze and bowed after clashing their blades once more.

"I bet you never learned that one, huh?" Veron said, leaning into Chelci as the crowd clapped. She laughed and hit him playfully on the arm.

The groups of staged fights continued as the village cheered on the young aspiring guards. When the pairings were complete, Russell, Aleks, and William stepped up and bowed to the crowd, generating a wild applause. "Thank you for joining us for this year's premweek of suether celebration!" Aleks shouted. "Now, enjoy the feast!"

Chatter erupted as most of the people surged toward the abundant display of food. "That was incredible," Veron said. "I can see why you enjoyed it."

"My nerves made me a wreck my first year," Chelci said. "I had to pair off against this young man who weighed twice as much as I did—and he didn't like me."

"How'd it go?" Veron asked.

"It was fine. I wasn't very good at that point, and I worried he would try to make me look like a fool. I did forget one of the parry moves we'd planned, but thankfully he stopped his own blade before it took my head off."

Finley bounced on the balls of his feet. "Maybe you all just want to talk, but I'm gonna go eat."

"I'm with you," Morgan said, following him toward the nearest table.

Veron chuckled as he and Chelci brought up the rear.

"Wow, this is good!" Morgan said as he took a bite of venison. He, Chelci, Veron, and Finley sat on a low stone wall while plates loaded with assorted food sat in their laps. The sun had ducked behind the trees, and freshly lit lanterns around the village center gave the area a warm, festive glow. On the far side of the green, the band played a lively tune. A few couples even danced through the grass.

"Did anyone try my mother's roasted tarrols yet?" Finley asked.

Morgan looked back at the table. "No, which were they?"

Finley pointed. "The flat dish at the end. I don't know how she gets them so good."

"I'll have to try some."

"I think I'm liking Nasco more and more," Veron said.

"You realize we don't have parties every day, right?" Chelci said with a quick laugh.

"I know, but . . . there's something about it here."

Morgan waved a hand in his direction. "I know what it is." He swallowed then counted out on his fingers as he spoke. "No one wants to ruin you. No one wants to steal your market. And no one wants to kill you."

Veron and Chelci burst into laughter. After a moment, a pang of worry filled Veron. *Someone out there does want to kill me.*

"Does the village guard not attend?" Morgan asked looking around. "Seems like the whole village is here, but I haven't seen many guards."

"Yeah, about half are on duty." Chelci pointed to the darkening sky. "New moon tonight. They wanted to make sure we're all safe."

Veron shuddered, thinking what it would look like for a valcor to tear through the middle of the village green.

A man in his late twenties paused while walking by. "Morgan, hi! You enjoying our party?"

"Hey, Philip! It's good to see you again." Morgan glanced around and nodded his head. "This is great. It sure beats anything I experienced in Karad."

"Did you try the bread yet?"

"Yes!" Morgan motioned to his plate, but stopped, glancing at an empty section. "Well, it's gone now. But it was incredible!"

"What was it?" Chelci asked.

"I took my honey and raspberry bread and added walnuts and a hint of coriander," Philip said, smiling with his shoulders back.

"Ooh, I'll have to try some of that," Finley said.

"Sorry, but I think I'll have to pass." Veron set his plate aside as he rested his hand on his stomach. "I'm stuffed."

"You better hurry, Finley," Philip said, glancing at the table as he walked away. "Looks like it's almost gone."

"Hey, Veron," Chelci said just to him. An odd grin crossed her face before she nodded her head toward the green. "You want to?"

Veron's blood drained from his face when he looked at the dancers twirling on the grass. "Want to what?" he asked, hoping she'd give an unexpected answer.

She beamed as she set her empty plate aside, stood, and grabbed his hand. "Come on. Let's dance."

Not wanting to release her hand, he found himself on his feet as she pulled him closer to the music. "But . . . I'm so full." Veron glanced back to Morgan with wide eyes, hoping for help, but his friend only grinned and raised his thumb in approval.

His hands began to sweat as she led him past the tables of food into the grass. He resisted halfheartedly, her resolve overpowering his hesitation. The music grew louder as they approached the band. Chelci dodged past twirling couples, refusing to release him until they entered the middle of the action. When she let go of his hand and turned to him, Veron's instinct to run abandoned him. Her eyes trapped him. The mischievous grin she held moments earlier had turned into a soft, welcoming gaze of joy. She rested a hand against his hip and grasped the other, intertwining their fingers.

His body was rigid and shoulders tight. Slowly, he settled his hand on her hip and squeezed lightly with his other. They intimately connected as he touched her hand and gazed into her eyes. Veron worried his heart would beat out of his chest. Soon, the thumping seemed to match the beat of the drum, and Chelci bounced to the rhythm—slowly at first then more pronounced as her smile grew broader. His shoulders and legs loosened, the hard line of his mouth cracking. With a squeeze of her hand, she moved first, stepping in time to the music.

The surrounding couples faded into blackness, and Veron saw nothing other than Chelci. They bounced and grinned, turning with the melody, yet he couldn't make out the beat. Flickering light from the lanterns danced across her hair. Her blue dress rippled and whirled in time to the music. Strands of curly hair freed themselves and dangled across her face.

Time seemed to freeze. His hesitation eroded the longer they danced until his inhibitions faded completely. He grasped both her hands. They both laughed as they twirled in a circle, spinning faster and faster. The world behind her blurred as they spun. Laughter sounded distant, as if it weren't real, but nothing in his life felt more real than that moment. The smell of trampled grass and sweat filled the air. His hands were slick, but he held on, unwilling to let her get away.

The music crescendoed then stopped suddenly, and the crowd exploded with applause. Veron stumbled, breathing heavily. He glanced around to reorient himself, surprised at the number of other dancers around them. Above them, the faint outline of a new moon left the sky dark and filled with stars. When he turned back to Chelci, she squeezed his hand again. Her soft smile mirrored what he felt on his own face. Before they released hands, a lute kicked off a new song.

Couples around them stepped in closer to each other and swayed to the gentle melody.

Chelci smiled at him. Her arms rested gently over his shoulders, wrapping around the back of his neck and pulling him closer. Their bodies touched and Veron swallowed to wet his dry throat. Without voicing his nervousness, he rested his hands on her hips, and the two swayed in time to the music, staring into each other's eyes.

"There's nowhere in the world I'd rather be right now," Veron said, his voice cracking.

A deep crease formed in her cheeks as she laughed. "Me neither, Veron."

His hands felt clammy. With his heart racing, he played the words he would say over in his head. He tripped on his own feet, distracted by his thoughts.

"Chelci," he said. Her soft smile and the sparkle in her eyes confirmed he was making the right decision. "I have something I want to ask you."

Her smile broadened. "Yes?"

"I—um . . ." His carefully planned words fled from his mind. He struggled to think of the right ones to replace them. "I . . . and you—I was thinking that . . ."

Chelci tilted her head, still smiling and listening intently.

Before he muddled out the next words, the look on Chelci's face turned. Her eyebrows furrowed, and her arms grew stiff.

"What I'm trying to say is . . . I—" Faint shouting tore through the night. The music paused, and a murmur grew in the crowd. Veron looked up toward the moonless sky. A rumbling sound grew until the deep peal of the village bell filled the air. Veron spun, and his heart dropped.

A contingent of Norshewan soldiers marched through the dirt street past the old wooden buildings leading to the village center.

Their torches' light gleamed off their shiny armor that chinked as they marched forward.

Veron tensed, and the crowd grew louder. People sitting on the outskirts came in toward the green.

"Veron," Chelci said in a wavering voice. He looked at her while feeling her hand tremble. Her eyes were open wide, and a nearly imperceptible nod turned him back around.

Two men rode on large black horses. Decked out in armor and wearing a red-and-black uniform, the man on the right sneered as he looked out at the crowd. The tangled brown hair and pockmarks on his face were unfamiliar, but when Veron looked at the other horse, he gasped. With short, blond hair and a proud look on his face, Brixton Fiero scanned the crowd. He wore a red-and-black badge on his shoulder, and a sword dangled at his hip.

14

Attack

Veron ducked as Brixton swiveled in his direction. His pulse pounded. When he raised his head, he sighed, relieved that he hadn't been noticed. "We've gotta hide," he whispered to Chelci before turning away from the soldiers and pulling her behind.

The two ran in a crouch between the gawking villagers standing on the grass. When they arrived at the far side of the green, Veron slunk along the buildings, trying to avoid the lanterns' revealing light. After rounding the corner, he and Chelci were startled at the sight of Morgan crouched in the darkness where they headed.

"Morgan! You scared me!" Veron said. He and Chelci pressed in to share the hiding place.

"How did he find us?" Chelci whispered.

"I have no idea," Veron replied.

"Your father was the only one who knew where we went, right?" Morgan said. "Could they have forced him to talk?"

Chelci shook her head. "I didn't tell him where we were going. Plus, even if he guessed, he doesn't know where this village is."

"I wish I had my sword," Veron muttered, glancing back to William's house just down the path.

On the far side of the green, Brixton held up his hands, and the people quieted. "Villagers of Nasco," he bellowed. "We come on behalf of King Edmund Bale, ruler of Terrenor." Several audible cries sounded from the crowd. "In case you aren't aware, Tarphan and Feldor have pledged fealty to Norshewa, and soon, Rynor will join them. As inhabitants of this land, you are now subject to Bale's rule."

Grumbling grew in the green. "We are subject to no one!" a voice yelled from the crowd. More indecipherable shouts joined in.

Brixton raised a hand again. "Bale does not intend to terrorize you. He desires a fair, peaceful, united Terrenor—one where all its inhabitants thrive."

In the front of the crowd, the elder, Peter, stepped forward. "What is it you want?"

"Who are you?" the pockmarked soldier on the horse asked.

"Peter Bebbington. I'm an elder in this village."

"Peter," Brixton said, projecting so all could hear. "I am Brixton Fiero, Commercial Envoy of Terrenor. This is Captain Forest Gannon, leader of the third battalion of the United Norshewan Army, and the fifty soldiers you see before you are under his command."

"We have lived in peace for many years, independent from Feldor or any rulers," Peter said. "We do not require protection and need no external governance. I ask again . . . What do you want?"

Brixton sat up straighter and rested both hands on his saddle's pommel. He spoke, directing his words to the entire crowd. "As part of unifying the land, bringing peace and stability, and providing the needed resources to the areas of Terrenor that need it, Bale has two requirements for all people in his kingdom." His voice turned quieter as he leaned toward Peter. "How many people live here?"

"Five hundred twenty," he replied in a clear voice.

"Is that exact? We will take a count."

"It is."

Brixton sniffed as he sat up straight again and looked at the crowd. "To fund the stabilization effort, Bale requires five tid per head each season from all citizens."

Angry voices roared in response. The soldiers in front of Brixton drew their swords and stood at alert.

"The amount is reasonable." Brixton raised both hands, but the murmurs did not subside. "For the size of your village, that amounts to twenty-six sol that we will collect today. It will cover your payment owed for suether."

"We don't have money like that here!" another elder shouted. "We barter, trade, and give to each other in the village."

"Then I suggest you scrounge up what you can and find something of worth to make up the rest," Captain Gannon said, leering at a woman with bright red hair clutching a man's arm at the front of the crowd.

"It sounds like they don't know you're here," Morgan whispered to Veron.

Chelci nodded. "We all need to stay hidden."

"Additionally, Bale requires workers," Brixton said. "Given the size of your village, we need thirty people willing to help bring the united Terrenor to its glorious destiny."

"Workers?" Peter said. "For what?"

"The volunteers should have strong backs and be able to do physical labor."

"Where will they go?"

Brixton adjusted in his seat and glanced at Gannon. "They will go wherever Bale decides they are needed."

"We're not going anywhere with you!" a man shouted from the crowd.

Veron's eyes drew to the side, where William hobbled with his staff. He met Russell just below the Academy patio, and after they spoke together, Russell popped his head up to scan the crowd. He gestured with a beckoning hand somewhere Veron couldn't see. William turned and left him, moving into the shadows.

"I think this is about to get ugly," Veron said. "I need to get my sword. Wait here."

Veron scurried down the path to William's house. Inside, he snatched Farrathan from where it leaned against the wall and slung the sheath over his shoulders. Before he barreled out the door, William popped out of the night, entering from the porch.

"William!" he gasped, bringing his hand to his chest.

"Sorry," his father said as he crossed the room to snatch his own sword. "Veron, wait."

Veron paused with his hand on the doorframe and looked back.

"This isn't your fight. Wait here out of the way. Don't risk your life getting involved."

"That guy out there, Brixton," Veron said, pointing to the village center. "He's the one who ruined my life."

William's eyes grew wide.

"He was my friend until he framed me for murder and sold me as a slave. He stole everything I had, then he told Bale where I was to have me killed."

"You can't let him see you then."

"This is as much my home as anywhere else," Veron said, looking his father in the eyes. "If I don't stand up to protect this, then what do I stand up for?"

William nodded after a pause. "All right but keep from being seen. And don't use the origine except as a last resort. We can't let them know."

Veron breathed in deeply. "Understood." Veron and William descended the steps and crept through the darkness back to the edge of the building where Morgan waited. "Where'd Chelci go?"

"I don't know," Morgan whispered. "She ran off after you did. What are you gonna do?"

"Russell is gathering the guard," William said. "I imagine there's about to be a fight."

Veron peered across the green. Gannon had dismounted and drawn his sword. He paced in front of Peter and the other two elders while Brixton remained in the saddle. "Resisting him is futile!" Brixton shouted with a tinge of desperation. "Bale will not make exceptions. This will not end well if you refuse."

The elders conferred while the surrounding villagers watched and waited. After a solemn look at the crowd, Peter turned back to the soldiers. "We mean no disrespect to Bale—"

"King Bale!" Captain Gannon shouted.

"Sorry," Peter said, standing tall with his chin extended. ". . . to your king, Bale." He shook his head. "But we can't agree to this."

A line of men with metal helmets and black uniforms streamed through the crowd. Close to thirty members of the village guard formed a line while many villagers backed away and began leaving the area. The guardsmen drew their swords, but the opposing soldiers outnumbered them nearly two to one.

"Stay here," William whispered as he left the shadow. "Only come out if it's absolutely necessary." He leaned on his staff as he walked to fall in line with the other guardsmen.

Brixton's chest rose and fell rapidly after the elder's refusal. Gannon drew next to him, and Brixton leaned over, speaking too quietly for Veron to hear. Veron's muscles coiled, ready to spring into action as tension filled the air. He leaned farther around the corner, but Morgan stopped him with a hand on his shoulder.

"Don't let him see you, Veron," Morgan whispered.

When Brixton straightened, Gannon returned to the line of guardsmen and stood in front of Peter. He narrowed his eyes as he stared at the village elder. "As we said, it will not end well," Gannon said before he thrust his sword into Peter's chest.

Chaos erupted. The soldiers jumped into action, and the guardsmen advanced to defend the rest of the villagers. People ran in every direction. Tables of food fell over. Women and children screamed. Bodies tripped over each other in a mad dash to flee the area.

"Scour the village!" Gannon shouted at the soldiers. "Take anything you find of value!" A dozen of the soldiers peeled off from the rest of the group, but Brixton stayed in the center.

Veron burned with anger, his father's entreaty to stay put losing its effect. "I'm going after them," he told Morgan before running across the path out of Brixton's sight.

Once away from the village center, the darkness grew. He hurried around houses to intercept the soldiers. A blur of torches crossed the path ahead of him as two men ran by. Veron pulled his sword from over his shoulder and followed. He leaned around the edge of the next house in time to observe a soldier kicking down the front door.

Veron tightened his grip on his sword and followed inside. The torch's glow arose from a smaller room to the left where a host of crashing and breaking sounds emanated. "There we go," a voice said.

Veron entered the room. The soldier stood over a chest, holding a small chunk of raw silver. He turned at Veron's footsteps, and his eyes grew as Veron directed an origine-powered kick into his chest. The soldier's ribs cracked as he crashed into the wall, dropping the silver and his torch. Veron scooped up the torch then dragged the unconscious soldier outside. When clear of the house, Veron snuffed the torch onto the ground and flung the soldier's body down the hill into the woods where his limp form collided with a tree trunk.

Veron heard multiple screams and turned back to the village. A loud crash and the clanking of swords sounded from the village green area. In front of him, a woman carrying two young boys ran past while, on the next street over, a house roared, engulfed in flames.

Two homes over, another soldier emerged from a house carrying an armload of brass fixtures while a large woman inside the house hit him on the back. Appearing fed up with the annoyance, he turned to the woman. She backed off until the soldier hit her in the head with a candlestick and threw her to the floor of the house. Veron paled when the man took his torch and hung it under the eaves along the house, which caught and began to spread.

While the soldier moved on, Veron ran to the burning home. Flames licked the walls and roof, spreading across the wooden structure. He ducked as he entered, running in a crouch to where the lady lay on the floor clutching her head.

"I've got you," Veron said as he scooped her up. He struggled to his feet under the extra weight, but the origine helped. He nearly stumbled as he exited through the open doorway, ducking his face to protect from the flames. She groaned as he set her on the ground at a safe distance. "Are you all right?" he asked.

Blood poured from a gash over her left eye. "I don't know. My head hurts."

Veron inspected the wound. "Press against it with your hand. It'll help ease the bleeding."

A crash sounded behind him, followed by a scream as glass from another house exploded outward. Leaving the woman, Veron ran toward the scream. When he entered the house, a massive soldier with a thick neck stood in the back corner, his sword dancing back and forth between a cornered woman and her son. "Which of you wants it first?" the soldier taunted, holding his torch in the other hand.

Veron's blood boiled as he stepped closer. The tingle grew in his gut as he lifted his sword to attack, but before he could move, a searing pain tore through his body. Veron yelled as he arched his back and stumbled away from the unseen weapon. He spun, losing his balance against a stool and falling, wedging himself between the wall and a chair. His sword clattered to the floor. A second soldier approached from the opposite corner behind the door and bore down on him. Veron's blood stained the man's sword as it approached his chest for a second attack.

Veron attempted to summon his energy to grab his fallen weapon and move out of the way, but there was nowhere to go. He fumbled to find his weapon's hilt, but it was out of reach. He tried to sit up, but the screaming pain in his back hindered his focus. His hold on the origine was weak, and his body fought to direct any available energy to healing his wound. He pulled harder, which only eased his back pain faster. *I need to move!* The soldier's sword continued forward. Fear rushed through him.

He watched helplessly, bracing himself for the worst, until another yell filled the room. Before he could identify the source, the soldier shuddered and stopped moving. His eyes lost focus as his sword drooped. The soldier's body went rigid then fell forward. Veron tried to get out of the way, but there was nowhere to move. In a moment, the heavy, armor-laden body collapsed on top of him. He moved the lifeless head out of his way. A knife stuck out of the back of the soldier's neck. Past the knife, wearing her light-blue dress, Chelci stood in a crouch, brandishing a sword pointed at the remaining soldier.

"Chelci!" Veron cried with relief.

"Leave them alone!" Chelci shouted at the man.

The soldier with the thick neck smirked as he turned to her. "Or what?" he asked, stepping toward her with his sword raised.

"Or you'll find my sword in your neck."

His eyes narrowed. Chelci didn't flinch as the beast of a man lunged at her with his blade. There wasn't much space inside the cramped room, but she dodged to the side while parrying his sword away. As the lumbering soldier stumbled with his weapon, she spun and drove the tip of her light blade into his unprotected thigh.

The soldier fell to one knee and uttered a furious yell. Using both hands, he raged as he swung his sword at her midsection. Chelci jumped back, the tip of the blade just missing her stomach. After the miss, she stepped forward, knocking his empty weapon away. Then she turned sideways and rounded her hips, delivering a swift kick to his face.

The metal helmet flew off the man's head and knocked into the wall. Something small and hard pinged against Veron's face before it bounced on the floor—a small, yellowish tooth. The soldier, without his helmet and less a tooth, crashed to the floor, dropping his sword. Holding his head with one hand, he used the other to lift himself back to his feet as he leveled his venomous gaze at Chelci. He growled as he charged with his head lowered. Without flinching, she held her sword straight. The soldier, decked in armor across most of his body, was not protected around his neck. The blade slid into the exposed skin, stopping the man in his tracks. His eyes rolled in his head, and he slumped to the floor.

Chelci panted as she pulled her sword free, blood pouring onto the wooden floorboards. She nudged the body with her foot, but the lifeless form did not respond.

"Thank you, Elise," the woman said, holding her son close. "I don't know what we would have done without you."

Veron raised a weak hand from behind the corpse pinning him to the ground. "Um . . . Can I get some help?"

Chelci sheathed her sword and helped pull the body off him, allowing Veron to sit up. "What happened? Is the origine gone?"

As Veron tried to stand, his legs wobbled. "Whoa!" He sank to a knee, leaning against the chair next to him. Turning his head didn't allow him to see the wound, but he felt for it with his hand.

"Veron!" Chelci yelled, running to him and lifting his shirt.

"How is it?"

Chelci's hand touched his back, then she chuckled. "Wow, I wished I had that ability. This *just* happened?"

"Yeah, the neck guy stabbed me before you got him. I tried to use the origine to move out of the way, but all the effort went into healing my wound. Now I'm exhausted."

"Well, the wound looks good. Can you walk?" she asked.

Veron frowned. He stood, keeping a hand on the chair. The room spun, but his legs held. "I don't think I can. I may need some help."

She came alongside him, placing one of his arms over her shoulder with the other wrapped around. "We need to get you somewhere safe." She turned to the woman and her son. "You two stay out of sight."

When they exited the house, three nearby homes blazed. Villagers ran through the street, shouting and crying. A Norshewan soldier emerged from behind a house with an armload of trinkets before he struck down a woman and hustled down another path.

"They killed the elder guy," Veron said as they hobbled along the path.

"Peter? Yeah, I saw. They'll take whatever they can and burn the entire village if we don't stop them."

"I don't think I can fight, Chelci."

She glanced at him while they continued. "How long does it take to be ready?"

Veron shook his head. "I'm not sure. It's been a while since I've felt this depleted. Five, maybe ten minutes?"

Two soldiers rounded a corner just ahead. One held a torch, and both carried swords. The soldier with the torch nodded toward

Veron. "Get him," the soldier said.

When the one without the torch pulled metal shackles from his belt, Veron's eyes grew. *No, not again!*

Chelci pressed against Veron's chest. "I've got this," she whispered. She raised her sword as she stepped in front of him.

15

Defending the Village

"Kill her," the man with the torch said.

"Chelci, no," Veron mumbled as he reached out to steady himself against the house, his vision spinning. To keep from falling, he allowed his body to slump to the ground. He pressed his eyelids together, trying to quell the dizziness. He ached to defend her instead of leaning against the wall, unable to stand on his own. When he opened his eyes, he found Chelci bending over, picking a torch up off the ground. *Where did they go?* Flickering in the light of the flame, the bodies of two unmoving soldiers lay in the street. She snuffed the torch in the dirt.

"Are you all right?" he asked with a proud smile.

Chelci sheathed her sword as she crouched before him. "Yeah, I'm fine." She offered a hand and helped Veron back to his feet. Before they moved, her eyes flitted above them. "Can you climb?"

Veron looked up. Rough logs extended from the wall of the house. Above them, the roof was pitch black. *No one could stumble into us up there.* He rested a hand on a log and brought a foot to another. "If you help."

Veron pulled with both arms and stepped. Chelci's hands supported his back, helping him ignore his weakness. After a bit of exhaustive pushing, he could swing his body onto the roof. A moment later, she joined him.

"Come on," she said, helping him move in a crouch to the highest point.

Peeking over the ridge revealed Nasco's true chaos. Village guards clashed with Norshewan soldiers in the town center. Dozens of bodies of villagers, guards, and soldiers littered the area with dark pools of blood reflecting the flickering lanterns. Looking over the rest of the village revealed torches moving along the streets. Soldiers moved from house to house, searching for anything of value. People screamed, dogs barked, and children cried. A group of six young men walked down a street with their heads lowered, their legs shackled together in a line with a Norshewan soldier at the front and back.

"We need to do something," Veron said.

"Yes, but what?" Chelci's grip on Veron's leg grew tight before she pointed. "There he is."

Brixton had dismounted. He held his sword at the ready but stood behind several other soldiers.

"Russell! Look out!" a familiar voice called below them.

Veron followed the sound to find his father, running across the green toward a skirmish just below the house they sat atop. His run's easy lope proved he relied heavily on the origine.

Russell and another guardsman he didn't recognize fought against five soldiers, but Chelci's host had fallen to the ground, holding his side where a red stain grew. While the Norshewans moved in for the kill, William arrived with a yell, blocking a sword arcing toward Russell's head. Veron's jaw dropped as he watched his father move.

With his artificial leg hidden underneath his pants, the casual observer wouldn't notice anything special—only that William seemed to know where to move and how to strike. Facing three enemies at once, he blocked or dodged every swing of the sword. The way he moved reminded Veron of water flowing around rocks in a stream. He was untouchable. When his foes had fallen, he turned to the other two, dispatching them in short order.

Remaining invisible, Veron and Chelci crept down the roof's backside, nearing the edge and listening.

"How bad is it?" William asked below, extending a hand to his fellow guardsman.

Russell cringed as he allowed himself to be pulled up. "It could be worse. How's the rest of the village?"

William leaned over with his hands on his knees. His chest heaved. "It's not good. Have you seen Veron or Chelci?"

Veron opened his mouth to speak until Brixton and the pockmarked captain approached with ten more soldiers. Chelci grabbed his leg then made eye contact as she put her finger to her lips.

"There's fight in these three!" the captain taunted, drawing the looks of the guardsmen below. He nodded to Brixton. "Let's bring them with us."

William bared his sword and stood solidly in dragon stance. He appeared strong, but his weapon's slight tremble and his deep breaths revealed his true state. When the Norshewans advanced, he sprang into action along with Russell and the other guardsman.

The third village guard fell from a blade through his chest. Chelci's grip on Veron's leg tightened as the man cried out. Russell fared somewhat better, favoring his good side while blood dripped from his shirt. Despite his injury, he held his own, keeping his attacker engaged. The other eight fighters seemed to realize William was the threat of the group, and all of them turned their attention to him.

The soldiers dropped from William's dancing blade. Four bodies soon piled onto the dirt. *I hope his origine holds out.* No sooner had the thought crossed Veron's mind than his father appeared to slump.

His body moved slower, and his feet stumbled. *Oh no!* Veron's eyes darted around, looking for something he could do, but his body was too weak.

While William faltered, soldiers again wounded Russell on the opposite side of the first. He reeled backward and fell to the dirt.

Below Veron, the soldiers surrounded William, who slumped on his knees. Veron clenched his jaw as a man took metal shackles and snapped them around each of his father's legs. "He won't be able to escape," Veron whispered.

Chelci's hand remained on his leg, but it shook. A low growl seemed to emanate from her. "What can we—" Veron's words cut off as Chelci released his leg and hopped over the edge. "Chelci, no!"

She landed on top of a soldier's neck, collapsing him in an awkward angle and knocking over the man next to him. She scrambled to her feet and drew her sword, brandishing it with ferocity.

Veron's lunge to grab her tipped his balance farther than he intended. His stomach jumped as he fell to the ground after her. He tried to stand like Chelci, but his legs collapsed beneath him.

"What are you doing?" Chelci asked, continuing to face the soldiers who had backed off.

"I fell after you. What are *you* doing?" Veron finally made it to his feet and tried to bring his sword into horn position, but the ground tilted and he had to flail his limbs to remain upright.

"You're not ready to fight!" she yelled.

Veron froze as his vision cleared. While Chelci was right, the one standing before him took precedence.

"Norshewans, to me!" Brixton shouted into the night. The whites in his eyes made a full circle as he stared at Veron. He held his shaking sword out, his arm straining even though he was well out of attacking range.

"Brixton, leave this village," Chelci said in a low, steady voice. "You know Veron's capabilities. It does no good for you and all your men to die."

"Soldiers! Come here!" Brixton's voice, laced with fear, cracked and shook.

Metal clanked as soldiers jogged toward them. Veron reached for William's shoulders and tried to help him up.

"I . . . I can't," William said. Veron staggered after a feeble pull, almost falling again himself.

"They're weak!" Captain Gannon shouted. "Attack them!"

"No!" Chelci growled. She stood in a crouch between Veron and the soldiers while their ranks multiplied. Swinging her sword brought laughter to the crowd, but it held the soldiers off momentarily.

Feet crunched in the dirt behind Veron. He tried to turn but couldn't get his body to respond. Suddenly, Finley and Aleks exploded into view, one on each side of Chelci.

"Back off!" Aleks shouted, brandishing a sword with flickers of a torch in his eyes. The three young adults stared down the Norshewan soldiers. Russell groaned as he struggled to his feet, wincing and holding his side. He stood behind Aleks, leaning against the house but holding his sword up.

"Morgan!" Chelci called over her shoulder, nodding her head toward Veron. "Get them out of here!"

Veron looked toward the left. Morgan ran out of the shadow.

"Are you all right?" Morgan asked.

Veron nodded. "We're just out of energy—" He turned back to Chelci. "—but I'm not leaving her." He attempted to lift his blade again, but the motion sent him stumbling into Morgan.

The grocer kept him upright while pulling William to his feet as well. He draped an arm around father and son and drew them away. Veron resisted, but Morgan won out.

The Norshewan soldiers charged with a roar. Chelci, Aleks, and Finley stepped in, meeting their attackers with a fierce intensity and clashing of steel.

With Morgan's arm around his back, Veron could move. They shuffled as quickly as possible down the street toward the darkness at the edge of the village. When the path ended, they turned right, away from the burning houses and screams.

"Over here," Morgan said, leading them behind a porch, where a short wall protected them from sight. Veron collapsed hard to the dirt along with William. "Did you use up all of that . . . thing you have?"

Veron took a deep breath. "The origine? Yeah. They stabbed me, and I used it to heal. I'm feeling slightly better though."

"Mine drains quicker because of the leg," William said, breathing quickly. "And now I have these shackles."

Veron looked at his father's restraints. He fiddled with the clasp but couldn't remove them without help.

"I think we need to stay out of sight for a bit," Morgan said.

"No!" Chelci's voice sounded behind them, closer than Veron expected. "Come back here and fight me, you cowards!"

Veron tensed at the sound of dozens of suits of armor close by on the other side of the wall. "She needs me," Veron muttered as he tried to stand. Morgan pressed an arm against him, keeping him down.

"You half, go that way. The rest, come with me," the captain called out.

William grabbed Veron's arm, his ragged breath sounding like an alarm in the darkness. In a moment, several pairs of legs marched past their makeshift hiding place. Although the light was dim, the soldiers' outlines were visible.

Move on! Come on, keep going!

A soldier turned and squinted in their direction. He stopped moving. Veron was sure his beating heart would give them away. The soldier's head extended forward as he stepped cautiously. He jumped back. "Here!"

The rest of the men converged on their location. Morgan jumped to his feet, but Veron and William took much longer to follow. As Veron straightened, he looked up to see the familiar short hair of his old friend standing a safe distance away, staring. Around him, the captain and seven other soldiers trapped them in their hiding place. There was nowhere to run.

"He's the one?" Gannon asked.

Brixton nodded after a long moment. "What are you doing here?" he asked Veron loudly.

"Does it matter?" Veron replied.

"Hiding from Bale?"

Veron clenched his jaw and exhaled through his nose. "Are you sure he's not hiding from me?"

"Why did you need Morgan to help you?" Brixton asked. "Does it really come and go? How does it work?"

"You don't deserve to know," Veron sneered.

"Enough of this! We have more work to do!" Captain Gannon looked at Brixton. "Are you going to kill them or should I?"

Morgan inhaled quickly, then took a step back, pressing against Veron's shoulder.

Brixton didn't reply for a long moment. Finally, his gaze drifted to the ground, and he extended a hand toward the captives, inviting Gannon to do what he wished.

Veron tested his energy reserve to see if he'd recovered enough, but a dizzy spell washed over him from the effort. He grabbed Morgan's shoulder to steady himself. "Don't do this, Brixton," Veron whispered.

Brixton's eyes flicked to his, but he turned away almost immediately. The captain walked forward, his boots crunching in the dirt.

He lifted his sword, pointing it at Veron's chest.

Sweat dripped down Veron's forehead. He didn't have the strength to fight back. "It's me Bale wants. Let them go, and you can have me."

Gannon sneered and continued forward. Veron pulled his sword from over his shoulder, but the movement made him wobble. He couldn't even hold the weapon straight.

What is that? Veron thought as a breeze picked up. A familiar odor reached him that made his insides turn, the decaying stench wrinkling his nose.

Gannon stopped and lifted his nose before turning back to his men with a pinched forehead. "What's that smell?"

Veron looked across the path to the woods just down the hill. The leaves rustled in the wind, covering the distant roar of flames and continued screams. He looked at the sky. Faint stars dotted the expanse and the new moon, barely identifiable by a sliver of a crescent shape, hung over the trees.

"The moon," William said.

"What's that?" Gannon asked.

Veron's stomach turned. *I remember that smell.*

William turned to the captain. "The moon isn't around to scare it off. We all need to get somewhere where there's light."

The captain chuckled. "Scare it off? What are you afraid—"

A deafening roar cut him off as a massive beast lunged into the crowd of soldiers, shaking the ground with its steps. Veron gasped. Norshewan soldiers flew in the air, batted by the animal like insects. The crowd of people yelled as they scrambled to flee. Veron still had nowhere to go, blocked by the enormous body.

Rippling muscles along the valcor's flank undulated as it moved. Veron stared at the long fangs and sharp spines running along its neck. A guttural growl seemed to shake his bones. The putrid smell overwhelmed him as it circled.

Gannon's sword hung limply as he stared at the monster with wide eyes. "Wh—What is—"

The valcor silenced him by grabbing his shoulder with one of its front paws and swiping across his chest with a back leg. The shriek of metal filled the air as the valcor's massive claw ripped through the soldier's breastplate, disemboweling the captain in one swipe. Gannon collapsed to the ground, shrieking and spasming.

Norshewan soldiers emerged out of the darkness, shouting and surrounding the monster. Their swords bounced off the thick skin one at a time while the valcor roared in defiance and lunged back. Bodies flung through the air with severed limbs. When the men tried to run, the beast grabbed their legs with its jaw, filling the night with horrendous screams.

Staying back from the fight, Brixton looked at Veron. His eyes were enormous as he seemed to waver with indecision. Finally, his body shifted, and he ran away from the valcor toward the village center, leaving his dying soldiers behind.

"We need to get out of here," Morgan muttered.

Veron snapped to attention as Morgan's arm wrapped around his back. He and William both stumbled two steps before the valcor turned its attention to their movement. A guttural growl rumbled at them, pressing their bodies into the wall as the beast stepped toward them. There were no more Norshewan soldiers to distract it. Its eyes bore a hole through Veron. The odor was oppressive as he struggled to keep his feet under him. Veron held his sword out, but it wobbled and took all of his strength.

"Back off, you!" Chelci yelled as she darted between the huddled bunch and the valcor. She brandished her sword in one hand and a flaming torch in the other.

The beast reared up on its hind legs and unleashed a deafening sound before it crashed back to the ground. Chelci waved the torch as she stepped closer. The animal turned its neck from side to side, trying to escape the harsh light. After backing up several paces, the valcor stopped. It looked at Chelci and lowered its head. Its eyes squinted. Its leg muscles quivered as if prepared to pounce. A guttural growl shook Veron's chest, but Chelci held her ground.

"Back to the woods!" she shouted.

The valcor leaned in and roared, blowing Chelci's hair behind her. The stench from the animal's breath made Veron gag. Just before the deafening sound ended, the blast of air snuffed out her torch.

The growling rumble returned. A grin seemed to pull at the beast's mouth, its white fangs shining in the dim light. The ground shook as it stepped forward.

"Chelci, leave!" Veron called, his weak voice lost against the deep reverberation coming from the monster. She tossed the extinguished torch to the side and held her weapon with both hands. Hard lines ran down her toned arms.

Veron's heart thumped wildly. His sword wobbled as he tried to hold it in front of him. He wanted to dash in front of her but didn't have the strength.

With a snap of its jaws, the beast lunged. Chelci rolled to the side, barely dodging its razor teeth. As she popped up, she swung at its leg. She grunted from the exertion, but her sword bounced harmlessly away.

Following her with a snarl, the animal swiped with a front paw. She cried out, her body flying against the side of a house, cracking the wooden sideboards.

"Chelci!" Veron stumbled toward her, but the animal was not deterred.

Chelci struggled to her feet, standing in time for the monster to arrive, cornering her against the wall with nowhere to go. It reared on its hind legs and swiped with a back claw. Her sword twisted, knocking the long talons back. It roared then attempted with the other leg. Chelci blocked it again. The spines on the animal's back shuddered. It opened its mouth and lunged for her head.

Veron's heart dropped. He struggled forward but was too late and too far away. Unexpectedly, a shriek filled the air, and the animal spasmed. Falling away from Chelci, it collapsed backward onto the ground. *What in the world?* Veron's eyes grew wider when he saw it. Chelci's sword stuck through its mouth as the beast frantically pawed at its face.

"Veron!" Chelci shouted. "Here!"

She ran toward the fallen animal but looked at Veron with her arms outstretched. He glanced at his weapon and understood. With a surge of effort, he tossed his blade to her. It spun once, and she caught it by the hilt. Without missing a stride, Chelci lifted it with both hands. She brought the sword over her head and heaved down in a massive stroke. The unearthly shrieks ended suddenly. Blood spurted into the air as the weapon cleaved through its neck, the head falling to the ground with a thud.

Chelci wrenched the sword out of the earth and pulled hers from the lifeless head. She turned back to their group, and Veron released his held breath.

"Are you all right?" Chelci asked.

"Me?" His mouth fell. "What about you? That was amazing. Are you . . . ?"

She glanced down at her body. "I'm fine. It didn't get me."

Veron looked at the others. "I think we're all right. I can move some."

"Me, too," William added.

Even without the light of the torch, a ghastly scene lay before them. Blood and corpses littered the grass. The beast itself lay headless, silent with a slight twitch in one of its back legs.

"Are there any soldiers left?" Morgan asked.

"I need to find out," Chelci said. She passed Veron back his sword. "You all stay here."

His legs more stable, Veron followed as Chelci jogged off.

"What are you doing?" she asked when he caught up to her at the edge of the village center.

Veron didn't answer as he sidled next to her. A hesitant grin grew on his face as he looked ahead. The village guardsmen had received new life. Organized into groups, they pushed back the soldiers. Several invaders fell, and some turned and ran. Shouts of celebration called out. Thundering hooves drew Veron's attention to his left. Brixton galloped by on his horse, fleeing the village and locking eyes with Veron as he passed. The look on his face held guilt, disappointment, and terror all at once. His horse paused at the lip of the rise at the end of the path then descended into the darkness out of Nasco.

Relief dissipated as Veron scanned the village. Flames roared in the night from multiple locations, crying voices filling the air. Chelci and Veron walked in a daze into the village center while bodies of villagers littered the paths.

"Chelci," a weak voice called, followed by a fit of coughing.

They followed the voice to where a young man lay in a pool of blood-stained dirt. "Reece!" She ran to kneel beside him. "No! Are you—" she stopped as she got a closer look at his body. A gaping wound marred his side. Her hand covered her mouth.

Veron hung back to give them space.

"I got three of them," he said weakly.

Chelci sniffed. "That's great, Reece," she said, her voice laden with emotion.

Reece turned his body, straining to look around him. "Have you seen Grace? I tried to find her. I wanted to make sure she was all right."

"Take it easy. You're going to be fine," she lied, resting her hand on his shoulder. "And I'm sure she will be, too, but you need to rest."

"Can you find her for me?" Reece asked before coughing again. Blood spattered his tunic.

"I can look," she replied as her head scanned the area. "I'm sure she's—"

Chelci stopped. Veron followed her gaze to where a young girl with short, light-brown hair lay on the grass. Her glassy eyes were open, her face frozen in agony. The shaft of a spear stuck awkwardly out from her unmoving body. *Grace.*

"The girl from the Academy?" Veron said, stepping forward. "I saw her a bit ago, down the path."

Reece turned to him. His eyes sparkled and a painful smile formed on his face. "Really? She's all right?"

Veron paused for only a moment. "Yeah, she had just chased a soldier away. She was fine."

Reece's shoulders settled against the dirt. He closed his eyes and leaned his head back. "Thank you," he said in a breathy voice. "Can you tell her I fought bravely?"

Chelci covered her mouth again as she turned and buried her face into Veron's pant leg. Her body shook with muffled sobs.

"I'll tell her," Veron said. With his eyes shut, Reece exhaled one last time before his chest stopped moving.

Chelci continued to shake, holding onto Veron. When she stood, Veron wrapped her in his arms, rubbing her back. She buried her face in his shoulder. While holding her, Veron's jaw fixed into a hard line.

"I have to stop him," he said.

Chelci pulled away. She sniffed, her eyes red and puffy. "Bale?"

Veron nodded. "I can't keep hiding out here. Brixton knows where we are. As much as I wanted to put it off . . . it's time to bring the fight to Bale. I must return to Felting."

Chelci exhaled a long sigh. "Then we go."

II

Reality

16

Aftermath

The sun peeked over the trees, casting a revealing light on the ghastly scene in Nasco. A dozen homes smoldered, reduced to piles of charred timber. Families picked through the smoking remains to salvage what they could of their property.

Large reddish-brown stains filled the dirt of the village center where pools of blood dried overnight. A young child with disheveled hair wandered through the green space. He stumbled through the overturned tables and piles of ruined food. Tears streaked his face as he muttered his parents' names.

In a clearing at the edge of town, villagers piled the bodies of dead soldiers on a stack of wood to be burned. Some died of battle wounds, but many were eviscerated by the valcor. Carrion birds swooped down, taking turns nipping at the mountain of graying flesh.

On the opposite side of the village, just past the garden, the villagers who died in the night lay by the graveyard's edge where a group of men dug graves. Some cried while they dug. Some worked silently, apparently in shock.

Veron gingerly set down the body of a small boy, whose long hair fell over his face. He brushed it back. The young boy looked at peace.

Chelci and Morgan approached, sharing the weight of a grown man. Morgan struggled under the weight of the shoulders while Chelci held up the legs. They set him down with the rest of the bodies.

William arrived, handing a skin of water to the group to share.

"Does anyone have a count yet?" Chelci asked.

William nodded with his jaw set. "Twenty-eight dead soldiers.

Morgan whistled.

"About half killed by the valcor."

"What about villagers?" Veron asked.

"I believe Henry was the last one," William said, indicating the man they'd just set down. "That makes thirty-nine from Nasco."

Chelci shook her head. "How many homes did we lose?"

"Fifteen homes burned. Plus, they lost the entire crop of cabbage."

"Ugh. That was meant to feed the village for the next several weeks."

"Julia would have hated to see it," William said, looking wistfully toward the charred field. "She loved cabbage."

"I can't believe it. What was Brixton thinking?" Chelci asked.

"It's not Brixton," Veron said. "It's Bale."

Chelci's forehead pinched as she snapped to him, wagging a finger. "Don't you *dare* defend him!"

"I'm not!" Veron replied, holding his hands up. "What he did is inexcusable, but I don't think he would get there on his own—that's all I'm saying."

Chelci's glare softened.

"How long until they're back with reinforcements?" Morgan asked.

"We won't have long," William said. "A week—two if we're lucky. Is there any chance he wouldn't report you back to Bale?"

Veron pursed his lips and exchanged a look with Chelci. "I doubt it, but . . . it's possible."

"The village is small enough they could decide to leave it be, but if

Bale knows you're here, he'll send his whole army. The village would be leveled."

Veron swallowed to wet his dry throat. "That's why we need to go after him," he said, sounding more confident than he felt.

"Brixton?" Morgan asked.

"No," Veron replied. "We need to go after Bale."

William nodded after a long moment. "Then we go after him," he said, adjusting his staff and stamping it into the ground. "When should we leave?"

"The village could use help to clean up today," Veron said. "We'll leave at first light tomorrow."

Lanterns hung around the graveyard even though the sun had not quite set. The village stood in silence, facing the thirty-nine freshly dug graves. Tears fell from much of the crowd. Villagers took turns speaking and sharing memories of the deceased.

A short distance away, Veron sat on a stump at the edge of the woods, unable to make out what they said. A stick cracked, turning his head. "Morgan. Hey."

Morgan approached and leaned against a tree next to Veron. "Not much for funerals?"

Veron kicked a stick on the ground. "I don't deserve to be a part of it."

"What do you mean?"

"It's my fault they died."

"What?"

"I should have killed Bale back in Felting, but I didn't."

"You couldn't! There's a difference."

"I could have," Veron said, dropping his head to the dirt. "But I gave up and went after Chelci."

"You did what you needed to do."

"I did what I *wanted* to do."

Morgan scoffed. "You didn't *want* any of this, Veron. You didn't ask to be the only warrior capable of saving the kingdom. I'm not sure you realize this, but you tend to place blame on yourself. It's not fair to *you*."

Veron shrugged.

"This is not your fault. Bale is the one driving it. You've done nothing wrong."

Veron sighed, unwilling to let himself off the hook. At the graveyard ahead, people dispersed. The service had ended.

"Are you sure you want to come with us?" Veron asked, looking at Morgan as he stood.

His friend scanned the village for a moment. "It's tempting to stay. I could see myself settling here."

"Then do it," Veron said. "As much as I'd love you to come, all we're going to find is danger and death."

Morgan nodded. "I know. You're the only family I have left, though. If I'm not with you, then what's the point?"

"The point is you can live a peaceful, long life."

Morgan chuckled. "I know, but if you're out there, fighting through danger, that's where I want to be. Where you go, I go. I may not battle next to you with a sword, but I can make a mean rabbit stew back at camp."

Veron chuckled. "That sounds good, Morgan." He rested his hand on Morgan's shoulder. "I'll be glad to have you with me."

"What do we need to pack?" Veron asked as he followed William into his house, setting his lantern on the counter.

William scanned the room then pulled a small trunk out from underneath one of the cushioned chairs. "Here, use this." He tossed a sack with straps to Veron. "Fill it with any food that fits."

Veron turned to the shelves. There wasn't a lot, but the dried meat and cheese should make for good travel food.

"I spoke with Philip, too. He said he'd have some bread for us in the morning."

Veron nodded, grabbing strips of dried pork. "How long do we need to pack for?" When William didn't answer, he turned to his father. "How long do you think we'll be gone?"

William stopped and turned to him with a grim look on his face. "As long as it takes."

A wave of cold washed over Veron. He clenched his jaw. "You don't think one of us will come back from this, do you?"

William breathed in deeply. "We'll see."

Veron placed the sack down as he crossed the room. He sat on the other chair and leaned in toward his father. "The origine can heal someone when they're close to death, right?"

William didn't answer.

"I had a Dream earlier this season where I thought I was going to die. When the day came, they stabbed me three times, but I lived."

"I heard the prophecy many years ago. It left little room for speculation. The Dream the woman had seemed very specific about the shadow knight dying."

"What if she saw someone die, but they could come back to life? What if she didn't see the complete story?" Veron asked.

"You can think that if it helps you feel better."

"You don't think it's possible?"

William sighed. "Dead is dead, Veron. Shadow Knights can do a lot, but they can't rise from the dead."

"What about that 'pure connection' thing? Maybe if someone can achieve it, revival is possible?"

"Veron," William said, looking him in the eyes. "Hope is a good thing. I want you to do all you can to unlock your full potential, but there are limits to our bodies' capabilities. Don't misplace make-believe for truth."

Veron looked at the rug on the floor and nodded. He rose and returned to the shelves while his father filled his own sack with supplies.

"Could you not do anything with the chains?" Veron asked over his shoulder.

"What do you mean?"

"While you had the shackles around your legs . . . last night." Veron turned around. "I know you used up your energy before they put them on, but can you not tap into the origine at all with something like that?"

"No, I can't. I've never known anyone who could. You've really been able to use it with something metal around you?"

Veron nodded. "Yeah—with my shackle on my ankle when I was a servant. I couldn't use it as freely as I do now, but if I tried hard, I could heal injuries. It used my energy in a flash though."

William furrowed his brow.

"Is there anything about that in the book?"

"I don't think so. Only that it's impossible."

Veron stepped closer to his father. "Tonight, after the soldier stabbed me, I tried to use the origine to keep fighting, but all the energy directed to healing my wound. Why was that?"

"Voluntary versus involuntary actions," William said. "You make a choice when you pick up a cup off a table. That's a voluntary action. But you don't have to choose to breathe."

Veron cocked his head. "I'm not sure how that applies."

"You can choose to breathe if you wish. But even without thinking about it, your body does it. It's involuntary. Healing is the same way. Normally, it happens without thinking because your body knows you need it. Being a shadow knight gives us the ability to choose to heal, but typically, it still happens without us thinking about it. When you flood your body with energy, that power will first take care of your most basic needs."

"So, if I have a wound, I won't be able to use the origine to do other things?"

"It's possible. It just takes a lot of focus. Healing uses up the origine rapidly—much faster than any other action. If you're injured in a battle, you need to hold off healing until the fighting is over. Otherwise it will leave you vulnerable."

"How do I do that?"

"Did Artimus put you through the knife exercise?"

Veron turned around with an eyebrow raised. "Knife exercise?"

"I guess not. How are you feeling now? Well rested? Plenty of energy?"

"Yeah, I feel good."

William stood and beckoned with his hand. "Let me see that knife."

Veron dropped his gaze to his hip, where the knife Bale threw at him in Felting rested in a sheath. He handed it to his father. "I'm not sure I like the sound of this."

"It wasn't my favorite exercise either," William added with a chuckle. "Give me your arm."

Veron's heart sped up as he stared at his father. His arm wobbled as he extended it.

William grasped his wrist and rested the tip of the knife against the outside of Veron's lower arm. "Are you all right?" he asked.

Veron swallowed hard, then nodded. Digging into the skin, William pulled the sharp blade along half the length of Veron's arm.

A sharp sting radiated through his body. Veron tried to reflexively jerk his arm away, but William held it in place. "Argh," he groaned, flexing his arm in response.

The knife stopped its cut, but William held the arm in place for an extra moment. A bright red line of blood appeared on Veron's skin. After beading for a second, it formed into a stream, falling down the side of his arm and dripping onto the floor.

"Don't heal it," William said, looking into Veron's eyes. "Not yet. Use the origine to run to the woods then to the Academy and back. Put all your energy into the speed of your body, but don't use any of it for healing. Got it?"

Veron nodded.

William glanced at the door. "Go!"

Veron looked at his arm. Every instinct in his body told him to stop the wound, so it took effort to leave it alone. *It's merely a scratch. It will be fine.* After another drop of red fell to the wooden floor, he jogged to the door.

When he pulled the energy, his body warmed and trembled with anticipation. Immediately, his arm tingled. The upper part of the cut hardened as a scab before his eyes. *No!* He focused on his legs and willed the energy into his muscles as he ran. The prickling on his arm stopped as he hit the dirt path. The surrounding scene blurred. He pumped his legs, moving to the woods then turning toward the Academy. He pulled enough energy to speed up but made sure not to overexert himself. When he reached the training building, he tapped the side and turned.

As he sped back to William's house, his arm prickled. *It's healing again!* Veron's legs slowed. Distracted by the battle inside him, he struggled to maintain his hold on the origine. What energy he found went to his arm. He tried to run as fast as he told his body to move, but his legs didn't respond. He stumbled, almost falling to the dirt before he caught himself.

When he pulled harder from his store of energy, it only increased the tingling in his arm. He couldn't divert it. As he emerged from the woods, fatigue caught up with him. His legs felt weighed down by stones, and his body leaned over his feet as he lurched ahead. With William's house in sight, his body gave out. Veron fell to the ground, planting his face in the dirt. Somehow, he rolled on his back as he gasped for air, but his arms and legs would no longer respond. The crunch of boots in the dirt approached. William looked down at him with his lips pursed together.

"I couldn't do it," Veron gasped.

William nodded. "How's your arm?"

Veron tried to look, but he couldn't lift it. His arm flopped at his side.

"Hmm," William mumbled. "Well . . . I guess we'll keep working on that one."

17

On the Road

Veron left William's home for what he expected to be the final time. The early morning air felt crisp, but his Shadow Knights cloak kept him warm. Farrathan's weight on his back comforted him. A bag filled with his clothes and the *Chronology of the Shadow Knights* slung over his shoulder while he held a bag filled with food in the other. Bale's knife was secured at his hip.

Just off the village green, Chelci and Morgan stood by the stables, tightening the straps on two mottled brown horses while talking with Aleks and Finley. Veron waved as he approached.

"Good morning," Morgan called.

Chelci left the horse and met him. She rested her hands on both of his arms and took a deep breath. "Are you sure you want to do this?"

Veron nodded. "It's time."

Chelci dropped her head.

"Hey," Veron said, lifting her chin. "I'm not gone yet."

A weak smile crossed her face. "I know." She rubbed his upper arms. "I know."

"Is this one yours?" Veron asked, motioning to the horse she had been preparing.

"Yeah, this is Nora. I've known her for a long time." Chelci patted the horse, rubbing along its flank.

"And this is *Firestorm*," Finley said enthusiastically, patting Morgan's horse.

Chelci rolled her eyes and looked at Veron. "His name is Clover."

"Firestorm sounds better though," Finley insisted.

"William's and yours are in there," she told Veron with a nod to the stable.

They both entered the dim stable, sheltered from the faint morning light. Two horses waited for them, tied to a post, saddled and ready. Specks of gray and white flecked the one on the left, while the smaller, inky-black horse on the right whinnied as they approached.

Chelci ran her hand along the black mane to calm the animal. "Steelmane is William's and this will be yours."

"Let me guess . . ." Veron smirked. "Slayer?"

Chelci smiled faintly. "No, Annie."

He ran his hand along Annie's neck. "Hey there, Annie. You ready to go for a ride?" He smiled as the horse nuzzled his chest.

They untied the reins and led the horses outside to join the others. Morgan finished strapping his bags to the side and took a drink from a skin of water. "You want some?" he asked, holding it out to Veron after he finished. Veron shook his head.

"You two dressing up as twins or something?" Finley asked.

Veron followed his eyes. William approached. A sword hung from his father's hip, a bag slung over his shoulder, and a coiled rope rested on his arm. A black cloak covered him from his shoulders almost to the ground. Over his heart, a white SK symbol with a sword stared back at Veron.

Veron grinned as he glanced down at himself, attired identically. "I didn't know you had one!"

"I didn't take much when I fled Felting, but I brought the cloak.

This is the first time I've worn it in fourteen years." William stood next to Veron while the rest of the group looked at them.

"Yeah, I see it now," Chelci said.

Veron raised an eyebrow. "See what?"

"The resemblance. You're a spitting image of him."

Veron and William looked at each other. His father's shaggy brown hair covered his ears, and his eyes twinkled. Around the same height, wearing the cloaks, they looked nearly identical.

"What are those for?" Finley asked, nodding toward the cloak. "What's that symbol mean?"

William laughed softly. "Don't worry about it. Just an old family heirloom."

"Are you sure you don't need help?" Aleks asked.

William shook his head. "They need you here. We lost a third of the village guard already in the attack."

Dirt crunching drew their attention in the other direction where Russell and Nevi drew near. Russell walked gingerly, holding his side while Nevi supported him.

"You weren't thinking of leaving without saying goodbye, were you?" Nevi asked.

"Of course not," Chelci said, giving them both a hug and mumbling things into their shoulders.

"Take care of them, Bensen," Russell said to Veron's father.

William nodded. "I will. I still feel badly about taking the horses, though. The village has a lot of work to do and could use them."

"We have more," Russell said. "You'll need them more than us."

With their bags strapped to the horses, they walked to the edge of town and mounted the animals. Veron looked behind him. The village green waited just down the path. A memory of the party flashed through his mind. He smelled the food again. He sensed the sweat on his hands while he twirled with Chelci to the music.

After blinking, the desolation jarred his senses. Bloody streaks still dotted the path. A trace of burnt wood reached his nose. A few dozen villagers stood watching, holding their loved ones silently. Some raised a hand to wave goodbye.

With a tight jaw and a soft kick of his heels, Veron urged Annie forward. He leaned back in the saddle, gripping the horse between his legs as they descended the rise to head into the woods. His heart felt heavy, but destiny could wait no longer.

The narrow trail through the woods opened onto the road by midday. Progress was good on horseback, but Veron's constant jostling in the saddle grew painful by late afternoon.

"Have you found a good way to sit yet?" Morgan whispered, adjusting his body as he came alongside Veron.

"No, I hope we stop soon. Those two must have been born on a horse or something." He glanced up at William and Chelci, surprised to find they had stopped just ahead. "What is it?"

Something on the side of the road held their attention. Veron angled Annie's reins to get a better look and gasped when the sign came into view. A wooden stake displayed it just off the ground—impossible to miss. A poster with the same inaccurate picture he'd seen in Felting identified Veron Stormbridge as a dangerous, wanted criminal.

"Apparently, your crimes have grown to include murdering babies and stealing from an orphanage," Chelci said casually, leaning forward toward the sign and squinting her eyes.

Morgan whistled. "And you're worth twenty gold sol now!"

Veron glanced warily between his riding companions. "Don't you three get any ideas." He chuckled nervously.

Chelci leaned over and rested her hand on his arm. "Don't worry. You're stuck with us."

William looked up at the sky. "The sun will set soon. We need to get off the road and find a place to camp for the night."

Veron brought up the rear, lingering to look at the sign. His chest tightened as he fought to tear himself away. After a swift kick, Annie trotted to catch up with the others.

Flames crackled as Veron stared into the depths of the coals. His hood covered his head, blocking out the wind while his mind flitted between thoughts of Bale, Chelci, and how he would miss Nasco. The rough log under him was no more comfortable than the saddle he'd sat on all day.

"Hey!" Chelci said, snapping her fingers in front of Veron.

He jerked to attention and lowered his hood. "Hey, sorry."

"I asked if you want some rabbit?" Chelci extended two sticks with roasted meat smoking from the end. "Sorry, the one fell in the fire. It's a little extra crispy."

"I'll take that one," William said, leaning forward and taking the ash-blackened meat.

Veron took the final stick, nodding in thanks. Chelci settled next to him on the log with her own skewer.

"Are you sure we're far enough off the road?" Morgan asked.

"Hills block us in either direction. We should be safe here," William confirmed. "We'll want to sleep in shifts, though."

Veron took a bite. The meat was hot and juicy, and his stomach rumbled in appreciation. Across the fire, his father sharpened a dagger on a stone while three more knives rested on a leather satchel.

"William," Veron said after swallowing his mouthful. "What was it like being in the Shadow Knights?"

Morgan and Chelci both looked at the older man, too. William halted his blade's circular motion and looked at Veron with flames dancing in his eyes. His shoulders relaxed. "It was like being in a large family."

Family. Veron winced.

"Most of the time, we lived in the training center in Felting. We ate, slept, talked, and trained."

"What was the training like?"

"Relentless," William replied. The corner of his mouth lifted. "But it was also incredible. We drilled all day—swords, knives, ropes, hooks, staffs. Anything you can picture as a weapon, we trained with it. We strengthened our bodies, and we practiced sneaking through the city."

Veron chuckled. "Yeah, I loved that part. How often did you go on missions . . . or whatever you called them?"

"Once every few weeks we had a task. Usually only a few of us were involved, but occasionally we would all go."

Veron's eyes widened. "What would it take for all of you to get involved?"

"Do you remember hearing about the Lorranis uprising? When a group of lords and their followers took over the port and tried to secede from Feldor?"

Veron glanced at the others. Chelci shrugged, and Morgan shook his head.

"There's a reason you don't remember. Ten shadow knights showed up in Lorranis before they made their first move."

"How did you know?" Chelci blurted. "If you stopped things from happening, how did you know when something was going to happen?"

"We had connections all over Terrenor—spies who reported back to us."

Veron's eyes lit up as he leaned forward. "So, you would go out as a group and—what—hide in the woods or in the cities? How long were your jobs?"

"Some took a day or two, but when we traveled, it could take weeks or months."

"Wow, that sounds exciting!" Chelci chimed in.

"It was at first," William said, "but taking lives carries a cost." Veron leaned back, sobered by the thought as William continued. "We usually slept outside of the cities, hiding in the woods. We'd come in at night."

"Did you always kill them?" Veron asked.

William stared at the fire and didn't answer for a long moment.

"I'm sorry. I was just curious. You don't have to talk about it if you don't—"

His father shook his head. "No, it's all right. Number seven of the code . . . 'Killing is always a last resort.'"

Chelci raised an eyebrow. "Last resort?"

"If they were trying to kill us . . . or if they could be as dangerous from a dungeon cell as they could be walking around." William looked back into the fire and took a long pause. "It wasn't a decision we came to lightly."

A piece of wood popped in the fire, causing Veron to jump. He stared into the coals as the group grew silent.

"Veron," Chelci said. He turned to her, their shoulders pressing against each other. "Can I look through the book?"

Veron's eyes widened. "Um . . ." He looked across the fire at William.

"I know he says I have less ability than anyone in the history of Terrenor."

"That's not what I said," William protested.

"Still, there's no harm in me reading . . . right?"

William raised both shoulders and turned his hands up. "Be my guest."

Veron leaned over and picked up his bag. After rummaging to the bottom, he pulled out the thick book and handed it to Chelci.

"Fair warning," Veron said. "It doesn't make much sense."

"You learned by reading it, right?"

"Well, yeah, but . . ." he looked at William again.

"I know. I know," Chelci said. "You are uncommonly talented."

Veron's face fell. "That's not what I was going to say."

Chelci laughed as she opened the book. "I'm teasing you. I get it."

"Veron," William called, beckoning with his hand.

Veron rose and walked around the fire, sitting on a rock next to his father.

William lowered his voice and leaned in. "When it comes time, I want you to leave Bale to me."

Veron pinched his eyebrows together. He'd expected to be the one to fight Bale for the last couple of years. The thought of another taking the mantle was a difficult adjustment. He couldn't bring himself to nod.

"Where do you think we'll find him?" Veron asked.

"At the castle, I would expect."

Veron stared into the fire, hoping the flames would provide all the answers. "We'll fight him together, Father," he said after a long pause. William fixed his jaw as he looked back. "Bale needs to be stopped. It may be you, but it may need to be me. We need to both try."

"All right, but if things get out of control, I want you to get out of there."

Veron nodded. "Agreed, but I've got a good feeling about it. Prophecy or not, with us working together, I think we have a good chance."

William laughed.

"What?"

"I used to be positive like that—always assuming things would work out."

"What happened?"

William exhaled. "Bale happened. Part of me died the day his men arrived. I don't think I've been the same since."

Both men gazed into the fire, mesmerized by the curling flames and crackling embers.

"If you all want to sleep, I'll take the first shift," Chelci said, looking up from the book.

Veron glanced at William, who shrugged. "We do need to get some sleep while we can," William said, putting his knives up. "I'll take the second."

Veron circled back around the fire to where he had laid a blanket out. "You sure you're all right, Chelci?"

She looked at him and flashed a grin. "Yeah, I'm not tired yet. Lots to read."

"You want me to stay up with you?"

"No, you try to rest. I'll be fine."

Veron lay on the ground and leaned his head against his bag. The fire was low, but the warm glow illuminated Chelci where she sat on the log. She flipped the pages of the book, poring over every word. Eventually, Veron closed his eyes and drifted to sleep to the crackling fire sounds.

18

Climbing the Castle

Ducking behind tall ferns, Veron joined the others at the edge of the woods. Next to him, William pushed a frond away, giving them line of sight to the city gate where two large Norshewan flags hung on either side. The afternoon sun shone on the open field ahead.

"There are only eight at the gate. You can take them, right?" Morgan asked, crouching beside Veron.

"We *could*, but we need to get in without alerting anyone," William replied.

"Can you just walk in?" Chelci asked.

William shook his head and pointed. Veron followed with his eyes and sighed. A poster stuck on each side of the gatehouse walls just behind the soldiers. "How many of those are there?" Veron groaned.

"They wouldn't think twice about me, but they'll be looking for our famous orphanage thief here," William said with a chuckle. He turned to Veron. "Can you manage to get over the wall?"

Veron nodded. "You?"

William pursed his lips. "I can, but it's best if I save energy for when it's needed. I'll walk through the front gate. I won't raise any suspicion."

"And I'll go with him," Chelci said.

"Chelci, you can't come with us," Veron said. "We're not planning to just walk up the castle steps. It's going to be dangerous."

She shook her head. "I want to see Father."

Veron breathed in sharply.

"Is that wise?" William asked.

"What if they're watching his place?" Veron added.

"For me?" Chelci asked. "I'm in Nasco. At least, that's what they will think. It'll be fine. I don't want to just wait in the woods with the horses."

Morgan raised his hand. "If you two are heading into the castle, I'll stay with Chelci and make sure she's all right."

William looked at Veron and Chelci. "Leave your sword with the horses then. That would draw suspicion." She nodded. "We move when it's dark."

Veron crouched behind a boulder, peeking his head around the side. The horses waited, tied in the woods, and the dark outlines of Chelci, William, and Morgan made their way along the road toward the gate. William limped, leaning heavily on his staff. Veron held his breath as they approached the soldiers at the gate and stopped. William gestured behind him toward the dark road. After a tense moment, the soldiers waved them on, and their figures disappeared through the stone wall.

Veron pressed his back against the rock and breathed in, trying to calm his nerves. All he could think of was the signs declaring him a wanted person and the problems it would cause if Bale knew he were coming.

He slunk low to the ground and ran across the open field, the darkness hiding him from sight. He scanned the empty wall above.

Only a few weeks before, he had walked along that wall, defending the city from invaders. He smirked. *Now I'm the invader.*

As he neared the wall, Veron jumped, pushing hard with his legs, using the origine to propel him into the air. His body flew, his cloak rippling behind him. The merlons rushed to meet him, and he grabbed onto one to stop his momentum. Dropping through the crenel, he pulled his sword and crouched on the battlements. Veron froze. A crossbow pointed directly at his face.

A soldier towered above him. His rough beard and scarred cheek formed a hardened face, familiar with the dangers of battle. His extended arm held firm. "Who are you?" the man growled.

"He's an intruder," another soldier called, leaning around the man's massive frame. "Kill him! I'll sound the alarm. There may be more." He raised a horn to his lips and inhaled as a bolt loosed from the crossbow.

Using the origine, Veron spun to the side and cleaved the projectile in half, splinters flying in slow motion. Before the crossbow-wielder had a chance to move, his head dropped from his shoulders, sliced cleanly by Farrathan. The other man's eyes slowly grew until Veron kicked the horn away, shattering it. He pushed the man into the wall, his head hitting the stone and body falling limp.

Veron spun, looking for others. His heart pounded and chest heaved. He was alone. Quickly, he tossed the bodies over the side, hearing a faint crumpling sound a few moments after they dropped.

He hurried down a set of stairs to the street. Across the cobble-stones, a man limped out of the shadows with two other figures by his side.

"Any trouble?" Veron asked.

"No," Chelci replied. "They asked some questions then let us past. You?"

"Nothing I couldn't handle."

At the intersection ahead, they stopped, and Chelci grabbed his arm. "Promise me you'll be careful?"

Veron looked into her eyes. "Of course I will."

"Remember . . . *your* Dream was different. It doesn't mean one of you has to die."

Veron swallowed as he held her other hand. "I know, Chelci. We'll both be careful."

She pulled him close and pressed her lips against his in a firm kiss. Veron's body melted into hers.

"Come on," William said, interrupting their moment.

Through much effort, Veron pulled away. Chelci rested her hand against his face before she turned, joining Morgan to walk up the side street toward her father's house. Veron sighed, watching her go. Finally, he turned to his father. They both raised their hoods and walked toward the castle, blending in with the shadows.

Ramparts loomed ahead, rising from the city, providing a faint silhouette against the sky. Red-and-black banners lined the main street's walls. Occasional groups of soldiers patrolled the streets, but the shadow knights eluded them, slinking through the darkness.

"Should we sneak through the entrance?" he whispered.

"No—too great a risk. If we're going to find Bale without one hundred men protecting him, we need to get to him without being seen."

"Do you know a secret way in?"

"Kind of," William replied. The little confidence Veron felt waned at the response.

When they arrived at the front of the castle, rather than head toward the gate, they skirted left toward the city wall where tall parapets and darkness waited.

"What if we get to Bale and he *does* have one hundred men?" Veron asked.

William's answer took a moment, giving Veron's anxiety a chance to grow. "Then we'll do the best we can," he said.

"Is there a strategy to fighting a force that large?"

"The strategy is to avoid it. But if you must fight, there are two schools of thought. One, preserve the origine. Fight using as little of it as you can to avoid running out while half the men remain. Two, use all the origine to put on an impressive display. Overwhelm their forces with a spectacular show of strength and count on them to give up and flee."

"Sounds risky."

"It is. If they don't run, you'll likely die."

"Which school of thought do you ascribe to?"

"Avoid it," William said with a smirk.

"So, if we meet Bale with a large force . . . should we run and hide again, or do we fight?"

William stopped walking and turned to Veron. "If we can't get an advantage of surprise, we need to leave and come back when we can."

Veron nodded then looked up at the castle. "All right . . . so how do we get in?"

William grinned, walking toward the castle wall. After leaving his staff leaning against the wall and looking in both directions, he bent his knees and jumped. Veron's jaw dropped.

His father landed on top of the ramparts, then looked down at him. After checking the street, Veron jumped.

"How's that on the leg?" Veron asked when he landed, resting a hand against the merlon for balance.

"It's tougher than it used to be," William confirmed. "It takes a lot more origine, both jumping and balancing."

"You're all right though?"

"I'm fine," William said, waving his hand in dismissal. He beckoned for Veron to follow as he crouched and worked his way along the wall.

On the opposite side of the wall, over a short alley, a visual cacophony of slanted roofs and towers filled their view. *I wish I could forget about Bale and just explore these rooftops.*

William stopped ahead. "Do you know the sunrise balcony?"

Veron nodded. "I think I know which one that is."

"The royal living quarters are on the floor just above that, with the wing for visiting dignitaries on the opposite side. Bale may take the royal apartments, but if he gave them to Fiero, then he should be in the dignitaries' wing. Either way, we'll find him on that floor."

"Any thoughts how to get up there?"

William looked toward the roofs. "We climb."

Veron's pulse sped as a grin formed on his face. "I was hoping you would say that."

William jumped across the alley first, with Veron on his heels. The slate tiles under his feet gave him a momentary flashback to Fend's fall in Karad a lifetime ago, but no fear entered his mind thanks to his discovered abilities.

A drainpipe running down the wall ahead gave them a straight-forward path to ascend to the next level. Veron didn't even use the origine. Topping out the pipe, a slanted roof made for easy traversing around the corner. They ducked past a series of windows where lanterns lit up a long reception hall with a throne at the end. The room was empty.

The next several minutes comprised of jumping, climbing, and scurrying. The two shadow knights were nearly invisible under their black cloaks as they climbed the exterior of the castle.

Veron paused as he held onto a small ledge with his feet perched on a window sill. Glancing down at the ground far below, a wave of dizziness washed over him. Arriving just after him, William took extra care when he set his feet. Sweat covered his father's forehead as he breathed heavily.

"Are you sure you're all right?" Veron asked.

"I'm fine," William insisted, wiping his brow with one hand while holding on with the other.

"How's your energy? Do you have to use too much?"

"I said I'm fine." He nodded up, just ahead of them. "The balcony's just up there."

Veron looked ahead and sighted his path. With a pull of origine, he leaped from his perch to a small ledge opposite the wall. Bouncing off the temporary resting place, he sailed to the balcony, soaring over the lip and landing on the stone lookout.

William followed the same path but faltered when he pushed off the opposite ledge. His trajectory was short. Veron lunged for the edge as William's arms grasped around the rail, his body dangling below. Veron grabbed his father's arms. William's muscles trembled until he rolled over the top, falling onto the floor of the balcony.

Veron and William lay on the stone, panting. When Veron sat up, he stared at his father. His chest heaved, and his face looked pale.

"Maybe you should wait here?" Veron suggested.

"No," William said, puffing. "Just give me a moment. I'm only partially depleted.

Veron stood and paced the balcony. He peered through the arched opening into the meeting room he knew well. The room inside was dark.

"How do you know so much about the castle?" Veron asked, keeping his voice down. "I'm guessing you lived at the Shadow Knights' training center, right?"

"That's right. But we covered every nook and cranny of the castle. A knight was always hiding in the shadows nearby whenever Wesley had meetings." William took deep breaths, his chest rising and falling smoothly.

They waited for several minutes until William groaned, raising himself to his feet. He steadied his balance with his hand on the railing then let go to stand on his own. He looked at Veron and nodded. "I'm good."

Veron allowed William to move first, entering the dark room through the middle archway. The oval meeting table materialized in the void. "There are stairs on the far side," Veron said. They crossed the room and paused. No sound came from above, so they ascended.

At the top, they both peered around the corner. To the left, at the end of the hall, two guards in Norshewan colors stood in position outside a large entryway, chatting quietly between themselves. A lantern hanging in the hall lit up the passage. To the right, a darkened set of double-doors sat alone a short ways away.

"To the left used to be the king's bedroom," Veron whispered. "He must be there." William nodded. "Should we charge the guards?"

"We can't risk it," William said. "An alert would endanger our mission."

"How can we get past them, then?"

William leaned his head out again. "How's your origine reserve?"

"It's good."

"Can you run to the doors on the right before they see you?"

Veron leaned to get another look. "Yeah, I think I can get there."

"With no guard there, I'm hoping it's empty. Inside the room, there's a door against the far wall leading to a short balcony. From there, leap along the outside windows. Rap on the glass of the third one, then come right back. That should get the guards' attention and draw them down that hallway, giving us a chance to enter."

"Sure. I can do that."

Veron peered around the corner again. The guards still conversed but hadn't left their post. He pressed a hand against the stone wall and evened his breath. The origine's warm tingle surged inside of him, waiting to be used. He looked at his father and whispered. "I'll be right back."

Veron ran. William's frozen face disappeared behind him as he flew down the corridor, pumping his legs as hard as he could. Reaching the doors, he ducked to the side in the darkness before releasing the origine. Veron strained his ears for any sign of alert. The faint sound of casual conversation reached him. He exhaled in relief.

Veron turned the doorknob. The door cracked, and ancient hinges creaked. Veron momentarily paused, but there was no sign of an alert. He pushed farther until the opening was large enough to slip through.

Shadows filled the room inside. A moonlit glow from the windows outlined the bed and furniture. Veron crept across the floor until he could see the bed more clearly. *Empty.* He exhaled.

He opened the door to the outside balcony, and the chill wind greeted him once more. The circular stone extension was small—only a fraction of the size of the one on the floor below. After climbing over the railing, he sighted three windows along the side of the castle. The distance between each was short, and graspable ledges surrounded them. Veron jumped, landing securely at the window, his hands clamped onto the stone edges. The next two leaps were just as smooth.

When he arrived at the third window, he peered inside, pressing his face against the glass. A lantern shined in the hall, illuminating the sides of the two soldiers guarding the door.

Veron adjusted his body, preparing to knock on the glass then jump out of sight. He raised his fist. With his body poised to leap, he paused. *How am I supposed to get back quickly enough? William's ready to make a break for the door, but I'm way out here.* Veron grumbled as he shook his head. *That was his plan all along. To be the one to attack and leave me behind.*

Holding on to the narrow ledge while his feet dangled above the nothingness below, Veron glanced around. Two windows ahead, a large balcony extended from the castle. *I bet that leads to the royal bedroom!* William was too weak to take on Bale on his own. As much as he appreciated his father's gesture, he had to be the one. "Sorry, William. Change of plans," he whispered to himself.

Veron pulled against the ledge and leaped twice in succession. He landed on the edge of the stone promontory and pulled Farrathan from its sheath. His heart pounding, he opened the door, squinting his eyes to peer into the darkness.

Velvet covered furniture greeted him as soon as he entered. He stepped around the furniture. Even without seeing the top, he sensed the high ceiling and open space around him. A smoldering fire in the far corner gave enough light for him to sneak by.

Holding his sword with one hand, Veron approached the bed. Thick, blue curtains draped from the railing of the four-post bed, shrouding any bodies within. Deep breathing rumbled behind the barrier. His heart pounded as he stepped up. He pushed the edge of the curtain. Two shapes with dark hair filled out the blankets, but the light was too dim to see. *Is it Bale?* Veron's hand was slick on the grip of his sword. He leaned forward to get a closer look, poised and ready to strike. *If I kill him now, is this the end? How would I die?*

The click of a door snapped him to attention. One of the double doors at the main entrance swung open, flooding the room with light.

Veron dropped to the floor, the end of his sword grating against the stone. He winced and steadied the bare blade with his free hand.

"Sire?" a guard called from the open doorway. "Is someone there?"

"What? Who's there?" a bleary male voice replied from behind the curtain.

Veron pressed against the floor and crawled underneath the bed, careful to keep his weapon from scraping. Above him, the bed jostled and curtains flung back.

"I was checking the room when I heard something," the soldier uttered while the second guard entered the room, backlit by the hall's lantern. "Was that you, Lord Regent?"

"Was *what* me?"

Regent? That's not Fiero's voice, and it doesn't sound like Bale either.

"I'm sorry, I . . . I thought I heard a metal sound."

"What's wrong, Gareth?" a woman's voice asked.

Gareth! Gareth Billings is the regent now? What happened to Fiero?

"Nothing, Vivian. Go back to sleep."

No one spoke while Veron tensed, hoping the darkness would conceal him. To his side, the outline of legs appeared on the floor as Billings stood. The tip of a dagger dangled just in his view. Veron's forehead exploded in sweat as he heard the unmistakable sound of the guards unsheathing their swords.

"Check the room," Billings said.

The three men spread around the room, looking behind furniture and checking the balcony.

Vivian's shaking voice spoke up. "Would Bale have sent someone to kill you?"

"Not a chance," Billings said. "Plus, he and his men left yesterday."

"What about Fiero?"

"I told you, Raynor's dead."

Raynor Fiero is dead? Veron's pulse raced.

"Not Raynor," Vivian replied. "His son. Could he be retaliating for you having his father killed?"

"It was Brixton's idea to kill him."

Veron gasped then quickly covered his mouth.

"Plus, Brixton left with Bale for Karondir," Billings added as the doors to his wardrobe flew open.

The men were quiet for a moment. *Are they done searching? Maybe I'll get lucky.* Veron's stomach turned at the next words.

"Did anyone check under the bed?"

From both sides, feet moved toward Veron. His hand grasped his sword tighter. When the men arrived at each side of the bed, Veron moved. He scurried straight ahead as fast as he could. When his body cleared the bed, he stood and ran, pulling from his supply of raw energy. He exited through the open door without pausing. When he flew past the lantern in the hall, his motion snuffed the light out. Veron stopped and ducked into the stairwell halfway down the passage.

William jumped, holding his hand to his chest. "What were you doing!" he whispered in a harsh rasp. "Why didn't you follow the plan?"

"What was that?" A guard called, his voice echoing down the hall.

"Someone was here!" Another voice shouted. "After them!"

"Bale's gone," Veron said, pulling his father down the stairs as they both ran. "He left for Karondir yesterday."

"You should have gotten me!"

"It doesn't matter," Veron said, puffing as they rushed, fueled by the origine and leaving the guards behind. "Right now, we need to get out of here."

19

A Visit Home

Chelci and Morgan walked the streets, with Chelci leading the way to her father's house. At each opening in the buildings, she glanced back at the castle. After crossing a street, she looked behind her and stopped with a gasp. In the distance, two dark specs scurried up the castle's outer walls.

"They're going to kill themselves," Chelci muttered.

"I'm sure they'll be fine," Morgan said. "I think William's done this a lot before."

"Hopefully no one else sees them." She sighed when the climbers disappeared around a turret, high up the castle walls.

"If there's one thing I know about Veron, he has a way of working things out," Morgan said.

Chelci chuckled, then wiped her clammy hands on her cloak as she resumed walking. "Yeah, I know. Still . . . I'll be glad when they're down."

Felting's streets felt different. Even that late at night, Chelci was used to taverns winding down and more people in the streets. An eerie quiet left her on edge. She turned her head on a swivel, unsure what danger to look out for. *As long as we avoid seeing Brixton, we should be fine.* The thought didn't quell her trepidation.

Her eyes widened as they entered Turba Square. Several of the shops she used to frequent contained broken windows and doors. Many of the carts normally in the center were either empty or missing altogether. The sign for Rosalie's Dress Shop hung askew, dangling over shattered glass and an empty shop inside. "Rosalie!" she groaned. "What happened here?"

In the center of the square, the centuries-old statue was missing. Chelci approached the empty plinth and rested her hand on the flat surface. Most of the statue was gone, but chunks of stone rubble remained on the ground.

"This used to be King Darrick," she said. "The statue had been here for hundreds of years. It celebrated our freedom as a kingdom."

"I guess Bale wasn't an admirer," Morgan said.

As Chelci gawked at the ruin, the hair on the back of her neck stood straight. *Someone's watching us.* She found them. Three soldiers in red and black stood by a wall, leering at her. *Norshewans.* "Come on," she whispered, pulling her cloak tighter and walking in the other direction.

"You've got a pretty little daughter there," a man said in a gruff, accented voice. The other two soldiers laughed.

"She's not my daughter," Morgan replied over his shoulder. He moved closer as they continued walking.

"Oh? Your wife, then?"

Morgan hesitated before shaking his head.

"Whoa! Hold on," the man called, jogging feet following.

Chelci tried to speed up, but a soldier grasped Morgan by the shoulder and turned him around.

"Wait, we have questions."

Chelci tugged at Morgan's arm. "Come on, we've got to go."

The man who spoke with Morgan held an arrogant smile while the two men in back sneered, resting their hands on their sword hilts. Chelci's stomach turned. The man's smile disappeared, and a club appeared in his hand.

Morgan raised his hands in front of him. "I'm sorry men, but—"

A crack to his head sent Morgan sprawling to the ground and drew a scream from Chelci. She scampered several steps back, the soldiers following, leaving Morgan moaning on the ground. The front man lunged for her arm, but she pulled it clear. The two with swords came at her from either side. She reached to her hip, but her hand found only air. She paled in a moment of hesitation. Morgan worked his way to his feet behind the men, but they continued toward her. She ran.

Chelci's heart pounded as she raced, her legs pumping. Just down the street, she ducked into an alley, pushing her momentum off the wall. Her speed was an advantage, increasing her distance, but the soldiers followed. She hesitated at the next intersection, but the pounding boots approaching forced her to choose a path.

Although she'd been to Turba Square plenty of times, she didn't know the streets around it well and approached a dead end. The end of the alley appeared to be a trash dump. Broken crates and forgotten furniture filled the area, providing several hiding places, though none satisfactory. She spun around, her frantic eyes dancing. A partially collapsed wall jutted from the side of the building. She slunk against it in the futile hope that it would be enough to hide her.

Her breaths heaved as she pressed into the darkness. Running footsteps slowed to a walk as the men's laughter returned. "Where'd you go, sweetie?" a voice called.

Her leg brushed against something, causing her to glance down. *A broken table leg.* She leaned over to grab it as the men appeared.

With a jerk of his head, one looked her way. "Hey, there she—"

Chelci pounced from her dark corner, clubbing the man in the side of the head and dropping him to the ground. Before the other men could react, she hit one in the side, causing him to groan and bend over. A swift kick to the gut sent him sprawling backward, where he collapsed on top of an old chair that splintered under his weight.

The last soldier sneered as he raised his sword, but Chelci didn't allow him to follow through. She struck his hand, sending the sword falling to the ground. Next, she spun and kicked his legs out from under him. He fell to the street with a sickening thud, and Chelci finished with a hard blow to his head from her makeshift weapon.

She exhaled and started to leave when her legs lost their footing. The ground rushed to meet her. Her arms softened her fall, but her face smacked against the hard stone.

"Gotcha!" a man yelled as he clawed at her legs.

Chelci turned over, kicking and thrashing, but the heavy man pinned her legs down.

Where's my club?

She inhaled to scream for help when a dull thud filled the alley. The soldier's eyes rolled as his body went limp, falling to the side. Morgan moved into the light, brandishing her lost club.

"Morgan! Thank you!"

The grocer grabbed her hand and helped her up as she looked around. The three soldiers writhed on the ground, moaning in pain. Chelci didn't wait to determine the extent of their incapacity. She and Morgan ran, retracing their steps. They didn't pause when they returned to the main road, but continued running, twisting, and turning through the city. Chelci looked behind her a few minutes later. No one followed. She ducked into a dark alcove along the side of the street, pulling Morgan after her.

Her body thanked her for the rest. Next to her, Morgan panted, his brow dripping with sweat. A red knot stuck out from the side of his head from where he'd been hit.

"I'm glad you came with me," Chelci said between breaths.

Morgan nodded and took in a deep breath. "I am, too. Are we near your father's house?"

Chelci laughed softly. "Not even close. We ran in the opposite direction."

They remained concealed for several minutes. Their breathing settled, allowing them to hear clearly. No footsteps followed. She poked her head out to confirm then waved Morgan to join her.

The walk back through the city took nearly an hour. They constantly checked behind them and took side streets where they'd be less likely to encounter anyone. She couldn't have someone follow them to her father's house. Chelci smiled when they finally arrived at the entrance. The house looked just the same as when she had left.

Her run-in with the soldiers left her shaken, so rather than walk down the long, exposed drive, she skirted through the trees on the side to be safe. After sneaking through the cover, they approached the side door to the basement. Her shoulders relaxed when the knob turned.

When Chelci entered the empty basement kitchen, the memory of Veron, weeks before, flooded back to her. She pictured the attackers they had to fight off. She closed her eyes, pressing them tightly together when she remembered the sound her dying mother made. "We need to find my father."

She led up the stairs, figuring her father would be in bed. The third floor was quiet and dark. She padded to his door and turned the knob slowly. The window coverings remained open along with the curtains to his four-poster bed. The bed was empty.

Chelci left the room and stood in the hall. *Is he not home?*

"Would he be somewhere else?" Morgan whispered.

Chelci didn't answer but led back to the stairs. As they arrived at the ground floor, furtive voices stopped her.

"Is that someone?" Morgan asked.

Chelci couldn't make out what they said. She tiptoed to approach the sitting room, then pressed against the wall. After a moment, a smile grew. *Father.* Leaning, she peered around the corner.

A faint glow filled the room from a lone candle on a table. Her father sat in his chair. She had only been away for a few weeks, but somehow, he seemed to have aged years during the time. Across from him, a man and woman sat together.

"Emma?" Chelci said, forgetting the desire to stay quiet as she took a full step into the room.

The woman turned. The shocked expression on her friend's face melted into joy as she jumped up. "Chelci!"

Her father gasped.

Emma and her father jumped up and ran to Chelci and Morgan. Chelci alternated hugs while they peppered her with questions.

"Are you all right?"

"What are you two doing here?"

"Where have you been?"

Chelci laughed, unable to lessen her smile. "We're okay. What about you? You look—" She stopped herself. Matthew stood by his chair. Both he and Emma looked like they'd been through a war. Nearly-healed cuts marked their faces and their cheeks sunk. "What happened to you?"

Emma looked at Matthew. "Brixton punished us for failing to comply with Bale's new law," she said.

Chelci's jaw clenched and eyes narrowed.

"It's a long story," Matthew added.

"If I ever run into Brixton again . . ." Morgan's grumbling words faded.

Matthew raised a hand. "To be fair, Brixton tried to get us out of it, but . . ." he shook his head. "Too little—too late."

"They've been in prison for the last four weeks and were just released this evening," Darcius said. "I picked them up."

"Your father generously offered us a place to stay and temporary work until we can establish ourselves again," Matthew said.

"We lost the bakery and the room we rented," Emma added.

Chelci exhaled. "We ran into Brixton as well."

"What?" her father said. "Where were you?" He cut himself off with a shake of his hand. "Wait! No . . . it's better if I don't know."

"It doesn't matter now. Brixton knows, which means Bale will know. We had to leave. We were in Nasco, the village I lived in. Brixton showed up with soldiers. They tried to collect a tax and take men as slaves."

Darcius raised an eyebrow. "Tried?"

"We fought back. They killed many people and destroyed homes, but we chased them away."

"So, what are you doing back in Felting now?"

"We decided it was time. We came back for Veron to go after Bale."

"Veron's here?" her father asked.

"He went to the castle," Morgan said.

Darcius shook his head. "Bale's gone. He took his slaves and most of the army. They marched toward Karondir yesterday."

Chelci groaned. "We waited too long." She moved to an open chair and sat.

"What will you do now?" her father asked. "Can you stay?"

Chelci shook her head. "We hadn't discussed what to do if he wasn't here, but I imagine we'll go after him. We were hoping to catch him with his guard down, since it had been several weeks."

"He's surrounded every time I've seen him," her father said. "It may still be difficult."

"Well . . . we've got to try. Maybe we can catch up with them on the road. Have you been all right, Father?" Chelci asked, noticing nearly healed cuts on his face she hadn't seen at first.

He smiled. "I'm fine, dear."

"Did they hurt you?"

He took a deep breath before speaking. "They asked me questions about you and Veron, but I had nothing to say." He fingered a scab on his chin. "They've left me alone since. They took two of the servants for their group of slaves though."

"Who?"

"Drevyn, the mason, and Nathaniel."

Chelci groaned before a noise drew her attention. Her head shot to the room's entrance as Veron rounded the corner with William just behind. She jumped up and ran to him. "Veron! You're all right!"

Veron nodded then looked at William, who leaned on his staff. "Yes. Bale wasn't there."

"I heard," Chelci said. "They left for Karondir."

"And Brixton is with them," Veron added. He nodded to her father with a tight smile. "Hello, High Lord Marlow."

Emma and Matthew stood. "Hello again, Veron," Emma said before glancing at Chelci with an impish grin.

"Emma," Chelci scolded her friend under her breath.

Emma shrugged her shoulders while her smile grew. "What?"

Veron and Matthew exchanged greetings before Veron turned back to Chelci's father. "Thank you again for helping us when we escaped."

Darcius nodded. "Chelci filled me in on your plans. But she didn't mention your friend." He raised his eyebrows at William.

A grin formed on Veron's face as he looked between the people in the room. "High Lord Marlow, Emma, and Matthew, I'd like for you to meet my father, William Stormbridge."

20

Tienn

Brixton's horse's steady gait caused his eyelids to droop. Two days of traveling left him tired and sore, and they were only halfway to Karondir. Around him, a few dozen men rode on horseback while most soldiers walked in formation. On either side of the road, fences held back cows, mooing at the passing army.

"How's the mare?" A deep voice asked, jerking him out of his drowsiness. Bale had sidled up next to him.

"Your Majesty!" Brixton said, sitting up straight in his saddle, then looking at the animal. "She's great."

"Ginger is one of my personal horses."

"I'm sorry. They told me to ride her. I didn't realize—"

Bale laughed. "It's fine, Brixton. She seems happy to carry you."

The chestnut mare's mane flicked at Bale's voice, and she whinnied. Brixton leaned over and patted her neck.

"I'm glad you returned when you did so you could come with us . . . even if it was empty-handed."

Brixton's throat turned dry. He swallowed, keeping his attention on Ginger's mane.

"You said the villagers fought back, and they killed over half of our men, including Captain Gannon?"

"That's right." Brixton's voice cracked.

"It makes you wonder what sort of training woodland men receive to defeat fifty battle-hardened soldiers."

Brixton thought of the monster's roar. He remembered the noxious smell filling the air as he watched his men die one after another. "They were fierce," he said.

He and the surviving soldiers had agreed to forego mentions of the beast, lest others find it unbelievable.

Bale nodded. "Defending your home is a powerful motivator."

Brixton forced his words out. "If Your Majesty would like, I would be happy to return to the village with more men to finish the job the captain couldn't complete."

Bale turned to him. Brixton's insides churned as he held his gaze. "Why do you think I sent you on that mission?"

"Um . . . you needed more workers?"

"Gannon could have done that on his own. Why do you think I sent *you?*" Bale asked. Brixton stared ahead, racking his brain. "It's because I see a leader in you. I wanted to give you a chance to develop that. It's too bad Gannon was inept at his job, but there's no need to return. One small village is nothing compared to what we need to focus on now."

Brixton exhaled, relieved to leave the village behind. What influenced him most wasn't avoiding the monster but staying away from Veron. He had intended to tell the king about Veron's location, but when they returned to Felting, he avoided the topic. Now, days later, there wasn't a safe way to bring it up without raising questions about his loyalty.

"Where do you think Veron is?" Bale asked.

"Veron?" Brixton repeated, a little too loudly. "What do you mean? I don't know where he is."

Bale cocked his head. "I didn't say you knew. I'm simply wondering. You used to know him well. Where would you guess?"

Brixton's stomach churned. *Is he testing me? Does he know that I know?* Sweat beaded on his forehead. "He's probably hiding in Felting. It's a big city—easy to hole up somewhere."

"But we have signs all over the city. Do you think people would protect him with a twenty-sol reward on his head?"

"Possibly. Veron has loyal friends," Brixton said. Bale narrowed his eyes as he stared back. "But if he's not in the city, he's probably hiding in the woods."

Bale's attention turned to the surrounding trees. "Well, either way, he's bound to find us at some point. And when he does, I'll be ready."

Horses' hooves filled the following silence. Brixton looked to the sky where the sun neared the horizon.

"Do you ever wonder why I do this?" Bale asked.

"Your Majesty?" Brixton replied, unsure what he referred to.

"Coming to Feldor. Conquering Terrenor. Why do you think I do it?"

Brixton's eyes grew. It was not a question he was prepared for.

"I could have sat in my castle in Daratill, riding out my life, yet I came over the mountains to be here. I risked my life and that of my people. Why?"

Brixton squirmed in his saddle. "You want power?"

"Power! Ha!" Bale laughed, causing Brixton to jump. "Power is a delusion, Brixton. It only exists because someone imagines it does, but it can be taken away in a moment. I would never waste my life on so fleeting a pursuit."

"Maybe money?"

"Money is also temporary. It's useless to keep and gone when it's spent."

"I don't know then. What?"

Bale lowered his chin as he spoke in an even voice. "I want immortality. To build a legacy. To create something great that lasts hundreds of years after I'm gone. I want buildings people can look at and remember that I'm the one who built them. When someone hears the name Edmund Bale, they should marvel, wishing they had lived during his reign."

"That sounds like quite a legacy," Brixton said.

"It will be," Bale said before he nodded ahead to the chained lines of men trudging along the road with their heads down. Over five thousand of them marched together, surrounded by soldiers keeping them in check. "These men will begin it for me."

"What will you use them for?"

"They will build the grandest palace Terrenor has ever seen. It will rise above Daratill so high that all of Terrenor will see it, even over the Korob Mountains!"

A pang of regret filled Brixton as he watched the enslaved workers. He recognized some from Felting or Karad. One had even been classmates with him at King's Academy.

"I thought you had a castle in Daratill?" Brixton asked.

Bale glared at him, causing Brixton to shrink in his saddle. "The new one will dwarf what I have now."

A young man caught Brixton's eye, looking over his shoulder from the line of workers ahead. *Nathaniel?* The servant from the Marlow house stared at him as the crowd marched along. Brixton averted his gaze.

Bale continued, "Stick with me and you'll see. You may live there one day."

The idea caught Brixton off guard. *Me? Live in Norshewa?* He hadn't considered it, but it made sense. Following Bale was likely to lead him there eventually.

"What created that drive?" Brixton asked, trying to look anywhere but Nathaniel.

"What do you mean?"

"Have you felt this way all your life? Or did something prompt you to want it that much?"

Bale looked to the north, staring into the distance. For a moment, Brixton wondered if he heard the question. He was about to ask again when a glint shimmered in the corner of the king's eye. Bale cleared his throat and wiped at his face. After a moment, he looked back to Brixton.

"I've worked for this all my life," Bale said, looking back at Brixton. He spoke with finality, as if he wanted no more questions on the subject. He kicked his horse into a canter. "Come. Tienn approaches."

Brixton looked ahead where buildings emerged from the hilly landscape. The previous night, the army had slept off the road in tents, eating dried rations—neither tasty nor plentiful. He assumed the second night would be like the first, so a grin formed when the army continued ahead into the city.

He had never been to Tienn before. Half the size of Karad, the town held the same feel, albeit without a castle or a wall. The main street ran through the town from south to north, splitting the city into halves. Stores and homes lined either side with alleys angling off in all directions. Instead of vendors in the street hawking wares, the people of the town cowered behind walls and windows.

As Brixton followed the line of soldiers up the street, a tower rose out of the buildings ahead. It grew in height the farther they progressed, until finally, they emerged into an open marketplace filled with shops, tables, and benches. Rather than being surrounded by buildings, the town square was open to the east, affording a striking view of the mountain range towering above the town.

Brixton gaped as he took in the scene. *This would be a magnificent place to have a house.* He turned around to find the perfectly centered tower. A large clock ticked away the time on its side.

The soldiers and their imprisoned laborers halted their march in the square. The sizable area quickly filled with people, but half had yet to arrive. Brixton turned his horse and trotted toward Captain Cyrus.

"Captain, why are we stopping here?" Brixton asked.

The captain scoffed and held out his hands, his thick, scraggly beard hiding most of his mouth. "Could you ask for a better place to settle for the night?"

"Yeah, it's great, but we can't fit here."

Cyrus scoffed. "You Feldorians have no creativity."

Bale's imposing form caught Brixton's eye as the king pushed his horse through the crowd to address a group of gathering towns-people. Brixton and Cyrus snapped their reins to join Commander Ryker next to the king.

"Villagers of Tienn, I am your king, Edmund Bale," he said in a booming voice. "Our army marches through, and we thank you in advance for your hospitality."

A murmur rumbled through the crowd before a middle-aged man with rust-colored hair spoke up in a trembling voice. "Your Majesty, I am Marcellus Shepley, Baron of Tienn, and we welcome you to our town. Tienn has a proud history dating back two thousand years, and we are proud to share it with you."

"I require food and lodging for my men. I trust your town will be accommodating."

"But you have many thousands of men," the baron said, his eyes shifting to his own people around him. "We can't feed and house that many."

Bale lifted his chin. "Oh, really?" He lifted his eyes to the tower behind them. "Tell me about this tower."

Shepley's eyes brightened. "The Talon Tower! This is the pride of

Tienn, built of solid marble! Outside of Feldor's castles, it's the tallest structure in the kingdom." He turned slightly and gestured above him. "It has looked over our town for nearly three hundred years."

"Interesting," Bale said in a measured voice. "How did it come to be built?"

"They erected it in celebration of when King—" the baron stopped and looked at Bale as if he'd swallowed a bug.

Bale raised his eyebrows and motioned for him to continue. ". . . when King . . . ?"

Shepley swallowed visibly after glancing at the surrounding people. He cleared his throat. "When they defeated King Vitrion."

"And when they pushed my people out of these lands," Bale finished, narrowing his eyes. "Tell me, was there a celebration after that?"

Shepley squirmed as he stood. "Yes, Your Majesty, there was."

"Was it called the Two Week Feast? Where the entire town ate and drank their fill for two entire weeks?" The baron didn't reply. "So, this monstrosity of a tower celebrates defeating my people and killing our leader, after which you gorged yourselves for weeks, but you stand there telling me you can't show enough respect to take care of my men for one night?"

"Your Majesty, I—we—" The baron stumbled for words. "I'm sure we can find *some* food, but we don't have even close to enough spare beds."

Bale uttered an evil laugh. "Who said anything about *spare* beds?" He nodded to the baron's side, where a young woman stood in a red dress. With her shoulders back and long, brown hair, she held an almost regal look. "And who is this? Your wife? Your daughter?"

"Leave her out of this," Shepley said, sliding to his left to stand in front of the woman.

"Perhaps she'd be willing to give me a personal tour of your town if you're unwilling to cooperate?" Bale said with a raised eyebrow.

The baron fixed his jaw and stared back. His chest rose and fell as his body trembled. Finally, Bale turned his horse around, facing the army surrounding him.

"The town of Tienn refuses to extend us the hospitality we require. That means we must stand up for ourselves. Find whatever food you can and take any bed you like. Enjoy the evening for tomorrow we march again."

A cheer rose from the crowd. Greed and hunger filled the soldiers' eyes as they turned in all directions to ravage the town.

Bale brought his horse to Ryker. "Collect our tax from the men's plundered loot."

"Yes, King Bale," Ryker replied. "What about the workers?"

Bale looked at the men in chains staring with wide eyes at the surrounding chaos. "Keep them chained in the square with men guarding them overnight. I want another five hundred added to their number by morning."

"It will be done."

Brixton's stomach roiled. The chaos and greed filling the air made him sick.

"Brixton," Bale said. He snapped his head to the king, who had a grin on his face. "Enjoy yourself tonight. You've earned it."

Bale trotted off but then turned in his saddle. "Oh, and Ryker . . ." He nodded to the tower. "Do something about this disgrace."

Brixton watched as the surrounding army descended into bedlam. Townspeople shouted and soldiers laughed. The shattering of windows rang over the roar. Brixton's shoulders slumped and chest tightened as he watched the chaos unfold.

21

Back on the Road

The sun peeked over the Straith Mountains ahead, lighting up the hills and Felting's exterior walls with an orange glow. At the lead, William eased Steelmane to a walk as he arrived at the bridge. The other three riders followed suit, and soon, the clopping of hooves on wood drowned out the gurgling of the Felavorre River below.

They passed a few early-morning travelers heading toward the city, but none gave them a second glance despite William and Veron's suspicious-looking hoods. Soon, the wide-open road on the river's east side welcomed them without another person in sight. Chelci's shoulders relaxed.

"What is it?" Veron asked, bringing Annie alongside her horse.

Chelci turned in her saddle, her eyebrows raised.

"You look relieved."

"Oh." She looked down, her cheeks growing warm. "I guess it's a relief to get farther from Felting and all of those posters listing a reward for your capture."

Veron chuckled. "Yeah, I guess so. Do you worry about me?"

She took a deep breath. "We can't know what's going to happen, and whether you or William will die like the Dream predicted." She turned and held his gaze. "I *do* know I want to be with you, for whatever time we have. But, yes, I worry about you."

"I worry about you, too," Morgan said, calling from behind. "Chelci, did Veron ever tell you about the time he ran off in the rain to rescue one of our market workers?"

"Was that the girl he had the crush on?" she asked, turning in her saddle with her mouth curling at the edge.

Morgan laughed. "Chloe? Did you have a crush on her?"

Veron's face paled as his head retreated.

"Why didn't you tell me?"

"I did get sent off into slavery right after that," Veron said. "Plus, she was married."

"Married?" Chelci put a hand on her hip. "Well, this is a whole new side of things."

"What's this, now?" William asked, turning around in his saddle in front of them.

"It wasn't like that, I promise," Veron said, holding up a hand.

Chelci raised an eyebrow.

"She kept it from us." He turned to Morgan.

"It's true. We didn't know she was married." Morgan shook his head. "Anyway . . . she was missing, and Veron took off, wandering the city to find her. It ended up being a trap, but of course, he came back in one piece. It seems no matter what trouble he finds himself in, Veron always finds a way through." His face darkened. "Still . . . this Dream feels like something else . . . and Bale is—"

Morgan's words choked off as his eye glistened. The others remained quiet as he composed himself. After a sniff, he said, "I feel so lonely with Catherine gone. I can't imagine losing you too, Veron."

Veron's mouth made a tight line. "I'll do my best to make sure you don't. I know no one will ever take Catherine's place, but one day, I bet you'll find someone to be with."

The group of four made solid progress through the day, alternating their horses between a canter and a steady walk. They passed farms and small villages, waving politely at the people they passed while Veron kept his face obscured. The low river lands gave way to rolling hills as they approached the foothills below the mountains. Just shy of Tienn, the sun fell against the horizon in the west, prompting them to make camp. They strayed from the road and found a stream to water the horses and rest for the night.

"I don't think I'll ever get used to riding all day," Veron said as he dismounted. He put his hands on his stomach and stretched backward, groaning. "My abs and thighs ache."

"I'm feeling it, too," Morgan said, tying Clover to a tree limb. "I'm sure it will get easier each day though."

Chelci smirked. She felt fine. *I have ridden a lot more than they have though.*

"I'm starving," Veron said. "More dried meat tonight, I guess. Chelci, is it in your bag?"

"Yes," she replied. "Give me a bit, though. Let me see if I can find something fresh."

While the men searched for firewood, Chelci strung a bow and grabbed a quiver. She slunk through the brush, taking care to dodge the dead leaves and twigs. Ducking around a tree, she nocked an arrow, holding it ready. A rustle of leaves turned her head. She stepped forward, moving up the edge of a flat rock. On the far side, scuffling through the dirt, the brown feathers of a garront brought a grin to her face. She raised the bow and pulled the string against her ear, sighting along the shaft. The bird popped its head up, turning its ear toward her. She loosed the string.

Veron dropped a load of dead wood on the ground as she approached their camp. "Nothing out there, huh?"

"I wouldn't say that," she said, tossing the dead bird next to his pile of wood.

"Nice! We can eat tonight."

"Yeah, but now we have to feather and clean it. It will be dark by the time it's ready to cook."

"I'll take care of it," William said, hobbling up with his staff and an armload of sticks. "You all relax. I'll let you know when it's ready."

Chelci smiled. "That sounds great, thanks."

"I'll help," Morgan chimed in. "I'll get the fire going while you prep the bird."

"Yeah, thanks, you two." Veron exhaled as he lowered himself to the ground and leaned against a rock. William had begun plucking feathers and Morgan bent over to grab some smaller sticks. He turned his head to Chelci. "What do we do then?"

Feeling full of energy, she pulled her sword and hit it against his shoulder. "We train. Come on!" She danced past him, skipping her way past a few trees to a cleared area. Veron followed. Well off the road, short grass grew in the clearing with a few rocks sticking out of the ground. Trees surrounded them and shadows of mountains loomed above the branches. Lingering twilight made the area appear to glow. Chelci rubbed her feet into the grass as she wound her hands around the grip of her sword.

"How should we train?" Veron asked, pulling his sword from over his shoulder and standing opposite her in the clearing.

"How about you try and get me." She smirked. ". . . if you can."

His eyebrow raised. "If I can, huh?"

"And *no* origine! That's not fair."

Veron laughed. "All right, let's see what you can do."

Chelci took a deep breath. Her legs were steady and arms taut. The light blade balanced in her grip, ready to spring into action. With a shout, she made the first move, stepping forward, striking at his side. He met her head on, knocking her blade away and spinning. Chelci was ready for his reverse attack, nimbly ducking, leaving his extended arms swiping nothing but air. She kicked his chest, pushing him backward.

"You've got to be faster than that," she taunted.

Veron's mouth formed a tight line as he stepped to the side, raising his sword above his head and pointing it toward her. They circled, keeping their eyes locked. Veron lunged and swung hard. She spun when his weapon passed in front of her, and, after a full pivot, she struck out with the flat end of her blade at his shoulder. His arm deflected hers, knocking the weapon harmlessly away. *He's so quick!*

The two traded blows back and forth for what seemed like forever. The glowing twilight gradually grew dimmer, but their duel's intensity didn't relent. Ducking below a high swing, Chelci rolled on the ground, popping up once she was a safe distance away.

"You can't get me if you just roll away," Veron said.

She narrowed her eyes and yelled, lunging forward. Veron jumped back, flinging his sword side to side to block her rapid attacks. The clang of the swords vibrated through her arms and filled the air. She didn't stop. Perspiration coated her palms, but she gripped tighter. Chelci continued forward, keeping Veron on his heels, his eyes wide, sweat flinging off his forehead.

I'm almost there! Veron's sword knocked to the side, and he nearly tripped, flinging his free hand in the air for balance. Chelci kicked his sword hand away and pressed forward. *This is it!* She stepped in, ready to press her blade against his chest and declare victory.

Suddenly, his body blurred. She held her sword forward where his chest had been, but Veron stood to her side with his own weapon held against her neck. Chelci froze. The guilty look on his face told her all she needed to know.

"You cheated!" Her mouth hung open with a trace of a grin. His eyes looked up and to the side, but he had no response. "How can it be a fair fight if you're using the origine?"

"Sorry. It's habit."

"Who won?" William's voice called through the trees from the growing fire.

Chelci glowered. Veron pursed his lips before yelling back. "I did . . . but I used the origine."

She raised her eyebrows. "And if you hadn't?"

Veron flashed a wry smile then spoke loudly enough for the others to hear. "If I hadn't . . . there's a *chance* she may have won."

"Gah!" Chelci said, punching him.

"Ow!" He laughed as he grabbed his arm. "Okay, okay . . . *more* than a chance."

"A chance," she muttered then pointed at him. "You know I had you."

His eyes held hers for a long moment. Finally, he nodded slowly and breathed, "I know."

She sheathed her sword and grinned as she returned to the light of the fire. *I had him.*

* * *

The hazy light was still young as Veron and his companions entered Tienn. Perched amidst the rolling hills of eastern Feldor, the small city majestically looked over the river valley below.

"Have you been here before, William?" Chelci asked from atop her horse.

"Yes, but it's been many years. Baron Shepley needed us when a miners' coalition conspired to kill him."

"What'd he do?" she asked.

"Nothing."

Veron turned his head as Chelci replied, "No . . . I mean, what did he do to make them want to kill him?"

"Like I said, he did nothing. They *wanted* him to give the miners more power in government. Mining these hills is their primary industry—silver, copper, even some baltham. The miners felt they deserved more control since they were the ones who brought in all the money."

"That doesn't sound unreasonable," Veron said.

"Except that the baron is specifically established to be an objective voice. There's an entire town of people living here. The miners wanted to change tariffs and fix the price of the ore to make themselves rich. The baron's job was to think of everyone—not just one group. Our team of spies picked up a plot to assassinate him, and we stepped in. Shepley was Wesley's personal choice for baron, and he's a good man."

"What did you do?" Veron asked, wide-eyed.

The horses' hooves sounded loud in the silence that followed. "We don't need to speak about that," William finally said.

Why are the streets so empty? Veron wondered. A town of that size would have people up and around by daylight. The few men and women he saw cast dirty looks in their direction. A woman carrying an armload of broken wooden pieces yelled in their direction, but he couldn't make out what she said.

"Not the friendliest town I've seen," Morgan said from the back of their train of horses.

Smoke trickled up from the center of town just ahead, giving Veron an uneasy feeling. When they emerged into the town square, his jaw dropped.

Several buildings bordering the square were burned husks that continued to smoke. Glass littered the ground from broken window panes in every direction. The square itself looked like a herd of rydanor had trampled everything in the area. A massive tower lay in ruins, crumbled on the ground. One side showed a clock face with hands bent and contorted. Scorch marks marred the stone.

William gasped. "The Talon Tower!"

"Did Bale do all of this?" Veron asked

"They would have just come through here," Chelci said.

Looking toward the fallen tower, William kicked his horse into a trot to cross the square. The others followed. Veron's stomach turned when he noticed what drew his father's attention. Next to the burned-out tower, a body hung from a rope, swaying beneath an archway. The man's feet swayed in the breeze, and his head drooped to the side. Chelci covered her mouth.

"This was Baron Shepley," William muttered.

"Who are you?" a voice shouted as a man approached from the side. "What do you want?"

The man was around thirty years old. His disheveled, dark hair didn't match his clothes' meticulous appearance. His face portrayed anger and suspicion as he glared at the four on horseback.

"We are from Felting," William said. "We're tracking Bale and his men. I presume all of this is their doing?"

The man fixed his jaw and narrowed his eyes. "They left here yesterday. What is your business with them?" Three other men with matching expressions seemed to materialize and stand around the horses. Their hands rested on sword hilts in their sheaths.

"Our business is to make sure they don't do anything like this again," William said, pointing to the hanging body. The man from Tienn's shoulders relaxed. "What happened here?"

"Bale and his army showed up two nights ago. They trashed the town—kicking people out of their own beds and taking their food.

They burned anything they didn't like, including our tower, and took five hundred men and women with them in chains when they left." He nodded to the swaying man. "And they killed my brother."

Veron's teeth clenched. He gripped the horn of his saddle, the leather creaking in his hand.

William's face turned down. "I'm sorry about that. Marcellus was a good man. You say they left yesterday?"

"Yes, midmorning."

William turned to Veron and the others. "They'll arrive at Karondir today. If we hurry, we can reach them by nightfall."

The man from Tienn stepped forward. "You say you want to make sure Bale doesn't do anything like this anymore. What are you planning to do?"

William grabbed his reins and sat up straight. "We'll do whatever we can." He turned back to Veron and the others. "Let's go."

22

Breaching Camp

U sing his elbows to pull him past the trees to the lip of the rise, Veron peeked over the hill and gawked at the valley below. All his life, he'd heard of Karondir's impenetrable walls, but seeing them in person still shocked him. They were twice as tall as those in Felting. Turrets lined the top, and a ring of torches made it look as if the wall were on fire. A closed drawbridge indicated the thousands of tents filling the plain were not welcome guests.

The tents surrounding the city stretched as far as the darkness allowed Veron to see. Red-and-black flags spread around the camp fluttered in the wind. Fires simmering in rings lit the camp and revealed the silhouettes of guards pacing between the tents.

"How do you think they plan to take the city?" Veron asked.

William exhaled. "I'm not sure. With those walls, they can defend themselves for a long while, but without Felting and Karad to back them up, they're stuck."

"Look," Morgan said, pointing past the camp. Barely visible in the darkness beyond the fires, massive structures sat in silence. "What are those?"

William sucked in a breath. "Siege engines . . . trebuchets."

"But they're *huge!*"

Veron squinted to see better. "How do they have so many?" Dozens of the enormous wooden constructions waited, ready to attack.

"They must have been building them for weeks," William said.

"What do you think *that* is?" Chelci said, pointing to a large tent in the middle of the Norshewan encampment.

The fire in front of it burned brightly, despite the late hour. A dozen men stood at attention in front of the opening and two more paced around the back.

"*That*," William said, "must be where Bale sleeps."

"There's only a handful of men." Veron said, looking at William, his heart speeding. "We could take them, don't you think?"

William nodded. "Yes, we could."

"I'm sorry," Morgan said, "but are you two thinking of trying to sneak into the middle of the enemy camp, dodging soldiers, and killing their king? How would you expect to get out of that? They'll surround you as soon as he cries out."

"*If* he cries out," William corrected.

Veron swallowed hard. *I wasn't even thinking about escaping.*

"Don't forget what they can do," Chelci said. The look on her face fell somewhere between pain and hope. "Sneaking in should be nothing, right?"

"We may not get a better chance than this," William said. "We've got to try."

Veron raised the hood of his Shadow Knights cloak. "Chelci and Morgan, you two wait here. We'll be back soon."

Veron grasped Chelci by the hand and looked into her soft, pleading eyes. "Don't worry. This will be easy," he said in a gentle voice.

"Be careful, Veron," she breathed in response.

"I will."

After scurrying along the edge of the rise, Veron and William peeked from behind a tree. The closest tent was a mere stone's throw away.

"Once we start, nowhere is safe," William whispered. "We'll be surrounded. There will be no chance to rest and recover our origine, so only use what you must. Even so, we'll have to hurry. And Veron," William grabbed Veron's arm, causing him to jolt. "No matter what happens, I'm the one to kill him." He inclined his head forward and raised his eyebrows. "Understood?"

He wants to be the one who dies. Veron took a deep breath before nodding. "Understood." He looked at the wooden staff lying on the ground. "Do you not need that to walk?"

William shook his head. "It will only slow me down. I'll be fine."

A few tents down, a soldier stood on guard, staring into the night. When he adjusted his stance to look the other direction, they bolted. Dressed in their black cloaks with their hoods raised, Veron and William ran in a crouch, using only a faint amount of origine until they passed the first tents. Loud snoring sounded from inside, but no soldiers were around to notice them.

"Walk casually now," William whispered. "It's less likely to draw attention."

The two walked, meandering between tents as they angled their path toward the camp's center. Veron tensed when a guard appeared out of the dark from behind a row of tents. He fixed his eyes on the ground and continued walking with purpose, hoping the man didn't inspect them. The soldier ducked into a flap just before they passed, without even looking their way. Veron's shoulders relaxed.

Light grew as they approached the center. William halted, pressing up against the closest canvas wall. Ahead, two guards passed each other, walking around the back perimeter of Bale's tent. His father panted heavily as he stood still.

"Are you all right?" Veron asked. "Can you do this?"

"You ready?" William whispered, ignoring the question as he drew a dagger from under his cloak.

Veron pulled out Bale's knife. He pressed his thumb against the flat metal, trying to think of anything other than what might happen, but the irony of killing the man with his own blade was not lost on him. "Ready."

With the guards ahead far apart, they ran. Veron moved so fast it appeared the guards froze. William reached the canvas first and cut a slit into the fabric, large enough to squeeze through but small enough to go unnoticed.

Veron stood after crawling inside. The light from the fire out front made the walls of the tent glow. The inside was sparse. Two chairs sat at one end of the small space with a portable desk, and a rudimentary bed filled the opposite end. Rhythmic breathing came from under the blankets, where a full head of black hair poked out.

Veron trembled. *I've waited for this moment for years, but it's nothing like I imagined.*

William's chest heaved silently as he approached the bed. Holding out his dagger, he paused for a moment while standing over the sleeping king. He looked Veron in the eyes and took a deep breath. He moved in a flash, covering the man's mouth with his hand and slicing his neck with the dagger.

Veron gritted his teeth as the covers writhed, and a moaning sound emanated from behind William's hand. After a brief struggle, the movement ceased and William removed his hand. *It's done!* He stepped closer as his father removed his hand and pulled the covers down. Blood glistened in the dim glow of the tent, and a lifeless stare looked back.

Veron gasped, and a watery feeling flowed through him. *Where's the beard? Where's the scar?*

"It's not him," William said as he jerked his head around.

Veron pinched his eyebrows together. "I don't understand. I was sure it would be him." William put up his dagger and pulled his sword from its sheath. "What is it?" Veron asked.

"It's a trap."

The edge in his father's voice stirred the embers of panic inside Veron. His gaze fell on the tent's back wall, where the light seemed to intensify. Veron ducked and peeked out the slit they had just come through. A wall of soldiers carrying torches and swords stood ready if they exited the way they came in.

"They're out there, waiting," Veron said, his voice shaking.

A horn sounded outside. The front flap of the tent drew back as Norshewan soldiers ran into the cramped space with a yell. Veron grabbed his sword while William went to work. His father hacked at the men, cutting through armor and breaking their swords. He kicked, sending them flying back through the tight opening and knocking others away.

Concerned by the level of fatigue his father already showed, Veron stepped up, allowing William a moment to move back and rest. It was an easy fight. The enemy's attacks were predictable and avoidable, and they couldn't block his own strikes. Bodies piled in the tent opening, but the wave of men continued to press in.

"We've got to . . . get out of here," William yelled between breaths.

He's right. After kicking the front soldier back and knocking down those behind him, Veron turned to the wall of the tent, slicing a long gash from top to bottom. "This way!"

Veron ran outside and gasped. He only got a glimpse when he looked through the slit, and the reality was much worse. A wall of soldiers, ten men deep, faced them from every direction.

"We can't fight them all," William said. The wall of men closed in, charging with a yell. "Jump!"

Veron sent energy to his legs and leaped. He sailed over the men and their outstretched swords. Unable to control his descent, he fell onto a tent that collapsed under him. He rolled across the bunched-up canvas then jumped back to his feet, looking around for his father.

A cry of anguish rang through the night. Veron jerked his head. William had fallen far short of where he landed, barely out of the Norshewans' reach. He grasped his good leg, his hand covered in blood.

"Father!" Veron yelled. He ran to him, arriving moments before the mob of soldiers.

"Go!" William yelled, waving his hand and revealing a fresh wound beneath. "Leave me!"

"No!" Veron turned his attention to the closing wall of swords. He lunged toward them, knocking weapons away and striking men down. Fear filled their eyes even though they had a staggering numeric advantage. Veron moved back and forth, keeping the men away from William. "Can you move?"

A groan came from his father. "Get out of here!" he shouted.

The Norshewan army surrounded them on all sides. Veron continued to jab, doing whatever he could to keep them away. They still pressed in.

Veron's insides turned to water. His feeling of invincibility waned. *My energy is almost gone! I can't keep fighting them forever!* He looked at William. His father lay on the ground. One hand clutched his leg, and the other waved his sword half-heartedly at the nearest soldiers. *I can't lose him like this!*

After a wide swath of his sword, Veron slid it into the sheath over his shoulder. Without pausing, he scooped William up in his arms. Using all the strength he had in him, he jumped just as the circle of enemies collapsed. The weight was immense. He could barely clear the men below, but it was just enough. He kept his feet when he hit the ground and continued running without glancing behind.

His source of energy was nearly depleted, but he held on as long as he could. After leaving the tents behind, he ducked into the woods and headed to Chelci and Morgan. He stumbled his last few steps until William's body fell from his grip and he collapsed on the ground.

Veron gasped for breath. He rolled side to side, seeking to replenish his depleted strength. In a moment, Chelci and Morgan's welcoming faces looked upside down at him.

"What happened?" Chelci asked. "Did you get him?"

After several more deep breaths, Veron shook his head. He could only manage a few words. "Need to hide."

23

Entering Karondir

Veron glanced up as a branch moved and William emerged from the thicket. He leaned on his staff as he hobbled into their excuse for a camp in the early-morning light.

"Anything?" Morgan asked with eyes raised.

"Nothing," William replied. "They searched around their camp but didn't come out this far."

"Why would they stop?" Chelci asked. "If all Bale cares about is killing Veron—or both of you now, I guess—wouldn't he send the whole army if he knows you're close?"

"They couldn't stop us when they had us surrounded in the middle of their camp," William said. "They won't want to stumble upon us spread out in the woods."

"Do you have any idea who you killed?" Morgan asked.

William shook his head. "One of their soldiers. Probably some low-ranking man Bale made sleep in his bed as a decoy."

"They know we're here now," Veron added. "That makes our job much harder." William nodded. "Any ideas?"

William rubbed his chin and jaw as he breathed in. "I wish we could speak with Karondir's army."

221

"To do what?" Veron asked.

"If we could get them to coordinate an attack, we could use that as a distraction. If Karondir can tie up Bale's men, fewer are left to defend him."

"We could talk with my brother!" Chelci said, raising her finger in the air.

"Your brother?"

"Jackson—he's a captain in the army, stationed here."

"That's right," Veron added. "I forgot about him. Could they let us in somehow?"

William chuckled. "They're surrounded by an army. They won't lower the drawbridge for someone who shouts they're a relative. But, we *could* use the river."

His serious tone gave Veron chills along his arms. "What do you mean?"

"The Felavorre River runs along the northwest side of the city. Upstream, a tunnel of water diverts and runs underground. It emerges behind the walls, inside a cistern."

"Perfect!"

"I'm great at swimming," Chelci said. "I can do that."

Veron's forehead creased. "Wait . . . Why wouldn't Norshewa or any invaders use it? Surely Karondir would see that as a vulnerability."

William pursed his lips. "For starters, they probably don't know about it. But even if they did, it's not exactly short."

"How long is it?" Chelci asked.

"Longer than a man can hold his breath."

"So . . . how can—" Veron stopped as a realization came to him. "But not longer than a shadow knight could?"

"Have you ever tried holding your breath using the origine?" William asked, and Veron shook his head. "It's like anything else.

You focus your energy on slowing down your body's need of oxygen, but—" His gaze drifted to the ground. "I don't know *I* could do it. Having one leg would make it difficult to make it through the tunnel."

Veron's hands began to feel clammy, but he swallowed hard and nodded. "I'll do it."

"It sounds dangerous," Chelci said. "What if his breath runs out?"

"Then he'll die," William said after a pause. No one spoke while the wind whistled through the trees.

"There's got to be another way," Chelci said. "What about the walls? Could you jump over them?"

William shook his head. "They're too high."

"What about . . ."

"This is the only way," Veron said. He turned to Chelci.

Moisture pooled at the corner of her eyes.

"It's all right. I can do this." He grabbed Chelci by the shoulders and pulled her into a tight embrace.

William sloughed the coiled rope off from around his chest. "Take this. Once you get inside, make your way to the wall, then lower it down to pull me up."

"Pull *us* up," Chelci added.

"You're not going," Veron said. "It's too dangerous."

Chelci scoffed. "If I remember correctly, *I'm* the one who saved *your* life in Nasco only a week ago. Plus, it's *my* brother we need to speak with!"

William raised an eyebrow. "It would be useful having her there."

Morgan raised a tentative hand. "I . . . don't mind watching the horses." The other three looked at each other and chuckled.

"All right then," Veron said, looking at each in turn. "Let's go."

Veron stood on the riverbank and stared at the circle of stones submerged just under the surface. Water rippled along, bubbling happily, but his stomach churned inside. He looked up to the city. The walls were a long ways away.

William rested his hand on Veron's shoulder. "Use your legs and arms, but don't use all your energy at once. Make it last."

Veron nodded then stepped into the edge of the river. Water seeped through his boots like icicles pricking his feet. He moved deeper, stopping at his waist and gasping from the cold.

On the bank, Chelci held William's hand, squeezing it tightly. She wore a feeble smile while a solitary tear creeped down her cheek. "Be careful," she managed in a croaking voice.

"I will." Veron returned a smile then cinched the rope around his chest.

William patted Veron's black cloak draped over his own shoulder. "I'll give this back to you once you pull us up."

Feeling naked without his cloak, Veron felt for the sword over his shoulder. He tugged on it to make sure it was secure. He took a deep breath and held it for a moment before letting it out. After a beat, he inhaled again, holding it a bit longer. After one final breath, he ducked his head under.

Despite the murky water providing little clarity, the foreboding black opening loomed clearly before him. Without hesitating, he kicked his feet to propel him into the tunnel. His sight turned to black as soon as he passed the opening. A current pushed from behind, helping him slowly move forward. The space was tight, but just large enough for him to kick his legs. He pulled himself with a hand pressed against each wall, the stones slimy and smooth. While he expected to need a breath, his lungs felt surprisingly good. The tingle he was used to in his body settled into his chest, keeping him from needing to suck in more oxygen.

Veron kicked along, throwing a hand forward after each stroke to make sure he didn't crash into an unseen object or a wall. He tried to estimate the distance he had traveled and imagine how close he was to the wall. A tug of pressure pulled at his lungs, and his stomach clenched. He squinted to try to make out anything ahead, but it remained black. A glance behind him revealed a pinpoint of daylight far in the distance.

Should I turn around? Veron pictured himself emerging, unsuccessful, back at the river's edge. *Could I even make it back?* The thought of Bale razing the town of Nasco flashed through his mind. *No, I've got to make it.* He turned toward the dark and stroked forward.

After what seemed like an eternity, a dim light grew ahead. Veron's heart surged. He kicked harder, renewed with hope. The tightness in his chest grew stronger. His body felt numb from the cold, but the light approached quickly. His lungs began to ache. His mind pleaded for him to take a breath, but he fought against the instinct. *Just a bit farther!*

The tunnel appeared to open up ahead. Veron stretched his arm for one last thrust, but his hand slammed into something hard. A round of bubbles escaped his mouth, then his head and shoulder slammed into a barrier. Metal bars crisscrossed the tunnel, leaving holes too small to swim through. He grabbed hold of the cold impediment and shook, yet the barrier held firm.

Veron panicked. His eyes darted across the opening. The metal sank into the stone edges on all sides. His lungs spasmed. The origine gasped inside, nearly depleted. Through the bars, just over his head, the water's surface taunted him. He stretched his arm through, flailing against the stone on the other side, desperately hoping to find something, but it was no use.

As his lungs pleaded with him, and his energy level grew perilously low, Veron calmed his mind. He took a moment and let his arms rest. His lungs momentarily softened their complaints. Focused, he turned around and pressed his feet against one side of the bars.

Leaning over, he grabbed the other side with both hands and pulled. The dregs of remaining origine protested, but soon his strength surged as his energy rerouted to his arms and legs. A crashing sound echoed underwater as the metal bars ripped free of their casing. Veron continued pulling until they swung free, creating a space large enough for his body.

His lungs were utterly spent. The origine was gone. With a last surge of effort, he pulled his body through the bars. He tried to kick, but his useless legs didn't respond. When his head breached the surface, he strained his neck and only barely lifted his mouth above the water. He gulped in air, the fresh infusion of oxygen filling his body with life. The darkness lightened.

The water's edge was near. He trudged through the shallow pool toward the dry ground. When he arrived, he rolled out of the cistern and lay on his back, sucking in heaving breaths with his eyes closed. His mouth curled in a smile. He rested for several minutes, allowing his energy to grow.

After a long rest, he opened his eyes, and the sight took his breath away. A large pool filled the room, the surface of the water lazily flowing from one end to the other. Tall, smooth columns spread throughout the pool, holding up an arched ceiling. Windows high on the wall let in light, which bounced off the water's surface and gave the room a glow.

Veron pushed himself to a sitting position and thought of Chelci and William waiting outside. After a few more deep breaths, he worked his way to his feet. The lack of energy left him wobbly. He pressed his hand against a nearby wall to keep steady. Water dripped from his clothes and the rope around his chest. Moving one step at a time, he pulled himself up a short flight of stairs and stumbled out of the cistern.

Sunlight greeted him when he emerged outside. People scurried through the streets with an anxious energy, but none took the time to pay attention to the soaking-wet stranger. Several chickens ran free, and a goat munched on a pile of trash, staring at him. The city wall towered above. Nearby, a staircase cut into the stone, and Veron moved in its direction. His legs struggled to support him, but he forced himself forward.

Halfway up the steps, a train of men, armed with pitchforks and wooden tools ran past him. The sudden rush of movement left him dizzy. Veron tottered, but he quickly kneeled on the step and touched his hand to the wall. A woman carrying a basket jogged down the steps. She slowed to pass, giving him a wary glance, but then continued.

By the time Veron made it to the top, what energy he'd built back was lost again. He leaned against the ramparts and took deep breaths. A glance over the wall brought a smile to his face. The river flowed past the city. He even saw the bank of the water where he'd entered the tunnel. The ground between, covered in grass and rocks, gave no indication an underwater passage lay beneath. He turned his attention to the left where tall trees grew. Keeping a hand against the wall, he plodded in that direction.

A few soldiers gave him wary glances when he walked around them. They watched the walls at regular intervals, but with Bale's army on the opposite side of the city, there was little for them to do. After passing a small building built up next to the wall, he arrived at the area where they agreed to meet. Veron checked in both directions. No soldiers were in sight. He peeked past the crenel and leaned over the edge. Two small figures looked up from below. Chelci raised her hands and jumped into the air at the sight of him.

He lifted the rope from around his chest. With it coiled at his feet, Veron lowered one end, feeding it as quickly as possible over the edge. When a tug confirmed it made it down, a wave of worry rushed through him. *I don't have the strength to pull them up.* He needed more time.

The rope rested in his hands when a gruff voice barked, "Who are you!"

He spun. Three Karondir soldiers stared at him, spread in formation with alert swords. More poured through the doorway to the room next to the wall. The quick movement caused a dizzy spell to hit him. He staggered and pressed a hand against the wall for balance. Soon, a dozen men stood before him.

"What are you doing?" the soldier in the middle demanded. He looked taller than the others and held himself as if he outranked the rest. "Drop that!"

"Whoa, whoa, it's okay," Veron said, sliding the loose coil of rope around the crenellations then holding up his hands. "I'm a friend."

"He's trying to let people in!" another yelled. "He's a Norshewan! Kill him!"

"No, I'm not!" Veron shouted back. None of the soldiers moved. "I'm looking for Captain Marlow. Do you know him?"

The leader's eyes flitted to the man next to him, and his shoulders relaxed the smallest bit. "What business do you have with the captain?"

"I worked for his family. I need to speak with him." Veron looked from man to man, but none seemed to believe him or want to do anything. "Please! It's about Bale!"

The leader turned partially without taking his eyes off of Veron. "See if he's free."

A younger man in the back of the group sheathed his sword and ran through the nearest archway.

A wave of weakness washed over Veron, and he wobbled. "Do you mind if I sit?" Veron asked, pointing to the edge of the wall while moving slowly. The others didn't object. Relief filled him as he rested on the stone edge. He chanced a glance over the edge. William and Chelci looked up, their arms held in a shrug.

"Where are you from?" The leader asked, sidling to the edge and keeping a wary eye on Veron. He took a quick look over the side. "Are they with you?"

"They are. That's William and Chelci. We come from Felting, and we're going after Bale."

The man raised an eyebrow. "You're . . . going after Bale?" He smirked. "Just for fun? What are you, some elite warrior?" The men behind him laughed nervously.

Veron swallowed hard, allowing the laughter to settle. "Yes . . . I am."

The men grew silent. A few glanced between each other as faces screwed up. The two soldiers closest to Veron puffed out their chests and flexed their arms as they extended their swords. "Nice try," the leader said. "Next time you—"

Veron moved quicker than they could see. He pried the swords from the hands of the two lead soldiers and moved back to his seat before he released the little origine he had saved up. The men staggered. Their faces jerked to each other before they stared at Veron, wide-eyed. He remained in his seat with both swords pointed back toward the men, who scrambled backward.

"How did you—" the soldier stopped, unsure what to say.

"As I said . . ." Veron began before moving again. He rushed through the small space, taking the swords from the rest of the men before returning to his seat. With the weapons piled across his arms and his energy depleted, he stared at the men as they gawked. ". . . I'm here for Bale."

The soldiers shuffled and stuttered. They glanced at each other, alternating between looks of fear and awe. Veron lowered his weak arms, allowing the weapons to clatter to the floor.

"I'm not here to attack you. I'm on your side, and I need to see Captain Marlow."

"This had better be good," an assertive voice called as two men proceeded through the archway. "Bale readies to attack, and I'm drawn away to greet people." The man in front was young, only a year or two older than Veron. His short brown hair crossed his head in a sharp line. Although his body didn't look like that of a soldier, the way he held himself commanded respect. The unarmed men averted their glances. A few shuffled to take back their swords.

"Jackson Marlow?" Veron asked.

"Captain Marlow, yes," the young soldier confirmed. "Who are you?"

"I've come here with your sister, Chelci." Jackson's head jerked while Veron continued. "I worked for your family for a while in Felting after you left. I was Chelci's wardman for a time."

Jackson's head tilted and face scrunched. "Veron?"

Veron grinned and nodded.

"Chelci wrote to me about you. What are you doing here? This isn't a good time. How did you . . . ?" Jackson looked around as his words trailed off. "You said you're here with Chelci?"

"I did," Veron said, motioning Jackson to the edge. When the captain looked over the side, Veron waved to the two watching from below.

"Chelci," Jackson whispered before turning to Veron. "How . . . did you get in the city?"

"It's a long story." Veron looked over the wall as he picked the coil of rope back up. "Can someone help me pull them up?"

Veron rested while the men of Karondir pulled Chelci up the wall. Even before she extricated herself from the loop of rope she sat in, she wrapped her brother up in a hug.

"I hadn't gotten a letter since the attack," Jackson said after they pulled back. "I feared the worst."

"Sorry about that. We've been in hiding. You got my last letter about Mother?"

Jackson nodded, pressing his lips together. "I . . . uh . . . wasn't sure how to feel about it."

"Yeah, me too."

"How's Father?"

Chelci perked up. "He's doing well. We saw him a few nights ago."

Jackson rubbed his hand along her upper arm. "It's so good to see you, Sister. It's been—what . . . ?"

"Six years," she finished. "I'm sorry for leaving you alone."

"It's all right. It's partly why I ended up here," he said, gesturing around him.

The men huffed as they pulled up William. When he arrived, Chelci introduced him as he recoiled the rope.

"We need to speak with the baron as soon as possible," William said. "We have an idea to defeat Bale, but we need Karondir's help."

"I appreciate you wanting to help, but Karondir's entire army is already on it."

William glanced at the other soldiers before leaning in to Jackson. "Can we speak privately?"

Jackson's eyes narrowed thoughtfully. "Leave us," he commanded. The soldiers filed out of the area, leaving Jackson alone. "What is it?"

William looked at Veron then back at the captain. "We're shadow knights, and it's our destiny to stop him."

Jackson's eyes grew. After a moment, he nodded then beckoned with a hand. "Follow me."

24

City of Chaos

Jackson led along the top of the wall as Veron, William, and Chelci followed. Rounding a corner, the plain filled with Bale's army revealed itself. Veron gasped. Seeing the camp in the light was much worse than in the dark. Tents stretched back as far as he could see.

"I'll take you to the baron, but I don't know how interested he'll be in listening." Jackson motioned to the army below. "We have our hands pretty full already."

"Where did they all come from?" Veron asked. "When they took Felting, they only had a fraction of this!"

The group stopped, and William pointed out a section where yellow-and-white flags rippled in the breeze. "Those are from Tarphan. Most are probably from Norshewa and Karad, but I bet the section over there is from Felting."

"How did they get so many siege engines?" Chelci asked.

"The first battalions arrived weeks ago and began assembling them," Jackson said. "We feared they were trying to draw us out from the walls, so we waited. More soldiers continued to show, and the machines multiplied. Now, meeting them in the open would mean certain defeat.

"There are over thirty of them!" Veron said.

William pointed. "See their pile of boulders?"

Chelci gasped. "They could knock down the entire city with that!"

"Like I said, we have our hands full," Jackson added.

Movement in the plain caught Veron's eye. Soldiers gathered around the trebuchets, and lines of men covered in armor moved into rows. "Are they . . . mobilizing?"

The four leaned forward, gazing intently. Jackson gasped. "They are. We need to warn the baron. Come on!"

Veron walked with purpose, following Jackson into the central keep. Passing through a doorway, a long room with tall ceilings revealed a handful of men gathered together. One paced at the end of a table.

"Baron Devenish!" Jackson shouted as they approached.

The pacing man stopped and looked their way. "Captain Marlow, what is it?"

Advanced in years, the baron hunched as he stood. His dark-gray hair was thick and wavy, but his beard was a lighter shade—almost white.

"Bale readies to attack!" Jackson breathed heavily from the brisk walk. "His men mobilize as we speak."

Devenish turned to the men in the room, who had already sprung to their feet. "Go, prepare the troops. Ready all the reserves."

"Also, my sister, Chelci, just arrived."

"Captain, this is hardly the time to—"

"She came with William and Veron Stormbridge." He leaned in and softened his voice. ". . . two shadow knights."

The baron's forehead pinched. "Shadow knights?"

William stepped forward as men ran through the hall, shouting orders. "That's right, Lord Baron. We need to speak with you."

"Shadow knights . . . Wasn't there a prophecy about you killing Bale?"

Veron and William exchanged a look. "We're working on that, sir," Veron said.

"But we're having trouble getting to him," William added. "We need your help."

Before the baron could respond, an enormous crash sounded outside and shook the building. Dust fell from the rafters. A second and third crash followed. Battle horns sounded from multiple directions, and the furious ringing of bells filled the air.

Jackson touched Chelci's arm. "I'll catch up with you soon. I need to go." He nodded to her before turning and running outside.

Veron, Chelci, William, the baron, and three guards trailed behind. The crashes continued. One after another, large objects collided into the city walls. Two men on top of the wall fell, crashing into the stone street below. The walls continued to shake. Rocks crumbled and fell into the streets, where Karondir soldiers ran, readying themselves.

A large boulder cleared the top of the wall and fell into the inner city, across the square from the keep. It landed at the base of a bell tower, destroying the foundation. The chime of bells dulled as the structure crumbled, collapsing into the street and crushing people below.

Screams filled the air while Veron watched. "What can we do?" he asked his father.

William shook his head. "We can't fight this battle."

"But, we could . . . go out there and try to stop them or something."

William's head continued to shake. "We have limits, Veron. Taking on an army is outside of our ability. We need to focus on Bale."

"Come with me. We need to get out of here," the baron said, turning back into the keep with his three guards in step.

William followed first. Veron turned to go, but Chelci caught his eye. She stared into the streets, where her brother shouted to a battalion of men waiting by the crumbling wall. "Come on, Chelci," Veron said, tugging on her arm. "We need to move." Her head remained facing the men as her feet followed Veron.

The baron led them through the keep as the crashes continued. They ascended what seemed an endless set of stairs. When there were no more flights to climb, they walked out on a platform looking over the city.

Boulders hurtled through the air, thrown by the trebuchets at various points of the wall. The massive objects spun as they flew, crashing into the outer fortifications or landing in the city with devastating results. The rest of Bale's army stood in formation, waiting.

Below Veron's platform, chaos reigned. The soldiers held their posts, but men, women, and children scattered in every direction. A young girl wailed next to a pile of rubble, pulling on a lifeless hand emerging from the stones. Down another street, a man held his wife. They both scurried down the street while pressing bloody bandages against their heads.

A boulder crashed into the open door of the central keep, where they had stood only moments before. Stones fell into a pile of rubble as a cloud of dust and terror filled the air.

"You said you need our help?" the baron said, keeping his eyes on the battle.

"We wanted you to lead a surprise attack on their camp to tie up their men," William replied. "But that's not possible anymore."

"What will it take for you to kill Bale?"

"We've tried to sneak up on him, but he's been hiding during our last two attempts."

"And when he's not hiding, he's surrounded by a small army," Chelci added.

A vertical crack formed in the wall ahead after a deafening boom. "They're going to burst through," the baron muttered to himself.

The hits continued, and the vertical crack splintered into a spiderweb. Stones from the top fell in large chunks as the wall crumbled. After one more massive collision, the cracked portion of the wall fell in a turbulent pile of rubble. Billowing fog and dust filled the air. Karondir's men held the street, ready to defend against the imminent invasion.

The crash of boulders stopped. An eerie quiet saturated the air as the city waited. Veron squinted his eyes to see through the haze. He looked for swords and armor coming over the wreckage. He expected shouts and cries of war, but what he heard were roars—gut-churning sounds penetrating the fog. At once, dozens of norsh bears streamed over the wall's remains, barreling through the haze toward the men inside.

"Bears!" Chelci cried.

The defenders below didn't budge, meeting the animals head on. Veron cringed as the gigantic beasts plowed through the men, knocking them to the ground and swatting them like flies. Surrounding their white fur, leather armor repelled arrows and swords. The bears didn't hesitate. They roared as they decimated the men, severing arms and legs and ripping open chests with their powerful claws. A woman below screamed as she ran down the street, trying hopelessly to outrun a lumbering beast with its teeth bared.

As soon as the bears dispersed to have their way in the city, Norshewan soldiers arrived with the blare of a war horn. A wall of men appeared in the gap before running into the city with a shout.

"Lord Baron, we need to get you out of here," a guard said.

William nodded. "I agree."

"Where's Jackson?" Chelci said. "I don't see him anymore."

"I'm sure he'll be all right," Veron said, swallowing the dryness in his throat.

The Norshewan army continued to stream in. The soldiers from Karondir had little chance to fight back. Outnumbered, with their formations in disarray, the invading army picked them apart. Bears continued to spread through the city, some even turning against the Norshewans, but the loss didn't matter. There were far too many of them.

"We need to go, *now!*" another guard said.

Tears filled Chelci's eyes as Veron again dragged her along. The group ran down a hallway, past the endless staircase. Shouts and footsteps sounded below. A guard stopped at the top of the stairs, looking over the edge. "Go! Go!" He waved his arms down the hall while he watched below.

Veron held onto Chelci as they ran. A guard pulled on the side of a bookshelf at the end of the hall, pivoting the wooden piece of furniture off the wall. When Veron arrived, a dark passage lay behind it. A musty smell wafted in the air. The guard went first, followed by the baron, another guard, then William. Veron and Chelci continued to hold hands as they entered the corridor. The final guard pulled the bookshelf closed after he entered, and a resounding boom echoed as darkness filled the space.

The group momentarily froze. Heavy breathing sounded like alarms as they remained where they were. Thudding footsteps and the metal clanking of armor rang out as what sounded like a small army spread through the keep.

"Find him!" a voice shouted. "We must have Devenish!"

Veron took a few silent steps closer to the entrance. Chelci's soft grip pulled on his arm, but he soothed her with a light touch. Running and shouting continued as Veron leaned his ear toward the back of the bookshelf.

A faint amount of light snuck in through cracks, and his eyes adjusted. The guard standing with him held his finger to his lips. He was young, maybe seven or eight years older than Veron. Well-built and confident, he held his sword firm.

"Commander Ryker!" a muffled voice called through the wall. Footsteps clacked on the stone floor. "We haven't found the baron. Either he's in hiding or he was never here."

"Keep looking. Bale wants him dead. He needs leaders loyal to him."

"We'll keep looking, sir. What should we do about the captured officers?"

"How many do you have?"

"Three captains so far. The Karondir soldiers are already surrendering though, so we should have more soon."

"Keep them in the dungeon. They could be useful for information. Once we've squeezed them dry, we can kill them, too."

Veron's body tensed. He glanced back toward Chelci but couldn't see her in the darkness.

"It will be done, Commander." A set of footsteps walked away.

Veron made to move back to Chelci, but the young guard held his arm fast.

What is it? Veron froze. The faint scrape of a book being pulled off a shelf vibrated through the wall. Veron clenched his jaw. His heart pounded. In a moment, the book slid back into place and a second set of footsteps walked away.

Veron sighed. Farther down the passage, flint scraped in succession until a bright light blinded him. A guard lit a torch. Chelci caught Veron's eye. Pressed against the wall, her jaw trembled. She stared forward with a dazed look on her face.

"Maybe they haven't caught your brother," the baron whispered.

"Come on," the guard with the torch urged before leading them farther into the passage.

Veron rested his hand on Chelci's shoulder as he walked just behind. "Chelci . . . I'm so sorry." She sloughed off his hand, continuing forward without turning around. Sniffs bounced off the walls.

The group followed the lone torch to a long-forgotten staircase. Veron leaned over the side and blanched. Rotten wood planks spiraled down, disappearing into darkness. With one hand on the wall, he followed behind Chelci who winced at each creak of the stairs.

Veron sighed when they reached the solid stone at the bottom. A loud creak filled the passage as the guard opened a rusted metal grate. Veron cringed at the sound, but there was no one around to hear.

Through the grate, a steep step dropped them into a pool of stagnant water, where Veron sank to his knees. A revolting smell filled the air, and the chattering of rats echoed somewhere in the dim passage. Some distance away, a grate on the ceiling let in a stream of light.

The lead guard waited for everyone to catch up. "These are the drains underneath the city. We'll follow them down to the river where an exit should get us outside the walls," he whispered. Then he pointed to the ceiling. "The street is above us, so keep your voices down."

Veron reached out to hold Chelci's hand. Her arm felt limp. Her eyes held a glassy look as she continued to blankly stare. His stomach churned. *What would it be like, hearing your brother was going to die?* He looked at the ceiling grate as the group moved. They stepped slowly, keeping the sloshing of water to a minimum. Veron's feet couldn't follow.

"Wait," he said, loud enough to be heard over the water. The group stopped and looked back at him. "I know we need to go after Bale. That's our priority and our destiny, but . . ." He looked at Chelci. She returned his gaze, her eyes growing wider and filling with hope.

"But I need to go after Jackson."

Her face softened. Creases formed at the corners of her eyes as her mouth turned up. "Thank you," she whispered.

The baron sloshed a few steps forward. "He'll be in the dungeon. You can't just waltz in there and get him out. Their men will guard it."

Veron nodded. "I know."

William stepped forward. "I'll go with you."

Chelci stepped forward as well but didn't speak. Veron wanted to tell her she couldn't come, but the gesture would be useless. He turned to the baron. "I know you need to leave, but where can we find the dungeon?"

The baron nodded then turned to the younger guard. "Patrick, will you lead them?"

"Sir? My job is to not leave your side. I—"

"It's alright. I'm asking you to help them. Plus, the captains need you."

The guard nodded after a pause. "Of course, Lord Baron."

William rested his hand on the hilt of his sword. "Let's go."

25

The Dungeons

Chelci crouched, her legs cramping. Ahead of her, a dim light danced across Veron's face as he pressed it against the grate above him. The passage was tight, but at least it smelled better than the ones they spent the previous hour walking and crawling through. Her feet and knees were raw and longed to be free of the sewers.

"I think it's clear," Veron whispered, leaning toward the rest of them.

Patrick nodded. "When you get up, hurry to your right. There will be a wall by a staircase you can hide behind."

William leaned against Chelci. "Are you sure you want to go?"

"Of course," she snapped, not wanting him to sense any hesitation. Only a tinge of fear crept into her. *I'd be more afraid if I didn't have two shadow knights with me.*

Veron lifted the grate and poked out his head. After a moment, he slid the metal barrier to the side. Chelci winced at the rough grating sound until he scurried out. As soon as his feet left the passage, a hand appeared from above. "Come on." His urgent whisper bounced through the narrow passage.

Patrick moved next, grabbing the hand for help. Chelci shuffled after him. A dim sky awaited as she looked up through the opening. She grabbed Veron's hand with both of hers. The strength with which he pulled launched her body in one smooth motion. She landed on her feet in a crouch.

They emerged in a small courtyard. Tall walls surrounded them on all sides, and passages shot off in three different directions. Laughter and chattering came from somewhere nearby, but she saw no one.

"Here," a rough whisper urged.

Chelci followed the voice and ran to join Patrick, where he ducked behind a short wall. Above them, stairs proceeded up, seeming to be the laughter's source. In a moment, Veron and William arrived, pressing their backs against the barrier.

"So far, so good," Veron said.

"Which way to the dungeon?" William asked.

Patrick turned and stood while the others followed suit. "The entrance is just through there." He pointed at the end of the passage where the flicker of torchlight bounced around the corner.

"I need a closer look," Veron said, leaving their hiding place and skulking toward the torchlight.

"Be careful," Chelci whispered.

With her eyes peeking above the low wall, Chelci's heart sped up as Veron crept closer. The corridor was dim, but she worried someone would see him. He leaned his body around a corner and held it for a long moment. Chelci's stomach churned as she watched. After a long moment, he tiptoed back. She started to sigh in relief until he turned toward the staircase.

"What are you doing?" she asked a little too loudly. William's elbow jabbed into her side.

Veron's hand rested on the side of the railing as he ascended the steps above. Around halfway up, his hand paused for a moment before retreating.

"What'd you see?" William asked when Veron returned to their hiding place.

"Only two soldiers guard the gate to the dungeon, but up the stairs, a large group of men gathers in the courtyard."

"People from Karondir?" Chelci asked hopefully.

"Norshewan soldiers."

William tensed. "How many?"

Veron swallowed. "Hundreds."

Chelci's pulse thumped. "Can you take that many?" she asked. Veron and William both shook their heads. "So, if something alerts them . . . ?"

"We run," William answered.

"Let's make sure we don't alert them," Veron said.

They looked toward the dungeon. "Can you take the guards without them calling out?" Chelci asked.

Veron bit his lip. "Maybe."

"Maybe?" William questioned. "Then we need another plan."

The group sat in silence while the noise from above continued to tumble down the staircase. Chelci poked her head over the wall and checked around. *The longer we sit here, the more likely we'll be caught.* She sighed, unbuckling her sword.

"What are you doing?" Veron asked.

"I'm going to give you the chance to take the guards out. Follow my lead." Chelci stood.

"Chelci, wait! Where are you—"

She pushed her hair back, running her fingers through it. While she walked across the exposed space, she straightened her clothes. The pants and rough tunic hardly fit the role she wanted to play, but they would have to do.

Chelci's heart pounded in time with her steps. When she turned the corner, the two Norshewan guards came into view. Swords hung on their hips, and a permanent scowl fixed on their faces. Behind them, a metal gate lay closed, and a burning torch hung on the wall. *No turning back now.*

Chelci forced a broad smile and allowed her body to sway as she walked. "Oh! Hello there," she said, giving a slight slur to her words while maintaining the grin.

The soldiers, surprised by the interruption, glanced at each other. "Be gone!" the shorter one with a beard said gruffly.

She faked a hurt expression while bringing her hand to her chest. Her steps continued forward. "I'm sorry, I got lost." She widened her eyes and lolled her head. "Were you two with the army that just came in? That was impressive!" *Is this what a drunk person would sound like?* She forced a hiccup.

The guards' shoulders relaxed. The taller of the two smirked. "Yeah, we were."

"I can't believe how you just . . . knocked down that wall." She modeled punching an invisible object, then faked sending herself off balance before catching herself. "I hope the new person is better than that baron we had. Ha! He didn't know a thing about ruling."

The guards shifted their weight. "Bale knows what he's doing, all right," the bearded guard said, his voice less abrasive than before. A peal of laughter echoed into the corridor from the stairs just behind her.

"Well, you two sure seem to know what you're doing. He must have chosen his most trusted men to guard the dungeon." She lightly ran her fingers across her stomach as she swayed, but her stomach churned. *This is stupid. It won't work. These men aren't—*

Grins grew on the guards' faces, and they moved in her direction. *Never mind,* she thought. She intentionally stumbled, taking her a few steps toward the opposite wall.

"Well, I'll leave you two to your jobs," Chelci said, swaying on her wobbly legs.

"Why don't you stay with us for a while, miss?" the tall one said.

"Yeah," the bearded one added, moving closer, "you don't have to leave."

She gave a playful laugh as she turned to go. "If you men ever—"

Her head deliberately bumped into the stone wall. She fell with a groan, flailing her limbs with her face to the ground. Scurrying guards rushed to her side.

"I think this is a sign that you need to stay with us," the tall one said, his rough hand grabbing her arm.

Okay, Veron. Now would be the time—

She barely heard the thuds and the soldiers' muffled cries over the nearby music. The grip on her arm loosened and fell away. She turned over. The guards' limp bodies fell back into the arms of two cloaked, hooded figures.

"Nice work," Veron whispered.

Patrick rushed up and handed back her sword and sheath. "Let's go," she urged as she strapped it on.

William and Veron carried the two guards as Patrick took the keys from the hook on the wall to address the locked metal door. The hinges creaked as it opened. Chelci cringed, grabbing the torch off its holder.

A pungent, decaying aroma hit her as she stepped into the narrow corridor. Stone walls lined each side, with metal doors arrayed along the dark, damp hall. Patrick tied gags around the guards' mouths before they tossed them into the nearest empty cell and locked it shut.

"Jackson!" Chelci called as loudly as she dared, rushing along the passage. "Jackson Marlow!"

"Chelci!" a voice answered from a few doors ahead.

Patrick used the key to open the door, and Chelci entered. The four men in the cramped cell shrank away from the light of the torch. Her brother lay on a bench, holding his side. He didn't rise when she entered.

"What are you doing here?" Jackson asked.

"We came to get you," Veron said, pushing his way into the room. "Are you all the captured captains?"

One of the other men nodded. "Yes, the rest are dead."

Veron's expression was grim. "All right then. Come on!"

The other three men jumped up from their seats, eager to leave, but Jackson only raised up on his elbow. Chelci stepped closer, extending the torch. Where his hand pressed into his side, a mess of blood and ripped skin shone back. A pool of red congealed underneath his bench.

"Oh no!" Chelci cried. "What happened?"

"A bear got me," Jackson replied with a wince. Chelci inhaled sharply.

"Can you move?" Veron asked.

Jackson groaned as he moved to stand. Chelci wrapped an arm around him to assist. "It's okay," Jackson said. "I think I can move. Let's go."

Chelci had the only light and squeezed back to the front of the line. She turned to Patrick and raised an eyebrow. "Back to the tunnels?"

"Yes, that's the best way," the Karondir soldier confirmed.

Chelci looked at Veron and William, who both nodded. She glanced at the captains, their bright eyes showing their eagerness to leave. Her brother grimaced, standing with a slight lean. Fixing her jaw, she hurried back down the corridor.

As she reached the metal door that marked the dungeon's entrance, a sight caused her to freeze. Ahead, four Norshewan soldiers approached cautiously with swords out and heads on a swivel.

"Where'd they go?" one of the men asked.

Chelci's breath caught as they turned toward the open door, looking straight at her. "Is there another way out of here?" she asked over her shoulder, her voice shaking.

"No," Patrick said, "this is it.

"Men! To arms!" the soldiers ahead shouted toward the stairs.

"Get to the grate! Run!" William shouted.

Chelci sprinted, wary of being the first of their group. The Norshewans pulled their swords and spread out, blocking her escape. Chelci skidded to a halt, and Veron collided with her back. In a moment, William and Veron both moved around her to face the men.

"Get ready to break for it," William said, half over his shoulder while monitoring the soldiers. A clatter of metal and a roar of men came from the stairs as soldiers descended.

"Bale has a plan for them," a tall Norshewan soldier in the front sneered while nodding toward the rescued captains. "You're going to pay for this."

William and Veron moved in sync, their movement blurring. The four soldiers fell, grabbing their wounds while crying out.

"Come on!" Patrick shouted, leading the rest toward the grate.

Chelci watched the descending reinforcements as they hurried across the room. The three uninjured captains moved well, but her brother struggled. Her heart dropped as a wave of Norshewan soldiers exited the stairs and spread out to attack anyone they could find. She didn't worry about Veron or William, but Jackson was unarmed.

"Keep going!" Chelci yelled, pulling her sword as she halted and pushed the captains past her. A Norshewan with a greasy beard ran at Jackson with his sword cocked. Chelci lunged forward, moving between them, parrying the blade away.

The man scowled at her. "Who do you think you—"

Chelci jammed her knee into the side of his leg, bending his joint in the wrong direction. The soldier howled, grabbing his leg and falling to the ground. She spun—a wall of men had moved between them and their escape. Jackson backpedaled.

Chelci frantically looked around. Veron and William continued to whirl through the mass of soldiers, piles of bodies in their wake. *We've got to get out!* She stepped forward and slashed at the nearest man. He blocked and circled around her. She pivoted to follow. The man lunged, but she twirled to avoid it, the tip of her own blade finding his side.

As he fell, clutching his wound, she turned to her brother. He had picked up a sword from one of the fallen soldiers, but his wince proved his lack of ability to wield it. A knot tightened in her stomach.

"Veron, help!" she shouted.

Two men lunged at Jackson. He avoided the blades, moving backward and groaning as he parried. Chelci jumped in front, engaging the soldiers.

She blocked a thin blade, but the second man swung a heavy two-handed weapon at her side. She barely had time to realize the inevitable—*I can't stop it.* In a split-second, the large sword crashed to the ground and the soldier who swung it wailed with pain as a splash of blood flew from his chest. *What in the—*

Veron was there. After knocking down the closest soldiers to her, he stopped. "Are you all right?" he asked, facing her while his chest heaved.

She swallowed, nodding her head.

Veron pointed toward the grate where the path opened again. "Run!"

Patrick peeked out from the storm drain, beckoning to her with the metal frame held open.

Chelci turned to her brother. "Jackson, come on—" Her words caught. She felt as if she'd been punched in the gut, knocking the wind out of her. Her brother leaned against the wall, his hand no longer staunching the bear wound. He held his chest where two red stains unceasingly grew. "No!" she screamed, running to him.

"Chelci, go!" Jackson sputtered, blood staining his lips. "Get out of here!" His eyes appeared glassy and listless.

"No, I won't leave you," she said, looping his arm over her shoulder. She took a step, trying to pull her brother along, but his weight collapsed as soon as he left the wall.

"I can't do it! Go!"

Tears blurred her vision. "Jackson, you're going to be all right! We just need to make it over there!"

Veron's hand rested on her shoulder. "I've got him." His words were soft, soothing the raw ache building in her. She let go of her brother while Veron bent to pick him up at the hip. He stood with Jackson draped over his left shoulder.

Chelci made a move toward the grate but hesitated at the sight of new soldiers arriving.

"William! Let's go!" Veron shouted, moving in front of Chelci to address the men.

Even with Jackson over his shoulder, Veron was an unstoppable force. His movement was slower but still plenty powerful to send bodies falling to the ground and flying through the air. As soon as an opening developed, Chelci ran.

Patrick moved out of the way, allowing her to slide into the tunnel. Veron was right behind with her brother. Jackson groaned as they passed his body through the narrow opening. Chelci moved out of the way, pressing against one of the rescued captains in the narrow space.

In a moment, William's boots thudded, and a loud clang indicated the grate dropped back into place.

"I found this," Patrick said, holding up a twisted metal object, passing it to William who slid it between the slats. Moments after tucking it to the side, the grate rattled but didn't budge. Voices from above shouted and William slid to the side as swords jabbed in a desperate attempt to hit something. The group of eight crawled as fast as possible away from the grate until it opened into a larger tunnel.

"I need a moment," William said, panting as he leaned against a wall.

"Me, too," Veron agreed, laying down Jackson's body.

As desperate breathing echoed around her, Chelci knelt by her brother while her tears returned. "Jackson, don't worry. We're going to get you taken care of." She held his trembling hand, her words choked with emotion.

He shook his head. "Thank you for trying to rescue me." His breath shuddered as Chelci's tears dripped on his arm. He managed a weak smile. "Mother would have been proud."

Chelci covered her mouth and pressed her eyes closed, sending a river of tears down her cheek. When she opened them, her brother's eyes didn't move, and his chest no longer rose. She bowed her head as a fresh wave of grief washed over. Without speaking, Veron's hand rested on her shoulder. She pressed hers against it and their fingers intertwined. She squeezed hard, trying to force away the pain.

After a long moment of silence, Veron crouched next to her. "Chelci, we need to go." She wiped her eyes and looked at him.

"He's right," William added. "We don't know how long that grate will hold."

She sniffed as she wiped her nose. "What about—"

"I'll carry him," Veron said tenderly.

"No. Please," one of the other captains said. "Let us."

The sun had set by the time they exited the passage by the river. The moonlight reflected off the water, illuminating the city's outside wall and surrounding land. Veron led the way as their group scrambled over rocks while keeping a wary eye out for Norshewan soldiers lurking in wait. They seemed alone.

Chelci had yet to speak after her brother's death. *Should I say something to her?* Veron thought. *Remind her we all tried our best?* He said nothing.

The moonlight dimmed as they trekked into the woods. The group climbed up the hill, away from the city. One of the rescued captains took a few quick steps to come alongside Veron.

"It's Veron, right?" the soldier asked. Veron nodded as he continued walking. "I'm Boyd. Thanks for coming for us."

Veron looked down and clenched his jaw, thinking of Jackson.

"I'm sorry about Jackson. He was a great leader and will be missed."

"I didn't know him, but . . ." Veron glanced at the silhouette of Chelci, walking behind with her head down. "I'm sure he was great."

"So . . . what was that back there?" Boyd asked.

Veron pinched his brows together. "What was what?"

"When you fought the Norshewans. How did you . . . ?" His question trailed off.

Veron looked up to William, who eyed him from a few paces away but didn't answer.

"They're shadow knights," Patrick said. Gasps sounded from the other soldiers. "Years ago, a Dream predicted one of them would kill Bale."

"That's amazing," Boyd said.

"And then they'll die." Chelci's voice chilled Veron to his bones. It was the first she'd spoken since her brother's death, and the subject was one he wanted to forget.

Conversation stalled after the revelation, and the group continued on in silence.

After crossing a rise and passing a large tree, they arrived at camp where Morgan sat around a small fire. The middle-aged man jumped and the horses neighed when the party entered the clearing. "Oh! You scared me! Are you all right? I saw the battle and feared the worst. Did you get to . . . ?" He stopped when one of the captains entered the clearing, carrying the body.

"It's Jackson . . . Chelci's brother," Veron said as William laid the body down.

Morgan turned to Chelci with soft eyes. "I'm so sorry."

Chelci replied with a nod.

"We didn't even have a chance to make a plan," William said. "Bale attacked as we arrived."

"We're going to need to find him again," Veron said as he sat on a log.

William nodded. "We need to find more help."

"It's got to be Rynor," Veron said.

William raised an eyebrow, the fire's light flickering on his face.

"They're the only ones with an army that hasn't been conquered yet. And I'm sure Bale will go there next, so it would be in their best interest to help."

"I agree," William added.

Veron turned to his father. "Do you have any connections there?"

William shook his head. "Artimus did. He met with King Petrous several times. From what I hear, he's a good man. I briefly met him once, but he wouldn't remember me."

"Are you men interested in coming with us to Rynor?" Veron asked, looking at the four Karondir soldiers.

The men glanced between each other with sheepish looks. "Blaine and I have families in Karondir," one of the men said. "We planned to find some plain clothes and make our way back into the city to join them."

"We know it's a risk, but . . . we can't leave them," the man next to him added.

"And my family is in Felting," the third captain said. I'll make my way down there.

Veron nodded before turning to Patrick and raising an eyebrow. "How about you?"

"My wife is in Karad. I think I'll find my way back there."

Veron tilted his head. "Patrick . . . Patrick Washburn?"

Patrick jerked his head. "How did you know?"

Veron chuckled. "Your wife is Chloe?"

"Yeah."

He smiled as he pictured dancing with Chloe back in the market. "When you see her, tell her Veron Stormbridge is doing great and says, 'hello.'"

The soldier's forehead wrinkled.

"If we're going to contact Rynor, we can't waste time," William said. "We need to leave tonight."

"What's the rush?" Morgan asked.

"We need to get there before this army does."

"I agree. But first, we need to collect stones," Veron said, his gaze shifting to Jackson's body. "We have a friend to bury."

26

Men of the Barren Hills

Veron pulled his cloak closer to ward off the cold as Annie clopped along through the Gap of Thardor. *I thought the afternoon sun would feel warmer.* He shivered as he craned his neck from side to side, stretching to loosen it up and ending in a great yawn. William had only given them a couple of hours to sleep during the night, and it had been steady progress since then. Mountains closed in on either side of the road, but along the path ahead, a small glimpse of the sea shimmered far in the distance.

"It's beautiful," Morgan said. "I never imagined I would lay eyes on it."

"Have you ever seen the sea, William?" Veron asked.

William nodded. "I was born in Rynor."

"Really?" Chelci said, her voice light and inquisitive.

Veron's ears perked up at her interest. She'd been stiff and curt all day.

"Yes, I grew up in Tolin," William said, "a small village nestled on the eastern slope of the Straith Mountains."

"How long did you live there?" Chelci asked.

"I was thirteen when Artimus found me. I made it to Rynor a few times after joining the knights—once on a job to Molvaigh, twice to Bromhill, and one time all the way down to Palenting—beautiful city."

"What about your parents?" Veron asked. "Are they still alive?"

William shook his head. "My father—your grandfather—Baloran, died when I was twelve, and my mother, Shylan, passed while I was gone—blue fever."

Veron frowned. *It would have been nice to meet them.*

"We leave the road here," William said, pointing to a rocky, overgrown path angling to the side. "It would take much longer to go through Molvaigh."

William led the way. The main road's hard packed dirt gave way to grass, weeds, and rocks. Hills and large boulders sprouted in their new direction. The footing was more difficult, but the horses didn't seem to mind.

As they settled in the new direction, Chelci dropped Nora back to walk alongside Veron. "How are you doing?" she asked.

Half a grin formed on his face at the prospect of her talking again. "I'm great," he said. His grin fell. "How about you?"

Her horse took several steps before she answered. "Sorry I've been quiet. It was tough losing Jackson."

"I'm sure."

"Throughout my childhood, he was always there. We weren't . . . best friends or anything, but whenever Mother flew into a rage, he always understood. If she made me cry, he gave me a hug and a shoulder to cry on. I hadn't seen him in years, but . . . I always knew he was out there."

Veron nodded, listening intently.

"I wanted him to be proud of who I was, what I grew into, just as much as I wanted it from my parents."

"I know he would be proud of you, Chelci."

She looked him in the eye and returned his smile. "Thanks. I like who I am, too."

Ahead, a field of massive rock formations littered their view. The faint path meandered between boulders forming sheer faces, towering over them. Tunnels poked holes in the stone, creating shadowy passages in all directions. Veron hung back, allowing Chelci to pass through a narrow space. When it opened up, he trotted up to come alongside her.

"Tell me more about the 'clearing your mind' bit," Chelci said.

"What?"

"I've been reading through the book more about the origine. It says, 'you must clear your mind of what you expect your body to be able to give,' but I'm not sure what that means."

Veron chuckled. "Yeah, I struggled with that as well. At first, I tried to not think of anything. That was a disaster—something always popped into my head. Eventually, I realized it was less about *not* thinking and more about not *limiting* myself by my thoughts. But it wasn't until my intentions lined up with the code of the knights that I found the origine."

Chelci leaned forward, her eyes full of life. "You can only feel it when your intentions are good?"

"I guess. That's the only time it works for me," Veron said.

William stiffened in his saddle just ahead.

"What is it? Am I missing something?"

William turned. "You can use the origine even if your intentions don't match the code."

"Really?"

"It's all about your heart. If you're filled with corruption and evil, power will follow. That's why we have the code. We want people's intentions to follow what is good. Tainted origine is dangerous . . . and incredibly strong."

Veron's body stiffened. "Stronger than us?"

William was silent for a long time. Veron was about to repeat the question when a soft answer returned from his father. "It lasts longer."

The words sent a chill through Veron. "You've seen it before?"

William shook his head. "No, but the knights have dealt with it in the past."

Veron opened his mouth to probe further but stopped as Annie's muscles tensed underneath him.

Just ahead, Steelmane snorted, lifting his head up. William bent down and patted his neck. "Whoa, what is it, boy?"

Steel scraped against stone in all directions as men jumped into view on various levels of the rocks, brandishing swords and bows. Ahead of them, three large men with clubs stepped in their way, preventing further progress. Their horses neighed, turning in circles.

Veron looked in all directions. A ring of boulders surrounded them. The only way in or out were the narrow passages behind and in front, but both were blocked. Chelci reached out and grabbed his hand.

"What is this?" William called out, his body stiff.

A man with a long, red tunic stepped forward. He perched on top of a boulder, putting him at eye level with those on horses. His shaven face revealed him to be no older than thirty. He held a sword loosely at his side. "I am Thorley the Just, and these are the Men of the Barren Hills. And you travelers cross through our land."

Veron tightened his grip on his saddle's horn. His other arm itched to release Chelci's hand and grab the sword over his shoulder, but he resisted.

"We didn't know it was your land," Morgan said. "I promise you we meant no offense."

Thorley laughed. "Oh, it's no offense." As his laugh faded, the creases around his eyes smoothed, and his face turned hard. "But it will cost you."

"Cost us what?" William asked.

"These are dangerous paths," Thorley said, stepping to the edge and leaning forward. His eyes darted around, and his voice grew low. "There are *evil* people out there looking for unsuspecting travelers. They lie in wait then, when least expected . . ." Thorley stomped a foot as he shouted. Chelci's hand jerked, but Veron held on. "They attack. They take everything from you and do . . . unspeakable things."

"It's okay," Veron whispered to Chelci. "I won't let them hurt you." He let go of her hand to ready for action.

Thorley's gaze settled on Chelci. "Trust me, you don't want to run into these men."

"So, what are you doing here?" Veron asked, his voice laced with a sharp edge.

"It's simple! We keep you safe!" The smile was back. Thorley pointed around to the men on the rocks. "The Men of the Barren Hills run off these evil brigands. But providing this safety takes a lot of effort, and we require a tax for our service."

"How much?" William asked, maintaining a conversational tone.

"Only two argen per person."

"You want eight argen for us to walk through here?" Veron shouted. "You're nothing more than bandits yourselves!"

Chelci pursed her lips while Veron's hand went to his sword's hilt.

Thorley chuckled, watching his hand. "Trust me, you don't want to do that."

"I think it is you who doesn't want to do this," Veron said, his mouth in a tight line.

The men on the ground with clubs closed in, and the ones on rocks stepped nearer. Veron pulled his sword from over his shoulder.

"Veron," Chelci whispered. "I don't think they—"

"Don't worry," he whispered back.

A tense silence filled the air. A breeze blew, rustling Veron's cloak. He ignored the cold, his rapidly pumping heart keeping his body warm.

Thorley sneered as he nodded to his men. "Let's show these travelers the consequences of their defiance."

Bows creaked as they pulled back. Veron's body tensed, his hand squeezing hard on the hilt of his sword. He looked at William, waiting for him to snap into action, but his father's casual manner made him wrinkle his brow.

William rummaged through the sack hanging from Steelmane's side. "Here, I've got it," he called.

"William, no," Veron said. "We can handle them."

The Men of the Barren Hills laughed in unison. "They can handle us!" Thorley shouted, bending over and hitting the side of his leg.

William jumped down from his horse, coins jangling in his hand as he used his horse to steady his balance. Favoring his good leg, he shuffled to the nearest club-toting thug and dropped the money into his hand. "We appreciate your help in keeping this area safe. I hope this helps compensate you for your trouble."

"William!" Veron's jaw hung open. His father looked back with a softness in his face he didn't expect to see.

"Here, take this, too," Morgan called from the back of the group. He jumped down from Clover and grabbed a spare cloak from his gear. He approached the rock where Thorley looked down on them with his eyebrow quirked. Morgan extended his arm, passing the cloak to the man in red.

"Thank you?" Thorley said questioningly.

"For the boy," Morgan clarified, pointing to the farthest boulder where a boy, who couldn't be over fourteen, stood shivering with a sword.

Veron hadn't noticed the boy, whose gaunt arms and legs revealed a starving body. His grip on Farrathan loosened, and the sword lowered to his side.

Thorley clenched the cloak and turned toward the boy, extending it in his direction. His face alight, the boy sheathed his sword and bounded down from his perch.

While the boy scurried around rocks to reach the cloak, Veron looked closer at the men surrounding him. Several were underdressed for the cold weather. The ones with enough clothes had loose threads dangling and mismatched patches. Hollow faces staring back showed they had probably gone days without eating.

The boy grinned as he joined Thorley on his boulder and took the cloak. After putting his arms through it, he tightened it around his body, and his face melted with joy. "Thank you, Father." A cough followed his scratchy, high-pitched voice. After battling away the cough, he turned to Morgan. "And thank you, sir."

Morgan bowed with a smile before turning back to his horse.

Veron looked at Chelci and shrugged sheepishly before sliding Farrathan back into its sheath.

"Do you need some food?" Chelci asked to the group. "We don't have much, but it looks like some of you haven't eaten in a while."

Thorley stood straight, blinking several times. "Um—" He cleared his throat. "We would appreciate that, yes." The surrounding men sheathed their weapons.

"Come then," she said, jumping to the ground and beckoning to them. The Men of the Barren Hills lined up, taking some food one-by-one.

Veron dismounted his horse and made his way to William. "Why'd you give them our money?" he whispered.

"I didn't want anyone to get hurt," William replied, watching Chelci at the other end of the rocky clearing.

"We wouldn't have gotten hurt. We could have defeated them easily."

His father turned to look at him. "I didn't want *anyone* to get hurt." His words were pointed, and his eyes seemed to bore into Veron. "Sure, it's not fair for them to take money from travelers, but they need it more than we do."

"But we're trying to stop Bale from taking over Terrenor!" Veron's voice drew looks from a few of the nearby men. "What's more important than that?"

"And they're trying to keep their children from dying of hunger. From what we started with, to the purse Lord Marlow gave us, we have enough."

Veron swallowed hard. After inhaling, he sighed. "I know you're right . . . but I don't want you to be."

A smile grew on his father's face. "Everything we have is a gift, Veron—our coins, our food, and our time. Use them wisely."

Use my time wisely. A pang of wistful longing filled Veron. He turned to Chelci, who traded words with one of the Barren Hills men. The large man's eyes twinkled as he listened to her with rapt attention.

"Were you really thinking of fighting us?"

Veron snapped his head to find Thorley standing in front of him. "Um . . ." he looked at his father. "Yeah, I considered it."

"Don't worry about him," William said to Thorley. "Sometimes he puts his sword ahead of his brain."

Thorley chuckled. "We've got a few of those ourselves." He leaned into Veron. "For your sake, I'm glad you didn't."

Veron took a deep breath. William caught his attention with a sharp shake of his head. "Yes, I'm glad, too," Veron said through gritted teeth. "I wasn't thinking."

His gaze drifted back to Chelci. That time, she looked back. A warm smile covered her face. *I don't know how much time I have left,* he thought, *but I know I want to spend it with her.*

262

27

Interruption

Veron watched the fire's yellow and orange flames curl around the burning sticks. *When are they going to go to bed?* he thought, sneaking looks at William and Morgan. Veron yawned. *Surely they're tired after last night's lack of sleep.*

After leaving the Men of the Barren Hills, they had traveled another couple of hours before settling in for the night. Veron thought about Chelci the entire time. So much had happened since he'd almost asked for her hand in Nasco, and there hadn't been a moment since that felt right to try again.

He looked to his right. She sat up, poring over the Shadow Knights book, reading by the firelight. Sitting around a campfire wasn't the ideal place to propose, but he couldn't wait any longer. *I just need the others to go to sleep first.*

Chelci closed the book with a thud and set it on the ground. She stood and kicked Veron playfully as she pulled her sword. "Come on. I need practice."

Veron looked at William, who raised his hands with a shrug. "Sure," Veron said, jumping up.

Their fire nestled between several large boulders, but just beyond, rolling hills opened up. The moon glowed in the sky, lighting the grass and dirt well outside the fire's reach.

"You're not tired?" Veron asked, pulling his sword from over his shoulder as he jogged to catch up.

Chelci grinned, the moon lighting up her face and glinting off her weapon. "What? Are you? Are you trying to make excuses?"

Veron chuckled, settling into a crouch and raising his sword above his head.

"No origine, right?"

"Maybe just a little?" he teased. Intending to defend, he lifted his blade sideways at chest level and settled into owl stance.

Her smile turned into a humorous scowl before she darted in with her blade. Veron parried and spun, their swords ringing in the night. He stayed out of her reach, moving in a circle, looking for any false step. After testing with a low swing, he followed with a kick to the opposite side. She blocked both, and he continued circling.

The cool air blew between them, rustling his cloak. Her hair waved in the breeze. A spark in her eyes clued him in a moment before it happened. They both moved. Their swords clashed, sending vibrations up his arms, but she had already spun away, her legs dancing across the grass. Instantly, she was back, the quickness impossible to anticipate.

She's amazing.

Veron's heartbeat followed in time with their blows of steel. His blood ran hot, drops of sweat rolling down his face. Her never-stopping blows continued to rain down on him. He parried and ducked, staying a hair away from her charges. The smile on her face transfixed him. The intimate dance between them drew him even closer. *Maybe I can ask her out here? It's nice under the moon, and—*Veron's sword flew to the ground.

"Haha!" Chelci shouted.

"But . . ." Veron sputtered, looking at his empty hand. A broad grin grew on his face.

"I did it!"

Veron chuckled. "You did. Nice work, Chelci." He fumbled on the ground to find his sword. *Here's your chance, Veron. Ask her now!* He found the handle and straightened. "Chelci, I—"

"Morgan! William! I beat Veron!" Chelci skipped back to the circle of rocks.

Veron sighed and sheathed his weapon, trudging after her. Grins met him around the fire, Chelci already back in her seat.

"It's true," he said, shrugging. "She beat me."

"Imagine if she had your abilities, too," William said.

"Yeah, that would be something." Veron glanced at Chelci, who winked at him as she picked the book back up.

He settled back into his fireside seat. Adrenaline coursed through his veins from the brief, intense skirmish, yet the anticipation of a proposal sent it coursing even harder.

Morgan leaned forward and shuffled some sticks around in the fire, sending sparks into the air which the wind blew out. The grocer yawned as he leaned back. "Well . . . I need some sleep."

"I don't mind taking the first watch," Veron offered. "Why don't you get some sleep?"

"Sounds good to me," Morgan said, laying back. "I can take the second shift. Wake me when it's time."

Perfect. Just one more. Veron grinned. "Are you going to get some rest, Father?"

William gazed at the fire and nodded. "Yeah, I need to."

Veron waited, but the man didn't move.

"We should make it to Bromhill by late afternoon tomorrow," William said.

"Hmm," Veron mumbled, trying not to start any conversation.

"You know . . . Meeting the men in the hills gave me an idea about Bale." Veron poked the fire with a stick but didn't respond. "Assuming we can convince King Petrous to help." A quiet moment followed until William broke it. "But I guess we can talk about it on the road tomorrow. What I'd actually love to hear about is your time in Karad—what happened to you there and how you met up with Artimus."

Veron internally groaned. "Yeah, that would be great to talk about."

A heavy silence settled. William leaned forward. "So, what happened when you got to Karad?"

Veron acted surprised. "Oh, you mean now?"

"We aren't going anywhere. What time would be better."

Argh! "Um . . . Can we do it tomorrow? I'm tired from the long day and don't want to think through all that right now."

William sighed. "Sure, that's fine. We can talk tomorrow." He laid back again. "Goodnight, Veron."

The grin returned. *Now, I need to give them only a few minutes to fall asleep.* No sooner did he think the words than Morgan began breathing heavily. Veron's heart pounded. He wiped his hands on his pants to dry off the sweat. His mind raced through the words he would say, but everything sounded stupid. *I can't plan it. I just need to talk.*

Over the light crackle of the fire, the second set of deep breathing began. His breath caught. *Wait!* He turned to the sound, and his shoulders slumped. Chelci was covered by her blanket. Her chest rose and fell in time to her breathing.

* * *

After an early wake and a meager meal of smoked meat and hard bread, the group mounted up for their final push to Bromhill. The ground grew smoother the farther they traveled, but Veron's saddle did not. He spent most of the ride in the back of the line, thinking about when he could talk with Chelci alone again. The farther the sun stretched across the sky, the more eager he became to arrive at their destination. He checked around each hill they passed for a sign of the walled city.

A shuffling of horses caught his attention. Chelci pulled in her reins, allowing him to catch her. She smiled as she kicked Nora back to a walk. "How are you doing?" she asked.

"I'm good. Didn't sleep great, but . . . I'm fine."

"What's on your mind?"

Veron inhaled and felt his eyes grow. *Can she know what I want to talk about?* He covered by clearing his throat and blinking. "On my mind? Nothing really."

"Hmm. I thought it may be those men of the hills."

"Oh, them . . . yeah." Veron chuckled. "I was ready to teach them a lesson."

"I noticed."

"I hate giving our money away, but . . . I'm glad William did. He's right. They need it more."

"I get it . . . why you feel that way." Chelci said.

"You do?"

"You grew up without money, fighting for everything you earned. Giving away eight argen would be unthinkable."

"Yeah, I guess you're right."

They were silent for a moment as a light breeze blew across the path. Veron looked at Chelci. Her long, brown hair rippled behind her. She closed her eyes and turned her face into the wind. His heart began to thump.

William and Morgan rode farther ahead, discussing something amongst themselves. His mouth felt dry, and he swallowed to loosen it up. "Chelci?"

She turned to him. Her face was soft and kind. Her eyebrows lifted while her eyes sparkled. Her horse's movements caused her head to bob up and down.

"I have . . . um . . . something I wanted to talk about."

"What is it?" Her smile grew.

Does she already know what I want to say? With his tongue loosened, the words flowed. "We've only known each other for a season, which could sound short to some, but I feel as if I've known you my whole life. I love everything about you—your kindness, your spunk, the way you stand up for yourself. I love that you could probably knock me on my butt even *with* me using the origine."

Chelci laughed, creases forming around her eyes.

"All my life I looked for someone like you, not even imagining it was possible for one person to be so perfect."

A drop trickled down her cheek. Chelci sniffed as she wiped it away, holding her reassuring smile.

"I have something I want to ask you, Chelci."

He reached out and took her hand. Her lips trembled as she nodded. "Yes? Ask me." she breathed.

Veron froze—not from cold feet but because of how enraptured he felt looking at her. Her eyes, glistening with tears, sparkled in the sun, and her smile radiated warmth. He wanted to remember the moment forever. Breaking free of his frozen stare, he opened his mouth.

"Hey! There it is!" Morgan's words tore Veron out of the moment. He looked away from Chelci to see the grocer pointing ahead. Around the hill they passed and up a steady rise loomed Bromhill's gigantic walls.

"Um . . ." Veron turned back to Chelci. His eyebrows knit together at the interruption, but hers remained lifted in eager anticipation. "I

. . . uh—"

"Come on you two, let's move!" William said, kicking his horse into a gallop.

Annie and Nora followed the leaders, jolting both Veron and Chelci out of their trance. Veron grabbed desperately for the saddle's horn to keep from falling off. Their horses galloping side by side, Veron looked at Chelci and shrugged. They both laughed.

"Hold that thought, I guess," Veron shouted over the rush of the wind in his face.

With the pressure off for the moment, the twisting in his stomach settled. *I was so close! Argh! Why couldn't Morgan have waited one more minute?*

Their horses thundered up the rise, catching Steelmane and Clover. Soon, William brought the group to a canter then back down to a walk as they approached the gate.

Bromhill's magnificence took Veron's mind off of his interrupted conversation. Roughly the same height as Karondir, the wall seemed taller because of the hill the city perched on. Battlements ran across the top where several guards patrolled.

A dozen soldiers stopped them at the gate. Forced to dismount, they endured an interrogation along with a thorough examination of their bags. Only after a lengthy side discussion between two leaders did the soldiers motion them to enter.

Inside the walls, the city reminded Veron of Karondir. Whereas Karad and Felting were spread out, Karondir and Bromhill felt tighter. Narrow streets and tall buildings filled his sight in every direction.

"Do you know where to go?" Veron asked.

William pointed ahead. "We'll find Petrous at the castle—straight up this road."

Wary faces glanced their way as they traveled up the main street.

Mothers pulled children close, and one man turned down a side street to walk away from them.

"What do you think is spooking them?" Morgan asked. "Are we that scary?"

Veron looked over at their company. He and William wore long black cloaks, and three of them had swords ready to draw.

"Six years ago, Bale's men ravaged their city," William said. "An experience like that leaves people skittish and unwilling to trust."

After crossing most of the city, the castle loomed ahead, rising from the tight streets to look down on the other buildings. They dismounted at the steps.

"Morgan and Chelci, do you mind staying with the horses?" William asked.

"No problem," Chelci answered.

William unbuckled his sword from around his waist and turned to Veron. "Leave your weapons behind."

Veron frowned.

"It helps them feel more comfortable. Plus, we don't need them."

Veron followed his father's example, handing his sword and dagger to Morgan. Free from their weapons, Veron and William climbed the steps and approached the guards blocking the entrance. William's staff clacked on the stone.

"Halt!" a guard with a large beard shouted as they approached. Two men held spears, while another two gripped their sword hilts. "What business do you have at the castle?"

"We need to speak with the king," William said.

The guard chuckled. "Oh, sure. Right this way." The others laughed.

"I'm serious. An army greater than any we've seen in Terrenor will be here soon, and King Petrous needs to know." The guards' laughter faded. "Is his advisor, Langham, here?" William asked, receiving shifting eyes in response. "Tell him we're from Felting and friends of Artimus. We have news the king needs to hear."

Large Beard looked at the others, shifting his weight. After a moment, he nodded to a man with a spear who turned and hustled into the castle. "Wait here," he said.

Veron exhaled as he and William exchanged a look. "Do you think they'll let us speak with him?" he whispered.

William glanced around. "I sure hope so."

Veron looked back at Chelci, who smiled at him. He tapped William on the elbow. "I'll be back in a moment."

"What'd they say?" Morgan asked after Veron descended the steps.

"They aren't too friendly, but I think they're checking with some advisor. We'll see what he says."

"What if they won't let you in?" Chelci asked. "Are you going to jump up the outside of the castle walls?"

Veron laughed. "I hadn't thought it through, but . . . that's a decent idea." His gaze fixed on the castle's exterior. He cocked his head, imagining potential routes. Behind him, carts rolled through the street. The faint hum of conversation blended into the background as the three stood at the base of the steps.

Chelci rested her hand on his arm. "Did you want to finish the conversation from earlier?" Her body swayed, and a crooked grin covered her face.

Veron eyed Morgan standing next to them but looking out at the surrounding buildings. "Um—" The thick beating of his heart returned, flooding his ears with a muffled thrum.

"Veron!"

He turned to the muddled voice. The guard from before had returned, and William waved for him. His pulse continued to thump.

Veron grasped Chelci's hand and raised his shoulders, angling toward the steps. "As soon as I get back?"

Her face fell. "All right. I'll be here."

He squeezed her hand, his chest tightening, then trotted up to join his father.

"They're letting us in," William confirmed.

Veron gave a relieved smile then waved at Chelci. The sweet look on her face melted his heart. *I think I know what she's going to say.* He turned and followed his father into the castle.

28

A New Alliance

Inside the castle, a servant led the way down a long hall with Veron and William following closely. A thick rug lined the corridor. Silver mirrors reflected them walking past.

After multiple turns, they entered an expansive room with a vaulted ceiling. Tapestries hung on three walls, and double doors filled the fourth. The surrounding windows revealed an outdoor patio beyond. Guards stood at alert in front of each closed door around the room. In the middle of the chamber, stuffed chairs grouped around tables, and a large chandelier hung above.

Two men stood next to one of the chairs. The shorter man had gray hair and a sharp beard. His brown coat was pressed and crisp. The other man wore a thick purple cloak decorated with gold lapels and buttons. Likely in his fifties, he held himself straight and proud with a crown on his head. A shining silver bracelet on his right arm caught a ray of sun from the window. Veron bowed, following William's lead.

"Please, please," the man with the crown said, motioning up with his hands. "There's no need for that." He beamed as they straightened. "Friends of Artimus arrive to bring me news—shadow knights yourselves from the looks of it. That is something worth hearing. Come, sit. Would you like a drink?"

"Water would be great. Thank you," William said, taking one of the chairs.

Veron sat in the one next to him. He puffed his chest out, feeling proud of how he and William looked in their black cloaks with the Shadow Knights emblems. A servant arrived presently and set down two pewter goblets on the table in front of them.

"I am King Petrous, and this is my advisor, Oswald Langham." The second man nodded. "It's been fifteen years since I've seen a shadow knight. I presume the rumors of your demise were exaggerated?"

William's face fell. "They were mostly accurate, Your Majesty. Only two of us survived Bale's attack."

The king grew solemn as he and his advisor sat opposite a table. "I'm sorry to hear that. What of Artimus?"

"He survived the attack but passed away more recently," Veron replied.

"Veron, here, is a recent addition, and my name is—"

"William, right?"

William's head tilted. "Yes."

Petrous continued, "I remember you. You're much older now, though. I'm glad to see you both alive. Terrenor could use your kind again."

"That's actually why we needed to see you. Bale is coming."

Petrous stiffened, his jaw firming. "I heard of Felting's fall and his march toward Karondir."

"They have fallen too, I'm afraid." William said. "We just came from Karondir. The Norshewan army now includes members of Feldor and Tarphan. Their numbers push twenty-five thousand."

The king gasped, turning to Oswald. "That's over double what they had last time they sacked Bromhill!"

"Rynor is the last piece of Terrenor. I'm sure Bale will come here soon if they're not already on their way."

Petrous flinched and looked toward the window to the west. His arm trembled until he held it with his other hand. "There's no way we can stop that." His words sounded distant and forced.

"We can, Your Majesty."

Petrous turned his head toward William. "How?"

"I'm sure you've heard of the Dream?"

"Yes," the king nodded. "It came out of Stonl, just north of Molvaigh." He inhaled as his eyes grew. "You think one of you will be the one to kill him."

William nodded. "We're trying."

"Bale knows we're after him but keeps himself surrounded by guards," Veron added. "We can deal with Bale, and we can fight a lot of soldiers, but . . . we could use help."

"What sort of help?"

William perked up. "You know the path that runs from the Gap of Thardor to Bromhill?" The king nodded. "We need Bale to bring him men down that route. Is there a way you could use your army to direct them that way? Maybe blockade the road to Molvaigh with trenches and barriers?"

"You would have me take my soldiers away from the city and convince an invading army to take a short cut to get here quicker?"

"The path through the hills grows narrow, and Veron and I could strike with the element of surprise."

The king thought for a moment then stood. "A moment, please." He nodded to his advisor, and they walked to the side of the room where they spoke in hushed voices. The advisor's face grew red as the volume grew.

"What do you think he's upset about?" Veron whispered.

William shook his head. "I don't know."

While they sat, Veron took a moment to look around the room. The door they entered a moment ago had been closed and was now guarded by four soldiers. He counted as he scanned the room.

"Why would Petrous have twenty-four guards in here?" Veron whispered, leaning toward his father.

William pursed his lips. "I'm not sure. He is the king, after all."

Petrous returned, his forehead wrinkled. "I'm thankful to have you here but, honestly, am somewhat skeptical of your intentions."

Veron screwed up his face. "Our intentions?"

"The Shadow Knights were always friends to Rynor, but it's been fifteen years. How do we know you don't have other objectives now?"

William straightened in his seat, his eyebrows pinching together. "I explained the reason for our absence. I'm not sure what designs you believe we may have, but I assure you, they are as we stated. We need your help to defeat Bale, which will help you keep your sovereign kingdom as well as your life."

Petrous nodded his head for a lengthy period. "And once Bale is gone? What about then?"

William's head jerked back. "I'm sorry . . . What do you imply?"

"What's to stop you from attempting a coup? It wouldn't be the first time such a thing had been done after a military victory."

William's face reddened. "That's ridiculous. We have no intentions of doing so. After Bale is defeated, we will return to Feldor."

"Are you both willing to swear vows of partnership?"

William glanced at Veron. "Of course, Your Majesty."

Petrous turned to Oswald and nodded. The advisor walked to the side of the room where a large wooden desk pressed against the wall. In a moment, he returned carrying a velvet pillow with two silver bracelets resting on top—bracelets that matched what the king wore. Several of the guards in the room drew close before the vow ceremony began.

Petrous motioned them to stand. "Would you both please rest your right hands on the pillow?"

Do they want us to wear those? Veron raised one eyebrow and watched his father. William stepped cautiously toward the king and extended his hand. Veron followed suit.

"Do the Shadow Knights, represented by William and Veron, agree to partner with the kingdom of Rynor?"

Veron swallowed his dry throat. He answered in unison with his father, "We do."

"Do you agree to defend our interests for the sake of peace and stability?"

"We do."

"Do you agree to *not* threaten Rynor's sovereignty?"

"We do."

Petrous smiled as Oswald selected one of the silver bracelets. When the king set the pillow down, he picked up the other, opening it up with both hands. "As a symbol of the renewed partnership between Rynor and the Shadow Knights, we bestow on you these bracelets of brotherhood." They moved the bracelets toward their exposed arms. "May they—"

Veron and William both jerked their arms back in unison. The king and his advisor flinched, their eyes widening. "What is it?" Petrous asked.

"I'm sorry," Veron said quickly. "We, uh . . ." He looked at William.

"We don't wear jewelry of any sort," his father finished. "It's part of our code."

The king frowned, tilting his head. "This is how we recognize allegiances in Rynor."

"We apologize, Your Majesty. I hope you can forgive us for skipping the symbolic gesture," William said.

Petrous furrowed his brow. "Did you not mean the words of

partnership you agreed to? Do you have other motives?"

"Not at all. We just . . ." Veron's voice faded, unsure what else to say.

"Please. This is Rynor tradition." The pained expression on the king's face made the decision difficult, but Veron wouldn't budge. He looked at his father whose jaw was tight. Guard's bodies pressed in closer from behind them. Veron's pulse sped. An unknown danger filling the air, he allowed the tingle of origine to simmer, ready to be summoned.

The look on Petrous' face changed. A sadness showed in his eyes as he mouthed the words, "I'm sorry."

Veron cocked his head. *About what?*

Strong arms grabbed him from behind as the soldiers converged. Two Rynorian men latched onto his arm, holding it extended as King Petrous and Oswald lunged with the bracelets.

Poised and ready for anything, Veron reached for the origine as he prepared to fling the soldiers away, but he felt a dull weight instead of a warm tingle. *What's wrong?* He looked down, shocked to find a loose metal chain encircling his waist, held in place by a Rynorian soldier. His stomach lurched as he pulled at his arm. It didn't budge, held tight by the men.

The bracelet surrounded his wrist, and a *click* reverberated through his arm. The same sound emanated from William—a metallic locking noise. Veron gasped and jerked his arm again, finally breaking free from the men. The loose chain around his waist fell free, but the damage was done. He pulled on the bracelet. It wouldn't budge. He turned his arm over, scrambling to find a clasp or a seam. William frantically struggled next to him.

"What is this?" William yelled, his voice tight.

A deep, bellowing laugh sent a chill through Veron's bones as a door slammed. He spun, his stomach churning.

Edmund Bale's hulking frame stood like a statue by the door they'd entered through minutes before. An evil grin covered his face, hidden partially by the black beard. A dozen soldiers stood behind him with swords bared. More doors opened and closed. Veron turned, finding dozens more men filling the room. Reaching over his shoulder from instinct, his hand stopped when it only found air. *My sword!* His breath grew ragged. His head jerked around, looking for a way out, but soldiers blocked every exit. William stood firm, staring back at the King of Norshewa.

"Good work, Petrous," Bale boomed. "As promised, your city shall remain intact."

Petrous's shoulders slumped, and he looked down at the ground. After a curt nod toward Bale, he and his advisor shuffled out of the room, Norshewan soldiers parting before him.

Behind Bale, a shorter, blond-haired young man caught Veron's eye. *Brixton.* Veron's lip curled, his teeth clenching together. His old friend momentarily locked eyes with him before looking to the floor, his face pinched.

Bale maintained his haughty expression but didn't take any steps closer. "It seems you tried to kill me in my sleep. I guess it's a good thing I didn't stop at Karondir. You can imagine my surprise when I heard there were now two of you. How many more shadow knights are there?" His eyes narrowed as he glared across the room.

"We have ten of us again," William replied, puffing his chest. "Five are back in Feldor, and the other three wait along the road to Daratill. Your time is finished, Bale."

Bale smirked. "You're lying."

William stared back without flinching.

"You are the only two, and you are about to die." He nodded to his men. "Kill them."

Veron's heart jumped. He pulled again at the bracelet to no avail.

Bending to the table, he struck his arm against the solid wood. The bracelet didn't budge. He struck harder. His arm ached, but the metal only dug harder into his skin. He spun, trying to find any opening, his breath coming in spurts. The soldiers in the room closed. "What do we do?" he asked.

"We fight," William replied, holding his staff with both hands, hopping on one foot to reposition his body.

Veron attempted to focus. He sought the well of energy hiding inside, resisting his attempt to call it forth. The first soldiers arrived. A vicious man with dark hair swung his sword, but Veron ducked then grabbed the pewter goblet from the table. He stood just as the next blade whistled toward him and blocked it with his makeshift tool. He kicked hard into the man's side, leaving him groaning and bent over in pain. Veron almost missed the next sword that jabbed at his side. Lurching his body around the point at the last moment, he slammed the mug down on the blade, knocking it free from the unsuspecting man. The clatter of steel on the hard floor filled him with hope.

He moved to scoop it up just as a large object collided into his back, sending him sprawling forward. He touched the hilt of the sword with the tips of his fingers before he fell to the ground, the weapon out of his reach. Veron rolled away from the unseen attack and jumped back to his feet. The chair that struck him lay upside down on the floor. Nearby, William whirled his staff at the soldiers, knocking them back and keeping them at a distance.

Veron blocked two quick strikes from his next attacker with his goblet, but the second hit sent the metal object flying across the room. The blade came at his head, and he ducked then swept with his foot, knocking the man to the floor. Veron turned to the upside-down chair behind him and yanked hard on the leg. With a crack, the wooden piece came free in his hand.

Veron spun with a grin on his face and a makeshift club in his hand. Five Norshewans prepared to attack but shrank back at his renewed confidence. He used the momentary lull to calm his mind. Straining through all the barriers and sluggishness holding him back, what he sought was there—the origine's familiar tingle.

With a roar, he pulled, fighting the resistance. Veron twirled faster than the men could react. He clubbed them down one by one, their weapons falling to the floor. Moving through the room, the soldiers paled as his lightning-fast form approached. Some fell where they were hit, and others stumbled away, holding their heads. Tossing the chair leg to the side, Veron scooped up a discarded sword.

Where are Bale and Brixton? he thought, turning. Against the far wall, the king pressed against the wall. At least twenty soldiers surrounded them. Through the gaps between their heads, Bale's eyes, wide and uncertain, locked with his. Veron smirked. *I've seen that fear before.*

Another soldier futilely swung at him, but Veron stepped to the side and ran him through with his borrowed blade. Suddenly, he shuddered as a familiar feeling of exhaustion caught up with him. *It can't be gone already!* He looked at his arm, cursing the bracelet.

William continued battling but struggled as he pivoted on his leg. *Half the men are still here. It's too many!* Veron thought. His breath shuddered. His arms felt heavy. *I can't let it go yet!* William looked at him, his brows lifted and forehead taut.

Veron's eyes flared as an idea came to him. "William!" He held up his own arm, then pointed to his father's and finally the table. William seemed to understand. With a flurry of vicious blows, he knocked back the closest soldiers then dropped to a knee. Pulling from deep within, Veron ran, closing the space in a flash. His legs lurched, and his vision spun. The origine was nearly depleted, and he struggled to even move. *Come on, just one more moment!* He cleared his mind, thinking only of his father's words. *Use the right amount of power.*

Using every reserve, Veron brought his sword down in a large arc. His father's extended arm rested on the wood of the table, his muscles rippling and his hand clenched into a fist. Veron's sword struck the bracelet, shattering the metal. In the fraction of an instant, he pulled back, keeping the blade from taking off the hand.

William gasped, pulling his hand back. The silver bracelet clattered on the table, and he flexed his hand, rolling it in a circle. Veron's vision blurred. With one final heave, he tossed his sword toward his father before falling to the floor. His head rolled to the side, too exhausted to lift it. Before his eyes closed, he glimpsed where Bale stood only moments ago. The wall stood empty. Veron exhaled as he closed his eyes.

Veron's body shook, slow and distant at first. After a long moment, he opened his eyes, blinking away the blur. His father let out a huge breath and stared back with a warm smile. "What happened?" Veron asked.

"Bale took off just before you passed out," William said. "I finished off the rest." He held up his arm and shook his bare wrist. ". . . thanks to you." He nodded toward Veron's hand. "I got yours off."

Veron looked at his wrist, relieved to find it bare again. A mangled silver bracelet rested on the stone floor. Veron managed a weak smile. He used an elbow to prop himself up, his father helping. "How long was I out?"

"Five minutes maybe. Can you move? With Petrous aligning with Bale, it's not safe here."

Veron allowed his father to pull him up. His legs wobbled, but he remained upright. "I'll need your help."

Sheathing the borrowed sword, William grabbed his staff off the ground and wrapped his free arm around Veron. The two dodged lifeless bodies and pools of blood, walking gingerly as they left the room and proceeded down the hall.

Ahead, a cluster of Rynorian soldiers grouped together. Veron tensed, but when they noticed Veron and William, they scurried away through the closest door.

"Ignore them," William said. "They won't mess with us."

When they made it out of the front doors, the guards from before gave them a wide berth. Veron struggled down the steps, scanning the street to find Chelci and Morgan with their horses. "They're not here," he said, his stomach dropping.

William ducked toward the side of the street, his head pivoting and eyes darting as he held up Veron. They checked in shops and down side alleys while keeping a sharp look for Bale or his men.

A shuffling sound drew Veron's attention. He looked up and gasped. Morgan limped as he approached, holding his head where a stream of blood trickled down. The shadow knights' weapons along with a couple of packs hung from his other arm.

"Morgan!" Veron said. "Where's Chelci? What happened?"

Morgan looked between them both. "I'm so sorry, Veron. I tried, but I couldn't stop them."

Veron's stomach turned. His voice caught in his throat.

"Was it Bale?" William asked in a grim tone.

"Him and his men. There was nothing I could do."

"What did he do?" Veron finally uttered. His body shook. "Where's Chelci?"

"Bale took her."

Morgan's words took a moment to register. Veron blinked, fighting to clear the haze from his mind. A stabbing sensation filled his gut.

"They beat me and knocked me over the head. Then they took our horses, storming toward the gate."

The weakness in his legs redoubled in intensity. *Anything but Chelci!*

"They took one other thing," Morgan said. "Veron . . ."

Veron held on to William's shoulder. His vision focused, framing Morgan in front of him.

"Bale has the book."

III

Destiny

29

Journey North

Chelci ground her teeth as she stared out the carriage window. She forced herself to look at the desolate hills, the jagged rocks alongside the road, the dimming sky—anywhere but at him. His intense stare from across the seat made her blood boil.

"It's going to be a long ride," Brixton said. "Sustaining that scowl may grow tiresome."

Chelci didn't move as the landscape flew past. She braced an arm against the wall as the carriage bounced over a rut in the road.

"I'll make sure they don't hurt you," Brixton said.

She turned. Brixton's eyes flared at her hard glare, his body leaning against the cushioned wall on his side of the carriage. She tilted her head and flashed a syrupy smile. "How kind of you. And how generous of you to offer to ride in here, keeping me company. I think that's what I needed."

Brixton swallowed and muttered toward the ground, "Someone had to keep an eye on you."

"I'm sure everyone else appreciates that sacrifice. You have to suffer in here on your cushioned seat while the rest get to sit on a hard saddle all day. I bet the good-natured citizens of Bromhill donated this carriage, didn't they?"

Brixton squirmed in his seat.

"They just love their new king so much." The corners of her mouth turned down as she looked back out the window.

"Bale controls the entirety of Terrenor now. There's nothing we can do about that."

"There's nothing you *choose* to do about that," she mumbled.

He rested his hand on hers. She jerked away, the cords of rope wrapped around both arms digging into her wrists. "Don't touch me!"

Brixton held up his hands. "I'm sorry! Look, Chelci . . ." He sighed. "I didn't want this to happen. I didn't want . . . *you* tied up or the trap for Veron."

She smirked. "Even after trapping him, you still couldn't kill him."

"Did Bale tell you?"

"He didn't have to. I saw it in his eyes."

"I didn't *want* to kill him. Look, I'm trying to do what's right here—"

"'What's right?'" Chelci's eyes bulged. "You turned on your friend! You sold out your country! And you sacked the village of Nasco, killing innocent people!"

"We lost at least as many of the king's soldiers there as we killed."

"And now Bale's running away at full speed." Another bump forced her to steady her balance. "He *knows* he's going to die!"

The carriage slowed, the horses' hooves settling to a walk. A hand landed on the window frame as a Norshewan soldier on horseback poked his head in, his beard pressing against the side. "Everything all right in here?"

Brixton jumped back. "Cyrus, you scared me. Yeah, we're fine, just talking."

The captain eyed Chelci, his mouth curling into a wicked grin.

"You want me to come and ride in here, too? I'd make sure you were nice and comfortable."

Chelci swallowed hard but refused to shrink away from his leering glance.

After a beat, he turned to Brixton. "Trade with me, will ya? You take my horse for a bit and let me ride with her."

Chelci's breath caught, her eyes wide, flitting to Brixton who didn't respond.

"Come on," Cyrus rasped with an air of longing. "We'll be stopping soon. Give me a chance to get to know this one."

"Bale told me to watch her," Brixton replied with little conviction.

"I'm a soldier, and you're just a commerce guy. I can watch her for you," Cyrus said, turning to her. "You know, I did already get to meet your father."

Chelci's eyebrows pinched as her nails dug into her legs.

"My first introduction was him nearly soiling himself when King Wesley died!" Cyrus burst into laughter. "You should have seen the look on his face! What a coward."

Spit flew from Chelci's lips, landing across the captain's nose and cheek. He stiffened and wiped his face, the humorous look gone.

"How dare you! Someone needs to teach you some manners!" Even though the carriage continued forward, the door rattled and began to open.

Brixton pulled it shut. "I said it's my job to keep her safe!"

"Bale never said she had to be safe," Cyrus sneered, leaning back onto his horse. "If you change your mind, Brixton, let me know." The captain edged away from the window but continued next to them.

Brixton exhaled and leaned back. "You're welcome," he whispered.

"Where are we going?" she asked without thanking him. "I know we're traveling north. Are we going to Daratill?"

He nodded. "We should catch up with the workers and their guards in a day or two. They headed there from the Gap. We should be able to travel at a slower pace then."

"What about the rest of the army back at Karondir?"

"What about them?"

"Are they remaining in Feldor?"

"Bale doesn't reveal all of his military plans to me."

"What about me? What's Bale planning to do with me?"

Brixton shrugged. "I don't know."

The carriage slowed to a stop. Brixton leaned to the window and called to Cyrus. "Are we stopping?"

"I hope so." The captain's attention turned. "Your Majesty!"

Both Cyrus and Brixton inclined their heads as a large black horse trotted into view.

"Should we make camp?" Cyrus asked.

Bale's deep voice bounced through the carriage window. "No, ten-minute break. We need to cover more ground before we stop." He turned toward the carriage, and a smile formed as he caught Chelci's eye through the window. "Ah, Miss Marlow! I hope your ride has been comfortable?"

She narrowed her eyes, trying to pierce him with her gaze. "I understand Veron gave you more trouble than you expected, huh?"

Bale's smile faltered.

"Why do you fight destiny? You know you can't stop him."

"Please, take a moment to stretch your legs," Bale said, wearing a forced smile that didn't reach his eyes. "I'm sure the carriage feels cramped."

"I'm fine," Chelci said sharply, lifting her chin. An ache grew in both legs as she considered how it would feel to move them.

"Chelci," Brixton said, nodding toward the door as he opened it.

Fine. It would feel good to stand.

Chelci descended from the carriage as Cyrus and Bale led their horses ahead. She extended each leg as she touched the ground. It did feel good. Away from the walls of the vehicle, a wind hit her. She pulled her cloak closer and shivered as she looked around.

Groups of mounted soldiers gathered in both directions. The sun lay below the mountains to the west. It would be dark soon. *They're going to continue for hours?* Chelci smirked. *Bale must expect Veron to come after me.* Looking to the south, she strained her neck, hoping to see a trail of dust kicking up from galloping horses. *Veron will be so angry.*

Sparsely-covered hills surrounded the road they traveled. Some men took advantage of the rest break to relieve themselves at the side of the road. Her own bladder screamed for relief at the reminder.

"Brixton?" she said turning to him and tossing her head toward a copse of bushes just down the hill. "I need to . . . you know."

Brixton's eyes widened. "Um, yeah . . ." He looked around as if to find someone to give him direction but didn't find an answer. "Sure. I'll walk down there with you."

She held up her hands to show the rope tied around them. "Can you help with this?"

"I . . . uh . . . don't think I can do that, Chelci."

"How do you expect me to go?"

He glanced around again. "I'm sorry, but I can't untie you. You'll have to figure it out."

Chelci huffed as they stepped off the road and walked toward the bushes. Her eyes scanned the countryside, hoping that somehow Veron's and William's black cloaks would pounce out from behind a rock. Her face fell as she remembered what the soldiers did to Morgan. *With how they beat him, I doubt they'd be able to make good time.*

When she arrived at the bush, she turned to Brixton. "If you think you're going to watch me while I go, you're—"

"I won't watch," Brixton interrupted. "But you have to promise me you won't try anything."

Chelci nodded. "Of course."

Brixton turned around as Chelci moved behind a large bush. The limbs held few leaves and didn't completely block visibility, but it was better than nothing. Maneuvering her arms to unfasten her pants wasn't as difficult as she wanted Brixton to think.

Before she began, she turned and looked through the bush. Brixton watched in the opposite direction as promised, but up the hill, the creepy soldier sat on his horse, nudging two other men who stood by him. Cyrus sniggered while pointing in her direction.

"Hey!"

Chelci jerked at Brixton's shout. He looked up the hill toward the soldiers and motioned with a hand for them to turn away. They gradually did. A reluctant smile crept on her face.

As she finished her business, her boldness grew. She fastened her pants quietly so as not to alert Brixton. *I know I promised him I wouldn't try anything, but . . ."* Farther down the hill, a small river filled the gully, surrounded by large rocks. *If I could make it to those rocks, they might lose what direction I'm heading.*

Her heart pounded. She glanced over her shoulder to confirm Brixton and the soldiers above still looked away. She took a soft step. The ground was free from sticks and leaves, and her feet were silent. At first, she moved sideways while watching her guard but soon turned. Her legs moved faster and faster along with her pulse's thumping. After a moment, she ran at a full sprint.

"Hey!"

Brixton's shout pushed her to run faster. She arrived at the boulders by the river and careened out of sight behind the first one. She paused in a rounded dirt area. Stones doubling her height surrounded her on all sides. Four distinct passages opened up between the boulders, all of which were dark where the diminishing sunlight struggled to reach. *I want to go upstream, back toward Veron, but . . .* She turned north, hoping the unexpected direction would throw her pursuers.

From the safety of the rocks, she couldn't see the train of soldiers up the hill searching for her. Chelci scurried as fast as she could to put distance between herself and them. The narrow path caused her to squeeze between rock walls and duck under low overhangs. She scrambled over stones and slid down the opposite sides. Her tied arms made travel difficult, but she compensated for it with her desperation.

Jumping across several rocks that poked out of the water, she made it to the other side of the river. A quick glance upstream revealed one lone soldier far away. Barely visible in the dim light, he searched along the bank, moving in the opposite direction. She grinned as she ducked back amongst the boulders.

A sheer edge of stone caught her eye. She tested it with her hand. *Is it sharp enough?* She placed the rope on the keen edge and moved her arms back and forth. The repetitive motion both warmed and tired her arms. She leaned to the side, checking around the wall of rock she had just passed. No one yet. She paused for a moment to rest her arms and inspect the ropes. A tight gash grew along the side. Her spirits perked, and she attacked the bindings with renewed vigor.

After a moment, a tearing sound grew more pronounced, and snapping threads reverberated through her arms. Sweat dripped down her face despite the crisp air. *Almost there!* She pushed her arms, leaning her entire body into the rock as she frantically rubbed against it. With a final snap, a cord broke. The pressure on her wrists loosened, and a soft cry escaped her mouth. Glancing around to confirm she was still alone, she contorted her arms to unravel the rope. It went slowly at first, but once she could grasp a loose end, the rest came.

Free from her bounds, she dropped the frayed rope to the ground. She rubbed her wrists, flexing them to work through the numbness. *Now I can move,* she thought. She looked downstream.

Just past the bank, the rocks ended, and a forest took its place. *Perfect, if I can get in there, I—*

A sudden jolt slammed into the back of her neck, dropping Chelci to the ground. Her vision disappeared, replaced by a blinding white light. The pain was so sharp she couldn't determine if it was real or imaginary. After a half-second of indecision, the agony settled in her body, confirming she did not make it up. She groaned as she rolled on the rocky ground, grabbing her neck.

When her vision returned, she looked up. The sky was nearly black. Above her, a bearded captain twirled a dagger in his hand.

"You thought you were clever, didn't you?" Cyrus' voice taunted.

Two other shadowy bodies stood next to him with swords of their own.

"Your pal, Brixton, isn't here to look out for you now, is he?" Evil laughs sounded from all three soldiers.

Chelci inhaled sharply, then frantically looked around. A rock wall lay to her back, and the three men blocked her only path of escape. Her heart continued to thud. Other than the discarded ropes, she could reach nothing.

With their weapons held lazily, she spun on the ground, kicking the captain's feet as hard as she could. An instant of resistance fought back until his feet gave way and flew out from under him on the smooth rock. A sickening thud sounded as he collapsed to the ground, the dagger bouncing away.

Chelci's pulse raced as she snatched the knife, but the other two men stepped in with their swords alert, forcing her against the rock. Escape was hopeless.

Cyrus groaned and held his hand against the back of his head. He turned his attention back to Chelci and drew a sword.

Chelci fingered the dagger, bouncing her gaze between the three men. *I can't take them all with this.* With a flick of her wrist, the knife flew, twirling end over end. The captain's eyes grew, and his body contorted. At the last second, his head jerked away, the small metal weapon clattering to the ground.

Cyrus regained his stance. He stared hard at Chelci while a thin line of red grew on his cheek. Faint drops of blood trickled from the narrow wound. The captain wiped his cheek with the back of his hand and inspected it. "Oh, you're gonna regret that. Grab her," he whispered to the other soldiers. They sniggered as they leaned in.

"I'm here!" Her hopeless call bounced off the boulders. "They caught me!"

The soldiers stiffened, stopping their approach. Cyrus' shadowy shoulders slumped, and the sword tip backed off. In a few moments, the cries and footsteps of new soldiers approached. Brixton rounded the boulder, his eyes somewhere between anger and worry.

"Get up," Cyrus growled, sheathing his sword.

Chelci struggled to her feet and rubbed the back of her neck, where a knot already formed. Suddenly, her head jerked, her scalp on fire as someone pulled on her hair.

Cyrus' beard tickled against her ear as he rasped, "Next time I won't care if Brixton is around or not." He pulled her hair forward, leading her back the way they came.

Unable to turn her head, Chelci's eyes flitted around, looking in the shadows, hoping for a surprise. *Veron, where are you?*

30

Pursuit

"I wish we could run through the night," Veron muttered, pacing at the edge of the small fire well off the road. "I can't stand the thought of her alone with them."

"I'll say it again. Leave me behind," Morgan insisted. "After the beating, I can't hurry. Even *if* they hadn't taken our horses, I'd need to be slow. You two should go on without me."

"We're not leaving you behind," William said. "I'm sorry, Veron. I know you want to get her back—and we will—but using the origine to sprint after them would be foolish. Even if we caught up, it'd be us two, with no energy, facing down however many men they have."

"But the bulk of their army is still back in Karondir. They can't have that many!" Veron protested.

"And how many would it take to stop you if you had no energy?"

Veron stopped moving and fixed his jaw. "They can't be far ahead." He sat by the fire in a huff and jabbed a stick into the coals.

"They'll be far enough," William said. "Their horses' tracks showed their speed, and Bale probably ran them well into the evening. They're likely close to Molvaigh by now and could change out their mounts there."

"We should have stolen horses from Bromhill! How are we supposed to catch up?"

William looked into the flames and paused for a beat. "We'll catch them in Daratill."

Veron's blood turned cold. "Daratill! No! She needs us now! We can run!"

"It's a bad idea. We need to travel at a regular pace so we can arrive ready to fight."

"How do you know that's where they're going?" Veron asked.

"It's what I would do. He's conquered Terrenor. Now he'll return home in victory."

"With his thousands of slaves," Morgan added.

"It will take us—what . . . a week or two to walk there at this pace?" Veron said. "That's plenty of time for Bale to . . . I don't know. Who knows what he may do to her?" He clenched his fists and groaned through gritted teeth. "We should go now! She needs us!"

William shook his head. "Take it easy. Bale won't touch her, trust me." His eye twitched at the words. "He needs her to draw us to him, and he thinks by controlling where we meet, he'll have the advantage. But we're capable of more than he realizes."

Morgan cleared his throat. "What about the book?" The question fell like an axe, filling the air with tension.

"Can he learn it?" Veron asked, looking at his father. "Not having any training, could he discover how to use the origine? Every day we're out here is another day for him to learn!"

William shook his head. "Not likely. He knows nothing about how it works. Reading wouldn't be enough." His father flinched as he spoke.

Veron swallowed hard. *He knows it's possible.* "That's how I learned," he said in a lifeless voice. The wind picked up, blowing his words away. No one replied.

Veron craned his neck, looking up into the inky sky. Clouds blocked out the moon and stars. A gust of wind whistled through the gully where they camped. His mind still raced at the thought of Chelci on her own, but he gradually calmed, his pulse returning to a regular beat. The breeze forced him to inch closer to the fire, rubbing his hands as he held them out.

"How did you use the origine when you had the bracelet on?" William asked.

Veron looked and took a deep breath. Smoke wafted his way, stinging his nose and burning his lungs. "I don't know," he mumbled, his mind still focused on Chelci. He sighed after a moment of silence. "It's like I told you before—it's there, just hard to use."

"Is the power the same?"

"It's less . . . I think. It's difficult to tell because it takes so much effort, and I wear out quickly."

"Back at the Academy, the knights talked about it sometimes."

"What'd they say?" Veron asked, interested in any information about past Shadow Knights.

"Just wishful thinking—trying to think of ways to counteract metal's effect. Artimus had a small group of them who practiced wearing metal to see if they could figure it out." William shook his head. "Nothing seemed to work though."

"What sets me apart?"

William sighed. "I wish I knew."

Morgan's yawn reminded Veron how late it was, but he was in no state to sleep. "I can take the first shift," he offered.

William nodded. "I'll take the second. Now, we need to get some sleep. The trip to Norshewa will be a long one, and Chelci needs us to be strong when we arrive. Wake me when it's my turn."

Veron dug a stick into the fire, sending sparks into the air and orange and red plumes twirling around it. "You know, I was about to ask her to marry me."

William's head cocked, and his mouth turned up in a half smile. "I thought you might. You'll get to ask her when you see her again . . . soon, I'm sure." His father lay back.

The thought of seeing Chelci soon soothed Veron's heart's ache, but he didn't share his father's confidence.

. . . If I get to see her again, he thought.

The fire's simmering light provided little warmth. Veron blew into his hands as he kept watch. After his father adjusted a few times, his chest rose and fell in a smooth rhythm. Morgan had long been out. *It's time.*

Moving as quietly as possible, Veron gathered his bag and a small portion of what food they'd saved. He slung his sword over his shoulder along with his bag of supplies. Neither William nor Morgan saw his pained grin. *I will miss you both, but I must do this.*

He turned away from the fire, and the night's cold hit his face. After a minute of stalking through the woods, he found the road again, the moon lighting up the path. Veron pulled his bag tight, reached inside himself for the origine, and ran.

The wind buffeted his face as he flew down the road. He tried to keep his hood up for warmth, but the wind knocked it back. The rocks and trees came and went. His legs pumped with just enough energy to sustain them. He felt like he rode on a horse at full speed, but the galloping legs were his own.

Not too much, Veron told himself. *I need it to last. If I can keep this up, I could reach them tomorrow.*

Whenever he tired, he slowed. After a chance to recover, he pulled at the origine again. For hours, he sustained his pace, alternating between a blistering run and a slow jog. When dawn peeked in the east, he felt even stronger. Energy surged inside of him. *I'm coming,*

Chelci. Just hang on. He chuckled as he ran. *William was just being cautious. He doesn't know how I can—*

Veron's eyes bulged. *What's happening?* His legs stumbled. He tried to steady himself but could no longer balance. The ground rose, his face sliding into the dirt and rocks of the path. Rolling on his back, he gasped for air. His lungs were empty, his limbs useless.

I was fine. I had plenty of energy . . . I thought. His chest ached. He tried to sit up but fell back again from the effort. The scrapes on his face stung, and he had no origine with which to heal. He closed his eyes. *Come on, Veron! Chelci needs you!* He deeply gulped and forced himself to a sitting position. A wave of dizziness washed over him. The road spun until his head hit the ground. The dull thud barely registered as blackness covered him.

* * *

A vague sensation of movement stirred his brain. Veron's mind urged him to open his eyes, but his body wasn't ready.

"I'm tellin' you, it's one of 'em," a muddled voice said.

The movement was back. Someone kicked his foot. He forced his eyes open and blinked away the bright light to find two soldiers leaning over his body. They jumped back, feet scraping the stones, and swords held erect.

"Don't move!" the taller soldier commanded.

Veron's heart pounded as he took in the soldiers with their stained uniforms and broad shoulders. Through much effort, he sat up, but his vision spun.

"Kill 'em now before he comes to!" the other said, his short body angled just behind the first. "He's s'posed to be dangerous."

"Doesn't look dangerous." He nudged Veron's leg with his foot. "He can't even move."

"Bale said the two men with black cloaks have special powers and they're trying to kill him. It's our job to stop 'em."

"But this is only *one* man, not two. How are we s'posed to know if it's him?" Both soldiers looked at Veron.

"Where am I?" Veron croaked.

The soldiers glanced at each other. The short one seemed to shake. "See that SK?" he muttered, pointing a wobbling sword at Veron's cloak. "I bet that stands for Shadow Knight."

"I bet you're right," the other said, standing taller and pointing his sword straight.

Veron tried to jump up and draw his weapon. He teetered on his feet but was too weak to unsheathe his sword. Sweat beaded on his brow. *I'm one of the most powerful people in Terrenor, and I'm helpless in front of a common soldier.*

"Kill 'em, quick!" the one in the back shouted. "Then we can take 'em in."

Veron used both hands, straining as he pulled on the hilt. The metal slid slowly, his arms weak and pitiful. The tall soldier reared back, holding his blade above his head. His teeth bared as he readied to strike.

A hollow thump made Veron flinch. He stared open-mouthed at the knife embedded in the man's chest, directly over his heart. The soldier's arms fell, and he stumbled backward.

"What's wrong?" the other said, moving out of the way. "What hap—" His words stopped when he saw the dagger and the trickle of red running down his comrade's tunic.

The tall soldier fell to the ground, grabbing at his chest. The other's knuckles grew white around the hilt of his sword. "What did you do?"

"Me?" Veron said, unsuccessfully trying to look around him. "I didn't—"

The soldier yelled as he ran at him. Veron flinched. He wobbled backward with no strength to run or fight. Moments before the blade arrived, a flash of steel and a sickening sound of cutting flesh filled the air. Veron gasped as the soldier's head fell from his neck, his body crumpling to the ground. In place of the soldier, William held his sword extended with his Shadow Knights cloak swaying in the wind. His chest rose and fell in deep gasps.

"William!" Veron's voice was hoarse.

"I thought you might end up like this, so we hurried as soon as we found out you left."

Veron rested his hands on his knees and locked eyes with his father. Guilt flooded through him. The shame of poor decision-making pressed on his shoulders. He dropped his head toward the dirt path. "I'm sorry, I should have—"

William cut off his words as he wrapped Veron in a hug, pulling tightly. He tensed for a moment but relaxed, giving in to the warm embrace. The scruff of William's beard pressed against his cheek. Veron closed his eyes, allowing the moment to wash over him. After a long moment, they pulled away. William's eyes glistened until he wiped at their corners.

"I should have listened," Veron said. "I'm sorry."

William nodded. "I should have listened, too. You brought up valid points about Chelci, and I shut them down. I'm sorry."

Veron chuckled. "You were right, though. I can't just run after them. Do you know what happened to me? I ran for hours, and then all of a sudden, my energy vanished."

"You can't sustain it for that long."

"But I took rest breaks and only used a small amount at a time—at least I tried to."

"After that much time, you're not only using the origine to give you strength, it also dulls your fatigue. You ran so long that your body didn't allow you to feel exhausted, even when your energy was nearly depleted."

Veron sighed. "And when it was gone, I collapsed and passed out."

"That's why we can't run to Daratill."

Veron nodded. "Thanks for coming after me. How'd you get here so fast?"

"A slow jog. You didn't actually make it very far. You must have been passed out for a while."

Veron looked around. "Where's Morgan?"

William nodded behind him where a dark spec traveled along the path in the distance. "Just a bit behind." Turning to the soldier on the ground, William nudged the first one with his boot before retrieving his knife. "Men must be scouring the road looking for us. We need to be careful. How are you? Can you walk?"

Veron took a deep breath and a few steps. "Um . . . If it's slow."

"Once Morgan catches up, we'll keep going."

Thankful for a moment to rest, Veron exhaled as he sat back on the dirt. *Sorry, Chelci, I'm still coming, but it will be a while.*

31

Molvaigh

Veron's legs ached as they descended the hill to the edge of the city, arriving just as the sun faded in the west. Molvaigh spread before them, vibrant and alive, a welcome change from the rocky path they had traveled for two days. Lanterns lit the streets, and the chatter of conversation greeted them the moment they passed the first stone building.

Next to him, Morgan walked with a pained expression. William had pushed to stop and rest several times, but Veron and the grocer always insisted they continue. From sunup to sundown, they walked at a brisk pace, traveling north toward Norshewa.

"Please tell me we can find a bed for the night," Morgan said. "The ground is great, but . . ."

"But a bed would be nice," William finished for him with a smile. "Yes, we should be able to find an inn." William stopped and stared at Veron's chest.

"What is it?" Veron asked before looking down. The embroidered Shadow Knights symbol stared back at him. His shoulders fell. "Our cloaks."

William stepped out of the center of the road and turned his back to a wall. He sloughed off the pack on his shoulder. "We should take them off."

Veron looked around and dropped his pack before uncovering himself. The cold air instantly made him shiver. He stuffed the thick fabric into his bag, now bulging.

William hoisted his load to his shoulders again. "Come on, let's go."

Veron held his arms against his body, trying to ignore the cold, hoping it wouldn't be for long. After a few more turns, a large wooden sign appeared, announcing the Mysfortune Inn. Two drunken men stumbled in the street, taking turns throwing knives at invisible hobbilade targets. Their raucous laughter covered the knives' clatters against the stone street.

"You sure about this place?" Morgan asked as William made to enter.

William shrugged. "If they have food and beds, it works for me."

Exchanging a look with Morgan, Veron flared his eyebrows. He extended an arm, allowing Morgan to enter first.

Ducking his head, a sweet, musty smell hit Veron as he stepped through the doorway. Warm lights hung on the walls around a large, open room. Tables and chairs filled the space while a high-top bar ran the length of the wall to his left. Half the tables contained people—mostly men—with tall mugs in front of them. In the back corner, a thin, young man with curly hair played on a lute, closing his eyes and smiling while his fingers strummed away.

Behind the bar, a man with a rag rubbed down a mug and nodded to their group. His welcoming smile overshadowed his stringy hair and gray beard.

William took the lead, his staff clumping on the wooden floor as they crossed the room.

"Looking for a room for the night," William said. "Three beds and a meal if you have it."

"Very good, very good," the man said, nodding. "One tid per person covers the bed and meal."

William fished coins from a pocket and dropped them into the man's hand.

"My name's Darian, and this is my inn. You are . . . ?"

"Bensen," William replied. "We're in town from Kandis, heading toward the Gap of Thardor first thing in the morning."

"Oh, yeah? What business do you have there?"

"Mining," William replied after a slight pause. "I hear the hills around the gap are bursting with baltham."

Darien looked just over Veron's shoulder and jerked his chin up. "Why the swords?"

Farrathan felt heavy on Veron's back. "Oh, uh . . . you can never be too careful, right? You never know where a bandit is hiding," Veron muttered.

"You two all right?" the innkeeper asked, pointing at their tunics. "You look freezing. Might want to pick up a cloak in town before you leave."

"Yeah, we were just talking about that," Veron said.

Darien ducked behind the counter. "Here you go," he said, handing a key to William and nodding toward the far wall. "Number six, just up the stairs. It's one of our rooms with three beds. Once you toss your gear, come back down, and we'll have a nice warm meal for you."

After momentarily dropping their bags and weapons, the three travelers descended the creaky steps to return to the common room. A reserved round of applause greeted them as they entered. Disoriented, Veron glanced at the lute player—the subject of the applause—who bowed in the corner.

"How about the one in the back?" Morgan asked, pointing to the far wall where an empty table waited without any close neighbors.

William led the way, leaning on his staff, and the three men sat around the table. Deep gouges raked the wooden surface. Veron touched his arms to the flat top, but the sticky residue against his skin forced him to put them down by his sides.

"Do you have any requests?" the curly-haired minstrel asked, looking to the half-full room of patrons.

"'The Long Lady of Wiether,'" a man suggested from a few tables down.

"Oh, that's so depressing. Anything livelier?"

A man at another table shouted, "How about 'The Dame and the Crooked Frog!'"

Bawdy laughter erupted around the room, and the musician pulled at his collar. "Whew . . . not a shy bunch, are you?" he said. "How about . . . 'A Bonny Bonny Prefinday?'"

The crowd mumbled. Veron took the response as dissatisfaction, but the minstrel launched into a lively tune with a grin on his face.

In a few moments, Darien arrived with three mugs of ale, froth pouring over the top. "Drinks to start you off, and I'll have hot plates for you soon."

"Thank you," Morgan said, picking up his mug and sipping the froth at the top.

"Is everything to your liking in the room?"

"Yes," William replied. "It will do just fine."

A bell rang as the door to the inn opened. Four large men entered with swords hanging from each of their belts. William's chest grew as he inhaled.

"I'll be back soon." Darien beamed as he trotted away, veering to intercept the newcomers.

"Are they trouble?" Veron whispered, leaning toward his father.

William shook his head. "I doubt it. Just men looking for something to drink."

While trying to act like he wasn't, Veron watched the new men who sat at the table next to them. Their loud conversation was easy to overhear. He sighed as they traded words back and forth about the merits of raising sheep versus cows.

"Why do I feel so tense in here?" Veron whispered again.

"I feel it, too," Morgan added. "Should we be worried?"

"I don't think there's anything we need to worry about, but stay alert," William confirmed.

"Rynor is our friend, right?" Veron asked. "We should be able to trust the people here."

William leaned in. "It *was* our friend. Don't forget, Bale controls everything now."

"But that just happened. The people here wouldn't even know yet, right?"

William leaned back with pursed lips. Before he could speak, Darien arrived with a plate for each of them.

Veron's mouth watered. Roasted chicken steamed as if pulled directly off the spit. Carrots, tomatoes, and a round roll filled the plate. His nose danced with happiness. He picked up the chicken by a leg and dove in, the juicy meat practically falling off the bone. He moaned as he swallowed.

"This is much better than any of our campfire meals we had back in—" A swift kick to the leg cut off Veron's sentence. He shrank a bit at his careless tongue. "It's good," he finished, picking up his mug to wash down the meat.

"Darien, I heard people saw Norshewan soldiers coming through these parts. Is that true?" William asked.

The innkeeper's face turned sour. "I'm afraid so. Marched right through Molvaigh, down this street. Apparently, King Petrous struck a deal with Bale and surrendered Rynor."

"We heard that rumor, but I could barely believe it was possible."

"I've kept this inn for thirty years—through Bale's siege on Bromhill, through the multiple times his army marched through Molvaigh, laying waste to the town. I can't believe Petrous turned it over, just like that."

"How long ago were they here?" Veron asked, trying to sound casual.

"It was early this morning. They tore through the city like they were running from a valcor."

"So, they were heading north, then? Toward Daratill?" William asked.

"It appeared so," Darien confirmed. "I saw a few still in the city today. Two are staying here tonight."

Veron inhaled sharply. "They're staying here? At the inn?" William's hand grabbed onto his leg, reminding him to act calm.

"Yeah," Darien leaned closer. "They give me the creeps. I'd prefer to turn them away, but times are tight and their coin is good. They had horses, so they must be officers of some sort. Not sure why they stayed behind."

Veron forced a weak smile, but his heart pounded. He opened his mouth to speak again, but William's firm hand again stifled his words.

"You may see them. They're in room five, just next to yours." A shout across the room drew the innkeeper's attention to the bar, where a man waved. "Well, enjoy your food," he said, taking his leave.

Veron, Morgan, and William stared at each other after Darien left, no longer paying attention to the food. "What do we do?" Morgan asked.

"I wonder who it is," Veron said. "Men on horses? They may recognize us."

After a long moment, William spoke up. "We should get out of the common room. We can't risk being seen."

Morgan swiveled his head around the room. "Do we need to leave?"

"We should stay up in the room then leave at first light."

Veron's heart sank as he looked down at his plate of delicacies. "Do you think we can bring—"

Loud footsteps and the scrape of a sword along a wall cut him off. The three turned to where two Norshewan soldiers stood side-by-side at the foot of the stairs. Veron propped an elbow on the table, resting his hand against his face to block their view of him. Peeking around his hand, he got a better look at the men. Clean-shaven with neat brown hair, the faces weren't any he recognized. He wanted to sigh in relief, but their smug faces turned his stomach.

"Hello, my countrymen!" the taller of the two soldiers called with a wicked grin.

The lively tune of the lute stopped mid-song, and the faces of the people scowled. No one replied.

"Now that's no way to greet your fellow citizen of Norshewa."

A muttered correction of "Rynor" came from somewhere near the musician.

"What was that?" the tall soldier shouted, his face hard as he took a step in that direction and rested his hand on his sword.

Whoever had spoken didn't repeat their mumbling.

"This land is now the property of Norshewa, as is all of Terrenor!" He scanned the crowd, but no one moved. His smile returned. "I am Sub-Captain Aric of King Bale's army, and we could use your help. We're looking for two men, and there is a large reward on their heads."

"Yeah," the other soldier added. "Twenty gold sol for their capture." Gasps echoed around the room.

Veron stiffened, turning to make eye contact with William.

"These men are dangerous. They were last seen traveling with black cloaks and swords and come from Feldor."

Veron clenched his jaw and took a deep breath. The innkeeper, Darien, stared at their table from behind the bar. He turned away as soon as Veron noticed.

"We also learned two of His Majesty's soldiers were killed on the road south of here. We believe the men we seek were the murderers. If anyone has any information, let us know. Who knows . . . it may lead to twenty sol."

"I think we need to get out of here," Morgan whispered.

Veron nodded. "How are we supposed to get up without drawing attention?"

"Keep eating," William said, picking up his chicken. "Be ready to leave as soon as we have the chance."

"Should we take them out?" Veron asked. "It's only two of them. It would be easy."

"We may have to, but I'd rather not draw the attention. Let it play out."

The soldiers meandered between the tables, looking closer at the people in the tavern and asking questions. The music picked back up, but at a lilting pace. Veron quietly ate while keeping an eye trained on the soldiers.

Across the room, the innkeeper wiped a mug with a rag repeatedly while he stared in their direction. Veron watched, but the man wouldn't take his eyes off of them. *He's probably mulling over the twenty sol.* A glance back toward the soldiers found Aric's eyes focused on the innkeeper. The soldier turned his head, following Darien's gaze until he stopped at their table. Veron's eyes widened. Aric stared directly at him. The two soldiers immediately moved toward their table.

"They've made us," Veron whispered, turning his head to his food.

"Do we run for it?" Morgan asked.

"Give it a moment," William said.

Veron forced a shaking carrot into his mouth.

"Hello there," Aric said, appearing next to their table.

"Hello," William replied with no smile or warmth.

"Where are you three from?"

"Kandis. We're just in town for the night—heading west."

"West, huh?" Aric raised an eyebrow.

Veron nodded. "That's right. We're going to mine baltham."

"It's cold outside. Where are your cloaks?"

Veron swallowed, turning to William. "We didn't bring any," his father said. "It's suether now, and we're from the coast. We didn't expect it to be so cold." He knocked against the side of his wooden leg, creating a hollow thump. "I rarely travel."

The soldier narrowed his eyes. "So, if we went to your room, you could show us your things, and we wouldn't find two black cloaks?"

"That's right," William replied after a beat.

The five men traded looks back and forth for a long moment until Aric nodded toward the stairs. "Let's see." Veron and Morgan made to stand until the soldier stopped them. "No! Just the cripple," he clarified.

William nodded to Veron. His staff punctuated his steps across the room, and his limp appeared more pronounced. The soldiers followed him up the stairs.

Veron's body shook, his muscles tense.

"Do you think he'll be okay?" Morgan whispered.

"He will," Veron replied confidently.

After watching the soldiers disappear upstairs, the rest of the room resumed their conversations, but Veron strained his ear. A distant thump and a faint shake of the lantern on the far wall confirmed his thoughts.

Morgan leaned in. "Was that William?" Veron nodded. "Should we go up to check on him?"

Veron shook his head. "He'll be fine. Finish whatever food you want to eat. We'll have to go in a moment."

He forced himself to look at his food but kept glancing toward the stairs. Seconds turned into minutes while they waited. *He should be back by now.*

A creak at the door drew his attention. The front door to the inn opened only a sliver, not even alerting the bell above it. Through a narrow crack, William's hand beckoned.

A relieved grin formed. "Come on," Veron whispered as he stood.

Ignoring the other patrons' glances, Veron opened the front door to find his father pressed against the wall in the street.

"What happened?" Veron asked as William handed him his pack and sword. Morgan picked up his pack on the ground.

"They won't bother us for a while. We need to get out of the city, though. There will be others looking, and word will spread."

Veron followed toward a side street. "Did you kill them?"

William scoffed. "They'll be out for a while, but they'll be fine."

"So, we won't be able to stay in an inn tonight, huh?" Morgan asked.

"I'm afraid not," William said. "We need to stick to the road."

Veron faintly grinned, thankful for the chance to make more ground. He followed William as he ducked through the darkened streets, moving from shadow to shadow. When they reached the far end of the city, they left the lighted warmth of civilization behind and forged ahead into the cold darkness.

32

The Land of White

The repetitive crunch of rolling over rocks and dirt changed to a soft, slushy sound. Chelci's eyes opened. She squinted at the bright light greeting her through the window. The sun was high in the air, and a blanket of whiteness surrounded everywhere they looked. She'd read of snow but had never seen it. Most of Feldor didn't get cold enough, but deep in the heart of Norshewa, the air was colder than she'd ever known—even though it was suether.

"Incredible," Brixton breathed on the bench across from her, exhaling a cloud of fog as he looked out his own window.

She sniffed, trying to ignore his presence.

Before long, inky black buildings passed by the windows. Faces of want gazed back from doorways as the army and their prisoners marched by. Even with her thick cloak, Chelci shivered, but many of the people staring back wore threadbare clothing with exposed skin.

Soon, the buildings grew dense, with buildings and alleys angling off in all directions. Most streets were clear of snow. A rotting smell wafted through the open window, wrinkling her nose.

"Why's everything black?" Brixton asked. Chelci rolled her eyes, drawing a glare. "What?"

She sighed. "Obsulom is found in plenty in the north."

Brixton's forehead creased.

"Obsulom? The hard, black stone?"

"Hmph," Brixton muttered after a moment of silence.

I guess King's Academy didn't cover Terrenorian minerals.

"Seems depressing," he said. "Who would want to live here?"

A river came into view, roaring around icy boulders and churning foam that disappeared against the snowbanks. The beginnings of a black structure caught her eye. It straddled the river and looked as if someone had planned an enormous palace but abandoned the project soon after beginning. Foundations grew out of each side of the river, and an arch spanned the turbulent water, contrasting the snowy land behind it.

"What's that?" Brixton asked. "Must be his new palace."

"I bet that's what he wants the *workers* for," Chelci muttered, shaking her head.

The Feldorian slaves angled off from the path their carriage took, following a group of soldiers toward the construction project. Their heads hung and shoulders heaved after the rapid escape from Bromhill. Few appeared dressed for the harsh weather.

Leaving the partially constructed palace behind, the road disappeared as the carriage crossed a bridge with the freezing river running beneath. After a brief section of stone passageway, the view opened up into a courtyard. The carriage turned in a circle and rolled to a stop. An unseen hand opened the door and Brixton motioned her to exit. Pressing her retied hands against the carriage wall for balance, she descended and looked up to take in Bale's castle.

Compared to the towering masterpiece of Felting, the surrounding fortress was barely half the height. Still, what it lacked in height, it made up for in design. Thick, black walls surrounded her. Towers shot up like weeds, with tiny walkways connecting them high off the ground. Pockets of snow lingered in the roof's shady areas.

"This way, you," a soldier said, grabbing her shoulder and pulling her toward a door. To her dismay, Brixton remained behind. Although she despised him, it pained her to be separated from her only semblance of familiarity and safety.

Two men led her through the castle, up winding stairs, and past frigid, empty halls. Passing through a doorway revealed a narrow bridge of stone leading to a tower ahead. The wind struck her as she reemerged outside. With her bound hands, she grasped the railing on one side of the bridge as she shuffled along. Halfway across, she stopped to lean over the side. A large interior courtyard with towering stone pillars lay far below. Her head spun from the height until a rough hand pushed her forward along the bridge.

"Keep moving," the soldier ordered.

At the end of the bridge, a spiral staircase wound up the tower. She trudged up with one man in front and the other behind. Her calves soon ached. Narrow window slits provided light in the otherwise dark stairwell. When the stairs ended, a grim, metal door opened with an exhausted groan, and the soldier ahead ushered her through.

The room at the top of the tower was bare. Only a hard wooden bench rested against the wall. A lever stuck out of the stone wall, and a grim looking hook dangled from the ceiling. Opposite the bench, a window with crossed bars looked south toward the mountains.

One soldier held up a knife. "Show me your hands."

Chelci lifted her bound hands, ready to jump back at any moment. The soldier slid the knife between the rope strands. After a few movements back and forth, it cut cleanly. She rubbed her wrists as the men left, closing the door with a slam.

She listened but couldn't tell if the soldiers walked away or remained to guard her. The door handle wouldn't budge. Bracing a foot against the wall, she jerked unsuccessfully with her arms.

"Hello? Is anyone there? What's going to happen to me?" She banged on the door to no response.

Giving up on the door, Chelci walked to the window. The metal bars sank into the stone at the window's edge. She grabbed a bar with her hand and pulled. It didn't budge, either. She pressed her face to the bars. A foreboding range of snow-covered mountains rose in the distance, reminding her how far away she was from home.

Chelci returned to the bench and sat where a thin gray blanket waited. She unfolded it and wrapped it around her body, somehow feeling colder with the added layer.

I'm sure Veron will come after me. The thought of him caused heartache. Her chin quivered as a tear built up, threatening to spill down her cheek. She wiped it away and sniffed. *What if he doesn't come? What if we never marry?*

She rubbed her hands together, cupped them in front of her mouth, and blew. Her fingers held a bluish tint from the cold, but the motion kept the blood flowing. With revitalized hands, she closed her eyes, sitting up straight.

Clear my mind. Clear my mind. Come on, Chelci. You can do this. She took a deep breath then exhaled, resting her hands on her knees. *Where are you, origine?*

* * *

Chelci's footsteps echoed as she followed her armed escort. Her breath fogged along the cold, featureless hallway lit only by torches. The man opened a wooden door with the outline of a bear carved into the surface. He ushered her into the room.

Walls of books and a roaring fire piqued her interest—a welcome change from the harsh cold of the tower, where she'd spent the previous night alone.

"The prisoner, Your Majesty," the guard said before ducking back through the doorway.

King Bale sat in an oversized leather chair, reading a book and stroking his newly-trimmed beard. Freshly cleaned, he wore a thick robe of yellow and red with black trim cascading to his feet.

When he looked up, a grin covered his face as his book snapped shut. "Chelci Marlow!" The king stood and approached. "I would ask how your accommodations are, but I can't imagine the east tower is particularly enjoyable."

Chelci clamped her jaw, forcing herself not to snap back.

"I would love to give you a comfortable, warm room to stay in with good blankets and a fire, but I'm not convinced you'd remain put."

"You can trust me," Chelci said, unconcerned that her tone contained not even a hint of truth.

"Hmm . . . We'll see."

"Why did you take me?" Chelci asked, folding her arms across her chest. "What good am I to you?"

Bale chuckled. "Maybe I enjoy your company?" Chelci's eyes narrowed, and Bale's face turned serious. "I imagine Veron would come whether you were here or not. If there's a knife at your throat, we'll see how willing he is to let you die." He extended his arm toward a chair by the fire. "Would you care to sit?"

Chelci's feet remained rooted as she stared at the chair next to the flickering flames of the fire.

"I assure you, it's no trap. You can warm yourself, and you're welcome to eat anything you like."

Chelci's eye caught the small platter of food on the table next to the chair piled with bread, cheese, and meat. Her stomach growled, directing her feet toward the chair.

When she sank into the cushion, the warmth hugged her body,

fighting away the chill that permeated her bones. Before Bale could repeat his offer, she attacked the plate. It had been days since she'd eaten, and her body ached.

While she gorged herself, the black-haired king settled into the chair opposite her, the fire's warm light dancing off the side of his face. "While you're here," Bale said, "I'd love to hear what you know about Veron Stormbridge." She paused with her teeth sunk into a chunk of bread. "For instance, how did he come to be a shadow knight?"

She tore a bite off and set the rest of the bread back onto the platter.

"Brixton tells me you and Veron are close," Bale continued. "Who was the second man in Bromhill? He's a knight, too? Are there others?"

Chelci extended her hand to select more food from the plate, but Bale was faster. He pulled the plate farther, just out of her reach.

"I'm happy to share my food with you, but it's only polite for you to share in return."

Chelci crossed her arms and leaned back.

"If you won't talk about Veron, maybe you can tell me what you know about this." His hand slid to the desk just behind them and lifted a large book. *Chronology of the Shadow Knights* covered the front.

Chelci's pulse quickened, and her eyes grew.

Bale leaned in. "I see you know this book. How does it work, this . . . origine?"

A laugh bubbled to the surface, and Chelci allowed a grin. "If I knew . . . I wouldn't tell you. But I have no idea."

Bale narrowed his eyes. "I encourage you to rethink that answer. While your stay in the east tower may not be glamorous, I assure you there are much worse situations. Captain Cyrus petitioned to visit you."

Chelci swallowed the lump in her throat.

"So far, I've denied him, but trust me, you don't want me to allow it."

While locked in a staring match, the door clicked open. Chelci turned her head, her breath catching. Dressed in a brand-new set of warm-looking clothes, Brixton's eyes flitted between her and Bale.

"Brixton!" Bale said before leaning toward Chelci. "Think about it." After a beat, he left the fire and walked to Brixton.

"You sent for me, Your Majesty?" Brixton asked.

"I did. I trust your accommodations are sufficient?"

"They're amazing! Much better than where I used to live, although cold at night."

"Did you keep a fire?"

"Yes, it helped."

Bale turned to the table next to him and grabbed a bottle. "I'll have more blankets sent."

While the king poured two drinks, Brixton's eyes jumped to Chelci. She narrowed her eyes and stared back.

I guess if you sell out everything you know, you get extra blankets and a fire. I hope he's still cold.

Bale handed a glass to Brixton. "I'm hosting a party tomorrow night, and I wish for you to be a guest of honor."

Brixton raised his eyebrows while Bale took a drink. "Me?"

"Yes, Brixton. I want to celebrate our victory over Terrenor, but I also want people to meet my new Commercial Envoy who was instrumental to our success."

Brixton's face lit up.

"I want you to get to know the people of Norshewa. You'll work with them to help build Terrenor into a united kingdom."

Chelci scoffed under her breath. *Playing right into his ego.*

"That sounds great, Your Majesty!" Brixton nodded his head. He raised the glass to his lips and took a cautious sip.

"What do you think of Norshewa so far?" Bale asked, walking toward two double doors against the back wall and opening them.

Chelci remained at her chair, grabbing handfuls of food while they were distracted.

A balcony waited outside, showing the extensive plains of Norshewa beyond. White covered most of the landscape with interspersed rocks and barren trees. A harsh wind rushed into the room. The dull roar of the river filled the room, and a crisp, clean smell singed her nose with cold.

"It seems . . . very nice," Brixton said, stepping onto the balcony.

Chelci almost choked on her laugh. *He sees how barren and awful this land is, same as I do.*

She didn't want to miss their conversation, so she stood and walked to the edge of the doors, peeking through the crack where the hinges rested. She strained her ears.

"I've only seen snow once before when I was young," Brixton continued. "It's beautiful."

"It will melt in a few weeks as suether warms up, but yes, it is beautiful." The two stood for a moment, surveying the land.

"Is that where the slaves—um . . . the workers will build?" Brixton asked, pointing to the right. "Looks like it was started years ago but abandoned."

Bale momentarily paused. "I decided to wait until the time was right. The new palace will be twice the size of this one and better in every way."

"It's going to span the river?"

Bale nodded. "It will be magnificent."

"How long will it take?"

"Years," Bale said without inflection. "Many years."

"The weather seems pretty harsh. Can the workers handle a project like that?"

"The work keeps them warm, but many will die, especially when wiether comes back. We have all of Terrenor as reinforcements, though. We'll send out for new workers each season."

Chelci's jaw clenched. His nonchalance chilled her. She thought of Nathaniel and Drevyn from her own family's house.

"Have you, um . . ." Brixton turned around, prompting Chelci to jump away from the crack, his voice dropping to a whisper. "Have you thought of what to do about Veron?"

Chelci could barely hear the question. She pressed her ear up to the edge.

"I have," Bale answered. "Let him come. We'll be ready."

Chelci shivered at his inflection. *Why does he sound so confident?*

"Do you know of any way to get *her* to talk?" Bale's whispered question chilled her anew.

She peeked back through the crack. Brixton's face wrinkled in thought. After a moment, he leaned in and whispered something in Bale's ear. Bale nodded before the two turned back toward the room, sending Chelci scurrying back to her chair.

"Have you decided you're willing to cooperate, Chelci?" Bale asked as he entered the room and closed the doors.

Chelci lifted her chin and fought hard to keep her voice from wavering. "I'll never tell you a thing," she uttered through clenched teeth.

Chelci imagined gears turning in Bale's head as he looked at her. Finally, he turned to Brixton with a tight nod. "Do it."

Chelci's breath left her.

Brixton's chest grew from a deep breath. His pained eyes flitted to Chelci before he turned and left the room.

The crackling fire soothed her as Bale stared at her, his lips almost a snarl. Her stomach churned as she withered under his gaze.

33

Stonl

"Do you think it's safe?" Morgan asked as the three men looked down the hill.

A few dozen buildings of wood and mud lay before them. Thatched roofs sagged, some appearing on the verge of collapse. Pens of goats, sheep, and a few cows surrounded the outer parts of the village while dirt paths crisscrossed through the center. Smoke puffed through several chimneys, reminding Veron that his stomach had growled the entire time they'd walked.

After they left Molvaigh the night before, they had continued for less than an hour before ducking off the path to find a place to sleep. Since men were searching for them, they decided to not risk a fire, so the bitter cold had seeped into his bones. After waking, he was eager to move, but they only got to eat a small amount of dried meat and nuts.

"I don't see any soldiers," Veron said, hopeful they'd be able to visit the smoking chimneys to see what was cooking.

"I think it's fine," William answered. "Keep a sharp eye out, though. The soldiers we met won't be the only ones looking for us."

Descending the hill after stuffing their black cloaks back into their bags, they came to a split-rail fence confining goats and chickens. Despite their innocuous presence, the bleating of the goats put Veron on edge. He scanned the area, looking for soldiers. Next to a house, an overhang covered a woman in her mid-thirties. She paused while milking a goat, and Veron hesitated mid-stride.

"Hello there," the woman called in a friendly voice. Her dingy, cream skirt draped in the dirt, and the sleeves of her faded-blue tunic were rolled to her elbows. Her wavy, auburn hair fell just to her shoulders, and rosy cheeks gave her a glowing look.

The three men stopped, and William rested his arm on the fence. "Good morning," he replied. "We've traveled quite a ways and would be interested in some warm food. Would you know of any place where we could find some? We have coin."

The woman stroked along the back of the goat's fur, the animal bleating in response. "I've got some pottage over the fire. I can't say that it's great, but it is warm."

"We would be most appreciative," Morgan said, flashing a smile.

The woman pulled a bucket out from under the goat and tapped it on the rump. "Go on, Annabelle," she said, the goat bouncing away. Hefting the finished bucket along with another, she stood.

Morgan opened a gate, holding it open for the lady to pass through. "Here, allow me to carry those," he said, reaching to take the buckets.

"Thank you. They get heavy," she said with a laugh. She tossed her head toward the house. "This way."

The house reminded Veron of the ruin he lived in with Fend back in Karad. The dirt floor grew weeds at the edges. Most of the ceiling was covered, but one corner had fallen in, the blue sky shining through. The room contained a table and a hearth, and a pot hung over the simmering coals of a fire. Through a doorway, Veron spied two straw beds. The fire warmed the room, but without his cloak, he still fought back shivers.

The woman grabbed three bowls from a shelf. Veron sat with William and Morgan while she went to the pot and filled them with a ladle. Steam rose from the bowl in front of Veron, and his stomach again grumbled.

"I'm Jeanette," the woman said, sitting next to Morgan. The men introduced themselves.

Veron raised a spoonful of the soup to his lips, bracing himself for the bland liquid. His eyes brightened as traces of sage and rosemouthe tickled his tongue. "This is amazing!" he said, looking at Morgan who nodded vigorously. Jeanette blushed. The warm liquid raised his spirits, and he attacked the soup. He cupped his free hand around the side of the bowl, trying to settle the bumps on his skin.

"Do you two not have something warmer?" Jeanette asked, nodding to Veron.

"Um . . ." Veron glanced at William, thinking about the cloaks in their packs. "We're fine. It's not that cold, especially when we're moving."

"Where are you all headed?" she asked, one eyebrow raised.

Veron paused with a spoonful almost to his lips.

"We're heading into Norshewa," William replied.

Jeanette tensed, her eyes shifting around the table as she leaned back.

"Don't worry," Morgan said quickly, "we're not Norshewan. We're from Feldor."

"Why do you head there?" Her question held a tremble.

William answered after a pause. "We have business to take care of."

After a moment of silence, she stood and walked to the other room.

Veron spun to his father, the muscles in his legs ready to act. "Are we okay?" he whispered. "Should we run?"

William motioned down with his hand, and Veron relaxed. Jeanette returned with two thick cloaks. One was brown, trimmed with some type of fur, and the other was a grayish color. She held them out, Veron's eyes growing. "Take these," she said. Veron's mouth dropped.

"We can't take these," William said. "Thank you for your offer, but—"

"If you're traveling north, the cold you feel here is only the beginning. You'll freeze to death without something like this."

"But they're yours," Veron said, looking around. "You can't—" he stopped himself, not wanting to offend the woman, but she had little to begin with.

"They were my husband's. He passed away long ago, and they've sat in a chest since."

Veron extended a hand and took the gray cloak. The thick fabric warmed his hand just to hold it. He slid his arms into the sleeves. William accepted the other.

"I'm sorry about your husband," Morgan said, his mouth tight. "My wife Catherine died this wiether as well—along with my children."

He bowed his head and Jeanette rested her hand on his shoulder. "There's nothing easy about it. I had two sons as well . . . but . . ." She wiped at her eyes after a pause.

"Did they catch ill?" Morgan asked.

She shook her head. "No." The look on her face said that was all she planned to say about it.

"What village is this?" Veron asked, attempting to lighten the mood.

"Outsiders call it Stonebridge. In Rynor, it's known by Stonl."

Veron's heart jumped. He snapped his head to William. "Stonl? Didn't Petrous say that's where the prophecy came from?"

Jeanette sucked in a breath.

"Do you know of the prophecy?" William asked.

Jeanette adjusted in her seat, glancing between the three. "About Bale?"

"Yes!" Veron confirmed. "Did that come from here? Do you know the woman who had the Dream?" She nodded her head. "Can we speak with her? I have so many questions!"

"She doesn't speak with outsiders."

"We *must* see her!"

"Veron," William said, short and firm.

Jeanette shook her head. "I'm sorry. It's not possible."

"Please!" Veron implored. "I—For years I've lived in the shadow of that Dream. Death followed all my life because of it. I only want the chance to ask questions. I beg you!"

Jeanette stared back but didn't speak. After a long moment, she nodded and stood. "Follow me."

Veron's heart pounded. He jumped up, eyes wide, and left his soup behind. All three men exited the house and followed Jeanette down a dirt path, passing mud homes on either side. Villagers paused in doorways and in gardens to stare. Veron continued after their guide.

"What do you hope to accomplish, Veron?" William whispered.

"Maybe we can find out more details about what's going to happen?" he replied.

His father's tight face did not reveal the same excitement. "Learning the future does not mean the news will be pleasant."

"Yes, but if we know what's going to happen, we can change it."

"Can we?"

The question caught Veron off guard. *Can I? If I know who is to die, I can make different choices, right?*

Passing the last house, they continued up a grassy slope. Having been distracted by hope, Veron suddenly grew wary of a trap. He looked at William, whose hand rested on his sword hilt and eyes darted around. Ahead, several large boulders rested on the slope. *Anyone could hide behind them.*

His muscles ready to leap into action, they walked between the rocks, but no one waited or jumped out. On the other side, dozens of gravestones rested atop the hill, looking down over the village. The stones were weathered and tinged with green. Etchings in the markers faded from time.

Jeanette stepped between the graves and stopped in front of a newer one, bowing her head. "This is the grave of my mother, Rose. She passed away five years ago." Stepping to the side, she motioned to the grave while looking at Veron. "Ask her anything you wish."

Veron sighed, his heart rate slowing and his hope of answers fading.

"She passed away during a harsh wiether. Harvest was poor that year."

"I'm sorry," William said.

Jeanette shook her head. "She had just reached sixty. After a full life, she was ready to go."

"Do you know more about the Dream?" Veron asked, unwilling to give up hope. A gust of wind crested the hill. He pulled his cloak tighter, thankful for the gift. "I've heard it predicted a shadow knight would kill Bale, and they would both die. Do you know anything more about who it was or how it would happen?"

Jeanette looked back at the gravestone and paused. She took several breaths before answering. "No, I don't."

Veron narrowed his eyes. William's furrowed brow showed the same skepticism.

He took a half-step forward "Are you—"

"Come," Jeanette interrupted. "We must return." Leading the way, she left the graveyard and passed through the boulders to descend the hill back to the village.

Veron's shoulders sagged as he walked next to his father. "I thought we might learn something. I feel like she knows more than she's saying."

"She *does* know more than she's saying," William agreed.

Veron's heart sped up again. "So, what do we do? Keep pushing?"

"The future is a dangerous thing, Veron. She doesn't want to speak for a reason, and I think we should honor that."

"But she may know something!"

"And we won't torture her to find out what it is."

Veron kicked a small rock on the path, feeling his chance slipping away.

Back at Jeanette's house, they entered to finish the soup. William handed her some coins as he sat. "For the soup and the cloaks," he said. "Thank you."

She smiled and nodded. "That one was Marcel's favorite," she said, pointing out Veron's cloak. "He died three years into our marriage, and I've thought of him every day since." She looked at Morgan, who scraped the bottom of his bowl. "What happened to your family—if you don't mind me asking?"

Veron paused with his spoon in the air and watched Morgan. The grocer smiled tightly and stared into his bowl. For a long moment, he said nothing. Veron prepped himself to change the subject when Morgan answered.

"People tried to get information, but I wouldn't cooperate. They were killed to get to me."

"Morgan, you don't have to talk about it," William said, his words sharp with an edge of warning.

"It's fine. I'm fine," Morgan replied, seeming oblivious to William's implied caution. "It was Edmund Bale."

William and Veron breathed in quickly, and Jeanette gasped.

"Bale killed them because I wouldn't tell him what he wanted. I—I didn't even have what he wanted, but it didn't matter."

Jeanette's breaths grew rapid, drawing Veron's attention. He looked at William, trying to ask with his eyes if they needed to leave.

"Bale was here," Jeanette said in a wavering voice, ". . . fifteen years ago. His men attacked our village. He threatened to kill my husband

and my two young sons if I didn't cooperate, too." She took a deep breath and exhaled while Veron snuck a look at William. "It wasn't my mother who had the Dream."

"The grave we visited? Whose was it?" Veron asked.

"That *was* my mother's grave, but she wasn't the one who had the Dream. I did."

It was Veron's turn to gasp. "But . . ."

"Bale threatened to kill my family unless I told him everything. After I told him, he was so angry he killed them anyway." Veron's heart pounded as Jeanette continued. "Sorry for misleading you. I wasn't sure I could trust you."

"I'm sorry about your family," Morgan said.

"Can you tell us more about the Dream?" Veron asked.

Jeanette nodded. "What do you want to know?"

"I heard Bale will die by a shadow knight, and that the shadow knight will die. Do you know—" He glanced at William. ". . . who or how they will die?"

"It's not that clear," she said.

"What do you mean?" Veron asked, leaning in.

"The Dream was . . . fuzzy. I felt it all, but the images were not precise."

Veron nodded along. "I've had one before, too. It felt real, but some things seemed blurred. How do you know it was a shadow knight?"

"I just knew it . . . somehow. The name fixed in my brain, although it was never said. Also, there was a symbol."

William turned to Veron. "Show her."

Veron reached under the neckline of his shirt and fished out the leather strap. At the end of the strap, the metal medallion reflected the light from the hearth.

Jeanette's hand flew to her chest and her jaw fixed in a hard line. "You're shadow knights?"

William nodded. "Veron and I are. We're tracking down Bale to kill him as your dream predicted."

She looked back to the medallion. "That's the symbol I saw. One of them had it on their black cloak."

"One of them?" Veron asked, sitting up straight. "How many were there?"

"There were two, and they both were knights."

William leaned forward. "You say only one wore a black cloak. Tell me, the one who died, were they wearing a cloak?"

Jeanette looked back and forth between Veron and William. "The one with the cloak lived."

Veron's breath came rapidly. His pulse thumped against his head. "Were we the two you saw? Which one of us dies?"

William rested his hand on Veron's shoulder. "Veron, we don't need that sort of information. It—"

"I don't know," Jeanette interrupted. "As I said, it was blurry. I couldn't see their faces."

"What did you see?" Veron asked. "How does Bale die? Tell us everything."

Jeanette leaned back in her chair. "Again, I saw very little—only a glimpse. It was in the middle of a courtyard, surrounded by castle walls. Ice and snow covered the roofs. Breath fogged when they breathed. Two shadow knights fought with Bale, circling him. One became injured, and the other had to fight alone."

"Which one was injured?" Veron asked.

"The one without the cloak." Veron glanced at William while Jeanette continued, "The other fighter was about to be killed when the Dream grew fuzzy again. The last two things I saw were Bale stabbed through by a sword . . . then the knight without the cloak exhaling their last breath."

Veron leaned back in his seat, taking a deep breath. "I had a Dream where I thought I saw someone killed, but they ended up living. How do you know Bale and the knight die?"

She shrugged. "I only know what I saw and felt. I can't speculate beyond."

The four people sat around the table, looking down. "Thank you for speaking of it," William said finally. "And I'm sorry about your family."

"How did you make it after the loss?" Morgan asked, his eyes pained.

"The ache never leaves, but I learned to accept it as part of my story. I can never change what happened, but I can make sure it doesn't define my future."

"You must be one tough woman, living on your own for so long."

She smiled. "Thanks. Sometimes I don't feel very tough. It gets lonely."

"Yeah, I understand that."

William stood, pushing his chair back. "We need to be off. Again, thank you for your hospitality and for sharing your Dream."

"If you decide you're interested in being around more people, you'd be welcome in Feldor," Morgan said, his half-grin giving him a goofy look. "With soup like this, you could make a good living."

Jeanette smiled back, nodding.

The three men stepped out of the house and proceeded to the village's north end. Suspicious looks followed, but they ignored them as they passed by, resuming their trek.

Anxiety gnawed at Veron. *The cloak-less one will die.* He looked down at the gray covering he wore, then ahead to the horizon fading over the hills.

34

Uncomfortable Party

Torches lined both sides of the passage, the windows dark with night. Sounds of the party trickled down the hall, causing Brixton's stomach to flit with butterflies as he approached. His new Norshewan formal outfit of black, trimmed with fur, fit his form. He had spent a long time looking in the mirror, admiring his powerful presence.

Three guards on either side of a doorway glanced over him. He angled his shoulder forward, showing off the Norshewan badge he wore. After a brief pause, they stepped aside to allow his entry.

The Hall of Dignitaries did not disappoint. Massive red-and-black marble columns flanked either side of the hall, extending to the high ceiling. Against the black wall, a blue relief of the Norshewan emblem of a bear and swords was set into the wall. *Is that ice? It feels cold enough in here to be ice,* Brixton thought.

Tables piled with food scattered throughout the room. Brixton's nose drew his attention to a surface filled with platters of roasted boar, chicken, and several other meats. Other tables contained fruits, breads, and vegetables. Inviting pastries covered an entire table as long as two men. Brixton's mouth watered.

Several dozen people milled about the room. Men were dressed in thick suits, mostly black like Brixton's. A few wore fur hats, giving an extra hand of height. Women wore elaborate, floor-length gowns. The varied blues, reds, and yellows filled the room. Shawls seemed in fashion in Norshewa as practically every woman wrapped a piece of fur around her neck that draped over her hands.

Brixton nearly tripped when he noticed another group at the party. Six or seven young women, likely around his age, meandered through the crowd. Their bare arms seemed to glisten in the torchlight. Tops of only a thin piece of fabric fell across their chest with glittering jewels. One faced away, allowing Brixton to see nothing more than a flash of fabric about her neck. He shivered at her exposed back. Some carried drinks while others talked, smiles on their faces.

"Brixton Fiero, the Commercial Envoy himself!" a voice shouted, faint among the crowd's roar.

Brixton tracked the sound to find Cyrus dodging a group of people. He shuddered at the man's presence but still welcomed the familiarity.

"Thank you, Captain," Brixton said, accepting a dark glass of red liquid. He sniffed the drink.

"Authentic Norshewan firetonic," Cyrus said, smacking his lips after drinking half his glass. "You can't get it anywhere south of the Korobs."

Brixton paled then handed his glass back. "I'll have to pass. Firetonic doesn't agree with my stomach."

"Suit yourself." Cyrus poured the glass into his own, smoke rolling over the side as it hissed. He led the way to a nearby table where he traded the empty glass for a plate. He nodded to a man behind a counter. "They've got ale over there for the girls, so help yourself."

Brixton clenched his jaw as the captain laughed. "Who are all the people here?" Brixton asked, grabbing a plate of his own and following the captain's example of piling on food.

Cyrus glanced up from the table to take in the room. "Some army leaders, nobles of the city, favored merchants."

Brixton smiled. *Just the sort of people I need to meet.* "What about the girls?"

Cyrus backed away from the table with a full plate and looked at him with a lascivious grin. "The palace girls? Nice, huh? Bale brings them in to help with the scenery."

"They must be freezing!"

Cyrus shrugged. "Nah . . . They like dressing like that. It gives them a chance to mingle with important people."

Brixton looked at the nearest palace girl. Her face glowed with excitement as she talked with an older, balding man. "Yeah, I guess so."

"Too bad that girl we caught couldn't join us," Cyrus said.

Brixton's brows narrowed. "Who? Chelci?"

Cyrus grinned. "That's the one. I bet she cleans up nicely. Maybe we could get her in one of those outfits. What do you think?"

The captain lifted his eyebrows, but Brixton's stomach turned at the suggestion. *Why do I feel so protective of her?* "Yeah," he mumbled. "I bet she'd love it."

Despite Cyrus' teasing, Brixton grabbed a mug of ale from the drink table. When he returned to the captain, the man had already stuffed most of his plate into his mouth.

"Hungry, huh?"

Cyrus shook his head while he chewed an oversized mouthful. "Eh," he muttered with a full mouth. "This is my third plate."

Brixton raised an eyebrow in question.

"It's here. It's free. Tonight is for celebrating. Tomorrow is for regretting." He chuckled before picking up his glass and taking another long drink.

After a swallow of his ale, Brixton turned to his food. It was delicious—much tastier than what they received on the road. The boar was juicy and filled with a smoky flavor. The cheeses were sharp, and the vegetables perfectly seasoned. When his plate was empty and stomach satisfied, he turned to the room, longing to meet the influential men and women surrounding him. Taking his leave from the captain, he walked through the crowd.

Bale caught his eye. The king beckoned to him from a raised platform with other men and women. Brixton's stomach jumped as he navigated the room.

"Are you enjoying yourself, Brixton?" Bale asked, halting the conversation between his group as Brixton stepped up.

"Yes, Your Majesty," Brixton replied. The men's eyes squinted at him as if inspecting a curious specimen.

"I'd love to introduce you to my wife, Juliette," Bale motioned to the woman next to him.

Brixton's eyes grew as he took in the stunning woman. Dressed similar to the palace girls but with more jewels, Juliette at least had a shawl draping her shoulders, which covered a few areas of bare skin. She couldn't be over twenty-five, but still held herself with a regal air, standing straight with one hand resting on Bale's back.

"Brixton, it's a pleasure to meet you," she said with a smile, her voice tugging at his memory.

He nodded in return. "The pleasure is mine. Are you from Norshewa? Your accent sounds almost Feldorian."

"A wife to the king has no home," Bale said, jumping in and looking pointedly at her, ". . . other than wherever her husband is. Isn't that right, dear?"

Juliette nodded, her smile never wavering.

"And this is Osvaldo McGreevy, Master of Smithing for Daratill," Bale said, directing Brixton to the muscled, middle-aged man next to him. His firm shake left Brixton's hand aching. "Then we have Lord Garland Emmins, Lord of City Affairs, and his wife Mildred. If you have a scandal to uncover, Garland is your man."

The elderly lord gave a wicked laugh and extended his bony hand. "I could use your help with some local businesses, Brixton."

"What sort of help?"

"I hear you did great work in Felting motivating people to pay taxes. With your help, we should be able to enforce some laws that have grown lax."

Brixton's heart sank. "Sure, I'll be happy to assist," he said with little conviction.

"And, of course, you know Desmond," Bale said, pointing to the last person in the circle.

"Of course," Brixton said, shaking the advisor's hand.

"I'll be interested to see what ideas you have," Desmond said.

Brixton titled his head. "What do you mean? What sort of ideas?"

"You are Commercial Envoy of Terrenor now, yes?" Brixton nodded. "Now we need to figure out how much we can squeeze out of these newly conquered lands. I can't wait to see how great Norshewa will be in a few years!"

Before Brixton could respond, Bale raised his hands and looked down the length of the hall. "Ladies and men of Norshewa, I welcome you all to this celebration feast!" he said in a voice that bounced off the walls, easily reaching the back of the room. Cheers echoed back. "After a tour over the mountains, through Feldor, and back, we return victorious! I want to thank Commander Ryker who remains in Feldor with most of our army. They bravely battled, taking down city after city, and will return once our replacement rule is stable. I do want to recognize Captain Cyrus." Bale gestured to where the captain had just finished his glass. "The captain helped to lead our men to victory. Also, I'm very thankful to have Brixton Fiero with us. We could not have had victory without him."

A smile curled at the corners of Brixton's mouth as Bale beamed, pointing toward him. Brixton turned on the raised platform and waved toward the rest of the applauding crowd. *This is what it was all for! My chance to be recognized and appreciated!* He pictured scantily-clad servant girls waiting on him and important visitors queued at the door to meet him.

"After realizing his own country was weak and pathetic, Brixton turned on them," Bale said, the words causing Brixton's smile to falter. "He will help Norshewa assert its dominance by exposing the weaknesses of the surrounding kingdoms. For this, we welcome the outsider as one of our own."

The renewed cheer bolstered him but couldn't chase away an unsettling feeling. He glanced around. *I'm the only foreigner here.*

"Our victory was swift and decisive," Bale continued. "The kingdoms fell before us like tall grass in a storm, trampled by the powerful army of Norshewa! They thought they could push us back hundreds of years ago when they rebelled against the Norshand rule—the benevolent leaders who united Terrenor into a glorious society. Their revolution set them on the path to destruction, and now, this is where they find themselves. They will all pay for the insolence they showed."

When the cheering and clapping settled, Bale raised his hands to quiet the crowd. "But, tonight, we enjoy a party. Drink, eat, entertain yourselves!"

Wanting to mingle through the room, Brixton thanked Bale for his words and took his leave. After descending the platform, he wandered through the crowd. Shifting eyes looked his way, but no one spoke to him. Whispered words of "traitor" and "Feldorian" seemed to follow him, but he couldn't pinpoint their sources. He attempted to listen in on conversation but met blocked bodies and raised noses.

Standing alone at the side of the room, Brixton finished his ale. Bale's words were supposed to help him feel like one of them, united in their goal, but he felt even more apart. *I expected they would focus on leading a united kingdom, but it seems they want to exploit everyone else.* Brixton took a deep breath. *At least I chose the winning side.* Forcing a smile, he walked to the man behind the bar and set down his empty mug with a thump.

"One firetonic," he said with forced confidence.

The bartender poured the smoking liquid from a curved bottle. Brixton stared at his glass for a long moment. He could barely hear the hissing of the liquid over the chatter in the hall. With his throat clenched, he lifted it to his lips and took a sip. Having a better idea of what to expect, his reaction was less violent than his first attempt, but the burning sensation still caused him to squint, grimacing in pain. When the feeling subsided, he expelled air and wiped his eyes. *Whew!* He took several breaths in and out. *Maybe I'll be able to fit in after all.* A foggy feeling crept through his mind like water trickling over a stone. The memory of the disastrous party at his house in Felting tried to enter his mind, but he pushed it away.

Leaning an elbow against the bar, he turned to find a palace girl approach. With a captivating smile, she came closer than he expected, her bare thigh pressing against his leg and her hand resting on the bar, touching his elbow.

"Hello, Brixton. Welcome to Daratill." Her smoky voice made her seem older, but she couldn't have been over twenty—probably around his sister's age. Dark hair fell to her shoulders. A touch of perfume washed over him, leaving him giddy.

"Hello!" He replied, a touch too loud given their distance, but she didn't seem to mind.

"I imagine you had a long journey to get here. I hope you're able to relax and settle in."

He grinned, feeling almost dizzy from the intoxicating perfume and the firetonic. "This party is great." He looked down to get a better look at her outfit. A thin top crossed over her chest and wrapped around her neck, leaving most of her stomach bare. A tattoo of a bear peeked around her side, and a metal ring pierced through her navel. Her skirt—if it could be called that—fell in gossamer folds midway down her thigh. A shiver ran through him just looking at her.

"Yes, it is," she replied, moving her hand onto his forearm. "I'm Chantel."

Brixton swallowed, straightening his posture. "So, uh . . . what do you do, Chantel?"

Her forehead creased. "What do you mean?"

"The palace girls . . . you, um—" Brixton glanced around. "You're not servers, are you?"

Chantel covered her mouth and giggled. "Not exactly. We're here to make sure guests feel welcome." She leaned in closer and traced the fine hairs along his arm, continuing in her sultry tone. "And you're an important guest. I saw you from across the room and haven't been able to keep my eyes off you since."

Brixton smiled, enjoying the compliment and the trace of honey on her breath.

She nodded to his glass. "How do you like the firetonic?"

He looked at his drink. "It's um . . . It warms you up, I'll say that. Would you like some?"

Chantel shook her head. "No, we can't drink—"

"Come on! I'm sure it could help keep you warm." He pushed the glass closer to her.

She halfheartedly pushed the glass away and pursed her lips. Her voice dropped in volume, losing its seductive flavor. "No, I can't.

We—" She cut herself off with a half-glance over her shoulder.

Brixton followed her stare to where an older woman stood against the wall, staring back. The lady's eyes bored a hole through Chantel's back.

"I can't," she repeated, pushing his hand back.

Brixton's brows furrowed. "Is everything all right?" He nodded toward the wall. "Who's that?"

"It's no one," she replied with a tight shake of her head. Her smile returned. She took a step even closer and rested her hand against the side of his chest. Her provocative voice returned. "Would you like to step into another room? Somewhere quieter where we can talk more freely?"

Her sudden change in demeanor disoriented Brixton. While confused, he didn't care as much about figuring everything out as he did about spending time with her. Just before agreeing to go off with her, her goosebumps caught his eye. "You *are* freezing!"

Her smile faltered as she lowered her arm. "I'm fine. Really, I am."

"How are you dressed like this? You look *great*, but you must be miserable." Brixton glanced around. "Can I get you a cloak or something?"

Chantel looked to the floor, her hair falling down either side of her face. Bumps covered both shoulders and arms, and she suppressed a shiver. "Thank you, but . . . we're not allowed," she muttered after a long pause.

"What do you mean? You can't wear cloaks?" She lifted her head, her eyes growing red and glistening at the corners. Brixton froze, holding his half-filled glass. His words failed him.

"Bale makes us dress like this—even in the dead of wiether." She sniffed and wiped at the corners of her eyes, her words barely above a whisper. "Our job is to make sure people feel . . . desired."

Brixton's eyes widened. "You're not interested in me at all, are you?"

She shook her head quickly. "That's not it. We—"

"Do you . . . *enjoy* this?" Her glance to the floor was an answer. "Why do you do it then?"

She looked up suddenly. Her whispered words carried an edge. "You think I chose this? They took me from my family in Nortris when I was thirteen. I haven't left the palace in six years."

"That's . . . awful," Brixton muttered. "I'm sorry."

She shook her head. "It's all right. I only have a few more days until I turn twenty. That's when they release us." Her smile was back. "But, enough about me. Let's talk about you." Resuming rubbing her hand along his arm, she lifted her chin to the doorway leading out of the hall. "You want to go find that quiet room?"

Brixton swallowed. *It's all fake.* His body begged him to go along with it, but he couldn't help picturing his sister. He shook his head. "No, it's all right. I think I'll stay here."

Chantel laughed softly and took a step away, returning a brittle smile. "Suit yourself."

Blundering through the crowd, a staggering Cyrus approached the bar. He set an empty glass on the counter and ordered the barman to pour him another. Only after he had picked up his refilled glass, smoke falling over his hand, did he look around.

"Chantel, my favorite girl!" he slurred, taking a quick drink then setting the glass back down. He grabbed either side of her bare stomach and pulled her close.

Chantel's eyes flashed regret for a moment before they lit up again, her smile redoubling its effort. "It's nice to see you again, Captain." Having nowhere to go, her hands found their way to rest on his shoulders, wrapping around his neck.

"Did you get to meet my friend, Brixton?" Cyrus asked.

"I did!" she replied, "but I'm so glad you came over, too. I've missed you."

"So stay with me for a while," Cyrus suggested. "Unless you're set on staying with this Feldorian."

Chantel glanced at Brixton, her eyes pleading for help. Jarred by the disparity of her words and actions, Brixton could only stare, mouth agape. He began to form words when Cyrus picked up his glass and pulled her away.

"See you later, Envoy," the captain called with a laugh as he and Chantel melted into the crowd.

Brixton shook his head and looked down at his drink. The red liquid stared back at him with a faint hiss. He raised it partway to his mouth but stopped. *Why am I here? To party with slave girls forced to fawn over me?*

He looked around the room. Plates filled with half-eaten food lay abandoned on tables, yet the piles of yet-to-be served dishes appeared even greater than when he arrived. Across the room, a drunk woman tripped on her own shoes, dropping her glass. Her laughter nearly covered the shattering sound.

I just need some time to learn this city and these people. Then I'll appreciate my power. His smile returned. Bracing himself, he tossed back the rest of his drink. The liquid burned through his body. He closed his eyes but relished the feeling. The glass clinked as he set it down. *Soon these people will all want their time with me.*

35

Applying Pressure

Lying on the cold, hard bench, Chelci draped an arm across her face. The late morning sun beat through the exposed window. Rather than hide from it, she craved its faint warmth. The nights had been brutal, wrapped in the thin blanket, her body shivering to generate warmth. Guards came once per day to bring her food but mostly left her alone. Footsteps sounded through the thick door.

The metal door groaned open, and Chelci sat up straight. Expecting to see a guard with food, she cringed as Captain Cyrus walked through the door, leering at her. She scooted to the back of the bench until the captain's attention turned back to the door.

King Edmund Bale entered the room. His massive frame blocked the sun from the window as he stood with his hands on his hips. "I have more questions about the Shadow Knights book. Are you ready to talk?"

Chelci's eyes shot to Cyrus, who sneered back at her. A lump formed in her throat. She clenched her jaw as she shook her head.

"Pity," Bale muttered as he nodded toward the open door.

Chelci's brows knit together as shuffling feet approached. Her jaw dropped. "Nathaniel!"

The servant from her old home in Felting shuffled in, the back of his shirt clutched by a guard who pushed him along. His eyelids widened, but he could only mumble through his gag. A deep bruise marked his neck and a nasty red-and-black gash traversed his forehead.

The guard looped his manacled hands over a hook dangling from the ceiling. After pulling a lever on the wall, his hands raised higher, lifting the servant to his toes. His frantic eyes looked around, his head on a swivel but body unable to move.

"Leave him alone!" Chelci shouted.

The guard stepped back, and Cyrus pulled out a knife, the blade as long as his hand.

"You'd like me to leave him be?" Bale asked, stepping closer to her. "Then answer my questions. Why will the origine not work for me? What does it take to draw from it?"

Chelci trembled as she locked eyes with Nathaniel. "I don't know," she uttered, forcing the words from her mouth. Bale turned away. "I told you before, I don't know how to use it. The book doesn't make sense. I've tried, but—"

A muffled scream filled the cell as Nathaniel cried out from behind the gag. Chelci spun as Cyrus pulled his blade out of Nathaniel's thigh. The servant's body arched, straining against the manacles.

"Stop it!" she shouted, tears filling her eyes.

"You're doing this to him!" Bale roared. "You can stop it by telling me what I want to know!"

Nathaniel continued to groan, his pant leg darkening with blood.

Bale leaned closer to Chelci. "Legs are easy to heal, but how do you think Nathaniel will feel when you cause him to lose his fingers?"

Nathaniel balled his hands into fists and moaned anew. Cyrus stepped in front of him and pulled on one of his hands to splay out the fingers.

"I'll talk! I'll talk!" Chelci blubbered. "Just leave him alone!" Her tears dropped on the wooden bench, and she wiped at her eyes.

"Good," Bale said with a smirk. "What am I missing?"

Chelci sniffed. "There's a trick to it. In order to connect with the origine, you have to be wearing something of metal. It's still difficult, but it's the only way—"

The back of his hand was like an anvil smashing into her head. Chelci's body flung off the bench, colliding with the stone wall beyond. Her vision blacked while she clutched the side of her face with her arm. She cried out in agonizing pain. When she regained her sight, her blurred vision revealed Bale bent over in her face.

"Don't take me for a fool!" he yelled before turning to Cyrus. "Take off his fingers!"

"Gladly," the captain sneered.

"No! No! I'm sorry!" Chelci bent over, tears streaming down her face. She grabbed at Bale's feet. "I was lying about the metal, but the truth is, I really don't know how to use it. I've read the book night after night, but I can't do it. You're supposed to quiet your mind and pull from your energy, but they say most people can't do it. You need to have certain abilities, which most people don't. I know it sounds like I'm just blowing it off, but I'm not! That's all I know about it. Leave Nathaniel alone. Please!"

Her tears dripped onto the cold stone floor and snot ran down her face. Continuing to hold Bale's feet, she strained her ears for any sound of pain from Nathaniel, but none came. A loud clanking noise jerked her head up as Nathaniel's feet fell to the ground. The guard had lowered his hands from the hook. No longer held up, Nathaniel groaned as his legs collapsed underneath him.

"Get up!" the guard shouted at the servant, kicking him in the side. Chelci's reddened eyes felt raw as she watched the two soldiers drag Nathaniel away. His pain-filled eyes expressed relief and gratitude as he disappeared behind the door.

Bale's hulking figure stepped in the path, lifting her chin toward him with his foot as he chuckled. "Compassion is a weakness."

Her eyes narrowed. "Why'd you show compassion to him then?"

"Ha! That wasn't compassion. That was practicality. I need him to build my palace. Plus, he makes a great motivator if you need persuasion to cooperate."

Her lip turned in a snarl. "How do you know I'm not lying now?"

"I can spot a liar," he said. "It's a pity you don't know more."

Chelci spit what saliva she could gather, leaving a wet spot on his boot.

Bale crouched in front of her, grabbing her face. "When Veron arrives, we'll see what he's willing to allow to happen to you. I wonder if he has the same amount of compassion you do?"

She clenched her jaw, jerking it free from his hand. With a smirk, the king left through the door, it clanging shut behind him.

For a moment, Chelci paced back and forth in the cell, breathing heavily. Her anger kept the tears at bay. Unable to take it any longer, she ran at the window, pounding at the bars and unleashing a primal yell. Her yell echoed back, bouncing off a castle wall.

"Veron, where are you?" she whispered.

* * *

Brixton tightened his cloak as he stepped out of the castle onto the bridge, his boots crunching in the snow. The white coating had fallen overnight, a fresh blanket of powder to cover the roads and buildings. Below the bridge, the river churned along, frozen at the edges. Before him, a long street with black-stone shops awaited.

He glanced at the shops and pulled a sheet of paper out of his pocket to remind himself of the name. Behind him, two soldiers followed, waiting for him to give an order. He relished the attention and power but dreaded the task.

The shops he passed looked grim. Long faces stared at him. A butcher stopped hacking at a frozen piece of meat and yelled at him to leave, waving a large knife in his direction. A cobbler stopped working on a shoe and put his arm around his young son, pulling him out of sight into the back of the shop.

The storekeepers bundled in thick furs didn't seem to mind the cold, but Brixton kept his hands in his pockets, trying to maintain feeling. His breath was a heavy fog.

"Should be just ahead," one of the guards said in a gruff voice.

Carriage wheels hung from the next shop's rafters. Brixton slowed. Behind the dangling objects, a woman in her thirties fitted spindles into a hub.

"Are you Chorley, the wheelwright?" Brixton asked, the woman's head snapping in his direction. Her straight, brown hair fell to her shoulders, and a pink scar followed the line of her jaw.

Her eyes narrowed. "Latrice Chorley, yes. And who might you be?"

"Brixton Fiero, Commercial Envoy of Terrenor."

Latrice's neck strained as her chest filled out with breath. "Mother! Mother!" A young girl called, running into the shop. "He won't stop hitting me."

The wheelwright turned to her daughter. "Tell him to come here." The girl eyed Brixton before running back the way she came. "How can I help you, Brixton?"

"As envoy it's my job to enforce policies equally across the united kingdom. Lord Emmins informed me you refuse to pay your taxes. The penalty—"

"It's not true." Latrice set down the wooden spindles and extended her chin.

Brixton cocked his head. "What's not true?"

"My husband died last year."

"I'm sorry to hear that, but—"

"After he died, I took over his work, but it took time for me to learn the craft. When the tax assessor came around—the premweek of wiether—I didn't have any money. As a compromise, instead of the tax, he accepted payment of new wheels for his own carriage—nice ones. I got better at my work since then, and last season was better. I paid the assessor for my taxes this season, but he got greedy. He demanded I pay him for the previous season as well."

"The one you paid for with the wheels?" Brixton asked.

She nodded. "I reminded him the wheels covered that payment, but he claimed he didn't remember. I told him I'd pay the taxes, but he'd have to return the wheels." She looked away and grew quiet.

"He didn't return the wheels?"

"No, but he gave me this," she said, tracing a finger along the scar on her jaw. "The king and the army were gone. The city has been in shambles. One poor wheelwright was low on their priority list, so they've let me be since."

Small footsteps approached. "I wasn't hitting her, Mother," a boy whined as he stumbled up, his sister pulling him. "She did it!"

"Nuh-uh!" the girl insisted, putting her hands on her hips. "He hit me in the stomach then laughed!"

The boy's eyes grew. "No, *she* was the one who hit *me* in the stomach!"

"Children!" Latrice said, silencing them both. "I don't care which of you hit the other. What I care about is that neither of you do it again. If you do, there will be trouble. Do you understand?" The children nodded their heads and looked at the ground. A warm smile formed on Latrice's face. "Ruby, I need you to be kind to your brother, and Matthew, you need to look after your sister."

Matthew. The name stung, reminding Brixton of the baker—the way he pleaded for help and the hurt look in his eyes when Brixton ruined him. His chest tightened.

The children ran off, and the wheelwright turned back to Brixton. "So, what are you here for, Commercial Envoy?"

Brixton swallowed. He blinked, trying to keep tears from his eyes. The soldiers behind him shuffled their feet, reminding him of his job. "I, uh . . . I have to make an example of you. Bale is back and we need stability in Norshewa."

The wheelwright stared hard with her jaw fixed, her eyes boring a hole into Brixton. "Fine. I'll pay your stupid tax."

She moved behind a counter to collect something until Brixton cleared his throat. "Um . . . I can't allow it."

"What do you mean?"

"If you pay now, your resistance becomes allowable." Brixton looked down at the floor. "There must be consequences."

The wheelwright breathed rapidly, but he refused to look at her. After nodding to the soldiers, he ducked out of the shop. His muscles clenched as he stood in the street. Behind him, crashing noises and the splintering of wood mixed in with Latrice yelling for them to stop. Brixton winced.

He turned back as a soldier backhanded the shopkeeper across the face, knocking her to the ground. Brixton flinched but did nothing to stop the madness.

Unable to watch any more, Brixton headed back toward the castle. The weight of his actions rested heavily on him but grew lighter the farther he walked away from the shop. When he arrived at the bridge to the castle, another party walking from a side street caught his eye.

"Juliette?" he asked.

Bale's wife stopped, with guards of her own trailing behind. She glanced his way with a reserved smile. "Brixton, what brings you out of the castle?"

He looked over his shoulder toward the shop. "Um . . . Some commercial issues I needed to handle. How about you?"

"I enjoy taking a walk after a fresh snowfall—especially when the weather is warm like this."

"Warm?" Brixton's eyebrows raised as his head leaned in.

She laughed. "Yeah, it's much colder in the middle of wiether."

"I guess I have that to look forward to."

She shrugged. "You get used to it."

Brixton pursed his lips. "So, I can't help but notice your accent. You're not from Norshewa originally, are you?"

After a moment's pause, her tongue loosened. "I was born in Karondir, but my family moved to Bromhill when I was still young."

Brixton smiled. "I knew you sounded Feldorian. How did you meet the king?"

Her smile tightened. She looked over her shoulder where the guards stood several paces away, then stepped closer to Brixton. "He chose me when his army took the city six years ago."

Brixton's eyes narrowed. "Chose you?"

"I—" She stopped herself, taking in a deep breath. "Edmund doesn't give options when he decides on a new wife. Camille and Abigail are from Rynor. Catina is from Tarphan, and Amelia—the newest—is from Feldor."

Brixton's jaw dropped. "He has five wives?"

"There were six until—" Her jaw tightened, and she shook her head. "Poor Alisha." She wiped away a tear.

"How do you . . ." Brixton faded out, unsure of what question to ask of the many floating in his mind. "Do you *like* that?"

Juliette breathed in as she stood straighter. "Of course. Edmund is a great man and a wonderful husband." The forced smile on her face did not extend to her eyes, and her body shook.

Brixton leaned in closer. "Do you . . . need help?" he whispered.

Juliette flinched. She opened her mouth to respond but stopped short. "What would you do?" she asked finally, her eyes glimmering with hope.

Brixton's heart thumped. *Bale would kill me if I interfered.* He shook his head. "I . . . I don't know. I'm sorry, but I can't interfere." He glanced toward the castle. "I need to return."

Leaving the shaken woman behind, Brixton hurried across the bridge. He forced himself not to look back. *I can't do anything to help her. That's not why I'm here.* The thought led to another which made his legs pause. *Why am I here?*

36

Men on the Road

After skirting the Korob Mountains' foothills, the cold weather turned bitter. Thankfully, Jeanette's gift was thicker than Veron's black cloak. Food was sparse, but the group got by. William caught a pair of rabbits that lasted a few days. Morgan found some edible plants and herbs to serve with the meat. Veron's legs ached from the minimal sleep and long days of walking, but he trudged along, wishing they could move even faster.

"What about this one?" Morgan asked, pointing ahead along the road where a small town revealed itself as they crested a hill.

William shook his head. "We can't stop. It's too dangerous, especially now that we're in Norshewa."

"But they would have food," Veron pointed out, his need for rest winning out over his desire for speed, "and beds."

"And rooms warmed by roaring fires," Morgan added.

"We could take any men who try to give us trouble," Veron said. "Just like those guys in Molvaigh."

"Probably," William said, nodding. "But is it worth it? Are you willing to jeopardize your chance to save Chelci for one night of warmth?"

Veron's shoulders sank. He sighed and shook his head. "No, you're right." His mind turned to Chelci, imprisoned in Daratill. He ground his teeth when he thought of Brixton near her. *Bale is going to die, and Brixton right after him.*

"Keep your hoods up and eyes down," William said. "And don't stop."

The path widened as they approached the village. Roofs sagged, stained black with rotting beams sticking out from the sides. The wind died as they stepped between the buildings, but the bitter cold didn't dissipate. Chipped pieces of stone walls littered the sides of the street. People frowned as they trod along the road, bowing under their burdens.

An inn's open doorway beckoned as they walked past. Trying to keep his eyes down, Veron's head turned to see a roaring fire in a large hearth on the far end of a common room. Morgan groaned, mirroring how Veron felt.

"Keep moving," William encouraged in a low voice.

Veron forced his feet forward, remembering how he used to live on the streets in much worse conditions. Plus, Chelci waited for him. He continued on.

In a moment, they passed a man sitting against a wall. Tattered blankets covered him, and a crooked grimace displayed snaggly teeth. "Please! Do you have any coin?" the man called in a scratchy voice, holding up a cup.

Veron's feet hesitated as he made eye contact with the poor man. His skin was loose, and black spots ran down half of one of his hands. Veron swallowed as he focused on the pleading eyes.

"Veron," a harsh whisper pulled his attention back to the street. William had frozen and nodded ahead. Four soldiers strode down the middle of the street, laughing and knocking into men and women as they passed.

"You there!" a soldier shouted, grabbing a man carrying a load of water over his shoulder. Water sloshed over the lip, dousing the dirt street. "Have you seen two men from Feldor with black cloaks?"

Veron groaned. His eyes flitted to either side of the alley, looking for a path. Appearing to have the same idea, William glanced behind him, but the look on his face concluded the same—there was nowhere to go.

"Do we fight them?" Veron whispered, leaning next to his father.

William shook his head. "Not if we can avoid it. Heads down. Let's go."

William took the lead, with Veron next and Morgan in the rear.

The cry from the poor man over his shoulder made Veron cringe. "Please! I lost everything to Bale's taxes!" the man cried out. "Can't you spare something!"

"Don't stop," William muttered.

The man's voice faded as Veron watched the back of William's legs. The gray hood from Jeanette's cloak prevented him from seeing much else, but the soldiers ahead grew louder as they accosted another villager.

Keeping to the far side of the street, William passed the men. Veron could see the tips of their swords dangling from their hips. His heart pounded, hoping they would pass unnoticed.

"You!" a soldier called.

Veron's adrenaline surged at the word. His foot hesitated, but he forced himself to keep his head down and legs moving. Behind Veron, a scuffling noise sounded as the soldiers' voices came in their direction. He looked over his shoulder. The men surrounded Morgan. One who had the look of a leader pressed a hand against his chest.

"We're looking for two men from Feldor. Have you seen any?" the man asked.

Morgan's eyes somehow remained calm. He shook his head. As he opened his mouth to speak, the poor man down the street called out.

"I've seen them! I know where the Feldorian men are!" The scratchy voice bounced off the buildings, drawing all four soldiers' attention.

The hand against Morgan's chest disappeared, and the soldiers left. As soon as he was free, the grocer caught up.

"Let's get out of here," William urged.

Veron lingered a moment, keeping an eye down the street. He strained his ear.

"What do you know?" the lead soldier barked when he arrived at the poor man.

"I'll tell you where they are, but first . . . I need some coin. What can you spare?" He held his cup out again.

The soldier struck the cup, shattering it into a wall and scattering a few coins. "We're not *paying* for information! Tell us what you know. Now!"

The man recoiled. "I . . . I . . ."

"He doesn't know anything," another man grumbled.

After a moment of silence, the leader reared back and kicked the man in the stomach. Veron cringed as the man doubled over and cried out. The other soldiers laughed, one spitting on him.

William's hand pulled against Veron's shoulder. "This isn't our battle, Veron."

Veron clenched his jaw but allowed his father to hold him back. His eyes grew as Morgan opened his mouth. "Morgan," he hissed. "What are you—"

"Excuse me, men!" Morgan called out.

Veron's head jerked, surprised by the grocer's convincing Norshewan accent.

"I have a shop just up the way. We sell the best produce in all the village! If you need tarrols, carrots, onions, we've got it all!"

Turning away from the poor man moaning on the street, the soldiers glanced between each other.

"Why don't you follow us up the way. You can shop for any dinner supplies you need, and maybe there will be other customers you can ask about these . . . Feldorians you seek."

The closest soldier pursed his lips and stared.

"Come with me! I guarantee you will be glad you shopped at my place!"

"Come on," the soldier growled to the other two, waving them in the opposite direction.

Morgan protested as they walked away but gave up the charade once they'd rounded the corner.

"That was brilliant," Veron said, his shoulders relaxing.

Morgan grinned. "It's tough to hold back the salesman in me."

"What if they said yes?"

The grocer shrugged. "Eh . . . I figured one of you two would have conked them on the head or something." William and Veron both chuckled.

The groaning man on the street coughed.

Veron looked at his father. "Do we have something we can give?"

William handed a small pile of coins to Veron. "Be quick."

Veron jogged to the man laboring to sit up.

"I'm so sorry," Veron said, pressing the coins into the man's hand. "Take this."

The man's eyes glistened, and a crease formed around his lips. A wince killed the attempt of a smile. "Thank you," he managed in a weak voice.

Veron walked back toward William and Morgan with renewed determination. "We must stop Bale," he said when he reached them, gesturing to the village around. "This cannot go on."

William nodded. "We will. We will stop him." He held Veron's gaze for a long moment. "Let's go."

* * *

"Should we go around?" Veron asked as the three men peered from behind the boulder.

Ahead on the road, a wagon stood immobile, listing to one side and blocking the path. Two men and two women worked—the women unloading goods from the cart while the men worked on a wheel.

"Surely, they're not Bale's people in disguise," Morgan suggested. "I bet they could use our help."

William nodded. "I agree. Let's see what we can do." He waved a finger at them. "Stay alert though."

After leaving the boulder's protection, they approached the path.

"Hello there!" William called, walking with the assistance of his staff while the stranded travelers looked in their direction. "Do you need some help?"

The men straightened, stretching their backs after bending over. The shorter of the two was missing the lower portion of his arm, and the other limped on his left side. "We could use it," the taller man with the limp and red hair replied, hitting the wheel before him. "The axle jostled loose. We could use more hands to lift if you're able. It's heavy."

"We're not the strongest, but we might help with that," William replied.

Veron grinned. They set down their packs and gathered around while the women finished emptying the heavy items off the cart.

The red-haired man continued, "We tried to lift the wheel, which should bring the axle close enough to reconnect it to the reach with this pin, but . . . it's awkward to lift. Plus, at least one person needs to be under the wagon to set the pin."

"Why don't you two get ready with the pin and leave us three to lift?" William suggested.

The shorter man's brows came together. "We could all help lift." He motioned to include the women. "It's tough to all get in there, but I think we'll need everyone."

William pursed his lips. "Let's try it this way first. It may be easier to lift with fewer bodies in the way."

The short man shrugged. "Sure."

The two men scampered underneath the wagon while Veron, William, and Morgan gathered around the wheel.

"You ready?" William asked.

"Ready!"

Veron lifted his side of the wheel, barely using any origine. He could tell William did the same while Morgan only acted as if he exerted any effort. The entire side of the wagon lifted with ease.

"Perfect!" a voice called from underneath. "Hold it just one moment."

Neither Veron nor William broke a sweat, but they grunted as if it were a great labor.

"Got it!" a triumphant voice cried. "Set it down!"

They lowered the wheel, gently setting it down. The wagon balanced, level once more.

"Thank you so much!" The red-haired man grinned as he emerged. "I'm Cliff, and this is Thad," he said, pointing at the man missing the arm. The men exchanged pumping of their hands. "Over there's Vivian and Delia—our wives."

Veron nodded to the women.

"Maybe the whole thing was lighter than I expected?" Thad said.

William nodded to the women. "I think it was the hard unloading work Vivian and Delia did that made the difference."

The women smiled.

"You three heading north?" Cliff asked.

"Yes, we just came from Rynor—heading to Daratill," William confirmed.

Thad scoffed. "Why would you go there?" he asked with a bite in his tone.

"Thad!" Cliff scolded before turning back to William. "Your business is your own. We don't mean to pry."

"How far is it?" William asked.

"Mmm . . . maybe a day." Cliff glanced up the road and pointed. "You'll hit snow after that rise, so your progress will slow, but . . . you should make it by nightfall tomorrow."

"What about you? Where are you all headed?" Veron asked, trying to take the subject off their mission. The smiles on the men's faces faltered as they looked at each other. "I'm sorry. I guess it's not our business either," Veron said, waving his hand.

"No, it's fine," Cliff said. "We appreciate your help. We're, uh . . ." He looked at the women, whose jaws made a tight line.

"We're leaving Norshewa," Vivian said. "We can't take it anymore."

Cliff nodded. "The taxes, the warring . . . We're living in poverty while the king builds a new palace."

"They kicked us out of the army years ago—injured fighting Bromhill." Thad said. "They left us to rot ever since."

"Since Bale returned a few days ago, he's picking up where he left off," Cliff added.

Unsure if he should say anything to sympathize, Veron turned to his father.

"I'm sorry to hear that. Hopefully, our presence here can help people instead of contributing to more rot," William said.

"Seems like you're already off to a good start," Cliff said with a smile.

A watery feeling of dread flooded through Veron as the clopping sound of hooves approached. He spun to look up the road as eight soldiers on horseback walked up behind them, coming to a halt just before the end of the wagon. Each wore thick Norshewan uniforms with swords dangling from their hips. Aric, the soldier from Molvaigh, sat in the lead with a bandage around his head. Veron moved to the side of the road, along with William and Morgan. All three pulled their hoods up. Veron dropped his head, looking from the corner of his eye.

"What do we have here?" Aric called out, looking at the wagon and the piles of supplies littering the ground.

"I bet it's more deserters," a bearded man on the horse beside him said under his breath.

"Are you folks leaving Norshewa?"

"We're heading north," Morgan said, motioning between Veron and Morgan with his face askew. "We paused to help these people with their wagon."

"And we're . . . traveling," Cliff said with a slight waver. "For supplies."

Thad jumped in. "We're heading to Molvaigh so we can bring back goods to sell at the market in Daratill."

Aric's eyes narrowed. "You're bringing goods back? Why do you have so much with you?" Cliff shifted his weight and glanced at Vivian. The soldier stepped his horse forward to get a closer look at the piles on the ground. "Clothes, canned food, blankets, chairs."

"It's everything they own," the bearded soldier said. "I'm telling you, they're deserters."

"By royal decree, no citizens of Norshewa may leave," Aric declared, sitting straight in his saddle. "You must turn around or face the consequences."

"Should we do something?" Veron whispered, but William shook his head.

Vivian and Delia moved behind their husbands. The travelers glanced between each other but didn't move. After a long moment, Cliff looked back, his jaw fixed in a hard line. "We cannot go back. There is nothing for us there but ruin and misery."

An amused look covered Aric's face. He chuckled as he leaned forward in his saddle, resting his hand on the horn. "The penalty is death, declared by the king when he returned last week. Are you sure that's the choice you want to make?"

The travelers' eyes danced around and feet shuffled, but they still refused to move.

"Very well," Aric said, dismounting from his horse in one fluid motion and pulling his sword. The other Norshewans followed suit.

"Now we do something," William whispered to Veron, pulling his own sword and hobbling forward, leaning on his staff. Veron readied his weapon and followed.

Aric stopped in his tracks and tilted his head. The men behind him laughed, holding their weapons at the ready.

"Out of the way, unless you want your fate to join theirs." Aric said.

William lowered his hood, Veron and Morgan following. Aric gasped.

"It's them," the soldier behind him said.

"We will not move," William said. "If you wish to pursue them, you will die. I suggest you turn around."

"You assaulted an officer in the king's army, and the penalty is death," Aric said.

Veron clenched his jaw. There was no wind—no rustling of leaves. Silence filled the road as the parties stared. Cold pressed in like an oppressive force, but Veron thought of nothing but the expected fight. His arms flexed, barely feeling the ruby-hilted sword's weight. In his stomach, a warm tingling waited on him to call it forth.

Aric chuckled, staring at William. After a pause, he looked back at his men, their swords out. The two men with bows had arrows nocked, ready to loose. With a yell, his face contorted and sword raised above his head to strike.

Veron's speed left the eight soldiers frozen with haughty looks on their faces. William stabbed Aric through the chest and Veron took off the head of the bearded man next to him. As he readied to attack the next soldier, a hand pressed against his chest. William held him back.

"Wait," he said.

Both men released their hold on the origine, allowing the crowd to cry out in shock. The Norshewan soldiers jumped backward as their comrades fell to the ground, spouting blood that stained the dirt.

"Turn and go or you will be next!" William's voice boomed unnaturally loud. The soldiers shuffled their feet and glanced between themselves.

"It's the shadow knights!" one soldier yelled to his companions.

"We can't let them go," Veron said urgently under his breath.

After putting more space between them, the soldiers resumed their fighting stances with arms and legs shaking. Some looked afraid of the knights. Others looked more afraid of what would happen if they ran.

The man in front moved as an archer loosed an arrow. Veron pulled from the origine, plucking the arrow out of the air before it pierced his chest. William knocked down the first soldier, and Veron stabbed the arrow into the upper arm of the next. Bending at the hip, he blasted his foot into another soldier. Ribs cracked before the man's body flew, knocking down two others. William's fist met one more man in the chest, who dropped his sword from the massive collision.

Resting, Veron took a deep breath, pushing air through his lungs and into the rest of his body. He bent over with his hands on his knees but kept his eyes up to watch the soldiers. A groan behind him spun him around. Morgan rested on his knees, clutching where an arrow pierced him below his shoulder.

"Morgan!" Veron yelled, running to crouch beside his friend.

The grocer gritted his teeth and drew rapid breaths. William arrived a moment later but kept his body angled toward the routed force.

"Don't worry, we can take care of this," Veron said, inspecting the wound. The arrow pierced his body with the tip poking out the back.

The galloping of horses' hooves spun Veron around. Two of the soldiers thundered away on horseback while the other ones struggled to mount and follow.

Veron stood to pursue until William pulled on his arm. "Leave them."

Veron's eyes grew. "They know who we are! They'll warn Bale we're coming!"

"Morgan's more important. Besides, Bale already knows. Let them live. Our battle is not with them."

Veron clenched his jaw as the other men clambered onto their mounts and fled.

"Are you two shadow knights?" Cliff asked, taking cautious steps toward them. Veron nodded before turning back to Morgan.

"Do you have any pliers?" William asked the travelers, "and a dowel or a stick?"

"Sure," Thad said, scurrying to rummage through their supplies. In a moment, he handed William a pair of metal pliers while Cliff gave a stick the width of his thumb.

William turned to Morgan, holding him against either arm. "We need to get the arrow out," William said. Morgan nodded with his jaw set tight and tears falling from his cheeks. "Bite down on this."

Morgan bit on the stick.

"Veron, I need you to grip around the arrow right where it enters his body," William instructed.

Veron looked at Morgan for approval. His friend's eyes watered, but he nodded. Veron took a deep breath as he rested one arm against Morgan's back and wrapped the other around the arrow. A fresh cry of pain uttered from Morgan, dulled by the stick in his mouth.

"Hold tight," William said as he readied the pliers. "First, I need to break off the shaft."

Nausea filled Veron. He turned away, gripping as hard as he could on the shaft. Morgan's body tensed and strained against his grip until a snap and a yell told him it was finished. After tossing down the broken end of the arrow, William moved to Morgan's back.

"Hold him tightly," William said.

"Can we be of any help?" Cliff asked, he and Thad lingering nearby.

"Can you help hold him steady? I need to pull it out, and it's better if he doesn't move."

Cliff and Thad joined Veron, holding Morgan by the arms, chest, and shoulders. The whites of his eyes showed. His chest heaved. The stick in his mouth crunched as he bit down even harder.

"One, two, three!" William counted, ending with a yank.

Morgan's body lurched. His neck strained and head flailed. As the tension lessened and groaning faded, they released his body. Morgan's limp form slumped.

Is he okay? Veron wondered.

The grocer eased his fear when he used the arm on his uninjured side to take the stick out of his mouth and tossed it to the side. "I hope we don't have to do that again," he said, causing William to chuckle.

"Here, we've got some spirits that will help clean the wound," Cliff said, returning to his pile of goods. When he returned, he held out a bottle of clear liquid along with a long, clean strip of linen.

William took the bottle, removed the lid, and sniffed. "This will do. Thank you."

After taking off Morgan's shirt, William poured the spirits on his chest and back over the injury sites, the wounds bubbling up under the liquid. Morgan yelled anew, grabbing Veron's arm and squeezing. When the sizzle subsided, he exhaled.

"Should have kept that stick," Morgan muttered with a laugh.

After wrapping the wound with the strips of linen and tying it off, William extended a hand to help Morgan up. "You're lucky it wasn't a hair lower. The wound should heal well if you take it easy for a few days."

Veron's eyes grew, turning to his father.

"What about Bale? We need to get to Daratill," a panting Morgan said, as if reading Veron's mind.

"Can you walk?" William asked.

Morgan nodded then gingerly slipped his shirt back on, pressing his eyes shut and grimacing. "Yeah, I think I can manage."

"Good. We can keep moving—slowly."

Cliff stepped. "Thank you for stopping them. You saved our lives."

"So . . . shadow knights," Thad said. "Does that mean one of you is going to kill Bale?"

Veron looked at his father. "We'll see," he said.

"What can we do to help?" Cliff asked. "We owe you everything. You can take anything you need."

William offered a half smile. "Thank you for the offer, but I think we have all we need for now."

"The only thing I need is in Daratill," Veron added.

After saying their goodbyes, Veron, William, and Morgan turned their feet north and continued along the road.

"Bale's going to be scared," William said. "He may grow reckless."

Veron's thoughts turned to Chelci. "If he hurts her, he's going to be in trouble."

"He's going to be in trouble no matter what."

Carrying both his and Morgan's pack, Veron bounced his legs, hefting them higher and trying to find a comfortable position. Grateful his friend was all right, he smiled despite the load. *Only one more day, Chelci. We're coming.*

37

Bath and a Meal

Chelci's nasal passages opened the moment she entered the room, her guard halting at the entrance and closing the door behind her. After days in the freezing tower, her body felt frozen and cracked, but the bathing room's warmth began thawing her immediately.

"Miss Marlow, welcome," an older woman in a plain robe said, bowing.

"I understand I am to bathe?" Chelci asked, glancing around the room.

A large basin with space for several people was sunk into the ground with steps descending into it. Steam billowed off the surface of the water while light from the walls' lanterns cut through the fog.

"That is correct. You are to dine with Commercial Envoy Fiero tonight, and he arranged for you to clean up."

"Hmm," Chelci mumbled, unhappy to do anything Brixton required of her, but secretly thrilled for a warm bath. "Who are you?"

"I am Anita, the bath servant."

"And what if I refuse?" Chelci asked, having no intention of doing so.

Anita pointed at the door. "If you refuse, your escort will have to see that you cooperate."

Chelci swallowed hard, not interested in bathing at sword point while a guard watched. "Very well." She looked around, wondering about the procedure. A table next to the servant contained a brush, a bar of soap, some bottles, and a towel. "Are those for me?"

"They're for *me* to use," Anita said. "Leave your clothes here, and get in the water, please."

Chelci felt the blood drain from her face. In Nasco, she bathed herself, usually with cold water from a bucket. In Felting, she managed by herself in their family's washing chamber. Her color returned and face flushed as she removed the clothes, lying them on the ground. After disrobing, she hurried into the water, partly to replace the warmth of her clothes, but mostly to hide her body under its surface.

Chelci's eyes lit up, and a moan erupted as her body sank into the warm pool. She dunked herself under the water, holding her breath and allowing the luxurious feeling to cover every portion of her skin. When she emerged, she threw her hair back with her hands and blinked the water from her eyes. "This is amazing!" she said.

Anita laughed, beckoning with a hand for her to approach the edge. She took Chelci's arm and rubbed a bar of soap along it. The scratchy texture scraped away the crusty cold which had settled on her skin.

Never having had a servant bathe her before, Chelci quickly grew comfortable with the arrangement and relished the unexpected luxury. Her skin tingled, feeling fresh and clean. After scrubbing her body, Anita went to work on her hair, dousing it with a liquid from a bottle and rubbing it in.

As Anita worked through her hair, the door to the bathing room opened, and a young woman entered.

"Anita, is it extra warm today?" the new woman asked with an eager smile.

Chelci jumped at the intrusion, wrapping her arms across her chest. Her worry over her modesty disappeared as the newcomer stripped off her own clothes in a fluid motion and tossed them to the ground. Chelci averted her eyes.

"I believe it should be to your liking, Juliette."

A splash indicated the woman entered the pool, laughing behind Chelci's back.

"Oh, it's perfect!" she shouted with glee before turning to Chelci. "You must be Brixton's girl. Chelci, right? I heard you were given permission to be here."

"I'm not his . . . girl," Chelci spat. She half-turned, looking out of the corner of her eye. The woman's stunning beauty gave her pause. Chestnut-brown hair draped into the water. Smooth skin, dark eyes, and a confident posture highlighted a woman not much older than herself.

The woman smirked, waving her arms across the surface of the water with little concern of protecting her own dignity. "Sure, you're not. I'm Juliette, one of Bale's wives." Chelci cocked her head. "How do you like the bath?"

Chelci's eyebrows raised. "It's . . . wonderful. I don't know if the cold inside me will ever go away, but for now, it's great."

Juliette's face fell. "I hear you're in the east tower. I'm sorry about that. Edmund is not—" She stopped herself.

"Not very caring toward others?" Chelci finished, causing Juliette to form a reluctant smile. "Yeah, I've noticed." Chelci turned fully, facing Juliette so Anita could work through her hair. Yellowish-green bruises marked Juliette's upper arm and the side of her neck. "Bale's doing?" she asked, pointing.

Juliette glanced at her arm with a strained look on her face. "How'd you put it? Not very caring?" Pushing her way through the water and coming uncomfortably close to Chelci, she lowered her voice. "Is it true shadow knights are coming?" The hopeful gleam in her eye told Chelci the prospect was not unwelcome.

Chelci nodded then shrugged. "Well . . . I think so. I was with them when Bale took me. They should come this way both for him and me."

Juliette's eyes grew. "Can they really do all the things they're supposed to do?"

"They're amazing. They can stop Bale if that's what you're getting at," Chelci said, a sobering smile coming to Juliette's face. "Does that please or upset you?"

Juliette glanced up toward Anita, who poured water from a bucket down Chelci's hair. "There are benefits to being here, but . . ." She drifted backward through the water. "I've not seen my family in Bromhill for seven years. I don't even know if they're alive anymore."

"That's it, Miss Marlow," Anita said. "Can you dunk one last time?"

Chelci submerged, relishing the wet engulfing sensation one last time before she came up, using her hands to throw her hair behind her head. Anita held out a towel and Chelci ascended the steps disheartened the bath was finished.

Chelci used the towel to dry her body and hair, relishing the scent of lilacs and honey filling the air. Her skin tingled, shining from the clean scrubbing. Once she was dry, her face fell as she looked at the crumpled pile of dirty and freezing, old clothes. She turned to the servant. "Am I to put on my old clothes again?"

The bathing servant was busy at work with Juliette, scrubbing her arms with the gritty soap. She looked over her shoulder. "No, dear. You'll find fresh clothing laid out over there."

Chelci walked where Anita's head indicated and found the promised fresh attire. She put on the undergarments before inspecting the dress—a full-length, jade-colored silk gown. Flowers decorated the neck and the end of the sleeves. Her heart jumped when she touched the thick, velvet fabric. Pulling the dress over her head, she worked her arms through the holes. The garment hugged her body with its warmth. The hem fell nearly to the ground, and the sleeves stopped at her wrists. *Perfect!* The neckline fell lower than she liked, but it would do.

"You look beautiful," Juliette cried from the pool.

Chelci blushed as she turned, averting her eyes now that she wore clothes but the other woman did not. "Thank you," she said with a coy smile.

"Let me finish with Juliette, then I'll help with your hair," Anita called.

Chelci nodded and took a seat in a nearby chair. Although she would never complain over the opportunity to get out of the tower, and she relished the clean and warm feeling, something tugged at her mind, making her feel uncomfortable. *What does Brixton want?*

Brixton stood, smiling in a crisp, umber-colored suit when she entered the intimate dining room. Candles decorated the table set with plates, glasses, and shining silverware. A fire crackled in the fireplace, filling the room with a comforting warmth.

"Wow, you look stunning," he said, his eyes lighting up.

Chelci glared, crossing her arms over her chest and wishing her neckline were higher.

With a quick wave of his hand, he moved toward a door. "Come, look!"

Reluctantly, Chelci obeyed. Brixton opened a door, revealing a balcony outside. When she stepped through the doorway, she gasped. Large flakes of white drifted to the ground from a thick blanket of clouds. The fading sun tried to find its way through the barrier, giving a muted glow to the scene of white. A biting wind chilled her, but she pushed the feeling away, entranced by the otherworldly scene.

"It's amazing," she whispered, a mild shiver spasming through her shoulders.

Chelci jerked when a cloak rested on her back. "Don't touch me," she growled.

Wide-eyed, Brixton stepped back, holding his cloak. After a shrug, he slung it back over his shoulders. "Suit yourself." He nodded back to the snow. "I thought you might enjoy seeing this."

"Hmph," Chelci muttered, resisting a second glance as she left the balcony to return inside. The door clicked shut behind her while she rubbed her hands for warmth.

"Please, have a seat," Brixton said, pulling a chair out from the table for her.

Not taking her hard gaze from his eyes, she walked to the other side of the table and took the chair opposite the one he offered. Brixton sighed as he settled into his seat.

Servants entered, pouring water into cups and a dark-red wine into slim glasses. They set down platters of bread and cheese, along with small bowls of steaming soup for each of them.

"Why am I here?" she asked after the servants left.

His head cocked. "Do you not wish to eat?"

"I can eat in my tower."

"Would you rather eat in your tower?"

Chelci didn't answer.

"I didn't think so." Brixton took a drink of wine while Chelci stared back. "I trust you enjoyed the bath and new clothes? I had to pull some strings to make that happen."

"How generous of you," she replied without inflection, hoping her eyes conveyed her inner dead, icy feelings.

Brixton ladled a spoonful of soup into his mouth. After swallowing, he followed with another swig of wine. "Please, eat. The soup is excellent."

Chelci's mouth watered. The spiced aroma filled her nostrils while the steam wafted through the air, but she kept her eyes locked on Brixton and her jaw firm. "I'm not hungry."

Brixton's spoon clanked as he rested it against the bowl. "Chelci, it does no good to be obstinate. I'm fighting to get you out of the tower . . . for *good*. But you need to behave. Stop arguing, trying to escape, and fighting back against everything."

"Veron's going to be here soon." Her voice was tight and low. Brixton flinched at the words. "When he does, he's going to kill Bale and rescue me . . . then he'll come for you."

A wistful smile played over Brixton's face. "Don't count on that, Chelci."

Her confidence faltered. "What do you mean?"

"Bale—" He stopped, shaking his head. "Nothing. It doesn't matter. You should expect to be here for some time so start thinking long-term. You can't live in the tower. The cold alone will kill you."

"If Veron doesn't rescue me, I might as well die."

Brixton pounded on the table. "Don't be foolish!"

She jumped at the outburst of anger.

"I'm sorry for that." He opened both hands and breathed out. "You can have a good life here, Chelci. It's not such a terrible place, and there are great opportunities. But, you need to move past Veron."

She laughed. "What would I do, huh? Wear thick furs and have a hut in the snow? Maybe raise children for some captain in the army so they can grow up to fight in more wars?"

"No." His eyes were soft, almost pleading. "Marry me."

Brixton's words struck her. She blinked several times, wanting to laugh but finding herself unable.

He leaned forward, his eyes filled with life. "Think about it, Chelci.

We're the only ones from Feldor here. I'm the commercial envoy for all of Terrenor. We can travel and live wherever we'd like. And technically, we are still engaged, so . . . it seems fitting. What do you think?"

Chelci's mouth hung open. She rested her arms on the table, intertwining her fingers. For a moment, she stared down at them, her pursed lips askew until she glanced back up. "I don't care if someone tortures me in that tower, tearing off my fingers and toes one at a time. I would *never* marry you, Brixton."

His eyes registered a moment of shock until they fell. His face displayed hurt and pain instead of the anger she expected. A glisten appeared at the corner of one of his eyes, and he wiped it away.

Chelci regretted her harsh words, her body softening. She reached out her hand on the table, not to touch him, but to let him know she cared. "I'm sorry. That was harsh."

"It's all right. It's how you feel."

"No, it's—" She sighed. "I don't know. There's good in you, Brixton. I see it, and I . . . love that about you."

He looked up, a faint smile pulling at his lips.

"But you've done horrific things. All you seem to focus on is fame and ego and money and parties, all at the expense of others' pain, but they don't matter!"

Brixton sighed. "It feels like they do, but . . . It's not what I expected." He looked around the room. "Here I am in this freezing land with a king who—" he cut himself off, shaking his head.

"I wish you would have become a baker," Chelci said. "You would have been happier."

Brixton pursed his lips. "You may be right."

"It's not too late, you know."

Brixton turned to the fire, silent. He took several breaths while he stared at the flame. After a long moment, he turned back to his soup and scooped more. "No . . . it is. I can't turn back now."

The two barely spoke after that. Chelci eventually ate, consuming all the soup as well as the chicken and vegetable entree. When they finished, Brixton escorted her into the wide hall and walked side-by-side to pass her off to the guard waiting at the opposite end.

While they walked, a young woman turned from an adjacent passage, walking with Captain Cyrus. She wore a cloak, but the opening at the front revealed an inappropriate amount of skin. Chelci cringed at the sight of the soldier, whose eyes narrowed when they caught her looking.

"Brixton!" the young woman cried. "I'm glad I got to see you before I left. Today's my twentieth birthday, and I'm being dismissed."

Chelci's head tilted as Brixton smiled.

"Congratulations, Chantel, and happy birthday!" he replied, slowing as the groups passed in the middle of the hall. He turned to Cyrus. "What are you doing? Taking her out?"

The captain smirked. "Yeah, Bale's orders. You can never trust them. Who knows what they'd steal on the way out?"

Chantel's smile faltered at the insult.

"How was your dinner?" the captain asked before turning to Chelci and leering. "Is it time for dessert?"

Chelci took a half step away from the man's gaze, but there was nowhere to hide.

"We just finished," Brixton answered before turning back to the girl. "Nice scarf."

The girl's smile brightened as she lifted the edges of a blue scarf. It wrapped around her neck and fell under her cloak, obscuring her barely clothed chest. "Thanks! The other girls got it for me as a going-away gift."

"What will you do now?"

The young woman shrugged. "I'll head back to Nortris to see my family. I'll figure things out then."

"Well, good luck to you," Brixton said with a wave as they continued along the hall.

"See you later, Chelci," Cyrus said with a crooked grin.

The parting words chilled her. "Who's the girl?" Chelci asked when they were out of earshot.

"Someone I met here in the palace. She's . . . a servant of sorts but is free now." He nudged her and whispered. "You see, Bale's not all bad."

When he and Chelci arrived at her assigned guard, Brixton stopped and extended his arm ahead. "She's all yours," he said, the guard grunting in response. The man motioned for her to lead the way up the stairs when Brixton touched her arm. His brows pinched together. "Don't forget what I said . . . about us. My offer still stands."

Unsure how to respond, Chelci nodded before ascending the spiral steps. No lanterns filled the passage, and the missing sun and thick clouds outside provided little light from the sporadic windows. Trudging up in darkness, Chelci moved her hand to her hip where the cold metal of the dinner knife pressed hidden against her leg.

38

Workers of Daratill

Night had long fallen by the time they arrived at the outskirts of Daratill. William insisted they keep to the woods, not knowing what sort of greeting Bale may have for them. Entering tree-cover, the falling snow lightened. Veron's feet grew cold, his boots from Felting unprepared for Norshewa's elements, but his gray cloak repelled the snow with ease.

William stopped at the front.

"What is it?" Veron whispered.

"Your cloak is too light and may attract attention in the woods. Change to your black one for now. It will be safer."

Veron tensed, eyeing his father as Jeanette's Dream ran through his mind. "Nice try, but you just want me to be the one with the Shadow Knights cloak when we meet Bale. Admit it."

William took a deep breath and straightened. "Yes, I do."

Veron shook his head. "No, you won't sacrifice yourself like that. Your cloak is lighter than mine. You should be the one to put it on." Father and son stared, neither moving to change.

"You should both change," Morgan suggested. "One of you needs to have it on, and it's better for both of you while you skulk around.

You can figure out the rest later."

Veron nodded, grudgingly lowering his pack from his shoulder as William followed. Putting on the cloak conflicted him. The familiar covering settled his heart, imagining he and Chelci could live and have a future together. But the thought of consigning his father to death troubled him. Attired in their Shadow Knights cloaks with their packs on their backs, they continued along. No one spoke, the snow crunching under their feet.

Progress was slow but worth the caution. Through the trees on their left, Veron made out the outline of Daratill's shops and homes. Smoke rose from chimneys, and lanterns shone through windows. A pang of jealousy for a warm room hit him until an opening in the foliage gave a better view. Walls crumbled. Roofs collapsed. Years of oppression had left the city in ruin.

William stopped ahead. The line of trees ended, and Veron and Morgan joined alongside him.

"Our cover ends here," William said.

Veron sensed the lurking danger as he stared ahead.

Past the trees, the city sprawled with more disheveled buildings. To the right, an icy river powered its way through the near-darkness, fighting to drown out their words. Ahead, what looked like a structure's ruins spanned part of the river. Curious dots of light gave the blowing snow a glowing feel, but it was too far away to tell what it was. Beyond the structure, black castle walls rose in the gloom, but the steady storm made visibility impossible.

"That's where she'll be," Veron said, "and we know nothing about it."

"We should cross the river. The trees on the other side will give us more cover to approach," William said, pointing to the right. He slipped his pack off and removed the coiled rope from across his body. "We need to travel light."

Morgan shifted his feet, glancing toward the river.

"Morgan, you stay here. They're coming for Veron and I. Plus, your shoulder pain is visible."

Morgan's shoulders relaxed. His forehead beaded drops of perspiration despite the frigid air. He didn't argue with the order to stay behind and gave each a hug. When he pulled back from Veron, tears pooled in his eyes. "Be careful, Veron," he said. "Kill Bale then find Chelci and bring her back."

Veron nodded. "I will."

"Also, don't die," Morgan added with a forced smile.

Veron clapped his friend on his good shoulder, squeezing hard. "Thank you for coming with us, Morgan. You're a good friend." His smile struggled to reach his eyes. *This may be our last goodbye.* "We'll see you soon."

His feet felt heavy as he turned away. Leaving Morgan behind along with their packs, Veron and William descended a short decline to approach the river. The dark water churned over rocks, icy along the banks. They cleared it with well-powered leaps, landing in soft powder on the far side.

Carrying nothing but his sword, Veron felt exposed. His black cloak contrasted with the white blanket around him. It gave him a sense of comfort, as if it were the only thing keeping him alive from what was to come. He dusted the snow off his arms and legs as they ducked back into the cover of the trees. They continued in silence through the edge of the woods, dodging trees and bushes. After several minutes of walking, they halted suddenly after cresting a short rise.

The black edifice emerged ahead, arching over the river with walls of a large structure growing at both ends. Awash in the hellish light of countless torches, laborers crawled over it like ants.

"That's what the workers are for," Veron said.

"He's building a new palace."

"Why would he work them at night in the middle of a storm? How long can they survive like that?"

William shook his head. "He doesn't care if they die. He'll just gather more people."

A break in the trees revealed a road where a team of horses approached slowly. They pulled a flat cart with black stones piled high. When the vehicle stopped, laborers trudged into the glowing torchlight. Several men and women were joined together by jangling chains. The workers lifted the stones, one at a time, then carried them toward the river.

Weighed down by a large stone, an older man's foot stumbled. He fell to the ground, the black rock cracking as it hit something hard.

"Watch your feet!" a guard shouted. He stepped in front of a torch, his silhouette looming over the man.

The worker tried to salvage the stone sections, but they wouldn't piece back together. A short whip tore through the air. The man yelled, his back arching.

"You're working an extra shift for that!" the guard growled. "You and your whole line. Now, get that rubble out of here."

The rest of the men on the line delivered their burdens to a stack not far away. When they returned, each picked up portions of the broken stone and took it to a rubble pile next to the woods.

"Can we do something?" Veron whispered, his fists clenched.

William hummed in thought. "By killing Bale, we'll be able to set them free."

"Assuming everything works out," Veron added. He scanned the worksite. "Can we free them now? I count no more than a dozen guards."

"It could cause a commotion and put the castle on alert."

Veron's eyes grew. "That could be good, right? We free them and send them on their way. Thousands of freed workers tear through Daratill, heading south."

"It could cause chaos."

". . . and divert soldiers from the castle."

William thought and nodded after a long moment. "All right. Let's do it."

The two shadow knights returned to the cover of the trees and slunk through the darkness. Their feet left indentations as they crunched softly in the snow. With a quick burst of speed, they crossed an open space from the trees to crouch behind the rubble pile where broken black stones piled. Horses snorted nearby, waiting patiently for their cart to be uploaded.

Chains clinked on the other side of the barrier. Veron peeked around the rubble. Lines of workers trudged by with their heads bowed. They wore ragged and thin clothes. Several faces carried a blueish tinge. No guards appeared in the immediate vicinity.

"Psst," William called.

The man at the back of the closest line turned his head and looked toward the woods.

"Here," William said, louder.

The rest of the line paused and glanced their way.

"We're here to help. We're going to get you out of here," Veron said. The workers' eyes grew. The other lines of nearby workers huddled around, leaning in.

"Who are you?" a woman in the closest group asked.

"We're friends," William answered. "How many guards are out tonight? And where are they?"

The group glanced between each other and mumbled. "Twelve or thirteen, I believe," a bearded man replied.

"Three are spread on the bridge," the woman said. "Then there are four or five on each side."

"Come on. We need to move," the man at the front of the line said, pulling lightly on the chains as he nervously glanced around.

"Can we help?" the woman asked.

William shook his head. "Just do what you're—"

"Hey! What are you doing?" A rough shout came through the night, and the lines of workers jumped before starting toward the cart. A guard emerged from the gloom, stepping into the light of the nearest torch. His whip dangled, tracking faint lines into the snow as he moved. He approached the woman and held out his whip. "Who were you talking with?"

She kept her eyes trained on the cart while the others grabbed stones one at a time.

"I said—" The guard let his whip fly, striking the woman across the back. She screamed, leaning against the wooden vehicle to hold her up. "—who were you talking with?"

Veron tensed. "I'm going to stop him," he whispered

The guard pulled her back by the hair. "You answer me when I ask you a question!" He threw her against the edge of the cart and reared his arm back.

Veron barely even felt resistance as his sword cut through the man's arm. The whip, still gripped in the severed hand, fell to the snow with a spray of blood.

The man's wail chilled Veron to his bones. He collapsed after a jab to the chest, his scream fading into gasping noises. William joined Veron, his own sword at the ready while he leaned on his staff. The alerted cries of multiple guards answered back through the night.

Veron crouched next to the gasping man and yanked the ring of keys dangling from his hip. He tossed them to the bearded man. "Unlock yourselves. We'll take care of the guards."

Before leaving the cart, he looked the woman who'd been whipped in her puffy, red eyes. "Are you all right?" he asked.

She sniffed then nodded. "Thank you," she said quietly. A hint of a smile tugged at her face.

Veron returned to his father. "You ready?"

William nodded. Veron led the way, rounding the cart and heading toward the torches. He ignored the wide-eyed faces of underdressed workers and continued forward.

"Who are you!" A guard next to a torch shouted, pulling his sword. Another man stepped to his side to spread out.

Veron and William moved in unison, pulling from the origine and striking opposite sides of each man before they could respond. The guards cried out as they fell to the ground.

"Guards! To arms!"

The cry drew Veron's gaze over the water where Norshewans dodged workers, running toward them with swords drawn. On their side of the river, two more guards' heads perked up from the partially completed walls.

"I'll take these guys," William said, lumbering forward. "Can you cover the bridge?"

"Sure." Veron ran ahead, ascending the rise of stone. He weaved in and out of chained workers, some gawking and others cheering.

Four guards slowed as he approached. At the river's far edge, four more hurried in his direction. A line of chained-together workers fell over when a rushing guard collided with them.

Veron observed the fanned-out guards. Their teeth bared as they held out their weapons, but he smelled their fear, carried on the wind. He stepped in. The first soldier's sword broke in half, cleaved by Farrathan's lightning-fast stroke. The man didn't even have time to cry out before he fell dead to the black stones. Veron jabbed the next man in the stomach. As the guard bent over, he grabbed him by the tunic and flung him into the others. Two of the men flew off the structure's edge, splashing into the icy water rushing below. The final guard cracked his head into the edge of a stone. Veron put him out of his misery with a swipe to his neck.

"Veron?"

The familiar voice spun him around. Veron's eyes danced between the faces of the crowd of onlookers until he found who he sought. "Nathaniel!"

His friend from Felting appeared a shadow of his former self. His face was pale and lean. A bandage wrapped around his thigh with a dark stain showing through. He shouted over his shoulder. "Drevyn, it's Veron!"

The name of the Marlows' mason surprised Veron once again as the other man emerged from the mass of bodies. "Drevyn? Nathaniel? What are you . . . ? How did you . . . ?"

Nathaniel shouted, "Look out!"

Veron ducked as a blade whistled over his head. He stabbed the guard who wielded it in the gut then slammed his foot into another, blasting him onto a stone promontory that stuck out high over the water. Two more guards fell quickly as he twirled faster than they could react.

He breathed heavily as he glanced around, looking down both directions of the bridge. No more guards approached. William appeared to be done with his men. His father loped up the slope with workers parting in front of him.

Veron turned back to Nathaniel. "I think that may be it."

Chains rattled and a young voice cried out. Veron's head snapped to the promontory.

A guard stood, hunched over. He held a hand against his chest, where Veron had kicked him. His other hand extended a knife to the neck of a grown boy a few years younger than Veron. The line of workers chained to the boy balanced precariously at the bridge's edge. The frigid river churned below.

"Who are you?" The guard winced at his own words.

"I am Veron Stormbridge, and I'm here to free these people."

"You can't—" The guard stopped and glanced around. His wary eyes took in the sight of thousands of workers surrounding him. "Back up! All of you!" He bared the lone dagger at the other workers. They scurried backward, giving plenty of space. The guard's voice grew weaker. "Bale is king, and the workers are his."

Veron weaved through the shuffling crowd, growing closer until no one stood between him and the lone guard.

"That's far enough!" The man pressed the dagger back to the boy's neck, causing him to whimper.

"All right! All right!" Veron stopped.

"Drop your sword!" The man grabbed the boy as if he planned to push him into the water. The other four men on the chain stared at the links connecting them to the boy.

Veron crouched slowly. Farrathan clanked when he laid it down. "They haven't done anything to you. You're not going to get out of here if you kill them." A gust of wind rippled Veron's black cloak behind him.

The guard's wild eyes darted around. His arm tensed. After one last glance to each side of the bridge, the guard pushed the boy.

"No!" Veron yelled.

The boy screamed as he fell. The men who shared the chain had their feet jerked out from underneath them in quick succession. The guard ran in the opposite direction, but Veron sprinted for the falling workers.

He fueled his legs with power and dove toward the edge of the bridge as the last man disappeared over the side. Veron lunged over the lip, wrapping his hand around the cold chain connected to the last man's leg. The weight of five men pulled him over the edge, but his other hand gripped the brink of the stone and held.

Dangling from the side, Veron chanced a look below. Stretched along the chain, five workers hung upside-down, shouting. The freezing river's frothing water rushed just below the head of the boy at the opposite end.

His arm screamed under the weight, but the origine kept him from giving up. Power surged through him as his own feet dangled precariously. *I can't hold this for long!* He attempted to fling the chained workers above him, but the weight was beyond what he could manage. He only succeeded in bouncing them in the air.

His fingers ached. The chain dug into his hand. One link slipped and his stomach churned. He glanced around, desperate for a solution. Another link fell through his sweaty hand. He mustered all the strength he could and lifted his arm. With a roar, he raised the chain to the lip of the bridge.

The leg of the man closest to him bumped into his body. The upside-down worker bent at the waist, trying to grab for the edge of the bridge, but his fingers fell short.

Veron's yell intensified. His energy was almost gone but he wouldn't drop the men. Having given up in his attempt to grab the lip, the man next to him fell back. The settling of weight intensified the burden, and Veron's arm began to lower. *No! I have to—*

Something clamped onto his arm. Veron looked up as his father's face leaned over the side. "I've got you, Son!" William's strong grip moved to the chain, taking it out of Veron's hand. With his burden gone, his body felt light. Veron pulled himself up to the bridge with two hands.

Panting for air, his body desperate to rest, he joined William at the edge. His father lay against the ground, straining to hold onto the chain. Veron bent down and shared the weight. Once both of them had a hold, they pulled. Veron walked steadily backward as he moved hand over hand, bringing the chain in. Bodies appeared over the edge every few steps, and other observers grabbed onto hands to help pull. Soon, the weight was light as the fellow workers dragged the rest up.

Veron expended all his remaining energy. He crumpled against the black stones, his chest heaving, desperate for relief. He rolled his head and looked to the side where the last guard ran down the bridge toward the shore. The man looked over his shoulder at Veron while continuing forward. With his attention distracted, a chain of workers nudged him. The man's arms whirled, but his balance was lost. The splash as he hit the water was inaudible over the sound of the river and the wind.

A cheer rose from the workers. Some attended to the line of men he rescued. Many surrounded Veron, but he only collapsed back on the bridge with his father panting next to him.

"Veron, are you all right?" Nathaniel asked, his voice close.

Veron opened his eyes to the sight of his two Felting friends leaning over him. He nodded and took a hand to rise to his feet.

"What are you doing here?"

"We—uh—We're going to find Bale and rescue Chelci," Veron replied between breaths.

"What happened to Chelci?" Drevyn asked.

"Bale took her. I think he plans to use her as bait or something. But how are you two here? They took you, I guess?"

"Yeah . . . when they rounded up people in Felting."

Nathaniel nodded toward William. "Who's this?"

A grin tugged at Veron's face as William gathered himself to his feet and leaned on his staff. Veron gestured to him. "This is my father, William Stormbridge."

Nathaniel's eyes grew. "I thought—" He shook his head. "It doesn't matter. It's great to meet you, sir."

"So, what should we do now?" Drevyn asked.

"Head south," William said, looking around the crowd. "The guards should have keys to free yourselves. The best thing you can do is get out of Daratill."

"Where are you going?" Nathaniel asked.

Veron looked at his father then glanced upriver toward the castle shrouded in blowing snow. "To kill Bale."

39

Freedom

Brixton paced his bedroom. Snowflakes collided with the window, illuminated by the candles. His whirring thoughts kept him from sleeping, and moving about helped him process them.

Would she truly rather die than marry me? Am I that bad of a person?

After he'd turned on his father and committed to following Bale, nothing had gone to plan. The position and money weren't as fulfilling as he hoped they would be. Norshewa was harsh and cold—a far cry from the familiar lush land of Feldor.

I wish I had friends here. I need people to talk to. Chelci knows me, but she can't stand me. Brixton sighed, frustrated with how things had turned out so far.

I need some air. He grabbed his black cloak and left his room.

The halls were empty as the castle slept. His feet clopped. The shadow of his body played across the walls as he passed lanterns in the passages. Laughter ahead piqued his interest. When he rounded a corner, two guards with bottles in their hands walked toward him.

"Brixton!" Captain Cyrus raised his hands in celebration and jostled liquid from his bottle. A dopey grin covered his face.

Brixton cringed at the sight of the soldier. He nodded slightly. "What are you doing up?"

"Hiding from Bale." Both soldiers laughed as they wobbled on their feet. "He wanted everyone to gather, but I said . . . *no!*" He punctuated the word by lifting his drink.

"What does he—" Brixton stopped. A blue scarf hung around the captain's neck. His forehead pinched together. "Is that Chantel's?"

Cyrus looked down. His eyes grew when they located the blue item. He grabbed the end of it and flopped it around. "Oh yeah! Forgot I had this."

"Did she give it to you?"

The captain chuckled while a wry grin smoothed over his lips. "Yeah, she did."

"Won't she need it? It's freezing out there, and she barely wore anything!"

Both soldiers laughed, glancing at each other. "She's not gonna need it anymore," the second soldier said.

An uneasy feeling churned in Brixton's stomach.

"You want a drink?" Cyrus said, words slurring as he held up his bottle.

Brixton shook his head. "Where's Chantel?"

Cyrus screwed up his face. "I took her to the Transitioner's Hut."

"Where?"

"It's where we help young women like her transition to life outside the castle."

"Oh!" Brixton said, his unease settling. "Where is that?"

With a weird smile, Cyrus pointed a wandering finger over his shoulder. "Across the bridge, take the first street on the right, near the end of the way." The soldiers stumbled away, giggling like drunken fools.

Brixton found himself drawn toward the castle's entrance. Billowing snow and a dark city greeted him at the doorway. *Why do I want to go out there? Why do I care what happens to her?* Despite his confusion, Brixton pulled his collar close and crossed the bridge.

Snow crunched under his feet as he turned up the first street. Sputtering lanterns protected by glass cut through the storm, providing minimal light. Brixton inspected the buildings he passed until a scrawling of "Transition" etched in a wooden sign caught his eye. The weathered, wooden door hung at an angle on its hinge. Gaps riddled the walls of the rickety structure.

He pushed on the door, and creaks announced his presence to anyone nearby. "Hello?" he asked into the gaping darkness. A decaying smell wrinkled his nose. He couldn't see anything. He stood in the doorway, mind spinning. Not wanting to enter the dark room, he grabbed a nearby lantern from its hook in the street. Holding it by the ring, he extended his arm as he crossed the hut's threshold.

A cramped room waited inside, but no one appeared to be there. "Hello?" he tried again. "Chantel?" Shovels hung from hooks on the ceiling, a stack of burlap sat in the corner, and a box with a loose lid pressed against a wall. He poked his head through an open doorway, but the smaller room to the side only contained empty shelves. Grit from the dirt floor rubbed into his boots. His nose turned, the rank smell growing strong the farther in he moved.

This is the Transitioner's Hut? The hair on his arms tingled, his senses attuned. He raised the box's lid and lifted the lantern to illuminate the inside. His muscles immediately seized. A lifeless hand lay next to a bear tattoo. His lungs no longer worked. He turned to the end of the box to find Chantel's pale face staring back at him and a tangle of bloodless limbs poking out from underneath her body.

Brixton cried out. He stumbled backward, dropping the lantern, the glass shattering and light snuffing out. He backpedaled until he rammed into the wall on the opposite side of the street. His pulse thundered in his ears, and he struggled to breathe.

When he felt about to burst, he leaned over and heaved. His hands rested on his knees while partially digested food and bile stained the pile of snow against the wall. Sweat covered his forehead, steam pouring off him. When he finished turning out the contents of his stomach, he stood and wiped the corner of his mouth with the back of his hand.

Why?

The question was all he could think.

She had done nothing. She was harmless—excited to return home.

Brixton's mind reeled. He replayed everything he'd done and seen over the last season through his head. When his breath settled, a tear rolled down his cheek. He sniffed, wiping it away with his sleeve. He fixed his jaw into a grim line and stared at the foreboding castle while his fists clenched into a frozen ball.

40

Searching the Castle

After leaving the freed workers behind and taking a few minutes to rest and recover, Veron and William used the wooded side of the river to approach the castle. Ducking in and out of snow-covered limbs, they came upon a rocky promontory with the fortress looming ahead. The storm abated, and the moon shone through the clouds, illuminating the landscape and allowing better visibility. Veron's jaw dropped.

Boulders speckled with white surrounded the base of the castle with the river curving around them, a finger of which diverted upstream to create a moat. The sheer black walls of the castle rose from the land. Towers seemed to balance in the air, connected by thin walkways high above the ground. To the left, leading up to the castle, the buildings of Daratill cowered at its feet. The rest of the city—mundane and impoverished—looked inconsequential compared to the fortress. Behind the castle, the Korob Mountains' shadows dwarfed everything, blocking the rest of Terrenor from the snowy land in the north. A simple leap from the narrowest section of the river brought them to the narrow, rocky base between the walls and the river.

The air grew colder as the spray from the water filled the air. Veron moved first, jumping from rock to rock while William moved slowly with his staff. Their target was the lowest part of the wall, where a tall boulder reached higher than the others.

The edge of the churning water threatened to pull them in. Veron tried to push away the thought of falling. *I'm not sure what the origine can do about recovering from that.* He paused, waiting for his father. "You coming?" he asked, his grin likely invisible. "Or are you going to hang back there, letting Chelci become an old woman while waiting on us."

William only grunted, taking time to brace with his staff while he moved. He used his free hand and good leg to stay upright, but the process was slow.

When he caught up, Veron turned and jumped, wanting to show how effortless the process was. His foot hit the rock and met a dark patch of ice, losing its purchase. His body fell, hands scrambling. Below the boulder, the river waited to pull him in, as if the rock were a trap to lure unsuspecting victims.

The origine froze time, stopping his fall. His mind scrambled for a plan, but the smooth, slick surface gave him nothing to use. He moved his hands and feet, trying different places, but his body continued downward.

His heart raced at an abnormal speed. His hand pressed against the icy surface. Beneath him, the boulder ended and his legs found nothing but air. He prepared himself for the biting cold of the river until a grip on his hand pulled his attention away from the water. William braced himself between two rocks and reached down to stop his fall. His father's eyes were warm, his arm barely straining as he held Veron's weight. A quick pull brought Veron back up to solid footing.

"Thank you," Veron panted. "I don't know what happened. I

thought I was fine."

"Even with your abilities, ice is still slick, and without a fire to warm by, a frozen river will still kill you."

Veron trembled inside. A sheepish grin formed. "I'll be more careful. I promise."

Moving more cautiously, Veron led the way to the tallest boulder, steadying his father as William joined him on top. Together, they looked up. The top of the wall would be easy to reach, but what lay beyond was impossible to see.

"I think I should leave my cloak here," William said as they craned their necks. "They'll be looking for two people with black cloaks, and we may sneak in better with only one."

"Nice try, but you're keeping it on," Veron said before taking a deep breath. "You ready?"

William nodded. Veron sent power to his legs and leaped. His hair blew back as the top of the wall hurriedly met him. He grabbed the top of the battlements as he floated past, rebalancing his trajectory. After a brief drop, he landed in a crouch, William's staff hitting the stone moments later.

"What the—" a voice yelled behind Veron.

He spun to find a Norshewan soldier standing with his mouth agape. Veron's hand moved to his sword, but a blur flew past him. Before he even touched his hand to the hilt, the soldier's neck twisted, and his body flew into the air toward the rocks and river below. William took the man's place on the wall.

Veron looked over the edge but lost sight of the man in the darkness. Whether he hit the rocks or the icy water, he had certainly perished.

The rest of the nearby battlements appeared empty. A shadow of another soldier a distance away appeared to pay no attention. Veron looked around at the black turrets and roofs. A nearby tower connected to the primary building by a precarious bridge. "Should we keep to the air?" he asked. "Maybe check out that tower?"

William followed his eyes and pursed his lips.

"Chelci could be up there."

William nodded. "Possibly . . . but unlikely. Bale won't be there. I say we start through there." He pointed to a door leading from the battlements into the castle.

Veron looked back at the tower. Something gnawed at him, but he couldn't place it. He shrugged. "Sure."

They hurried along the wall, away from the distant soldier. The door opened, revealing a lantern-lit hall. They pulled their swords as they entered.

"Do you have any idea where to check?" Veron whispered.

"He'll probably be sleeping, so we're looking for his bedroom. Look for guards."

They padded along the hall, walking as quietly as possible. "You know," Veron said. "If we found Chelci first, she could help us if we ran into trouble."

"I'm sure she could. If we find her, that would be great, but the longer we're here, the more likely we'll be caught. Bale must be the priority."

Passing a railing, they paused. Veron looked down from the top of a massive hall with columns along either side. The room was dark, but a Norshewan bear symbol shone against the wall.

"Let's keep going," William said, tugging on his arm.

Around the next corner, a door caught their eye. The intricate carved bear and silver inlay gave the impression of an important room. "Should we try it?" Veron asked.

"No guards . . ." William muttered, appearing deep in thought. He jerked his head. "Check quickly."

Veron turned the handle, and the door pivoted smoothly. Inside, walls of books greeted him. The fire's simmering remains lit the room. Rich furniture and warmer air beckoned him to relax. The maps on the tables invited him to explore. He drifted along the bookshelves, eying the titles.

"We're not here for books," William whispered.

Veron pulled himself away. "Yes, but this looks like a king's chambers, doesn't it?" Stepping away from the books, he traced his hand along the tables with maps and led them through an open doorway on the far side of the room. A luxurious bed awaited in the chamber. Thick tussled blankets rested on top, and a nearly used up candle glowed on the side table. The tiny flame illuminated a slight woman, her brown hair emerging from the covers.

Veron froze. He backpedaled when the woman turned over, pulling at the blankets. She gasped and lurched to a sitting position.

"Who are you?" Her voice trembled as she held the blankets to her chest.

Veron's pulse thumped in his ears. William's sword raised next to him, but Veron held his hand out. He put his own sword back into its sheath. "It's all right. We're not here to hurt you. I'm sorry for the disturbance."

"She can raise an alarm," William muttered, still holding out his weapon. The woman's eyes reflected the candlelight, quivering in terror. Her smooth skin showed her youth.

"It's fine," Veron said to his father while nodding. After William sheathed his sword, Veron took a few slow steps toward the bed. "We're looking for Edmund Bale. Do you know where he might be?"

A nervous laugh replied, then she nodded toward the rumpled covers next to her. "He was here until . . . a half-hour ago. What business do you have with my husband?"

Veron stiffened and turned to William. His mind raced, knowing they were so close, but jitters filled him. "We . . . um . . ."

"He took something from us, and we're here to get it back," William said.

The woman nodded her head. "You're looking for the girl."

Veron gasped.

"Chelci? Is that her name?"

"Yes!" Veron shouted. "Do you know where she is?"

"Veron, keep it down," William scolded.

The young shadow knight moved forward, touching the side of the bed. "What's your name?"

"Juliette."

"Juliette, please, you must tell us."

Her shoulders relaxed and eyes softened. "I'm sorry about what Edmund did—taking her. I met her earlier this evening, actually. You'll be glad to know she's healthy."

"Where is she?" Veron asked.

"Edmund has her locked in the east tower." Juliette pointed toward the far wall. "After you leave, follow the hall to the right. Two flights of stairs will lead to a long, narrow passage. Halfway along, a door on the left will bring you to a bridge over a courtyard. Cross it and you'll be at the eastern tower. She should be locked at the top. Be careful, there will be guards."

A grim smile formed as Veron took a step back. "Guards we can handle. Thank you."

She raised her hand before he left. "Are you the two shadow knights?"

Veron's breath caught, and he glanced at William. His father nodded. "We are."

"I don't know what Edmund will do, but he's been preparing for you. He has some sort of plan."

"Why do you offer this information?" Veron asked, his eyes narrowed.

Juliette looked down at the blankets. "I've waited for this moment since the day he took me—the Dream to be fulfilled. You come for him, but you also come to free me. Good luck."

Veron solemnly nodded. His heart rate increased as they left the bedroom and made their way back to the hall. "I know Bale is our primary goal, but—"

"We should go for her," William whispered in return. Veron's head snapped toward him, his eyes eager. "We still don't know where Bale is, but we know about Chelci. Something tells me we may end up finding both."

A twisting pain turned Veron's stomach. He hurried along the passage and up the stairs, dreading whatever trap Bale may have waiting for them.

Halfway along the passageway, William opened a door. A blast of cold air hit them while flakes of snow drifted in. Veron went first. A narrow stone bridge, barely wide enough for one man, arced over a courtyard. Sticky snow covered most of the stone, and the black tower rose ahead of them.

While the sight of the bridge and tower made his heart pound, looking over the side of the bridge made his legs weak. A large courtyard was situated beneath them. Decorative pillars dotted the space, and stone surrounded it on all sides. Covering the entire courtyard, a massive force of soldiers waited at attention.

"What are they doing?" William whispered, crouching in the darkness.

A sinking feeling filled Veron's gut. "I think they're waiting for us." Hearing his own words left his arms shaking.

"There must be close to two hundred of them."

Veron nodded. "And I guarantee Bale is nearby." He looked back at the tower and took a deep breath. "What do we do?"

"Go after Chelci or Bale?" William sighed. "You make the call, Veron."

His gut felt like it would split. *Why do I have to decide?* "I was in this place back in Felting. I had Bale before me with only a handful of men to protect him. I could have killed him then, but . . ." He hung his head. "I left to save Chelci instead."

"Hey," William said. "It wasn't a bad decision. It was what your heart told you to do."

"But I could have stopped him from taking over Terrenor. We wouldn't even be here, now."

"Could you have, though?" William asked. "Jeanette's Dream saw us here . . . together." He motioned with his hand. "The snow. The courtyard. The icy walls." His breath fogged as he spoke.

Veron tightened his jaw. "You're right. This is where it happens."

"And now, *you* have a choice to make. Do we go after Chelci, or do we head down to the courtyard to take care of Bale for good? I'll follow whatever decision you make."

The weight rested heavily on Veron. He looked up at the tower, picturing Chelci behind the blocks of stone at the top, alone and scared. *Can I put her over the needs of the kingdom again?* The wind buffeted him, and he grabbed the rail for support. Looking at the courtyard below, his mouth curled into a grin. He spun to his father. "We go for Chelci."

William's eyebrow raised, but he didn't speak.

"We know we're going to meet Bale sooner or later, might as well be later."

His father chuckled. "That's a good point." He gestured ahead with his hand and a smile. "Lead on."

Veron held to the low, stone sides as he walked to keep the wind from knocking him over. The icy path caused unstable footing. She was so close. He could feel her presence. A faint woman's voice mixed in with the wind, calling his name. He looked around and saw nothing but black stone and blowing snow.

As he passed the bridge's highest point, a gasp from William made him look up. He froze. A man stood, blocking the entrance to the tower on the far side. He looked like a statue. Leather and fur wrapped around his broad shoulders and chest, and a massive sword hung at his hip. His thick, black hair waved in the wind. A smirk covered his face, tugging at the unmistakable scar. Bale waited for them.

Veron pulled his sword. The wind blew his cloak, rippling behind him. His heart pounded as he faced his destiny. He wanted to run at the man and cut him down before he took another breath, but he hesitated. *One of us will die.*

Something fluttered behind him. A thick, black item of clothing flew from the bridge, passing in his peripheral vision. Veron spun. His father stood with his sword ready in one hand and staff in the other. His jaw set and muscles rippled. The cloak was gone.

"What are you—"

"It's done!" William's eyes didn't leave the far end of the bridge. "Focus on what we must do!"

"Father no! I—"

A deep laugh stopped his words, his heart aching from the thought of his father's death. Veron spun around to see Bale's shoulders bounce. "Father and son? Interesting." Veron gritted his teeth while Bale continued. "Let me guess. You met Juliette, and the soft-hearted fool told you where the girl was?"

Veron kept still.

"I thought she might. It's a pity she'll have to die now. I liked that one."

"It's over, Bale!" Veron crouched, holding out his sword.

Bale roared with laughter. "I think not." He nodded upward and behind him. "I hold something you want. And you'll have to get past me to get to her." He pulled his sword and dropped into a crouch, as if taunting them to attack.

Veron's stomach turned, his sword arm faltering at the king's confidence.

"What's he hiding?" William whispered over his shoulder.

"Should we run at him?" Veron asked back, but his father didn't reply.

Metal footsteps turned him around. On the side of the bridge they left, a half-dozen men with spears lined up in full armor, paused, waiting for something. A fresh laugh spun him back as Bale faded into the tower's darkness. Another half dozen armored men took his place. With a yell, the men charged from both directions, metal spear tips closing fast.

41

Gain and Loss

Chelci lay on her bench in the freezing tower. The threadbare blanket covered her new jade dress, but she still shivered. The bath's warmth had long since faded. She tried to sleep, but her stomach kept her up, gurgling, not used to the rich food.

She sat up with a sigh, then pulled the blanket over her shoulders as she stood. *Maybe movement will warm me up?*

Outside the door to her cell, someone coughed—one of the two guards who remained stationed outside her room at all times.

Chelci stopped moving and closed her eyes. She extended her hands and focused on her breathing.

Clear my mind. Clear my mind. Give me your energy, body.

She flexed her arms, searching for any sign of power, but nothing returned.

I want this to stop Bale. I want to help people. I want it to stay alive.

Her motives were pure, but nothing seemed to work. She sighed and sat back on the bench.

Hustling footsteps came muffled through the door. Mumbling voices were too quiet to hear. Chelci sprung to the door and crouched at the slit at the bottom.

"He's in the castle," a voice said. "He's coming to the tower, so be ready."

Chelci's eyes grew. *Veron?*

"What's Bale gonna do?" another asked.

A moment of quiet followed, her ears straining for any sound. The words were too quiet for her to make out. When the footsteps walked away, she scurried away from the door, her heart pounding. *He's here!*

She lunged for the bars over the window and sucked in a lungful of air. "Veron! I'm in the tower! Veron!"

A key clanged in the lock as someone worked to open the door.

"Bale knows you're coming! Veron! Be care—"

A club slammed the side of her head, knocking her to the ground. Chelci cried out, grabbing her temple when a boot collided with her stomach. She yelled, curled up in a ball, waving her hand to fend off any further blows. She blinked her eyes, but the blinding white behind her irises hadn't faded. Her head pounded as she sucked in rapid breaths.

"Quiet, you!" a guard growled.

Her sight returned. One guard stood over her, with the other behind. On the opposite side of the room, the door hung ajar, her eyes lighting up at the glimmer of hope. *Veron is near, and my door is wide open.*

The guard leaned forward, shaking a hand in her face. His mouth moved, but her mind didn't listen to what he said. Behind her back, her hand gripped the knife from dinner. The cold metal pressed against her skin as her arm flexed. The guard grabbed her by the hair. She followed to her feet while the man lifted. Her head screamed in pain, but she kept her mouth shut as she glared back. Holding onto her hair with one hand, the guard cocked his club back. She lashed out with her arm, stabbing toward his exposed neck. She wanted to look away but needed to ensure the blade found its mark. His skin waited, unprotected. Her knife grew closer.

Suddenly, the tension on her scalp faded. The soldier let go of her hair, and his arm blocked hers. She screamed as he thwarted her surprise attack.

A knee buried into her gut, followed by a bludgeon to her back. Her breath gone and back screaming, she fell to the cold stone floor, gasping for breath while the guard knocked her paltry weapon away. The knife scraped on the stone as he picked it up. Laughter faded as the two men left through the door, the cold metal clanging shut behind them.

Chelci remained on her knees, coughing and wheezing. Once her breathing was under control, she rolled onto her back. Her head pounded and stomach still ached from the blows. She focused on her breath while she rested.

A smile grew on her face. *Veron is near.* She inhaled with a start. *What if he's the one who needs me? Bale's supposed to kill either him or William. What if I can save them?*

She rolled over and scrambled to her feet. Her jaw clenched as she pictured Veron somewhere in the castle, about to fight Bale. Her breath was even, pulse calm. All she could see was him. *He's a good man and needs to live. If only I could—*

Chelci gasped. Her eyes opened wide. Deep in her chest, a warm tingle grew, moving outward along her arms and down her legs. Her mind sharpened and eyes grew keen. Her heart sped as it swelled.

The origine!

It waited for her to call it forward.

Veron tensed, feeling the precarious nature of the bridge holding them.

"We can't stop them all!" William shouted.

Veron held his sword in both hands, waiting for the right moment. The soldiers charged with abandon, their boots shaking the bridge. The moment they arrived, he pulled on the origine. He kicked the tip of the first spear out of the way and sliced his blade hard against the soldier's thick armor. The sword cut into the metal, sending the man careening over the rail of the bridge. Veron's arm yanked, the metal gripping the blade, threatening to pull it from his grip. He held on, pulling it free as the soldier fell toward the courtyard of men below. He dodged the next spear by angling his body to the side, but the barreling soldiers' bodies came too quickly. The mass of armor collided with him.

Veron steeled his legs using the origine, but the snowy walkway gave him no purchase. His legs pressed against the low wall, his center of gravity shifting. He shouted as his body tumbled over the side, his weight disappearing. Upside down, but still using the origine, he sighted his path as he fell. The soldiers in the courtyard below had moved out of the way. They all watched with swords ready.

Veron brought his feet around as he met the stone courtyard. His legs bent to absorb the shock, and his cloak settled around him. His sword remained in his hand, held out toward the hundreds of wide-eyed Norshewans. William landed a moment later, but his landing was more difficult. He favored his good leg but used the other for balance. A loud crack echoed through the courtyard as the wooden leg splintered, and William collapsed on top.

Veron scrambled with his free hand to lift under his father's arm. "Are you okay?" he asked without taking his eyes off the men surrounding them.

"Yeah," William panted, balancing on one leg, his breath heavy and deliberate. "I'm all right."

Veron chanced a look at his father. William's strong and confident face didn't hold any doubt or fear, and the lack of a cloak didn't seem to bother him. A tear formed in Veron's eye. "You shouldn't have taken off the cloak, Father."

William returned a reassuring smile and rested a hand on his shoulder. "This was always how it had to be, Veron. I wasn't there for you through most of your life, but I can be here for you now."

Tears fell down Veron's cheeks, but he wiped them away. He sniffed and nodded. "Thank you."

A slow clapping turned their attention upward. Looking down from the bridge, Bale applauded with his hands raised. "Impressive!" he boomed. "But I expect no less from two shadow knights. Or should I say . . . one-and-a-half?"

William bounced on his good leg, adjusting his stance while keeping a hand resting against Veron for support.

"You've come so far—all the way from Feldor. But I'm sorry to tell you there is nothing but disappointment for you here. Now, you must die."

Veron's muscles tightened as the soldiers drew closer. He clenched his hands around Farrathan's hilt. William pushed off to put space between them, balancing on one leg as he limped a few steps away, leaning on his staff. For a moment, the soldiers paused as if waiting for another to move. Most held swords, and several carried strings of chains or thin metal strands they twirled slowly in the air.

Kill them!" Bale shrieked. With a sudden roar, the men in front charged.

The roar faded in Veron's brain, and his body responded. His sword sang as it sliced through the air, faster than any could hope to avoid. His brutally efficient arms and legs broke limbs and flung bodies. A metal breastplate cracked under his pounding boot. A flying soldier knocked several behind him to the ground before crashing into a stone pillar. Swords came at him from all directions, but he ducked and twirled out of their reach. Chains slung toward him, but Veron slashed them away, preventing them from wrapping around any part of his body. The metal links rattled as they fell in heaps.

His own blade found the cracks between the men's armor, the feel of his blade piercing flesh and drawing blood. Their cries blew away on the wind while others took their positions. The origine trickled through his body as Veron used only what he needed. Sweat dripped down his face, the salty residue touching his lips while the tang of blood filled the air. Splatters of red littered the snow where the Norshewan soldiers stumbled away, providing space for reinforcements.

William held his own. He moved slower than Veron but used his sword and staff well. Relying more heavily on his blade than movement, fallen men piled high. Others had to climb over bodies to get to him. Despite the missing limb, William remained upright.

Brandishing his sword with a yell, Veron stared down the soldiers, keeping them at bay while he rested. His chest heaved, the exhaustion telling him to sit and recover. He spun, keeping his blade up, his body soaking in every breath it received.

A shout turned his attention to William. His father clutched his side where a blade tore a gash, the soldier responsible already falling to the ground. William stumbled, leaning over with his sword hand resting on his knee while keeping himself upright with the staff. While he panted, another soldier lunged, the blade piercing William again in the side. A penetrating cry from his father rang in the air.

"No!" Veron yelled, pulling again from his well of energy.

The soldiers closing on his father froze while Veron jumped into their midst, moving swifter than they could process. He struck them down one after another, pressing the ring of men back. A woosh of air caught his attention. With a sickening feeling, he turned to follow the sound, and his heart dropped. His father teetered on one good leg, leaning on a staff. A spear stuck through his chest, over his heart, the point sticking out the back. William's eyes rolled in their sockets as he fell to the ground.

"Father!" Veron yelled. He yanked out the spear and scooped him up with his free arm, tossing William over his shoulder. His father groaned. The soldiers surged forward, but Veron leaped. He cleared the unsuspecting men below and landed outside of their formation. Summoning his strength for another jump, Veron targeted a lone balcony peering over the courtyard. He landed hard on the elevated ledge, dropping William, giving in to exhaustion and collapsing to the floor.

After sucking in several deep breaths, he rolled to his knees. "Father?"

William looked back, eyes pained. He tried to speak but only sputtered blood. Underneath his body, a red pool formed on the balcony floor.

"Heal! Use your energy. You can do this!" Veron insisted.

He pulled up his father's shirt. One cut in his side had healed into a tight scab while the other still trickled blood. His chest wound was another matter. A dark red puncture glistened in the moonlight. Blood ran down his bare chest, surging with his heartbeat.

"Father! You need to close your wounds!" Tears dripped down Veron's face.

William shook his head. "I don't have anything left. I can't heal any more." His weak voice scratched. "It was always meant to be this way, Veron. I needed to be the one . . . for you."

"Father, no!" Veron grabbed his father's hand and gripped hard. "The Dream doesn't have to be true! Neither of us have to die!"

A weak smile played across William's face. "It's all right, Son. You were made for this. Kill Bale, rescue Chelci, and embrace your destiny."

"Veron Stormbridge!" a voice boomed from the courtyard, causing Veron to flinch.

He straightened and peered over the balcony's edge. The bulk of Bale's force remained ready to fight, while Bale called from the back.

"Come down here and fight!"

"Veron." William's hand squeezed his with fading strength, and Veron turned back to his father. "I wish I could have been there from the beginning. I should have come for you immediately. I should have never left. Can you forgive me?" His words cracked with emotion.

"Of course." Veron sniffed and wiped at his face. "I forgive you, Father."

A peaceful look settled on William's face. "I love you, Son."

Veron's teeth clenched to keep from weeping, but tears still flowed. His chin wavered as he squeezed his hand. "I love you, too."

William's eyes closed. His chest fell as one last breath whispered from his lips. His hand grew limp, but Veron held on. His tears had run dry. His father made the ultimate sacrifice so he could live.

The origine's power simmered inside of Chelci. Her ears hummed and mind sharpened. The pain faded. Her eyes bored into the door, the obstacle keeping her from Veron. She crossed the room and tried the handle. It didn't budge.

She closed her eyes and took a deep breath. With one foot pressed against the wall, she grabbed the handle with both hands. Her body begged her to act—to use the energy. She pulled at the origine, willing it to flood her body. Her mind exploded. Every detail of the cell came into sharp focus, and her arms felt as hard as stones. She pulled on the handle. The door groaned, but nothing budged. She pulled harder. The groan turned into a creak, and the metal handle vibrated.

The edge of the massive door bowed, the creaking intensifying. She pushed against the wall with a foot, yelling as she pulled even more energy. Her arms shook. Snapping sounds filled the cell as the door shuddered. With a massive crash, the cell door exploded out of its frame. The metal edge rippled, and the hinges shattered.

Chelci fell to the ground, the heap of a door toppling toward her. *Oh no!* The metal nearly crushed her into the stone floor. She pulled from the origine again, and the door slowed, almost freezing in mid-air. She rolled away and released her energy, the massive object crushing the stone floor she had just left. Chelci laughed. *I can't believe it!*

Her smile faded as exhaustion took over. Her lungs seemed to empty of oxygen at once, and her arms and legs felt like lead. She tried to inhale, but could only bring in short, ragged gulps of air. She closed her eyes.

"Wh—What was th—that?" a quavering voice uttered.

Her eyes popped open. The two guards stood in the gaping doorway, holding trembling swords. She took a long moment to gather herself to her feet.

"Stay back!" a guard said, his sword lifting higher.

Chelci sighed. She closed her eyes and extended her arms. The tingling returned, fainter than before, but ready to be used.

The guards looked like statues as she moved toward them, brimming with power. She kicked the swords from their hands, but they didn't even budge. Defenseless and still frozen, Chelci kicked each in the chest, their bodies ramming against the wall and heads slamming into the stones.

Is that enough? She released the origine, and their bodies crumpled, breathing but knocked out. "I guess it's enough," she said out loud.

Exhaustion swept over her, stronger that time. She rested her hands on her knees and leaned against the wall. *I need to conserve my power!* Deep breaths filled her lungs. Her arms and legs shook. She glanced down the stairs. *Where's Veron?* With hands on both walls, she descended the steps, taking care not to trip on her weakened legs. She arrived at the bottom, and the bridge loomed before her. Snow fell in a slanted fashion, and the wind howled. The bridge was empty.

Chelci stumbled outside. She gripped the railing, her velvet dress billowing in the wind. In the courtyard below, a mass of soldiers surrounded two men. One pivoted on one leg, and the other wore a familiar black cloak. Her heart soared. *Veron!* The excitement waned as she took in the scene. The array of Norshewans surrounding them seemed endless.

"Veron!" The weakly shouted name vanished in the wind. "Veron!" *He can't hear me. I need to get down there.* She turned her attention back to the bridge. Gripping the rail, she stumbled across the span. Her sight twirled before her, threatening to send her over the edge. Her legs felt like blocks. Almost to the end of the bridge, she gasped, stopping short. A soldier before her narrowed his eyes as he pulled his sword with one hand and held onto a bottle with the other.

"Cyrus," she muttered.

"Who let you out of your cell?" the captain growled, his words slurring. The wind's whistle was the only response. The captain walked forward with slow, deliberate steps. "What happened to your guards?"

Chelci tried to suck in air, but her weakness and the shock of finding the captain were too much. She leaned against the side of the bridge to keep from falling. *I only need enough to fight one more. I can do this!* She searched inside but couldn't find the origine's warm presence. Cyrus held the tip of his sword up as he approached. *Why didn't I take those guards' swords?*

She strained, wincing to summon what energy she could, but

nothing changed. *I need time!* Standing as erect as she could, she lifted her chin and met his eyes. "Why aren't you down there with the rest?" she asked.

Cyrus glanced over the side of the bridge and shrugged. "I wanted to come and check on you. I didn't want you lonely in that tower." A smirk covered his face before he hiccupped. He stepped closer.

"If you like . . ." Chelci's fast words and raised hand stopped his movement. She softened her face, forcing a playful smile. "We can go back to the tower. But first, I have a question for you."

The captain raised an eyebrow and relaxed his stance. He took a swig from his bottle, draining its remains. "What?"

I have no idea. "What was . . ." *What might get him talking that will buy me time?* ". . . your life like when you were little?"

His casual look hardened. ". . . when I was little? What is this?" He glanced around. "Are you . . . stalling?" He tossed the empty bottle to the stones, shattering the glass. Chelci flinched. He raised the sword and approached again.

Chelci scrambled backward until her feet skidded on an icy patch. She fell backward, hitting the hard bridge on her rear. The sudden motion sent a wave of dizziness through her. She tried to gather herself, but Cyrus was there. His face twisted as his sword extended toward her. The tight scar across his cheek flinched. "Maybe I should just kill you now and be done with it?" His lip snarled and body tensed.

Chelci strained for the origine, but nothing answered her call. She lay against the cold stone but had nowhere to go. *I tried, Veron. I'm sorry I couldn't get to you!*

"Cyrus! Leave her alone!"

Cyrus spun as Chelci leaned around his body. Her eyes grew at the sight of the blond-haired young man who shouted from the end of the bridge. "Brixton," she breathed.

"What do you want, Commercial Envoy?" the captain spat.

"I want you to leave her alone."

"Why? Because you *like* her. Ha! Go back to your room, Feldorian." Cyrus turned around, the snarl returning to his face.

"I won't leave." Brixton's voice carried an edge.

Cyrus turned again, but more slowly. "What do you intend to do?"

Brixton pulled a sword from his sheath. "If I have to, I'll make you leave her alone."

Cyrus bellowed in laughter. "Please. You insult me."

Brixton stepped forward, his sword held high, and his body nearly touching each side of the bridge. With a swift movement of his hand, he ripped the Norshewan badge from his shoulder and flung it to the ground.

"You're serious?"

Brixton's intense stare served as an answer.

Cyrus sighed. "If Bale gets upset at me for your death, it's going to be your fault."

Chelci's eyes jumped between her two enemies. The thought of cheering for Brixton turned her stomach.

Brixton moved first, stepping in and swinging for the captain. Cyrus parried the blow and countered, forcing Brixton to jump back.

"You *are* serious," Cyrus said, his laughter gone. The two stared silently.

With a sudden flurry of movement, both men attacked. Their blades clashed in a frenzy of steel. They danced forward and backward, limited by the line of the bridge. The captain swung hard, groaning as he heaved his blade, but Brixton was fast, ducking and deflecting to keep from being hit.

With a cry of triumph, Cyrus pinned Brixton's blade against the side of the bridge. He pushed against the younger man, forcing his torso to lean precariously over the side. "Give it up, Fiero! You're no match against me!"

Brixton brought up a knee and jammed it into the captain's side. Cyrus groaned and stepped back, freeing both swords. Brixton ran at him with a yell. His sword danced side to side, forcing the captain to backpedal. Brixton's hardened face revealed a long-pent-up fury. Cyrus nearly backed into Chelci when a thin blade emerged out from his back.

The captain's body stiffened and hunched forward. His head looked down then back up to Brixton's face. No cry uttered from him, only a faint gurgling sound.

The blade disappeared back through his body, and the soldier collapsed in a heap. Chelci gasped as Brixton stood alone.

"Are you all right?" he asked, sheathing his weapon and extending a hand.

Chelci shrank back as if the hand were poison. Her hand scrambled over the fallen body next to her until she found the hilt of Cyrus' sword. She held it up with the little strength she had.

"I'm not here to hurt you."

She exhaled, staring into his eyes. After a beat, she allowed him to take her free hand. With great effort, she stood, touching the bridge for support. "What are you doing, Brixton? You . . . killed him."

He looked at the body and the blood running across the packed snow. "I've had enough."

Chelci's eyebrow raised. "Enough of what?"

"Of him. Of Bale. Of Norshewa." He swallowed. "Of who I've become."

His eyes carried a haunted look. *Is that regret?*

"They killed that girl—Chantel—for no reason. They stole her from her home and used her for years. They could have just let her leave. Bale is an awful man, and I can't follow him a moment longer."

"What are you going to do now?"

Brixton sighed. "I want to help however I can."

Chelci narrowed her eyes. "I don't trust you."

Brixton nodded, looking down. "Fair enough. I've earned that. I've done so much that I can never undo—to you . . . to Veron . . . to my country—but I want to try. Even if I'm executed for treason, I have to do what's right."

Her jaw clenched as she stared at him. *He's deceived me before . . .* She turned to the courtyard and nodded. "Well, if you want to help, now's your chance."

Veron and William were no longer in sight, but the Norshewan soldiers stared at something around the corner.

"Veron's here?" he asked.

Chelci nodded. "And he could use your help."

He rested his hand on the hilt of his sword and gave a tight nod. "Let's go." Brixton turned and hurried toward the far end of the bridge.

Chelci remained frozen, hesitant to move her feet. After a few steps, Brixton turned back. "Everything okay?" With a start, he tilted his head. "How'd you get out here, by the way?"

Chelci chuckled. "I, uh . . . I kind of learned the Shadow Knights' power." Brixton's eyes widened. "But I used too much energy breaking out of my cell and knocking out the guards."

"That's amazing!"

"I'm too weak now. I need time to recover."

"How long?"

She shook her head. "I don't know."

Brixton returned. He approached her with slow steps until he stood next to her. "Do you mind if I, um . . ." He moved his arm around her back but hadn't touched her yet.

"That's fine. Thanks."

His supporting arm helped her stand without the railing. The dizziness seemed to be gone, and her legs felt stronger. "I can feel it's already getting better. I just need more time."

He led her across the bridge. Chelci looked over her shoulder before they entered the building. The soldiers remained gathered below, ready to fight, but there was still no sign of Veron. *I'm coming, Veron. Hold on.*

42

Reinforcements

The stone wall rubbed against his back as Veron shivered from the cold. His father was gone, but he used the moment to rest and allow his energy to recover.

"Are you a coward?" Bale taunted from below. "Will you come and face your destiny? Or would you rather we come up there? Maybe pick up Chelci along the way?"

Veron's breath caught. "Leave her out of this," he whispered to himself, clenching his jaw.

Veron crouched next to his father's body. He rested his hand on William's arm, the skin already growing cold. "Goodbye, Father." After a quick squeeze, Veron rose and jumped down from the balcony, landing with a solid thud in the courtyard.

The soldiers tensed, raising their weapons. Veron breathed evenly, energy surging within.

"Kill him, now!" Bale's face twisted in fury as the mass of soldiers moved.

Veron didn't rise to the anger, accepting whatever was to come as anger and desperation seethed off the king. The men arrived, but Veron barely noticed. Warm tingling filled his gut. His sword arced and body spun. His limbs oozed power while he slayed man after man. He didn't think about breathing. He felt one with his sword, purposeful in his destiny. The Norshewans fell, but not quickly enough.

There are too many. The thought didn't contain fear—only acceptance. *My energy will deplete soon, and I won't be able to get to Bale.* The king paced behind his men, but Veron continued fighting, worried that every swing of his blade would be his last.

After knocking a group back, Veron released the origine to take a quick break. He gulped in deep breaths to recover as quickly as possible. The remaining mass of Bale's guards rushed toward him without missing a beat. *I need more time!*

Using as little energy as possible, Veron swung into action, striking down soldiers and dodging their attacks. The barrier of men between him and Bale grew thin. Hope flooded through him as he pictured opening the door to the tower to rescue Chelci.

Lost in his thoughts, a weight wrapped around his leg. The speed of his thoughts and power in his body faded as the surrounding soldiers sped up. Veron looked down. A link of chain wrapped around his calf from where a soldier had thrown them. He scrambled to disentangle himself. The links fell from his leg the same moment a metallic click sounded from his other ankle. Sweat dotted his forehead. *No!*

A man had crept up and clasped an anklet around his other leg while he was impaired. The memory of his time as a slave flooded his mind. His head spun. Thoughts came slowly. He pivoted, keeping his sword raised, but the Norshewans surrounded him. Bale's black hair towered behind them. His eyes held a patient fury while his mouth smirked at the change of events.

"What will you do now, Shadow Knight?" Bale shouted.

Veron's breath grew ragged as his exhaustion caught up. He struggled to even keep his sword raised. With men on all sides, he spun while grabbing at the metal clamp with his free hand. The icy band gripped his skin tight. He slid a finger between it and his body but couldn't break the lock. He groaned as he pulled, to no avail. The lunging men forced his eyes to stay up, focused on them.

"The Dream proves I will kill you, Bale. You can do whatever you like to me, but it will happen in the end."

The soldiers paused. Bale chuckled as he walked closer, through his wall of men. "Dreams don't always come true."

Veron's chest rose and fell in heaving breaths. Face-to-face, he stared Bale down. "Yeah? Then why are you terrified?"

Bale's eyes narrowed. "You had your father to save you before. Who's going to rescue you now?"

A crash sounded to the side as two of Bale's men flew through the air. Others knocked down as a blur sped between them to stand beside Veron. When the figure stopped, Veron's jaw hung agape. Chelci Marlow crouched next to him in a flowery jade dress, holding a sword and baring her teeth at Bale. Her fierce look forced the closest soldiers to step back.

"I will rescue him," she said, her quiet, menacing tone piercing through the courtyard's sudden silence.

A grin covered Veron's face, his mind reeling.

"As will I," a second voice announced as another figure jogged to catch up.

It took a moment for Veron to recognize the black-clad young man, but when he stopped next to Chelci, baring his own sword, the blond hair gave him away. "Brixton?"

Chelci and Brixton stood next to him, stalwart and focused. Shaking away his conflicted feelings for his old friend, Veron summoned his remaining strength and straightened, holding his sword out. He locked eyes with Bale. The king's sharp jaw clenched, and his chest rose and fell rapidly.

A grin came to Veron's face. "You still so sure about that Dream, Bale?"

The sea of soldiers mobilized, spreading out around the three.

"Chelci! You found the origine?" Veron whispered, keeping his sword up and eyes focused on the soldiers.

"Yeah, it's incredible!"

A lone soldier lunged at Veron's side. He knocked the strike away, sending the man scuttling back to the others. Chelci, Brixton, and Veron moved into a triangle formation, their backs to each other, facing out.

"Rest every moment you can, and when you act, only use a small amount," Veron said.

"I'll try."

Veron's mood soured as he bumped shoulders with the young man on his other side. "Brixton, what are you doing here?"

His old friend feigned a lunge at an encroaching soldier, creating more space. "Making amends," he replied.

"He claims he's finished helping Bale," Chelci whispered.

"Yeah, we'll see," Veron said. "Any chance either of you can help with these anklets?"

"Let me," Chelci said quickly, dropping to the ground at his feet.

Veron kept his sword up, pivoting with only Brixton at his back while Chelci tugged at his leg.

Bale's booming voice filled the courtyard, "And this is how you repay me, Fiero?" Veron looked to the side where the king stood just behind his men.

Brixton's feet scraped on the stones of the courtyard. "I'm through, Bale!"

"Through? Ha! You can't be through!"

"I'm done with your lust for a legacy. The cost is too great!"

"There is always a cost to achieve greatness."

"You throw away people like garbage! They only exist to serve your needs, then you toss them aside."

Bale roared with laughter. "Tell me you're so different, Brixton Fiero. You, who turned on your country and betrayed your friend. You even killed your own father in order to rise in power. Don't lecture me on tossing people aside."

"Like I said, I'm finished," Brixton said.

"I'm sorry, Veron. I can't get it," Chelci whispered, standing again.

His heart sank, the fatigue intensifying. "That's all right. I can still fight."

"It's a pity, Brixton," Bale shouted. "You could have been by my side and had it all. Now I must kill all three of you."

For a moment, no one spoke. The wind whistled. Veron stood in dragon stance with his cloak fluttering around his feet. His body felt sluggish. *At least I know my way around a blade.*

As if deciding in unison, the Norshewan soldiers advanced.

Chelci moved first. To his side, Veron caught the blurred image of her rapid movement. Three soldiers fell by her sword in the blink of an eye.

"Take it easy, Chelci!" he shouted.

Brixton engaged on his other side, crossing blades with two soldiers coming at him.

A soldier moved at Veron, drawing his attention back. He brought down Farrathan, stepping forward and crashing into the man's blade. The sword glanced to the side, and Veron elbowed the man's face, his nose crunching. Veron ducked under the next attacker's blade and stabbed into his gut. The soldier keeled over and fell to the ground.

Come on, origine. I need you!

Veron pulled from within. Despite the metal band, the power was there. He strained and fought to use it, and it was just enough to help. Moving faster than the men expected, he knocked back blades and struck down soldiers as they continued charging.

"Argh!" Veron cried out. He spun where a man nicked him in the side, the sword slicing just above his hip. He staggered as Brixton's blade entered the soldier's neck, dropping him to the ground.

"I'm sorry, Veron. I missed him," Brixton said, his eyes wide.

Veron grimaced. Pain shot through his body. The faint trace of origine he summoned begged to direct itself to the wound.

No! Let it bleed! Don't use the energy!

He held the wound with his free hand, keeping all his energy to fight. Blood dripped through his fingers. He pressed harder, ignoring the agony.

Chelci was a sight to see. Having slowed her speed down, she almost appeared as a regular fighter, but was always one step ahead of the Norshewans. They frantically attacked, but their blades hit nothing but air. The soldiers fell one by one, piling around her. The hem of her dress danced, decorated with splatters of blood.

"Careful, Chelci!" Veron shouted after running a man through the chest with his weapon. "Make it last!"

After the last man fell before him, Veron spun. Brixton had just struck down a soldier and turned to him. His old friend's pile of bodies was smaller but still impressive. Veron nodded to thank him. They both turned to Chelci. Moving again in a blur, she sliced a man's sword in half before her blade cut into his side, uttering a ferocious roar as she did. Four soldiers remained, but when Veron, Brixton, and Chelci faced them, they turned and ran.

"Where are you going? Cowards!" Bale shouted.

Chelci's blur solidified, and she moved to Veron's side, resting a hand on her upper leg. Her chest rolled with heavy breaths.

"How's your level?" Veron whispered.

The strained look and tight shake of her head was a sufficient answer. *She's nearly empty!*

"That was impressive," Bale said casually. He kicked a lifeless body to the side, allowing him to approach. One of his fallen men reached out a trembling arm and groaned. Without a change of expression, Bale stabbed him in the neck, the soldier's body falling limp.

The trio stepped backward as the massive king neared. An enigmatic smile covered his face. Veron's stomach turned. *We killed almost two hundred men*, Veron thought. *Why am I nervous about one more?*

"Chelci, I see you've escaped your tower and that you *were* lying about the origine," Bale said.

She stared back with tight lips, her neck straining as her quick breath fogged the air.

"Or did your reading of that book finally pay off?" Bale's mouth tweaked in a smirk.

Why does he look so confident?

Bale's eyebrow raised. "You're not the only one who can learn from a book."

The words hit Veron like a club, knocking his breath away. *No! He couldn't have!*

"What do you mean?" Brixton asked. "What does—"

The air shimmered as Bale's form blurred. Brixton's words gurgled as the king's obscured body stabbed him through the stomach before darting back out of reach.

"No!" Veron yelled. His face twisted and mind scrambled, unsure of what he should feel.

Brixton fell next to him, clutching his stomach. Holding his sword toward Bale, tense and ready, Veron glanced down. His friend and betrayer lay against the bloody stones, staring back at him. "I'm sorry, Veron," he sputtered, "for everything."

Veron swallowed hard as a tear built.

A deep chuckle grew from Bale. "You can't use the energy, your father is gone, and your girl is exhausted."

Veron glanced at Chelci. Her shoulders hunched as she rested an arm on her knee. After Bale's taunt, she straightened, lifting her chin and readying her sword. "I'm not tired," her defiant words echoed back.

Bale's smirk remained. "Meanwhile, I am brimming with power." His mouth curled into a snarl as he stepped behind a pillar next to him. After a push, the colossal stone structure tipped, falling toward Veron.

He scooped up Brixton and jumped in the opposite direction of Chelci. The pillar slammed to the ground with a mighty boom, shaking the stones beneath his feet. Dust filled the air as the column crumbled. Brixton groaned when Veron set him down. "Lay here, Brixton. We can patch that up once we're done with him."

"This is incredible," Bale said, looking at his own arms as he raised them and flexed. "I'm invincible!"

Veron made eyes with Chelci as they both walked closer, the crumbled pillar between them. She still panted, but her posture looked stronger.

Bale grabbed a battle-axe from a dead soldier's hand, the metal scraping as it dragged along the stone. He hefted it to his shoulder.

Veron jogged, moving closer as Chelci followed suit. Straining to reach the origine deep inside, he jumped atop the pillar and ran along its crumbled length, racing toward Bale. Chelci sped on the ground, leaping into the sky as she neared the king. When the pillar ran out, Veron jumped, his sword cocked, ready to strike. Bale crouched on the ground with sword and axe in hand as Veron and Chelci flew.

43

The Final Battle

Bale exploded as they collided, blocking both attacks with his weapons before spinning out of the way. Veron hit the ground hard, barely able to strengthen his legs enough to absorb the blow. The wound in his side throbbed, but he pushed it from his mind.

Chelci moved like lightning, but Bale responded like thunder. His immense axe would cut through anything, but she avoided each swing. A blow from his elbow landed on her chest, sending her flying and crashing into the broken column.

Bale turned to Veron, lunging with his sword nearly faster than he could see. He managed just enough energy to dodge, rolling away, but the strain was incredible. Veron tried to attack, but Bale parried the weapon away, chuckling.

"You'll have to do better than that," the king taunted.

Veron fixed his jaw as he moved in a circular motion, sword at head height, poised in dragon stance. Chelci had collected herself and circled opposite him while Bale pivoted between the two, never losing his haughty smile. Veron's cloak swayed beneath him in time to his steps. The Shadow Knights medallion bounced against his chest. *This is my destiny. I know I will beat him. I'm destined to live and—*

His thoughts jarred, and he nearly stumbled. He shot a look to the balcony where his father's body lay.

From the village of Stonl, Jeanette's memory of the Dream came to his mind. *"Two shadow knights fought with Bale, circling each other."*

Veron couldn't breathe. He looked past Bale where Chelci circled, baring her sword. Her dress moved with her. *A dress . . . not a Shadow Knights cloak. William died, but that wasn't even part of the Dream. Chelci's the one!*

"No!" Veron cried, turning both heads his way.

Chelci seized the opportunity to fly at Bale, but the king was ready. He spun and stabbed, glancing across Chelci's shoulder.

"Argh!" Chelci yelled, dropping her own sword as she stumbled away, falling to her knees.

Veron tried to run for her, but Bale appeared between them, stopping him in his tracks.

"Worried about your girl, Veron?" Bale taunted. He stepped forward, forcing Veron to walk backward. Bale's chest rose and fell as his lungs heaved.

The metal brace on Veron's leg clanked as it hit a chunk of the stone pillar. His back stopped against it, the still-bleeding wound in his side screaming. His shoulders fell. *I don't think I can kill him like this.*

The king halted just over a body length away. Veron held his sword up, his jaw tight, straining to summon any origine. Bale grinned, wielding his sword and axe.

A groaning sound reached him. "Chelci, are you all right?" Veron asked, not taking his eyes off the king.

"It's not deep," she called back. "And it's healing."

Veron's stomach turned. "No!" he yelled. "Don't heal it! Let it bleed." Bale's eyes narrowed, and his head cocked.

"It's fine," Chelci called. "It's all better now, and . . . Whoa!"

Bale spun. Veron leaned around him. Chelci tried to lift herself to her feet, but her arm waved. Her wobbling legs seemed to collapse, and she fell to the ground.

"Veron, I can't move!" she shouted.

Jeanette's words returned. *"One became injured, and the other had to fight alone."*

Bale turned back to Veron with a wicked grin. "This may be a good time to finish her." He turned toward Chelci.

Veron's heart pounded. He'd long ago made peace with his own death. He shook his head. *Anything but her.* With labored breath and weak arms, he ran after Bale, swinging his sword at the man's back, his mortal attempt knocked away by a flick of Bale's sword and a kick to the gut. Veron fell to the ground, what little breath he had knocked away. "Leave her alone!" Veron choked on the words, leaning over his knees. "Kill me but let her live!" Tears fell from his cheeks.

Bale laughed and continued forward.

"She deserves to live," Veron whispered, salty drops falling on his hand as he bowed his head. He couldn't watch.

A tingling in his body caused his hair to stand on end. His eyes grew. His breath was even. It came to him with instant clarity, almost knocking him over. *The origine! It's here!* He should have been at empty. The metal brace should shield him, but the energy flowed, strong as ever. Tingling filled his entire body from his fingers to his toes.

A pure connection renders the mind and body with nearly unlimited capacity. The book's words filled his mind.

Veron pulled at the origine. It flooded his body as if he'd rested for hours. His arms flexed, muscles hard as stones. A broad grin covered his face. Bringing his leg up, Veron grasped the anklet with one hand and pulled it off as if it were made of paper.

The wind died just before the metal cuff clanked across the stone courtyard. Bale stopped a few steps from Chelci. He spun toward the noise, his jaw tight.

"You underestimated what it means to be a shadow knight, Bale," Veron said, advancing closer while Bale's eyes grew. "It's not about power. It's about purpose. The origine is only a tool, but what we do with that tool defines our legacy."

"Legacy, bah! You can't even imagine what I'm capable of." Bale's face didn't match his confident words.

"No, Bale, it's you who underestimated my capabilities."

The king blanched. His mouth opened, but no words came out.

Veron darted between Chelci and Bale, his raised sword making the king jump back a safe distance from her nearly lifeless body. Bale alternated his weapons, but Veron was far too fast. He dodged the king's slow-moving attacks. None even came close. Veron pulled more energy than before, but his well felt fuller than ever. Bale desperately struck out with his sword, but Farrathan cleaved it into pieces. Bale roared, his eyes wild as he scrambled toward the crumbled pillar.

"It's no use, Bale. You can't defeat me."

The king's hair fell crooked across his face, plastered with sweat. His chest heaved as he gulped in breaths. His eyes flicked to a section of pillar that came to his hips. A smirk grew on his face. "One of you still needs to die."

Veron cringed.

Bale bent over and put his arms around the sizable chunk of broken stone.

Surely he doesn't expect to—

In a surge of motion, Bale lifted the stone and heaved it through the air. Veron thought it a joke until he noticed the boulder's trajectory. *Chelci!*

Using all the energy he could muster, Veron darted to her, arriving just before the crumbling piece of rock. He braced his legs and leaned forward, desperate to stop the massive object. When it hit, the force nearly knocked him off his feet. He kept one foot down as he pushed against the hurtling piece of stone. He moved its bulk away from Chelci, but the awkward motion left him without purchase. Veron's stomach dropped as he hit the ground, the boulder crushing his leg moments later.

His scream echoed from all sides of the courtyard. The searing pain chased away any origine. He pushed against the rock, but it didn't budge. He huffed, breathing in rapid bursts as he propped on his elbows. The fiery pain faded as he lost feeling in his leg. Farrathan lay pinned beneath the stone. He pulled at the hilt, but it wouldn't move. Veron reached inside to find the origine but could only manage a trickle. The stone still wouldn't budge.

Chelci lay a body length away. She stared at him with pained eyes as she strained to move, but she only managed to flop an arm across her body before her head fell back.

Bale strolled up, standing between Chelci and him. "Well, well, look how things can change." His battle axe rested against his shoulder. He still panted, but his confidence had grown. "The powerful shadow knights reduced to a pile of weaklings."

Veron scrambled for energy. His eyes grew as Bale stared at him, raising the axe with both hands.

Movement caught his eye behind Bale. A staggering Brixton held his stomach with one hand and a limp sword in the other. His steps were quiet as he crept up to the king. When he reached striking distance, both hands gripped his sword, and his body tensed.

Come on, Brixton. You can do it!

Bale's eyes flicked.

No!

Bale spun, catching Brixton's weak attempt at a killing blow with the edge of the axe. "Brixton, I thought I finished you," he growled. He pushed the sword away and unleashed a swift kick to his sternum. Brixton flew through the air and landed against the remains of the stone pillar, his head thumping against the column and falling limp.

Veron cringed. He pushed against the ground, trying desperately to move.

Bale turned back to him. "Enough of this! Now, you die!" Rage filled his eyes as he lifted the axe again. His arm muscles rippled. His chest expanded as he inhaled to prepare for the killing blow.

Is this where I die?

Veron's arm hit a lump at his hip. *The knife!*

Bale lifted on his toes, the axe above his head poised and ready to strike.

Veron pulled any trace of the origine he could find and slid Bale's knife from its sheath. The king seemed to freeze in time as Veron cocked his arm back. He adjusted his aim, zeroing in on the soft target, and flung the silver weapon.

A faint swish filled the air as the knife flew. Spinning once, the blade found its mark, settling into the king's exposed neck, burying itself to the hilt.

Bale staggered from the impact. His eyes rolled and blood trickled down his neck.

A smile erupted on Veron's face. "Yes!"

Life drained from Bale's body in a flash. Veron froze, his arms in mid-air, when his heart dropped. Bale's lifeless hands released their grip on the handle. The king fell, but so did the massive axe blade hovering over Chelci.

"No!" His scream rang through the night, but it didn't stop the blade from falling. Veron strained with all his might to pull his leg free, but it wouldn't move. In the split-second before his world ended, he looked at Chelci, processing everything in an instant. Her eyes locked with his, the softness showing a peace unlike anything inside him.

When the blade entered her stomach, he screamed again. "Chelci!" The axe buried deep, blood rushing down the side of her dress. Her body lurched, but she didn't even cry out.

Tears sprung from Veron's eyes as he wailed. He thrashed his arms and tried to move his feet, but they remained pinned. His guttural roar echoed through the courtyard.

Sucking in quick breaths, he forced himself to calm. He held out his hands and closed his eyes. When his breath slowed, the warm tingle of the origine returned. Summoning what he could, he pushed with everything he had. The massive boulder rolled to the side, off his legs, booming as it fell away. His numb, crushed legs refused to work. He pulled himself along the ground, pushing aside Bale's lifeless body to get to her.

"Chelci?" he whispered.

Her eyes blinked and hand twitched. "Veron," her raspy voice replied.

Veron scrambled, pulling closer. "You're still alive! You need to heal! Here, let me . . ." He turned to the axe, bracing an arm against the ground. "This might hurt."

"Veron, no just leave—"

Veron yanked the weapon out of her stomach, eliciting a moan. He looked at her, eyebrows raised. "Use everything you have, Chelci. The origine can heal you."

Her head wobbled. "I don't feel anything, Veron. There's no pain, but there's no origine left."

"There has to be," Veron said, his voice strained. He grabbed her hand and squeezed. "Find anything you can. The wound isn't that bad. You can—" He choked up after his eyes drifted to the wound. Dark red filled the wound's cavity. Blood poured over the side of her body and pooled beneath her. Tears sprung anew. "You can still recover. You can stop the bleeding." His words quivered.

Chelci's eyes closed, pinching tight. The tendons in her neck strained until she sighed and opened her eyes again. Her head shook. "It's no use, Veron."

"Chelci . . ." Tears poured. Veron grabbed both of her hands, holding them over her chest. "It can't be this way. You can't be the one."

"Veron, it's okay." She weakly smiled. "You did it. You stopped Bale. Now, you can help make things right again."

"But I don't want to do it without you. I was—" Veron stopped. He squinted to fight back the tears. "I was going to ask you to marry me."

Chelci managed a weak smile before drops sprung from her eyes. "I was going to say yes."

Veron's chin quivered. He managed a feeble smile in response. "I love you, Chelci."

"I love you, too, Veron."

They squeezed hands. Veron's sight blurred. He blinked to clear it. Her weak breath fogged the air. Letting go with one hand, he brushed the side of her face, wiping away a tear. Her skin already felt cold. The only person he'd ever truly loved—the one who seemed made for him—took her last breaths. Veron leaned forward and touched his lips to hers. He was gentle, but she pressed back into him, her lips sweet and tender. Tears fell down his cheeks when he pulled away.

"Chelci?" he started. "I'm sorry that I—" He looked at her eyes, and his words caught. She stared past him, unblinking and lifeless. No fog came from her breath. Her chest no longer rose. "Chelci?" His voice trembled as he shook her arm. Nothing.

Tears sprang again. Veron hung his head, wracking sobs filling his body. He wailed, gripping her limp hands. He glanced desperately toward the balcony, hoping his father would somehow leap down and come to him. The wind was all that stirred.

Veron turned back to Chelci and pulled her eyelids shut. Staring at her lifeless body, he wiped his eyes and sniffed. He spoke as if his father were with him. "I thought somehow the Dream would be wrong. I even found the pure connection. So much power flowed through me, but what did it get me?" Veron pounded the ground with a fist. "Nothing! I don't care about being a shadow knight or Bale. I only care for her!"

Veron's legs tingled. Momentary pain soothed, allowing him to move his toes and bend his knees. The hole in his side was next. Having stopped the healing while he fought, blood covered his side. He inhaled while scabs prickled. His entire body felt full of power, but his sorrow remained.

I have more than enough power. He turned to Chelci. *But I'm not the one who needs it.*

Veron raised on his knees and leaned over Chelci. Her face was pale, her hands across her chest in a peaceful pose. *She was the perfect person—selfless in all she did, brave in the face of danger, and wise when all others were foolish. She deserves to live.*

He took a deep breath and exhaled. "Chelci," he said in a slow and deliberate voice. "You can heal."

An imagined voice in his head told him to give it up, but he pushed it away.

"Come on, you can do this."

Veron placed his hands over the gash in her stomach, pushing into the sticky blood. His breath was steady as he closed his eyes.

"Chelci, you were made to live, and you have more to do."

Veron cleared his mind and thought of the only thing that seemed to matter. *Chelci needs to live.* The origine swelled inside of him. His entire body tingled, his hair standing on end. His hands trembled, but he held them firm.

Like a raging torrent, the origine burst from him. His mind exploded with clarity. Veron's eyes popped open, greeted by a blinding light. He squinted. Power flowed through his hands, causing Chelci's skin to glow, warming beneath his touch. A faint crackle filled the air, and a tickling sensation feathered his palms. *It's healing!* Veron pressed in harder. His arms shook. The tension grew in him until the pressure escaped his throat with a yell.

As suddenly as it had arrived, it was gone. Veron slumped forward, wheezing. The light faded. The tingling vanished. *What just happened?* He looked at Chelci's face, and his heart stopped. Her soft eyes, filled with peace and love, stared back at him, bewildered.

"Chelci!" Veron gasped. He put a hand underneath her head, helping her sit up. His heart pounded. "Are you . . . all right?"

Bracing an arm behind to prop her up, Chelci looked down with wide eyes. She touched her stomach where a tight scar ran across her stomach. "Yeah, I think so. What did you do?"

Veron's eyes widened. "I—I don't know. The power . . . came out of me, I guess. I'm not even tired."

"Is Bale dead?" Chelci asked.

Both heads turned to the large body splayed across the courtyard. "Yeah, he's dead. We did it," Veron whispered before turning his attention back to Chelci. "So, you're really all right? Is there pain? How's your energy?"

"I'm okay. I don't feel any pain at all. Help me up?" Her reassuring smile eased his fears.

Veron stood, making sure his once-crushed legs worked as expected before he offered a hand to Chelci. She pulled against it, popping up as if she were never injured.

"Your dress is quite the sight," Veron said with a laugh.

She scowled. "You're not going to make a crack about me wearing a dress now, are you?"

"No! You look beautiful in it! It's just that . . ." He motioned to her lower half, where blood from various sources left it a reddish-brown color.

"Oh." Chelci chuckled. "Maybe I need to find some new pants to wear."

Butterflies filled Veron's stomach. "So . . . before you . . . sort of died, we were talking." He rubbed his hand behind his neck and looked at the ground. His pulse thumped wildly. "I mentioned I had kind of planned to ask you something."

She touched under his chin, lifting his eyes to hers. Her other hand grasped his. Her gentle expression soothed his fear. "My answer is yes, Veron Stormbridge, I will marry you."

A wave of warmth rushed through his veins. His heart leaped, barely contained by its body. Veron broke into a relieved grin and squeezed Chelci's hand. She stepped closer, wrapping an arm around his back and pulling him close. The fog from her breath in the icy air obscured her face's radiant smile. Veron leaned forward and met her lips.

The falling snow disappeared. The wind vanished. Veron's memory of pain and setbacks faded into the distance. The kiss felt like the end of a journey—a celebration of everything he never knew himself capable of wishing. Veron gasped when it ended and leaned his forehead to hers. Chelci laughed, and the soft, giddy melody made his spirit soar. Tears of joy cascaded down his face.

Holding tight to Chelci's hand, Veron looked around. Dead bodies and crumbled stone filled the courtyard. He pictured Morgan waiting in the woods and the rescued workers already heading south.

"So, what do we do now?" Chelci asked.

Veron squeezed her hand. "Now, we head home. Bale is dead, and Terrenor needs to know."

44

A Welcome Return

"You nervous?" Chelci asked, snapping Veron out of his daze. Blinking, he grabbed her hand, holding it as they walked next to each other. Dust from the road kicked up from the line of freed slave workers stretching in both directions. "A little," he admitted, looking ahead to the walls of Felting looming in the distance. "I've thought about it for the last couple of weeks since we left Daratill. I don't know what to expect."

"There's nothing to be nervous about," she said. "The kingdom will celebrate what you did."

"What *we* did," Veron corrected.

"Yes, but it was mostly you and your father." A melancholy smile formed on her face. "He will be missed."

Veron's face drooped. The crunch of footsteps on the road filled the air. "We were a team, and we all played a part," he said finally. "We couldn't have stopped him without you, Chelci."

She blushed.

"You arrived to rescue me just when I was about to be killed."

"I guess I did," she said, her voice softening, "along with Brixton."

Veron's gaze fell to the path. "Yeah, him too."

"So, what are you nervous about?" Chelci asked, perking up. "For years, you've had this destiny hanging over your head, and now that's in the past. You saved Terrenor from Bale, and you're free!"

"Yeah, I am. But what do I do now?"

"Um . . . you get *married* for starters."

He laughed, settling into a warm smile. "I know, but after that. What do we do then?"

"You could start another market!" Morgan's voice called from behind him.

Veron spun. His friend rode in the front of a wagon with a horse's reins in his hands. His ever-present smile reminded Veron of simpler times. Jeanette from Stonl sat next to him, closer than the width of the wagon required.

"Veron here started the most amazing market in all of Karad," Morgan said to Jeanette. "You should have seen it. People came from all over the city."

"He's exaggerating. It was just a market," Veron added.

Jeanette's smile brought creases next to her eyes. "I hear Morgan only speaks of things he believes in. So, it must have been something."

Veron chuckled.

"Jeanette and I may open a store in Felting. I'd sell groceries, and she'd make soups and prepared meals."

She rested her hand against Morgan's arm. "You were all so generous to invite me to come with you. I needed a change. Thank you."

"We're just glad you came!" Morgan said with an awkward grin. The two wagon riders looked at each other and blushed.

Veron shook his head and chuckled. "How's your shoulder?" he asked, pointing to the linen wrapped around Morgan.

"It feels fine. I think this will be my last bandage."

Veron nodded. "How about our other patient?"

Morgan's smile soured. He glanced over his shoulder before turning back. "Unfortunately, still breathing. Check on him yourself if you like."

"Go ahead," Chelci said, squeezing his hand.

Veron stopped, allowing the wagon to catch up. At the far side, he grabbed on to the railing and hopped up, crouching against the wooden clapboard rail amongst the newly recovered Shadow Knights book and the rest of their supplies.

Brixton Fiero propped himself on his elbows and grimaced. "Are we almost there?" he asked, his voice weak.

Veron nodded. "Yes, it's just ahead."

Brixton sighed. "What do you plan to do with me?"

Veron stared. *I don't know.* Ignoring the question, he pointed to Brixton's stomach. "How's the wound?"

"It's feeling better. That potion you made helped."

Veron chuckled. "Magic water," he muttered to himself. "Thank you, Artimus."

"My head's doing better as well. It only hurts when I move it . . . or breathe."

Veron laughed and shook his head. "I'm glad."

"Veron," Brixton said, drawing his eyes. "Thank you."

Veron's jaw tightened, and he swallowed hard.

"I'm shocked you let me live after all I've . . . You know. Nothing I do could ever make up for the wrongs I've committed—to you, to everyone."

"No, it couldn't," Veron said. "You can't take what you did back, and you can't undo it with good."

"You must hate me! It eats me up knowing what I did to you."

"So, don't do it anymore."

Brixton's brows narrowed. "Yeah, but—"

"I forgive you, Brixton." The words were short, but it took a great deal of effort to say. Brixton's eyes widened at the revelation. "I release you from your guilt. In my eyes, what will define you is what you do going forward from here."

Tears welled as Brixton stared back, his lips parted. He wiped at his face. "Thank you," Brixton said, barely above a whisper, his mouth trembling.

"Your fate will be up to Feldor law now," Veron said. A solemn look fixed on Brixton's face. "But your condemnation won't come from me."

Brixton managed a nod. "I understand."

Veron looked ahead where the walls grew larger. "Rest for the moment. We'll be there shortly."

Veron blushed as they entered the city. Rows of people lined the streets, cheering and shouting.

"Hooray for Veron Stormbridge!"

"Cheers for the Shadow Knights!"

Banners celebrating their return hung from buildings and in windows. Young girls ran up to Chelci, handing her flowers.

"I guess the rider we sent ahead told more than just my father," Chelci said, laughing as she balanced the colorful, growing bouquet.

The remaining slaves who didn't go to their homes along the trek dispersed as they walked through Felting. Cries of joy echoed through the city at the family reunions. People waved thanks to Veron with one arm as they hugged their returning family members with the other.

When they arrived in the square in front of the castle, an even larger crowd greeted them. Rows of people packed together to be as close as possible to the high lords standing on the steps before the castle. At their center, Darcius Marlow beamed, shaking with excitement. Before they stopped, he ran to Chelci, wrapping her in a hug.

"Oh, Chelci! I worried I'd never see you again!"

"We're back, Father," she said, "and we're alive."

"I heard news of Jackson, and—" He paused, lowering his chin and swallowing. "I feared the worst." He freed an arm and clasped Veron on the shoulder. "Thank you for keeping her safe."

Veron chuckled. "Actually, sir, it was I who needed to be kept safe." He nodded to Chelci. "She saved my life."

Geoffrey Bilton, the High Lord of Defense, approached, clearing his throat. "Is he truly dead?" he asked, his face expectant.

Veron turned to Morgan, who remained on the cart. The grocer reached behind him and grabbed a burlap bag. He extended his arm, holding the sack out with a disgusted look. Veron took it from him then tossed the sack forward. It landed with a thud and rolled to the high lord's feet.

Bilton crouched to peer in the opening. With a groan, he cringed and turned his head away, nudging the sack farther away with his foot. "Yes," he said, turning to a line of high lords behind him. "He's dead."

Edgar Weatherbee, the High Lord of Justice, turned to Veron. "I underestimated you, Young Veron. I—"

"His name's Veron," Chelci said, interrupting. "Not, Young Veron."

Weatherbee smiled and nodded. "Of course. Veron, thank you for what you did. We all owe you."

Veron blushed, nodding. "So, what will you all do here, now?" he asked.

"Gareth Billings is in the castle dungeon until we decide what to do with him," Darcius replied. "And I hear you have Brixton Fiero with you?"

"Yes. Brixton turned against Bale in the end. He saved your daughter's life as well as my own, and he helped us kill Bale."

"Hmm," Darcius mumbled, glancing at the high lords. "Sounds like we need to bring back the Advisors Council meeting."

"Agreed," Bilton chimed in. "We have a lot to discuss."

Veron stared at the palace wall, sitting on the stone bench, his leg bouncing up and down. Chelci rested her arm on his knee, prompting him to stop shaking. "Sorry. What do you think they want?" he asked.

She moved her hand along his leg, the motion comforting him. "Probably to hear our account of what happened. They have quite the mess to clean up here in Feldor with the king dead and Bale gone."

"I wonder what they'll do with Brixton?"

Chelci sighed. "He murdered the king . . . and his father."

"And his fiancé," Veron added.

"I think there's only one thing they *can* do."

The door clicked as it opened, and a guard motioned them to enter. The familiar oval table filled Veron with a swirl of feelings. High lords of Felting sat in the room, talking in hushed tones. Brixton stood with his back against the wall, covered by a guard. Veron's old friend looked down at the floor after they made eye contact.

"Veron and Chelci, thank you for coming!" Darcius said, beaming. The rest of the men nodded. "Edgar?" He said, turning to the High Lord of Justice.

The man stroked his beard as he stood. "We've spoken with Brixton Fiero about last season's events, and we wanted to get your input—see if anything is missing."

"What has Brixton shared?" Veron asked, glancing at his old friend.

"He shared how he sold *you* into slavery and how he worked with Bale to sneak his men into the city. He admits to murdering King Wesley, along with his role in his father's death. But, he insists he's changed—that he fought alongside you two in Daratill against Bale."

Veron looked at Chelci. Her fixed lips didn't move. "I can't refute any of that," Veron responded. "I can't speak to the piece about his father, but I know the rest to be true. And, yes, he fought with us in Norshewa. He gave up his position and killed one of Bale's captains. By our side, he helped us face down a hundred men. If it weren't for him fighting in the face of certain death, neither Chelci nor I would be here today."

Weatherbee turned to Chelci and raised an eyebrow.

"I agree," she said. "He protected me and saved my life. I—" She paused to take in a deep breath as she looked toward Brixton. "I do believe he had a change of heart in the end."

Weatherbee took a deep breath. "Veron, if it were up to you, what would you do with him?"

"It's not my place to dictate the laws of the land."

"Please, Veron. We want to hear your perspective," Darcius prompted.

Veron looked at Brixton, who met his eyes. He expected to see him pleading, but the young man's face was placid—accepting.

Chelci squeezed his hand. "Be honest," she whispered.

Veron inhaled, looking at each of the men. "I'm sure the penalty for killing a king is death," he said. Murmurs of approval rumbled around the table. "But, if that is the determining factor, I deserve death as well." Those around the table jerked toward him. "I killed Bale."

"Come, now," High Lord Bilton protested. "That's entirely different."

"Is it though? While his claim to Terrenor was suspect, he was the rightful king of Norshewa."

"He attacked us. We were at war," Bilton added, several others muttering.

Veron shrugged. "I'm not trying to put myself on trial but only sharing my perspective on Brixton. He was my friend, one of my oldest ones. We laughed and ate and drank together. We spent birthdays together. Then, he threatened my business in order to make money for himself. He killed someone and framed me. He sold me as a slave. He told Bale where I was. I've forgiven these offenses. If you want justice, please don't take it on my account."

Weatherbee sputtered. "B—but his crimes were not only against you."

"And I'm sure you must dole out consequences as you see fit. He knows his choices were wrong. But I've seen his change, and I've heard where his heart is now. I'm proud of him for making the hard decision he did even if his prior actions come with consequences."

The high lords looked between each other. None spoke.

"For what it's worth . . ." Veron added, "Bale defined his rule by fear and selfish ambition. As we build something new, I think it could be wise to lean more toward forgiveness and compassion instead. What better time to start than now?"

Silence continued to blanket the high lords until Weatherbee spoke. "Fiero, do you have any final thoughts to share in your defense?"

Brixton cleared his throat. "Nothing I haven't already shared, High Lord, except that I place myself in your hands and accept whatever decision you find appropriate."

"Very well," Weatherbee said, nodding to the guard.

Brixton left the room under tight watch, giving a weak nod of thanks to Veron before he left.

"Before we consider what to do with Brixton, we have one more topic we wanted to discuss with you, Veron." Weatherbee nodded to Darcius.

"We will all miss King Wesley. He was a kind but just ruler who will be difficult to replace. It is the high lords' job to choose his successor, and the decision must be unanimous—not a simple task." A grin grew on his face. "However, we have agreed. Veron, we would like *you* to be the next King of Feldor."

Veron's jaw dropped. Chelci gasped. Applause rang from around the room, but it sounded muddled in his ear.

"I, uh . . . I can't . . ."

"Of course you can. You're *perfect*, Veron!"

"Why me?"

Darcius gestured around the table as he spoke. "You've shown your wisdom to the council. You care more about others than your own fame and glory. And you killed Bale. The people already *love* you!"

Chelci covered her mouth, muffling a laugh. The rest of the council stared at him with eyes of anticipation. Veron's chest pounded.

Darcius placed his hands on Veron's shoulders. "The council trusts you, Veron. They are ready to follow wherever you lead them."

"If I'm king, would that mean the decision about Brixton rests with me?"

Darcius pursed his lips before looking to the others. "That call lies with the High Lord of Justice."

Veron nodded, looking around the room. "Can I, uh . . . think about it?"

Darcius chuckled. "Sure. Think about it. Can you let us know by tomorrow? We have a kingdom to rebuild."

Veron's eyes struggled to focus. The winding paths of the Marlows' plant garden passed underneath his feet, but his mind was elsewhere. Chelci squeezed his hand and offered a faint smile.

"No matter what is to come, I couldn't be happier than being with you, right now," she said.

"I remember the last time we held hands walking these paths," Veron said with a grin.

"After Emma's wedding?"

Veron nodded. "With the rain."

"When you kissed me."

"Uh, I think *you* were the one who kissed me," Veron said, raising an eyebrow.

Her playful grin made him feel warm inside. "You kissed me, too."

Veron laughed. "That seems so long ago." Pebbles crunched under their feet as they walked. "You realize if I accept this, that will make you queen after we marry?"

Chelci nodded, kicking at the rocks while they strolled.

"How do you feel about that?"

"It's exciting—I can't lie about that. There are so many things I would love to do as queen."

"But you hesitate?"

She paused. "I'm not sure it's what you want."

"Yeah! What do you want?" Morgan called from up the path.

Veron and Chelci approached the end of the garden, where Morgan sat on the edge of the stone patio.

Veron sighed, sitting next to Morgan while Chelci leaned against the wall. "Honestly, I hadn't thought about it. I always figured I would die defeating Bale. Had I come up with a plan, it wouldn't have involved a crown. I still can't believe they offered it to me. I feel like I should be more excited."

"You're not excited about being king?" Morgan asked.

"Oh, I am! It just . . . It doesn't seem real. Having the responsibility of a king is something I'd never thought about."

"You know," Morgan chuckled. "Most people might have said, 'Having the *power* of a king is something they'd never thought about.'"

Veron shrugged. "I just don't know if I would be any good."

"You'll be good," Chelci said.

"Do you think?"

"A good king cares more about others than himself," Morgan said. "He doesn't spend his money and power building riches and comfort.

He'd be humble, like one of the people. He needs wisdom—the ability to see what needs to be done and figure out how to do it. You'd be perfect."

Veron looked at each of them. "Thanks for your words. I think—" He jerked his head.

"What is it?" Chelci asked.

Veron broke into a grin. "I just had an idea."

"What?" Morgan asked.

"I know exactly what I want to do."

* * *

Veron stared over the castle balcony's edge. The sun peeked above the Straith Mountains, and a crisp light fell across Feldor, sprawling before him. Chelci stood next to him, quiet but supportive.

"It seems so long ago when we stood on this same balcony," Veron said, "the night Wesley died."

"Yes, it does. Now they need someone new to take his place," Chelci said. "Are you sure about this, Veron?"

He squeezed her hand. "Yes, I'm sure."

Darcius Marlow poked his head through the arched doorway. "They're ready," he said.

Veron kept ahold of Chelci's hand as they entered the council room. The five high lords settled in their seats and eagerly looked at Veron.

"Before I give an answer, I'd like to know what is to be done with Brixton," Veron said, turning to High Lord Weatherbee.

The man's eyes widened as the rest of the room turned to him. He cleared his throat. "About Brixton Fiero? I've given it some thought since we met yesterday. His crimes amount to treason and deserve death."

Veron inclined his head forward. The high lord had more to say.

"However, your standing up for him yesterday made me think. With the change of power we've seen, it may be worth showing some compassion as a gesture of goodwill to set apart this rule from Bale's. He won't be allowed to run a business, have any authority, or even think about holding a weapon. If so, he'll find himself rotting in the dungeon. But . . . if he can behave and live under a supervised probation, Fiero may live."

Veron nodded, a faint smile tweaking his face. "I'm glad to hear it."

"Now, to the question at hand . . ." Darcius said, leaning forward.

"Of course," Veron said. He glanced at Chelci, who squeezed his hand before letting it go. Veron walked around to the end of the oval table and held on to the back of the chair. "You ask me to be king—a young man who has barely lived twenty years. You say that I care more about others than my glory. I believe you are right. I do care more about others. It's for this reason that I cannot accept your offer."

The high lords gasped. "But, why not?" Darcius said, standing to his feet.

"I have something else I need to do—rebuild the Shadow Knights Academy."

45

Two Years Later

Veron leaned against the wall, the warm breeze wafting over him, rustling his tunic and tickling his hair. His hands rested on the stones, stacked in the same places for hundreds of years. They observed silently while generations of shadow knights came and went through the academy, trained within those very walls. In the west, the sun settled low, past the woods on the other side of the river.

Footsteps sounded behind him. Veron turned as Jacob Lipton walked up the steps, holding a hammer.

"You finished?" Veron asked.

"It was only a few tables—much easier than the bedrooms we refurbished and way simpler than building rooms out of the loft at North Karad Market."

The carpenter's smile took Veron back to when they first met in Kulling Square. "Perfect timing. We'll use them all tonight—should have a large turnout," Veron replied. "You're coming back for the feast, right?"

Jacob scoffed. "I wouldn't miss it! Mary's been looking forward to it for a while. Few people get to spend Deliverance Day with the shadow knight who actually delivered us!"

"Ha! It wasn't just me. It was a team effort."

Jacob flipped the hammer in his hand. "Well, I better go get ready. See you in a bit!"

Veron waved as the carpenter left. His eye drew to the courtyard below, where a boy and a girl stumbled through a doorway with large stones balanced on their shoulders—Gavin and Dayna. They trudged across the dirt with heads down and lumbering steps. Reaching a corner of the courtyard, Dayna dropped her stone onto a pile of others, moments before Gavin.

"Beat you!" she shouted before collapsing on the ground, her chest heaving.

Veron chuckled. "Dayna, you don't like to lose, do you?" he said to himself.

Sweat covered the top half of Gavin's tunic. He fell next to Dayna, panting and devoid of response. As they writhed on the ground, another boy and girl entered the courtyard carrying stones of their own. With red faces, they added them to the pile. Bradley leaned over with his hands on his legs while Ruby dropped to her knees.

"Not quick enough," Veron called, moving down the steps.

The boys and girls groaned. "That hourglass is too fast," Gavin protested. "There's no way we can get back by then.

"Really?" Veron said. "If that's the case, maybe you don't belong in the Shadow Knights Academy. What do you think, Dayna?"

Dayna sat up. "I can do it, Shadow Master! Give me time and I'll prove it's possible!"

Veron laughed. "All right, you four. That's it for today. We'll end early so you can get ready for the feast."

The students sighed before stumbling off, complaining about their aching legs.

Chelci walked through the doorway, passing the exiting students.

"Ruby, how'd you do?" she asked.

"Last," Ruby muttered, shaking her head as she passed.

"That's all right," Chelci encouraged. "Tomorrow we get back to sword fighting, and you'll show them a thing or two." She turned to Veron after the others left. "They're so competitive!"

"Ha!" Veron laughed. "I can't imagine anyone else was ever like that."

She narrowed her eyes and put her hands on her hips. "I like being competitive."

Veron grabbed her arm and pulled her to him, causing her to squeal. "And I happen to like *you*."

She smiled as she wrapped her arms around his waist and gave a quick kiss on the lips. "No sign of your friends yet?"

Veron shook his head. "Not yet. They should be here soon, though."

"Who should be here soon?" a voice called from just beyond the doorway.

Veron spun as Danyel Barton, Emma, and another girl he didn't know entered the courtyard. "There they are!" Veron shouted, running and embracing his friend from Karad in a great hug, while Chelci embraced Emma. "What took you so long?"

"Sorry," Danyel said, pointing to Emma. "Had to stop by to see my cousin first."

"You must be Lynnette," Veron said to the other girl.

Danyel grinned, rubbing a hand on her shoulder.

"Lynnette Barton," she said, "Nice to finally meet you, Veron."

"Wait! Barton?" Veron turned to Danyel. A creeping grin grew on his friend's face. "Why didn't you tell us?" Veron asked, hitting Danyel in the chest.

"We talked about having a big wedding and inviting everyone, but . . ." He looked at Lynnette with a sheepish grin. "But, we couldn't wait."

"We got married last season," she added.

"And . . ." Danyel stepped closer to his wife and rested a hand on her belly. "Barton number three should get here sometime this wiether."

Veron's eyes grew. "No way! Congratulations both of you! That's great."

"What about you, Emma," Chelci said. "Have you decided if you want a number three?"

Emma rolled her eyes. "You can ask Matthew when he gets here with the bread. I'd love to hear his answer."

Chelci narrowed her brows. "He'll be here soon, right?"

"The bread was in the oven—should finish shortly."

Chelci nodded. "That's fine. We still have a few things to prepare. Any chance some of you could help?"

The crowd headed inside to the common room. Danyel and Lynnette moved tables and chairs out into the courtyard, and Veron and Emma stayed with Chelci.

Veron's mouth watered at the scent of roasting meat and vegetables. "It smells amazing!" he said, making Chelci blush.

A fire roared in the hearth, where two chickens turned on a spit. A large iron pot to the side sizzled with smoke. Chelci took a wooden spoon and stirred the contents.

"Veron, can you chop those vegetables?" She nodded to a pile on the counter.

"Sure." Prepared bowls and platters of sliced meats and cheeses decorated the flat surface—enough food to feed an army. Veron took the knife and cut up the large leafy greens before placing them in a bowl. Next, he went to work on the pile of bright, purple verquash. A wooden rapping sounded in the hallway.

"Is that someone knocking?" Veron made an awkward show of wanting to go to the door but realizing his hands were covered in verquash juice. "Chelci, do you mind getting the door?" he asked.

Chelci sighed, handed the spoon over to Emma, and wiped her hands on her clothes.

Veron's mischievous grin grew as she passed.

"What is it?" Emma whispered after Chelci left.

His smile grew broader. "Wait just a moment." He tilted his head, training his ear. Presently, a shout rang down the hall. The high-pitched squealing approached, and soon Chelci re-entered the common room with her arm over an older woman's shoulder.

"Nevi! Russell!" Veron cried with mock-surprise. "Wow, who would have thought you would be here?"

"Don't forget us!" Finley said, trailing the couple with Aleks behind.

"Did you know?" Chelci asked, staring at Veron while his smile steadily grew. "How did you know?"

"I invited them," Veron said. "I hope you don't mind."

"Of course not!" Chelci turned to the visitors. "I had no idea you were coming. It's been, what . . . ?"

"Three seasons," Russell said.

"Since your wedding," Nevi added, smiling broadly.

"It's good to see you again, Veron," Russell said with a nod.

"Yeah," Aleks chimed in. "I told the candidates at the Academy we'd take a break for us to come and visit the famous Veron and Chelci Stormbridge. They all begged to come. I kept looking over my shoulder while we traveled to make sure they weren't following."

"Sorry we arrived just before the feast with nothing to contribute," Nevi said. "It looks like you're busy. Is there anything we can do to help?"

"Could one of you set up lanterns out in the courtyard?" Chelci asked.

"Sure, we'll find them," Finley replied, heading down the hall with Aleks on his heels. Nevi and Russell took a seat at one of the tables.

Emma rubbed her hands together. "I think this is about finished, here."

Veron returned to his cutting board and slid the verquash onto an empty platter. "We're good here, too."

Chelci spun around, nodding. "I think all we're missing now is . . ."

"Bread's here!" Matthew's voice called down the hall. Emma's face shone as Matthew entered the room. More footsteps followed.

"Morgan! Jeanette!" Veron greeted them as they entered. "You're just in time."

"We smelled the bread, and just had to follow it," Morgan said with a chuckle.

Matthew carried two large loaves in his arms, which he set on the counter.

Chelci's face pinched. "The bread smells wonderful, Matthew, but do you think that will be enough?"

The baker returned a casual smile. "Oh, there's more." He nodded toward the door where a young blond man carrying a large basket appeared.

Brixton Fiero plunked the basket on the counter and dusted off his trousers. A proud grin covered his face as he peeled back the cloth covering the basket. "These may be my best yet! I took Chelci's Nasco roll recipe and infused it with roasted tomatoes and barkleaf seeds."

"Barkleaf?" Veron asked. "In a roll?"

"I know, it sounds strange, but trust me, they're *so* much better."

With a hand on her hip, Chelci raised her eyebrows in mock hurt. "So, you're saying my rolls needed improvement, huh?" Brixton pursed his lips and froze. His eyes darted around the room before Chelci burst into laughter. "I'm only teasing you, Brixton. I can't wait to try them."

"Are you going to make those for our wedding in a few weeks?"

Morgan asked, grabbing Jeanette's hand and holding it tenderly.

"I can, if you like," Brixton said.

"You know . . . Deliverance Day is not the only thing we celebrate today," Matthew said, projecting his voice. "This week marks the end of Brixton's probational supervision." A cheer filled the common room. "I must admit, I wasn't happy at first when they appointed him to our shop, but he's won me over since."

Brixton blushed. "Thank you, Matthew. And thank you for giving me a chance. Pairing me with you two was the perfect assignment."

"Agreed," Emma said. "We can turn out twice as much with him around. You should see how his eyes come alive when he has a bowl of flour."

"Not even my father had such passion," Matthew added.

While most of the room scurried around to continue preparations, Veron pulled Brixton to the side. "Thanks for coming," Veron said, his voice earnest. "I'm sure today brings up a variety of feelings, and I'm glad you came to celebrate with us." Brixton nodded. "Also, I'm proud to see how you've grown."

"I couldn't have done it without you standing up for me," he replied with a weak smile. "You had every right to give up on me, but you didn't."

"And I'm glad I didn't. I always knew you had great things in you. I'm thrilled to see you finding something that brings you joy."

Chelci approached, running her arm around Veron's. "We're about set here. Should we get her?"

Veron smiled. "Sure. I get to wake her though."

Veron and Chelci ascended the steps at the end of the hall, leading to the upper floor. The line of rooms held living quarters, empty but waiting to be filled with aspiring shadow knights. Veron entered the second door on the left. The setting sun cast an orange glow through the window, lighting up the simple bedroom. Through an open doorway, a smaller room held a crib with a padded rocking chair.

"Where's my girl?" Veron said in a high-pitched voice. A cooing noise answered back from the crib. He leaned over the side, and his daughter's smiling face beamed up at him. "There you are! Did you have a good nap?"

Chelci's hand rubbed his back as he picked her up. "I can't believe we let her nap this late. We're going to pay for it tonight."

"Maybe," Veron said. His cheeks puffed from a playful grin as he held his girl against his hip. "What do you think, Lia? Do you want to stay up late and celebrate with us? Are you gonna make us pay tonight?"

"I call not being in charge at midnight when she's still wide awake," Chelci said.

Veron tickled Lia under her chin, "Are you ready to go see everyone?" He made his way toward the door when Lia frowned and turned her head back to the crib. Her arm reached out, and she pouted.

"Wait!" Chelci said, leaning over the crib. She returned to Veron, handing Lia a small stuffed cow. "You can't go without Mr. Butters!" Lia cooed, breaking into an infectious grin.

"Isn't she getting a little old for that?"

Chelci's head jerked, her forehead pinched. "Uh . . . *No!*"

Veron's eyes grew. "Whoa! I'm sorry. I thought—"

"You thought *wrong*! Lia, you can keep Mr. Butters for as long as you like—until you're grown and married with children of your own if you want."

"That's . . . fine . . . I guess."

With a scowl, Chelci took their girl from Veron. "Come here, Lia. Don't worry, I won't let him take Mr. Butters away."

"I wasn't—" Veron stopped his protest since his wife and daughter were already gone. He chuckled as he followed out the door.

Back in the courtyard, the feast was ready. People brought platters of food and set them on the long row of tables placed end-to-end. Lanterns hung around the courtyard, giving it a festive mood in contrast to the dimming sky. Jacob and his family had arrived and the shadow knights-in-training drooled over the feast.

"Do you think he's going to make it?" Chelci asked, looking toward the doorway when Veron arrived next to her. I think we're all ready to eat."

Veron frowned, following her gaze. "I was hoping, but he's probably too busy. It would have been nice for one of our fathers to be here." A tear came to Veron's face after a moment of silence.

Chelci rested a hand on his shoulder. "William would have loved to see this—" She motioned around the courtyard. "—what you're building. He'd be proud of you."

Veron wiped his cheek, gave a weak smile, and said, "We should get started."

He walked to an open seat at the end of the table. Chelci joined, taking the chair next to him with Lia on her knee. Veron took in a deep breath and beamed as he looked down the row. Friends and family found their seats, laughing and joking. Food and wine lined the cobbled together tables. Chelci squeezed his hand and smiled, her dimpled cheeks glowing in the light of the lanterns. He picked up his glass and let the crowd settle.

As he opened his mouth to speak, trumpets sounded. Veron's heart leaped, the liquid in his glass jostling and almost spilling on Chelci. He turned to the courtyard doorway as four royal guardsmen adorned in gray-and-blue tunics with black berets and metal breastplates entered. They moved in step and kicked to a halt with their hands resting on their swords.

The man in front announced in a clear voice, "His Majesty, King

Darcius."

Darcius Marlow waved the guardsmen away as he passed through the doorway, shaking his head. "I'm so sorry. I tell them not to play those silly trumpets, but they won't listen."

Chelci beamed and approached, wrapping her father in an embrace with Lia pressed between them. "I worried you wouldn't be able to make it."

"Are you kidding me? I wouldn't miss this for anything. Plus," He tickled Lia under her chin and smiled, "the castle's a little too stuffy. I try to get out into the city any chance I get."

"We're getting close to adding some new knights," Veron said, nodding down the table toward the younger trainees. "Hopefully, we can help around the kingdom more soon."

"Sounds great," Darcius said. "Any luck on figuring out how to repeat that pure connection thing yet?"

Veron pursed his lips and shook his head. "I keep working on it, but . . . I haven't been able to find it since that night."

"That's too bad. I'm looking forward to you rebuilding your group. Terrenor will need you."

"Thank you for honoring us with your presence tonight. Your timing is perfect. I was about to propose a toast." Darcius' face turned hard, and he shook it. Veron's brows knit together. "What is it?"

"It is *I* who am honored to be here tonight. Please allow me to give the toast."

Unsure how to reply, Veron took his seat. Brixton brought a glass for Darcius as Chelci pulled up a chair next to her.

The king remained standing and held his glass, drawing the eyes of everyone around the table. "Thank you all for allowing me to join you tonight," Darcius began. "Today, on this second observance of Deliverance Day, we remember the bravery and selflessness shown two years ago when Veron, Chelci, and William Stormbridge fought and defeated the usurper king, Edmund Bale."

"Don't forget about Morgan," Chelci added.

Morgan pursed his lips together. "True. I was in Daratill, hiding in the woods, nursing my injured shoulder while they took down two hundred men." The crowd laughed.

"Also, I want to recognize Brixton Fiero," Darcius added. A few mutters rumbled around the table until the king held up his hand. "No one is ever too far gone to change, and I applaud you for your bravery to make amends, Brixton. May we all be so humble to ask forgiveness for the mistakes we have made."

The crowd was silent for a long moment until Veron broke it. "Here, here!" his lone voice echoed. Brixton nodded with a smile of thanks from down the table.

"Here, here!" several other voices chimed in.

The king continued. "Although we celebrate Deliverance Day, I want to toast our friend, Veron Stormbridge." Heat creeped up Veron's neck as the other heads turned to him. "All of us here have known him for years. He extended a hand and helped many of you get back on your feet when you went through a difficult time. Everywhere he's gone, he made a difference in the lives of the people he met, putting their needs over his own—in Karad, here in Felting, and in Nasco. He was even willing to sacrifice his own life for the rest of us.

Heads nodded, and Chelci squeezed his hand under the table.

"Some of you may not know this, but the high lords offered him the crown." A few surprised faces dotted the courtyard. "It's true. They saw his wisdom, leadership, and humility and wanted him for the job, but he turned it down. He didn't want the fame and glory. It turns out he was the smart one. This job is exhausting!" The crowd laughed.

"So, this toast is for Veron. To the young man from the dirty streets of Karad, who grew up to advise kings and lords. To our friend, who has a dear place in all of our hearts and to whom many of us owe our lives. To the warrior who saved our kingdom. Veron, we thank you for being you."

Veron held the king's gaze for a long moment until a tear welled in his eye. Darcius' noble smile filled him with a warm sense of belonging. He scanned the room where his friends held glasses up, nodding in his direction. Morgan shed a matching tear, and Chelci beamed with pride. He wanted to say something in response but was too choked up. He merely nodded. *Thank you. Thank you all.*

* * *

Rosalik ground her staff into the hard packed snow where she'd paced along the ridge of the Straith Mountains. Past the fog of her breath, down the precipitous slope, the kingdom of Feldor extended beneath her. The Felavorre River cut through the valley, leading toward the horizon. On the clearest of days, she could see the Westfale Ocean at its end.

Hidden in the faint wind, a sound caused the hair on the back of her neck to prickle. She tightened the grip on her staff. Power in the guise of a warm tingle simmered inside her, waiting to be used. She spun toward the faint crunch of snow.

A man walked up the slope with a thick cloak wrapped around him and a hood obscuring his face.

"Who's there?" Rosalik called.

The man continued to walk as he looked up, his blue eyes connecting with hers. He was older than her. Gray hair fell down the sides of his face in long strands. His short, thick beard was blacker than gray. On his exposed neck, a dark spot showed like a stain over his throat, matching her own. Dangling from his neck, a necklace ended at a red crystal with a faint glow.

"Talioth! I'm so sorry." She bowed slightly. "I didn't realize it was you."

"It's fine, Rosalik," he said as he crested the ridge to join her.

"What brings you up here, Sir?"

He sniffed as he took in the view down the slope to the west. A moment of silence lingered as he scanned the valley. "I wanted to see if it would be stronger here on the ridge."

Her breath caught. *Is he referring to . . . ?*

"Have you felt it?"

A chill ran up her spine. "The power waning?"

His piercing gaze confirmed her guess.

Clenching her jaw, she nodded tightly. "I have. Their numbers grow again."

"A few years ago, it felt like the Shadow Knights had been wiped out, but now . . ."

"Where do you think they are?"

He sniffed again. "They could be anywhere." He spun, scanning the maze of peaks behind them.

"Should we do something about it?"

He turned back toward Feldor and paused for a long moment. Finally, he cleared his throat. "No. Not yet. But if they continue to grow, we may be forced to intervene.

Her eyebrows narrowed. "In what way?"

"Eliminate them."

The End of the Shadow Knights Trilogy

Are you curious about what happens next? Check out the next trilogy, Shadow Knights Generations, coming 2023.

The Shadow Knights Trilogy is Charlie's favorite book series of all time. After he read it, he went and told all of his dog friends. The one thing he always asks his puppy pals to do is leave a review. "If you don't leave a review, how can other readers know how doggaly-great my dad's books are?!"

PLEASE leave an honest review on Amazon or wherever you got the book from. Do it for Charlie.

For behind the scenes writing updates, follow **@michaelwebbnovels** on Instagram or Facebook.

Acknowledgments

This book marks the end of a monumental goal for me. October of 2019, having no idea how to write or how much work it would take, I set a goal of writing a novel. As I began to outline what that story might look, the framework of a trilogy formed in my head. I began to write and soon realized it was much more work than expected. My high ideas of writing a trilogy became more tentative. Would I finish the series or call it quits with one book? After I published the Last Shadow Knight, I knew I had found an exciting new passion. I had no idea whether the hard work would pay off, but I did know I loved the process, so I kept at it. This book completes that original story I planned (what seems like) so long ago.

I want to thank all my readers. Your support and encouragement help me daily to keep at it. When the 5 am hour rolls around, the excitement you share about my story is what helps get me out of bed to write. I hope you find this final chapter of the trilogy worth the wait!

I want to give a special thanks to my Alpha Readers, Eli, David, Mom, and Dad! You all had a huge part to play in crafting this story along with me. Some of the scenes in the final book are there because of you. I value your input incredibly, even if I didn't cut some of of the dying scenes. Haha. :-)

Also, thanks to Tara, Sara, and Cody, my Beta Reader team! You're feedback was extremely useful in helping me polish out my writing and pick up on missing details. I feel this is the stage where it really starts to feel like a book, and you were vital to this!

Thank you Dan and Ian, my editors. I'm always amazed at the level of detail you pick up on, and I almost ALWAYS agree with your suggestions.

Thank you Julia for supporting me in my dream! You never complain when I work, and I can see the pride in your eyes when you speak with other people about my books. I couldn't do this without you in it!

9 781737 578833